CIRCLES OF CONFUSION

a novel by
Doug Wicken

ISBN: 978-0-9691228-4-5 Paperback
ISBN: 978-0-9691228-5-2 eBook

Published by Doug Wicken, 2024

Circles of Confusion is a work of fiction. Names, characters, places, and incidents are the product of the author's imagination and are used fictitiously. Any resemblance to actual events, locations, or persons, living or dead, is entirely coincidental. In some historical references, events, locations, and public persons are identified for the sole purpose of background reference. No judgemental attempt is intended.

During my sojourns in Nicaragua as a photojournalist, I encountered several people named Azucena. The Azucena in this book is not any *one* of them, but *all*. *Compañera Azucena* is a composite of many amazing women in Nicaragua who were, and are, committed to the cause of human dignity, equality, education, and a better life for women and the poor.

Warning

This fictional work contains references to the subjects of sexual assault and suicide.

Cover image, 'Circles of Confusion,' painted by the author.
Photograph of the author by Scott Wicken at Café O.
Formatting by Chrissy Hobbs at Indie Publishing Group Inc

DEDICATIONS

To my loving family:

Scott Wicken, Shelley Young, and Rowan

Craig and Nena Wicken, Luka, and Gabrijela

Gudrun Heiss

I also honour the friendship and influence of the following very special people who, while they no longer walk the planet with us, continue to dwell in my memory. By entering my life, they have shaped my thoughts and values in so many positive ways.

The spirits and their legacies live in these pages.

Ron Wakegijig, Jim Maiangowi, Phillip Pitawanakwat, Albert 'Hardy' Peltier, Grace Peltier, Genevieve Peltier, Eugene Manitowabi, Kryn Taconis, Barry Wills, Dave Drew, Pastor Valle-Garay, Ernesto Cardenal, Fred Miller, Daniel O'Hanley, Peter Brysky, Joy Middleton, David Wicken, Beatrice Wicken, Leonard Wicken, and George Hickox.

During my lifetime, I have witnessed and experienced the loss of cognitive abilities in many close friends and relatives, including both of my parents. I dedicate this to them, and to the important work done by PSWs, volunteers, nurses, physicians, and other practitioners in the medical field, and especially to the family members who care for patients and loved ones living with dementia.

ACKNOWLEDGEMENTS

Many thanks to Catherine Muss, a 'forensic' reader who has guided me through the editing process. Initially, I presented her with an 87,000 word manuscript. Her sharp eye and encouragement over an intensive six-month spree resulted in this 140,000 word novel of which I am very proud. Her valuable suggestions have made this book possible and have contributed to a much-improved reading experience.

A very special thanks to fellow author, Lindsey-Anne Pontes (deSousa), a trusted and helpful reader, friend, and source of publishing information. She has unselfishly volunteered her time and knowledge to my writing projects.

To Irina and the wonderful staff (Abigail, Brooke, Emily, Hope, Kadence, Kendra, Ljiljiana, Mark, Miranda, Susan, and others) at Café O in Kitchener, Ontario, my all-time favourite café and writing space. Without the dark roasts and delicious baking, and especially the friendly smiles and unlimited openness to writers, many book projects would have been short-changed.

To all of my fellow writers of Kitchener-Waterloo Writers Alliance for their comradery, advice, and encouragement to experienced and novice writers alike.

Thanks to Chrissy Hobbs of Indie Publishing Group Inc for her valued assistance with the formatting and design.

A special thanks to the following people who assisted me in so many ways by reading early drafts and offering comments, assisting with research, formatting and design, holding hands when needed, being a friend at critical times, and accommodating my endless rants and relentless philosophical meanderings.

Deborah Polzin, Amy Prendergast, Bill Van Dyk, Jody Swannell, Javier Vera, Howard Pell, Mamoon Chakhansuri, Maureen Duffy.

And to my dear special friend, Sher Kariz.

MEMORIES

Pellets of colour and random shapes rain down on Duncan MacGregor as he gazes toward the last remnants of his memories hanging on the wall. Labyrinthine details — questions more than answers — litter his vision like the kaleidoscopic compositions of his childhood.

Extemporaneous sounds blend the cacophonous irritations from traffic and verbal disagreements, with sighs of still vivid ecstasies, and harmonious laughter. Duncan's senses explode in a relentless audio-visual confusion, a thunderous big bang of destruction and new creation.

Love, compassion, revenge, mystery, all components of his obsessive passion for being, rotate like comets, planets, asteroids, and cosmic dust, in some pre-ordained circle of confusion around a life force; a fire that flickers before the final embers succumb to the freezing night and the black hole that sucks the debris into nowhere; or to somewhere else.

Memories: a collaboration between the facts and the fictions of our life.

The completion of another circle.

Such is life.

PART ONE
1965 – 1971

CHAPTER 01

DUNCAN

Hamilton, Ontario, 1965 – 1968:

Black and orange goblins and witches adorn the walls of the high school gym. Costumed students, ignoring the pungent odour of sweaty socks, grind and twist their bodies in the darkness, while being watched closely for any unacceptable behaviour by masked chaperoning teachers. The Beatles rock through tinny over-worked speakers with 'Twist and Shout' echoing between steel roof rafters and the hardwood floor.

The tall, fair-haired, 17-year-old Duncan MacGregor, awkwardly slouches on the perimeter with his wall-hugging buddies, staring vacantly into a labyrinth of bouncing zombies, trolls, wizards, princesses, and assorted celebrity look-alikes. His blue eyes focus on a blond-haired classmate sporting Playboy bunny ears, currently twisting and shouting while her bunny-tailed derriere vibrates to the music. She fascinates him although the shy Duncan has never gained enough courage to speak directly to her.

After a quick cigarette escape outside, Duncan and his buddies return to the gym just as Mr. Hanson, their Physical Education teacher, doubling as tonight's emcee for the Halloween Dance, announces, "The next dance will be a Sadie Hawkins dance, a lady's choice. Here's your chance girls, to haul the boy of your dreams out onto the dance floor."

Penny, the Playboy bunny look-alike, the gleam in Duncan's eyes, turns and struts confidently toward him, her right arm extended, her fingers drooped and fluttering.

"C'mon, Duncan. Take my hand. I've been waiting all evening for you to ask me to dance. Now you have to."

Duncan's lanky legs weaken at the thought of dancing with Penny. Shyness kicks in. "I-I-I'm not a very good d-d-dancer. Maybe you should ask another guy."

"Nope. I want to dance with you." Penny grabs his hand and pries him forcefully away from the wall as The Animals begin singing, 'The House of the Rising Sun.' She draws him close to her for the slow dance.

"I warned you. I'm not very good at this," Duncan confesses, as his dress-up brogues stomp down against her instep.

Penny places her head on his shoulder and whispers in his ear, "You're doing just fine, Duncan."

After continuing in silence, Penny confides, "I heard you play the piano at last year's music night. That jazz piece you played was really cool."

Duncan's voice cracks, searching for words. "Thanks," he offers, followed by more silence before adding, "I saw you sing and dance in that musical. You looked really nice."

"Which one?"

"Um ... I don't remember the name of it." Duncan starts to panic. "You know, the one you were in last year."

"Oh, that was L'il Abner," Penny laughs. "I was Daisy Mae. It looks like I'm going to have to teach you something about musical theatre."

Duncan interprets that as a promising sign that he'll be seeing more of her.

The Animals wrap it up and another song begins. Duncan turns to leave the dance floor but Penny holds him tight while Bobby Vinton croons, 'There, I've Said it Again.'

They continue dancing as a couple for the remainder of the evening, and their conversational topics broaden. Gradually Duncan's shyness loosens. He buys Penny a Coke from the machine, and they take a short stroll around the schoolyard while he inhales an Export A. Penny steals a few drags as well before they return inside for the last dance. She pulls herself tighter to Duncan and closes her eyes.

"Would you like to walk me home, Duncan?" she whispers seductively.

Duncan's heart pumps faster. "Sure, I guess, if that's OK?"

As they leave, he suggests, "I hope you have a coat, you're gonna freeze out there dressed like that." He points to her flimsy Playboy bunny costume. Penny stops at her locker and dons a short jacket before leaving.

Their walk is quiet, allowing each of them to privately review their assessment of the evening, and to ponder their anticipations. After dancing together most of the evening, they neglect to hold hands while walking.

"There, that's my house." Penny points to a humble wartime bungalow. She turns to face him and holds both of his hands. "Can we get together again? Soon? Maybe we can go out on a date?"

"Yeah ... sure ... I guess. Where do you want to go?"

"How about taking me roller skating?"

Duncan has never tried roller skating and worries that it might even be worse than his ice skating. "How about a movie instead?"

"That's even better," she answers.

She wraps her arms around his neck and pecks a short kiss on his lips. "I had a great time tonight," she says.

A sudden warmth surges through Duncan's blood stream. "So did I," he responds, blushing. He hesitates before admitting, "I'm looking forward to the next time. How about a movie this Saturday night?"

"What's playing?" Penny asks.

"I have no idea. Does it matter?"

Penny snuggles close, framing Duncan's face between her hands. Her lips connect with his, soft and inviting, a prolonged and affectionate kiss. When it's over, Penny promises, "Sweet dreams." She touches her lips with her forefinger and passes it to Duncan's. "Until Saturday."

Penny and Duncan continue dating and soon become 'steadies.' Their naïve first date blossoms into a full-blown intimacy within a month. During Christmas they exchange gifts and join each other's parents for their respective family dinners, Penny's on Christmas Eve and Duncan's on Christmas Day.

On Boxing Day, stuffed with turkey, they meet to walk it off. Bright sun reflects off the fresh layer of snow that fell heavily overnight, making it appear warmer than the sub-zero temperatures that force them to bundle up. They walk arm-in-arm toward Inch Park to watch their friends skating and to join in snowball fights.

"Your folks are so cool," Penny offers. "Your father tells those weird Scottish jokes and your mom's French accent is fun, especially when she mixes up the two languages."

"Yeah, she's from Quebec City. If you listen closely, Dad only reverts to a Scottish brogue when he's been drinking."

"I thought he was born in Canada," Penny says, "That's what he told me."

"He was," Duncan answers, laughing. "That's the funniest part. He doesn't even know when he starts talking like a Scot. It just comes out. I guess it's in his genes."

"What do you think about my folks?" Penny asks.

"Your dad is pretty serious, eh? I'm not sure whether he likes me or not."

"Oh sure he likes you." Penny squeezes Duncan's hand through two layers of woolen mitts. "Dad always wants to be taken seriously; that's just the way he is. Mom's the one you have to look out for,

Duncan," Penny warns, laughing. "She makes all the major decisions in the family. She's the General; Dad's just a Corporal."

"So I have to suck up to your mother then, right?"

"If she likes you, you'll have no problems."

"What do you think? Does she like me?"

"You're all set. She loves you."

On New Year's Eve Penny and Duncan declare their undying love for each other by exchanging class rings.

In the new term at school, they only share a few courses together. One of the classes they share is algebra, where Duncan's participation is obviously minimal.

"Don't you like math, Duncan?" Penny asks outside their adjoining lockers during a break when their separate schedules allow. "You're always screwing around during class and you never have any of the homework completed."

"It's boring," Duncan admits, forcing his face into a grimace. "I just don't get it. Besides, when will I ever use it in real life?"

Penny turns it around. "When will you ever need baseball?"

"Whew. That was a low blow."

"You know what I think, Duncan? I think you have trouble conceptualizing abstract principles. Even though algebra is one of the secrets to logic, it's more abstract than you're accustomed to. You need to stretch out a bit; loosen up."

"Easier said than done."

"I can teach you. I love math," Penny offers. She pokes him in the ribs. "Of course I love you more."

Duncan leans over to kiss Penny.

"Tut-tut. None of that in the halls," Mr. Hanson warns in passing.

Penny's tutoring gradually has a positive effect on Duncan's attitude toward his education, not only in math classes but in other subjects as well. His grades and enthusiasm for learning improve. Before meeting Penny, Duncan was in danger of dropping out of school altogether.

While at high school, Duncan starts playing music gigs, as a piano soloist and with various groups around the city. He's drawn to the challenges of jazz music, takes a subscription to Downbeat magazine, and considers enrolling in the jazz program at Berklee School of Music in Boston.

* * *

They graduate together in 1967. Penny's desire is to pursue a career in theatre arts. Duncan is, of course, following his dreams in music. They have both worked hard preparing for their goals.

Penny has been working as a waiter in a fine restaurant where the tips are plentiful. Duncan has been saving the money he's received from music gigs and has been teaching some younger students at his family home.

Penny is already accepted at a university in England and plans to start classes in September. Duncan is accepted into Berklee.

Finally, before the summer comes to an end, they spend their final week together at a lodge in Muskoka. Duncan manages to talk his father into loaning him the family car.

While the other vacationers are swimming and playing tennis, Duncan and Penny make passionate love, day and night. They agree to avoid conversation about their future together, understanding that it's too far away to make any firm plans. This week is for frivolous activity and to confirm their undying love for each other.

On Labour Day weekend, Duncan relocates to Boston and Penny departs for England. Duncan is immediately thrown into a chaotic class schedule with workshops, band rehearsals, visiting lecturers, and attending as many live performances as he can afford. He consumes the latest recordings by Miles Davis, Thelonius Monk, and John Coltrane, and buries himself in texts on jazz, practises etudes, arpeggios, chords, and scales, learns all the jazz standards, and absorbs George Russell's new manual, 'Lydian Chromatic Concept of Tonal Organization' like a sponge.

Penny's schedule is also heavily booked with classes and workshops on theatre design, playwrighting, and the history of British theatre.

A regular correspondence between them is well-intentioned, but it wanes as the weeks pass. By mid-December, Penny stops replying to Duncan's letters, despite his frantic attempts to remain in touch. He phones her, but it seems she doesn't receive his messages. 'At least I'll see her at Christmas,' he rationalizes.

When Duncan arrives back home for the holidays, he phones Penny's parents' home hoping to find Penny there, but no one answers. He leaves messages to no avail. Finally, in desperation, he arrives at Penny's house. Her father answers the door; his usual happy smile is replaced by a stern serious response.

"I'm terribly sorry Duncan. Penny isn't here. She's staying in England for the time being. She asked me to tell you that she no longer wants to see you. She hopes that you will understand, as difficult as that may be." Penny's father apologizes again, as if it's somehow his fault.

Duncan is totally frustrated, depressed, dejected. Convinced that Penny has found another lover, he buries himself into his studies. During Christmas dinner with his parents he hardly touches the turkey. On Boxing Day, he returns directly to Boston to spend New Year's Eve alone in his dorm room. A final attempt to contact Penny by phone proves futile. He imagines Penny dancing at a New Year's party with some actor or playwright.

Depression sets in. Duncan's studies begin to crumble, his passion for music is put aside. Instead of practising, he stays in his room alone with his thoughts. A week later, after battling the cockroaches and hearing rats gnawing in the walls, he grabs his belongings and rushes home to move in with his parents. He ignores all outside communication with old friends and turns down offers for music gigs. His only activity is sleeping, watching TV, and thumbing through old Life and Look magazines.

Duncan's parents worry about him. They suggest he take a trip somewhere, a road trip perhaps, if only to clear his mind. He immediately considers travelling to England to confront Penny face-to-face, but quickly abandons the idea as an exercise in futility that would probably prove embarrassing.

* * *

'There has to be more to life than this,' he agonizes. With so much time on his hands, Duncan attempts to make sense of his life. 'As long as I can remember, I've focused on two things, baseball and music.'

When Duncan was a toddler, his dad dressed him in a Brooklyn Dodger cap and jersey. Number 42 was printed in large numbers on his back.

'Jackie Robinson, the first African-American to play in the major leagues, was my idol,' Duncan recalls. 'Still is, I guess. Dad took me to see the movie, 'The Jackie Robinson Story' when I was just six or seven and my life hasn't been the same since.'

His mother, Sophie, was responsible for his love of music. 'Mom sat me down at the piano before I could even walk, at least that's what she always told me. I use to bang away on the keys as if I was composing music. Before long I was studying with a teacher and playing recitals. By the time I entered high school I'd completed all my Royal Conservatory credits. I was a child prodigy, for Christ's sake. That's what the newspapers wrote about me.'

Duncan stares blankly at the walls in the room he's called his own since childhood. Posters of Jackie Robinson and Miles Davis stare back.

'Why do I feel so shitty? Everything was going great, but I just threw in the towel at Berklee, the gateway to my musical career. For what? Surely it wasn't just because Penny dumped me. There has to be more to it than that.'

* * *

After a few more weeks in the doldrums, Duncan suddenly awakes with a smile of determination on his face. He announces to his parents over breakfast, "I'm travelling to Florida."

"Well, that's a surprise," his mother reacts in her Quebecois accent. At least it's warmer there." She turns to her husband who's face is hidden behind the morning paper. "Did you hear that, Mac?" she shouts, pulling his newspaper down. "Duncan's going on a holiday."

"Where?" his father asks.

"I'm going to Florida to watch spring training. I've decided to check out the Pittsburgh Pirates training camp. Since the Dodgers moved to L.A., I've lost interest in them. I've been watching the Pirates lately. I hope to meet Roberto Clemente. He's hot right now."

"Wow." Mac puts the newspaper down. "I'm envious. I wish I could go with you."

"What about your music?" his mother asks.

"There are pianos in Florida, Mom."

"When will you be back?"

"I have no idea, Mom. After training camp, I think I'll just hit the road. You know, like Jack Kerouac. I don't have any plans right now; nowhere special to be. I'll just wander about, see where fate takes me, one day at a time. I'll come home when my money runs out."

A worried frown frames Sophie's forehead. She touches the back of Duncan's hand.

"Are you sure that's what you want to do, Duncan? There are a lot of troubles down there in the States these days, with all of those riots and stuff."

"Oh for crying out loud, Sophie," Mac interjects, suddenly adopting his Scottish brogue. "Let the lad go. He's 20-years-old for Christ's sake. There's nothing better to get over a lost love than to travel. After all, that's how I met you, don't you remember?"

"Of course I remember, you Scottish rogue." She pokes a jab at Mac's shoulder. "You never told me that you were escaping a lost love though."

Duncan breaks into his parents' free-for-all. "I promise you, I'll keep in touch and let you know where I am."

As a going away gift, Mac and Sophie give their son a new Nikon camera, so he'll have a photo record of his trip. In mid-February 1968, Duncan boards a Greyhound heading south, with an open-ended itinerary.

Duncan's first stop is Terry Park in Fort Myers, Florida, the spring training park for the Pittsburgh Pirates. With a concocted story about being a sports reporter for a small Canadian newspaper, he manages to secure a press pass that enables him to photograph and interview the players with very few restrictions. Despite an unfamiliarity with his new camera, he attempts to capture some action shots. He meets and photographs the great Roberto Clemente, who immediately becomes Duncan's new hero.

Duncan confides his ruse as a reporter to a photographer from Sports Illustrated, who gives him some valuable tips and offers to process his films. To Duncan's surprise, the first few rolls of film reveal his raw talent for timing, the secret for great action shots.

"You have a good eye, kid," the Sports Illustrated photographer also compliments Duncan on his composition. "You'll do just fine. Just keep working on it."

From Florida, Duncan hitches a ride with a trucker to New Orleans, where he hopes to hear some great jazz. For twelve hours, however, he endures the unrelenting torture of trucking music blasting from the radio over a grating chorus of meshing gears, CB lingo, diesel engine rattling, and shouting conversation with a southern drawl.

He arrives in New Orleans in mid-morning, exhausted. Luckily, the trucker drops him off at a budget-priced hotel where he can catch up on sleep. He finally wakes up at 7:30 pm, takes a quick shower, and searches the hotel for a restaurant. A jazz quartet is performing in the lounge that sounds solid to him, so he grabs a drink and orders a roadhouse meal. After some brief conversation with the musicians, he's invited to sit in for a set.

Duncan is comfortable playing with the band and is familiar with the tunes they call. After the set, the bass player buys Duncan a drink. "Great job, man. If you're ever back this way, drop in." Duncan and the bass player share a cool 'hooked-thumbs' jazz handshake.

While sitting at the bar, Duncan is approached by an appealing older woman, possibly mid-to-late-30s; a blonde southern belle whose drawl invites him to spend the weekend with her, frolicking, sipping mint juleps and fornicating.

"Oh Christ," Duncan says. "Forget it. The last thing I need is a hooker."

"Don't worry, I'm not a prostitute. No money needed. In fact, I'll give you a hundred dollars, just give me your weekend. I'll even supply the safes."

"There has to be a story here somewhere," he tells her. Duncan always wants to know the story behind everything. A voice triggers Duncan from deep inside, 'Curiosity kills the cat,' a phrase his mother used when he was an inquisitive child.

"So, what's the catch then?" Duncan queries.

"There is a story, if you want to hear it." She doesn't wait for Duncan's answer.

"I'm married to a marine. They called him up last month for special training; they're shipping him out to Vietnam. I have no idea whether I'll ever see him again, or what shape he'll be in when he returns."

"Oh shit," Duncan says with a sad face. "I'm sorry."

"Don't be sorry. Listen to this, you won't believe it," the blonde continues, clutching Duncan's arm. "I just found out today that he was getting it on with my younger sister. Do you believe that asshole? So-o-o, I'm here to meet someone for a few drinks and to have a good time, that's all. I won't even ask you your name, and I won't tell you mine. No declarations of love and all that crap."

The blond leans her face close to Duncan's and lowers her voice to a whisper. "I just want to fuck somebody, and from all the guys in this bar, I chose you. Don't that just make you feel re-e-al good?"

"I'm flattered," Duncan blushes, "but I'm leaving town in a few days, so I'm not looking for any relationship. You're a beautiful woman, and I'm sure you'll be great in bed, so …" Duncan inhales to pump up his confidence. "OK, let's make some memories together."

"Whew. I thought you were going to tell me to fuck myself."

"That would be a waste," he answers, proud of how quickly he responds with a sharp comeback line. 'Christ, I've been reading too many Mickey Spillane novels,' he ponders. 'I'm beginning to talk like Mike Hammer.'

It's Duncan's first intercourse since Penny left for England, pure and simple lust this time, much different than sex under any illusions of falling in love. They frolic at all hours of the day, unrestricted to schedules. The blonde's seniority teaches Duncan that lovemaking is an art form, one that could easily compete with baseball and jazz music.

When she leaves the hotel two days later, she kisses him fondly, thanking him for the wonderful weekend. Duncan grabs his camera and prepares to become a tourist. He reaches into his gadget bag for a fresh roll of Tri-X film. An envelope drops to the floor. There's a C-note and a brief letter. "Thanks for straightening out my life. Happy travelling kid."

Over the following week, Duncan visits several blues bars, a Dixie tavern, and a rock club. While enjoying a drink at the Dixie tavern, he asks where he can find some bebop in New Orleans. He's directed to The Ebony Room, an obscure bar on the other side of town. He hails a taxi. Before leaving the cab, the driver asks if he's sure he wants to be dropped off here. Duncan naïvely asks him why.

The cabbie offers, "I don't mean to scare you sir, but in the last 10 minutes, have you seen any folks that look like you?"

"Thanks for the heads-up, but I don't have any issues. My idols are Jackie Robinson, Roberto Clemente, Miles Davis, John Coltrane, and Martin Luther King. None of them look like me. I don't give a shit what colour people are. Besides, where would we be without jazz … and baseball of course?"

The cabbie chuckles. "I hear you, man. I wish all people could say the same," adding, "some people won't even get into my cab because of who I am. Do you believe that?" He accepts Duncan's generous tip and shares a cool handshake. "God bless and good luck sir."

The club is dark and smoky, with an ambience of skunk-weed lingering. It's damp and muggy, and hotter than Hell. Patrons assess Duncan as he enters and assumes a stool at the bar.

'The cabbie was right, nobody looks like me,' Duncan ponders. A bartender approaches, swiping the bar with a damp towel. "You lost mister? Looking for directions?"

"I'd rather have a drink. What's good?"

The bartender serves Duncan a Jack Daniel, his eyes revealing an uncertainty about what the stranger is doing in the bar.

"I hear the band here cooks, like Bird," Duncan offers, snapping his fingers.

"You're not lost, man. You're in the right place." The bartender's worry lines dissolve. "They'll be back on the stand in a few minutes. Where's your accent from anyway?"

"I'm from up in Canada, just travelling around, hearing some music, taking some pictures, watching some baseball. You know, touristy things."

"What do you know about bebop?"

"I play bebop piano," Duncan responds. He spreads his hands out against the edge of the bar, like it's an imaginary keyboard. "I'm into Bird, Monk, Miles and Trane. You ever hear of Oscar Peterson? He's from Canada too."

"All right." The bartender introduces Duncan to the band when they return. "Check it out man, this cat plays bop piano."

"If he's sober, he can sit in," the tenor sax player offers.

It feels great to be playing some real music again. The set begins with a medium blues. The tenor player is dynamite and the drummer puts down a solid pulse. The bass player, a keen listener, immediately senses Duncan's approach to the changes and digs in, offering musical suggestions of his own. They follow the blues with a ballad that gives the tenor player some room before blazing through Oleo, a Sonny Rollins bebop classic.

When Duncan steps down, the band members high-five him. "Where did you learn to play like that, man?" the tenor player asks.

The bass player says, "You come back here anytime, you hear?"

CHAPTER 02

EPIPHANY

1968:

After being exposed to some great music, Duncan has doubts about his decision to quit Berklee, but travel and photography are starting to occupy a larger portion of his interest. He lingers in New Orleans for another week to photograph the city and its culture, particularly in the historic French Quarter where the architecture reminds him of Old Québec.

A fleeting memory emerges of his grandfather when Duncan and his parents travelled to Québec to visit his mother's family home and his French-speaking grandparents.

'I was just a child, maybe seven or eight,' Duncan recalls. 'Grand-Papá was a strange but fascinating old man who dabbled in folk art, making sculptures of people and *objets d'art* from discarded junk. His brightly painted workshop in the back yard, with the old woodstove, was crammed with antiquated tools and weird handmade animations that swirled when the wind passed through them. He designed and built rough-hewn kinetic machines that, when connected to other pieces, passed on their energy and movement but accomplished nothing at all. He seemed to understand me despite his inability to communicate in English. What small smatterings of French that I picked up from my mother were of little use.'

His memories touch something inside. 'I wish I could have taken photos of my grandfather.' Duncan ponders. 'He was small, like a gnome, and became so excited while showing me his art pieces, talking wildly in French and waving his arms about. It would have been a challenge for me though, to freeze the action of his animated gestures and the expressions on his face as he nattered on wildly in French while describing his creations.'

Duncan's reminiscing morphs into a philosophical self-examination of why he chose to become a musician and how he feels about it now.

'While there is incredible personal satisfaction playing jazz, there is little opportunity for me to explore my interests in the human condition. Sure, I'm performing with musicians, both black and white, with whom I share the intensity and pulse of the music, primarily an African-American art form. Together we contribute and benefit from the interaction, but that's solely between us, the musicians. What I'm not doing, however, is contributing toward a better world. Sure, I can compose a piece of instrumental music and title it, 'Ode to Integration,' or something similar. The only reference to improving the human condition is in the title. If I took the same composition and called it 'I Love Lucy,' it would mean something about a TV sitcom.'

Duncan ponders his thoughts, attempting to rationalize his new attraction to photography.

'Writers write masterpieces about famine and poverty, about war and peace, and the words make people think, or become inspired to do something about the problem. Painters show the public what they're concerned about and people weep. Jazz musicians pour their soul into a tempo-burning bebop tune and the audience thinks it must be good because the musicians are sweating.'

It isn't until the following morning, while Duncan is taking travel photographs in the streets of the French Quarter, that it strikes him. His camera snaps random images of ordinary people going about their normal routines. He challenges himself to capture their gestures and interactions. Some of what he witnesses before him are humorous anecdotes of normal behaviour: a man jumping over a puddle and two people bumping into each other on a crowded street. Others are tender moments: lovers holding hands and a mother wiping remnants of chocolate ice cream from her child's frowning face. He begins to recognize the role photography can play in expressing his concerns for the human condition, something his music doesn't deliver for him.

'I want to show the world what I see, what I feel, and what other people feel and how they express themselves.'

In a local library he peruses issues of Life Magazine, paying close attention to the impact of the images. The photo essays of W. Eugene Smith touch an emotional chord. He's drawn to the strength of composition and perspective and wants to learn more about the craft. At a bookstore, he buys a photo magazine and picks up a 'How-to-Take-Better-Photographs' textbook with dozens of graphs and diagrams of apertures and shutter speeds.

As a balance to the technical material, he also buys a book of photographs from the Farm Security Administration and is immediately moved by the 'Migrant Mother' photo by Dorothea Lange. A desire to follow a similar path consumes him. He revises his itinerary from baseball and jazz, to concentrate more on human condition issues.

'Right now, I'm in the south,' Duncan acknowledges to himself. 'where civil rights are the big issue. What can I do with that? The touristy French Quarter is quaint, but other neighbourhoods will show the issues more bluntly.'

Realizing that Mississippi is constantly in the news for its resistance to integration, the naïve Duncan boards the next Greyhound to Jackson.

Upon his arrival at the bus station he's immediately exposed to the state's segregation policy through 'white-only' signs in restaurant windows and public washrooms, and he witnesses a white policeman pushing an older black man to the sidewalk for no apparent reason. Fear exists with every corner he turns.

From a table in a 'white only' restaurant, he observes street life passing by a window. 'Is it the fear that pushes me along and can that be a problem, or is it just me paying some dues?' He pauses his thoughts. 'If I'm experiencing fear, what about those poor bastards who are living it every day, being told what they can and cannot do? How can I photograph that without offending anyone? Is that even possible? Should I even worry about offending anyone? Maybe that's a reason to do it.'

Back in the streets, Duncan watches for local contrasts that identify segregation, mainly contradictions to the way he was raised. The 'white only' and 'colored only' signs that appear at doorways and above water fountains do the job, but what Duncan is hoping to see is someone challenging the message of the signs.

'What's the penalty for disobeying one of the signs?' he wonders. 'Does a white person entering a 'colored only' establishment suffer the same punishment as the opposite? Not bloody likely,' he concludes.

As he turns a corner expecting more of the same, he's confronted with a young, mixed-race couple heading toward him. They're holding hands and smiling to each other. Duncan snaps a quick photo that also includes several bystanders sneering at the couple from the edges of his frame. 'It's a keeper,' Duncan notes.

Further along the street, he raises his camera to photograph some kids playing baseball. They too are a blend of skin tones, doing what kids do by nature. As he's taking some photos he's approached by a large white man with a tattoo of a Confederate flag on his arm and a pack of Marlboros stuffed up his sleeve.

"What are you doing? Get the fuck outa here."

On another street, he's told the same thing by an African-American woman.

'At least that part is equal,' Duncan concludes.

While spending a week at a downtown hotel, he's treated with wonderful southern hospitality until he helps a black porter lift some heavy baggage in the lobby. There are looks from bystanders and hotel employees, but nothing is said at the time. When he asks to extend his room booking for two more days, he's refused. The manager suggests that it's time for him to move on, adding, "We don't want any trouble here."

Duncan leans across the desk and quietly suggests, "You got all the trouble you need already."

Before leaving the hotel in the morning, while cleaning his camera gear, Duncan is still unsure where he will travel to next. The television news is focused on Martin Luther King's meeting with striking sanitation workers in Memphis and on the riots that ensued. A 16-year-old is killed by police. Thousands of National Guards are called in to quell the violence. In the morning Duncan is on a bus to Memphis with hopes of witnessing the aftermath.

When he arrives in Memphis, he hears about the funeral of the young man, Larry Payne, at Clayborn Temple. Duncan has no intention of trying to enter the temple and is satisfied to watch from a distance. He takes a few photographs to establish a wide view of the event without inciting any undue antagonism.

Martin Luther King arrives the day after the funeral to deliver a speech.

"I've seen the Promised Land. I may not get there with you. But I want you to know tonight, that we, as a people, will get to the Promised Land! And so I'm happy, tonight. I'm not worried about anything. I'm not fearing any man. Mine eyes have seen the glory of the coming of the Lord!"

The power of King's speech roils in Duncan's chest. Tears emerge uncontrollably. Duncan has been following the events of the civil rights movement for several years but always from the distant and comfortable isolation of his family's TV in Hamilton. This is real.

Duncan manages to secure several photos of Dr. King from a distance. He also takes images of the people in the surrounding crowd, white and black together, all sharing the emotions and joyful tears of the moment.

The following evening, when Duncan arrives at his next destination, Nashville, the news is catastrophic. Martin Luther King is dead, assassinated by a gunman on his motel balcony in Memphis. Again the emotion overtakes Duncan. This time the tears are not joyful. He can't stop staring at the TV in his room as response to the assassination erupts into chaos throughout the country.

'This violence is not what Dr. King would have wanted,' Duncan reflects.

There are monumental events in each person's life when one is steered toward a new direction; turnaround moments, forks in the road. Duncan isn't sure where his life is heading, but he understands that it will be in a different direction than it was yesterday.

* * *

Duncan experienced enough country music to last him a lifetime while travelling with the trucker to New Orleans, but he stays in Nashville another night before moving on to Louisville Kentucky, home of the Louisville Slugger, the baseball bat of choice for his idols, Jackie Robinson and more recently, Roberto Clemente. He visits the factory and museum, adding some touristy photos to his ever-growing collection.

Curious about the Kentucky Hills, Duncan takes a detour to Lexington, home of the Kentucky Derby and to some very wealthy people, and then hitches a ride, stopping at Corbin for some chicken at Harlan Sanders Café. Another ride takes him through the strip-mined coal-country hills of Harlan County, recognized as one of the poorest counties in the U.S.

He books into a motel in the town of Harlan where he tries to take photos around town after breakfast but is met with some local resistance that involves the threat of weaponry. He packs his camera away in the gadget bag and asks, jokingly, "Is Harlan Sanders named after the county and the town, or are they named after him?" His humour is unappreciated.

He hitchhikes a ride through Cumberland Gap that returns him to Lexington. Finally, he books a Greyhound to Cincinnati and northeast to Cleveland before stopping for a rest. A day later he's off to Rochester, the home of American photography, and Kodak. There's an exhibition of Farm Security Administration images showing in the gallery.

Duncan recognizes the power they project when he stares at an authentic print of Dorothea Lange's 'Migrant Mother.' His new direction in life is beginning to materialize. He discovers the world of documentary photography.

The FSA exhibit provides an emotional strengthening for him, but it is Robert Frank's book, 'The Americans,' discovered in the Eastman bookstore, that creates the biggest impression. He's also attracted to the introduction by Jack Kerouac, the author of 'On the Road.'

"What a piece of shit," Duncan whispers aloud.

"I thought the same thing as you did when I first laid eyes on that book," a woman in the bookstore tells him, "but it'll grow on you, I promise. Now, I can't even put my copy down. I wish I had the guts to shoot that way myself. If I were you, I'd get a copy now, it's going to be a classic and hard to find in no time, and it'll change the way you see."

It's in the streets of Rochester that tests Duncan's mettle. Although he's a mere 50 kilometres from home, he's a foreigner. There are differences.

'Hamilton is a city of white faces,' Duncan recognizes. 'Everybody I know is white. This is a society of mixed faces, but they don't share the same terrain. Oh sure, they all shop in the stores and work in the same factories, but they don't all live in the same neighbourhoods, or socialize together.'

Duncan creates a personal project. 'I want to capture the nuances of difference between a typical American city (Rochester) and my

Canadian home (Hamilton). Both are factory towns and the people are mostly blue collar.'

He wanders into bowling alleys and laundromats, snapping candid photos of people playing and interacting. He observes people at bus stop lineups and shoppers pushing carts of groceries through supermarket parking lots. He takes photos of workers as they leave their shift at one of Kodak's factories.

Later, in his hotel room, Duncan forces himself to take another look at Robert Frank's book. They are images of the same subject matter that he's been encountering in his travels, but 'Frank has torn moments from the tapestry of the American dream, and has revealed the truths hidden behind it,' he concludes.

Duncan concentrates too hard to organize his naïve vision into compositional perfection. The immediacy and the rawness of Frank's images, however, inject an indelible impression on his soul.

'I have the same problem with my music,' Duncan realizes. I have a constant conflict between textbook perfection and emotional truth.'

In his quest, he's understandably drawn to Frank's subject matter: diners, racial segregation, complacency, the melting pot, etc. His newfound excitement, and the knowledge that his odyssey will soon be over, keep him in Rochester for several more days as he wanders through a variety of districts and neighbourhoods capturing the diversity with his camera.

Late one evening, Duncan hears loud music emanating from the Upper Falls district and strolls there to check it out. While walking through the African-American neighbourhood, he encounters a street dance in progress. Before he can use his camera, he's surrounded by a group of young men demanding money. To avoid any physical violence, Duncan empties his wallet.

One of the men steps forward and confronts him. "You're in the wrong place, *honkie*," he says, pushing Duncan backward. The others laugh. Fortunately for Duncan, they are satisfied with his cash and depart into the darkness.

He arrives safely at his parent's home in Hamilton the following day, convinced that the altercation won't deter him from continuing his new passion. He invests in darkroom supplies: film processing reels, tanks, and chemistry. The clerk at the camera store provides him with basic instructions. In advance of his upcoming birthday, his parents buy him an enlarger and trays for printing.

Duncan has a new plan. He applies to a college for photography and is accepted into the full-time program on the basis of a portfolio he's slapped together from his travel photos. He hopes to major in documentary photojournalism. For the balance of the summer, he prepares a stronger portfolio that displays the uniqueness of his photographic vision and the variety of his subject material.

In September 1968, Duncan relocates into a small apartment in Toronto and quickly finds a part-time job working in a camera shop. He also secures music gigs as a solo pianist in an upscale restaurant that allow him to purchase a used VW Beetle and cover his basic living expenses.

Jack Bryant, the editor of 'Human Interest,' a lifestyle and travel magazine is impressed with Duncan's portfolio and offers him freelance assignments while he attends college.

Duncan finishes the freshman year at the top of his class.

His instructor advises him to make a choice between his music and his photography. "You can't serve two masters, Duncan. You'll have to make a choice."

CHAPTER 03

WISDOM

Toronto & Manitoulin Island, 1969 – 1971:

Documentary photography has also been referred to as Visual Anthropology by academics. The respected American anthropologist, Margaret Mead, used photography extensively to document her studies in Samoa and Papua, New Guinea. One of Mead's studies punched holes in the theories, current at that time, that intelligence could be measurable by race.

With a keen interest in cultures other than his own, Duncan is influenced by 'The Family of Man,' a widely-published collection of documentary images from photographers around the world. Many photographs from Mead's projects appear in the 'The Family of Man.'

"I'm moved to tears by how these photographs powerfully demonstrate how people from different cultures are so very much the same in all respects," Duncan writes in one of his class papers. "Regardless of where we are born, and into what culture and faith, we all share the same values: family, activities, the arts, and we all have the same needs: sustenance, shelter, work, friendship, and survival of the species. All children are created in the same way, through love and desire. One must question what we have against each other. Why do we hate when all we want is a decent life for our children?"

The instructors at the college are aware of Duncan's strong interests in the documentary tradition. During a week-long college field trip to Manitoulin Island in his final year, Duncan is assigned to document the Indigenous people of Wikwemkoong Unceded Territory, a community of three thousand people.

To create a 'real world' example, Duncan is dropped off at the community by his instructor. It's a blustery October day. He wanders around the small town before seeking out the band office for information, and hopefully, permission to stay for a week and take photographs. The instructor promises to pick him up in a week.

Duncan is introduced to the Chief who, sceptical of the unannounced visitor from the south, peppers Duncan with questions.

"Who are you? Why are you here? What are you looking for? What did you expect to see, and who do you want to photograph?"

Before Duncan can answer the first question, the Chief adds, "I already heard reports that you were wandering around as if you were surveying the area. Some people reported a strange white man in town acting as if he's looking for somebody. They thought you were an undercover cop or an agent from Indian Affairs."

Before attempting to explain himself, Duncan removes his portfolio from its case and passes it across the desk. The Chief looks impressed as he slowly turns the pages. Wisely, Duncan remains silent until the page turning is completed.

"OK. You obviously know how to use a camera, so why are you here?"

"I'm Duncan MacGregor. I'm a college student and ..."

"If you're here to conduct some kind of sociological or psychological study, you should probably start returning home. We've been studied to death, and we never get to see the results. They end up being buried somewhere in Ottawa so nobody can find them. To be honest, nobody really wants to read them anyway."

"Like I said, I'm a photography student at college and I've always been interested in cultures different from my own. I would like to take photos of whatever I get to see, just as if someone from another culture would want to see how I live in mine." Duncan smiles and adds a humorous observation, "If it's of any value to you, I always cheered for the Indians at the movies when I was a kid."

The Chief laughs and calls out through his office door. "Hey Eugene, we've got a live one here." Eugene joins the discussion and looks through the portfolio.

The Chief queries Duncan further. "You said you want to photograph whatever you get to see. What did you see when you were walking around before you came in here?"

Duncan tells him, "So far, a new school, some kids playing baseball, an old mission church, a new lodge for elders, a corner store with kids hanging out, some new houses and some old houses, pretty much the same as my own neighbourhood so far."

Without further delay, the Chief says, "You can take photos anywhere you want. If anybody gives you a problem just tell them that I said it was OK. Hopefully, I'll get to see some of the pictures. By the way, I always cheered for the cowboys; those damned Hollywood Indians were all Italians anyway."

The Chief adds, "If you're looking for a place to stay, I recommend Jeannie's place. She sometimes takes in visitors and she could use some company these days. She's also a great cook."

The Chief drives Duncan to Jeannie's farmhouse on the edge of town. He opens the door and shouts some words in his native language. A plump, white-haired woman wearing a handmade apron covered in flour, meets them in the hallway. Duncan estimates her to be in her mid-70s. She communicates with the Chief. The only word Duncan recognizes is 'photographer.'

"Oh my," Jeannie turns to Duncan, her hands covering the sides of her face. I'm not ready to have my picture taken," she chuckles. "I'm just dressed in my working clothes. Today is my bread-baking day."

While the Chief explains that Duncan needs a place to stay for a week, Duncan inhales deeply, filling his nostrils with the sweetness of fresh dough baking in a huge country wood oven.

"This smells like heaven," Duncan utters.

"That's the smell of my special wood. I only use it for baking bread, once a week."

The Chief leans closer to Duncan with a grin on his face. "You won't starve here." He turns to leave. "I'll see you around town. If anybody wants to know what you're doing here, just tell him I gave you permission."

Jeannie struggles with arthritis to show Duncan to an upstairs bedroom. The brass bed is covered with a substantial soft mattress and three hand-sewn quilts adorned with Indigenous patterns. The heaviness of the quilts keep Duncan from rolling in his sleep but are welcome protection against the cold unheated upstairs of the old house.

'I feel like I've just stepped back into the 19th century,' he considers while staring up at the open uninsulated beams in the bedroom ceiling.

Most of Duncan's early images are observations from a distance: kids in the school playground, teens hanging out at the store, a few 'take my picture' portraits, some sports photos of a sandlot baseball game. Gradually, the inhabitants become as interested in Duncan as he is in them. Even Jeannie, despite her early resistance, becomes an ideal subject, especially in the photos taken as window light passes through the curls of smoke encircling her from her special bread-baking wood.

Within a few days, the school principal invites him to photograph in the classrooms. He attends a birthday party for a senior citizen at the Elder's Retirement Home and joins two families for dinner at their invitations.

Duncan returns home at week's end, a few pounds heavier from Jeannie's home cooking. He brings with him, a bag full of exposed Tri-X black and white film and enough stories and experiences to feed his desire to continue the project.

* * *

In February, he returns to Manitoulin and arrives at the band office with a set of contact sheets and selected 8 x 10-inch prints for the Chief.

"This is everything I saw," he says.

The Chief stares intently at a print of a young boy. "This is the first photo of a real Indian I've ever seen taken by a white man. This kid's definitely not Italian. You have talent my friend. Can I keep this print?"

"It's yours," Duncan answers.

"I know. He's my son."

Eugene brings in coffees and they sit around a table passing photos back and forth.

"Look at this one of Rachel," Eugene points at the photo. "She's my cousin, eh? Here's one of Jimmy, he's my uncle." There's laughter, followed by some tears. "Oh Jeez, here's Jeannie baking her bread. She looks so good in the photo." Eugene's face saddens. "We just lost her two weeks ago in a fire."

"Oh no, really?" The news of Jeanie's passing strikes Duncan hard. She was like a substitute mother to him when he stayed there. "I was planning to visit her this afternoon."

"Come with me," the Chief says. "I'm taking you for a ride around the rez. It's time you met some important people."

They arrive at a small Insulbrick-sided cabin on the edge of town. Wood smoke billows from the chimney. Inside, the sweet smell of apples cooking is inviting. A small, wizened woman, not unlike an apple doll, is baking pies in the oven of the woodstove. An old man, presumably the woman's husband, enters the room. He walks tall and proud, despite evidence of arthritis in his gnarled hands.

The Chief utters some words to the old man in their own tongue and the man responds, "Aha."

The old man points to a chair for Duncan to sit in and begins to speak slowly in English.

"This island is the place where The Great Spirit chose to create natural man. For our people it is a sacred place, a place not unlike the white man's Garden of Eden. Our beliefs are very similar to yours." He continues, providing details about life on the Island of the Great Spirit.

"There are medicines growing here that are provided for our well-being. If you become ill from something you ate, or suffer from poison ivy, the antidote is within a few feet of the cause. We know this to be true."

The old woman serves tea and a slice of pie, still warm from the oven. *"Miigwetch,"* the Chief utters. He explains to Duncan that the old man they are visiting is one of the community's most revered elders, a medicine man who is respected by his peers across the entire continent.

"He is a man of great wisdom; a keeper of the knowledge that has been passed down orally through many generations. It is important that the elders pass their knowledge on to the younger people for our culture to survive. They used to do that in the home while taking care of their grandchildren. Then the white man took our children from us and taught them about the white man's ways in his own language. Finally, after many years of suffering in those damned residential schools, we have our own schools and many of our own teachers, and the elders now teach traditional ways and languages to the children in the schools, the same new schools you saw when you were walking around. In some respects, we are completing a circle."

The elder continues. "We are the people of the Three Fires, a treaty agreed upon by three tribes sharing a similar language: the Ojibwe, the Pottawatomi, and the Odawa. This island was the natural home of the Odawa. We were entrusted by the Great Spirit to be the guardians and keepers of this sacred place. Once, a long time ago, when our people were being threatened, we were forced to evacuate the island of the Great Spirit. As we were leaving to travel further north and join our brothers, we set fire to the island, to leave nothing of value for our enemies. Several generations later, we returned to reclaim our original home. The trees and medicines had regrown, and the animals had returned. It was like a rebirth."

Duncan stops to eat some pie and to sip his tea before starting to ask another question, but the Chief places his hand on Duncan's arm. "Wait. The elder hasn't finished talking yet."

"Fire is a natural event," the elder continues. "Just as the forests need regeneration, so does man. New growth begins after a fire. We place our faith in the circle, where birth meets death and rebirth begins. It's one of the reasons we dance in a circle during the powwow. A circle completed is an event to be celebrated. It is about leaving and returning, losing and finding, wondering and discovering. You can also find these values in your white man's Bible; they are universal truths. Everything is according to the Great Spirit's design. In our language there is no word for coincidence. There are many things that are just not intended to be explained or understood."

While the elder is speaking, Duncan is reluctant to put the camera to his eye. During a silent moment, he asks the elder if he minds having his picture taken.

"Of course I don't mind," the elder answers, relaxing the seriousness of his face to display a grin. "Speaking is what I do. Taking pictures is what you do. The Great Spirit has given us these gifts. We must use them. I'm not one of those Indigenous people who thinks that a photograph will take away my soul. Nothing can do that. We can never lose our soul. We can, however, share it with others. This is how circles are completed."

Before they leave the elder's house, the Chief leans over to Duncan. "Do you mind taking some photos of Jim and his wife? Today is their 56th anniversary. I wouldn't mind you taking a couple of photos with Jim and me too, for posterity. He's my mentor. He teaches me everything he knows about traditional medicines, and he knows a lot."

The Chief opens the elder's closet and removes a headdress of eagle feathers. He places it on the elder's head for the photos.

"You have just made a new friend with the most revered person in the Indigenous community," the Chief tells Duncan. "He likes you. He said you are an honourable man."

The elder takes Duncan's hand with a long firm grip. Duncan fails to hold back the tears.

The photographs Duncan takes in Manitoulin become very personal to him. He doesn't offer them for sale to any magazines for a long time, until he can fully comprehend the wisdom entrusted in him.

The deeper he probes into documentary photography opens windows to other worlds for Duncan. Each new experience connects to another, creating an endless string of possibilities for him to discover. Curiosity is a driving force for him. Every opportunity to explore a new culture or social circumstance draws him further into the story behind it.

A chance meeting with an international student in the journalism program catches Duncan's interest. He is from Nicaragua and seems to be well-versed in the country's politics, but it is the student's obsession with baseball that initially attracts Duncan's attention. Over coffee, they compare baseball stats and players.

"How is it that Nicaraguans love baseball?" Duncan asks. "I thought soccer was the game of Latin America."

"It's all political, *amigo*," his friend suggests. "Everywhere the *yanquis* ruled, their baseball took over. In Nicaragua, they governed from 1912 to 1933, and introduced baseball. The same thing happened in Cuba, Puerto Rico, and Dominican Republic. It even happened in Japan after World War Two, right?"

"How is the baseball there, in Nicaragua?" Duncan asks.

"Fantastic, *amigo*. It's on a par with the major leagues in the U.S. You should go there. But you should learn some Spanish before you go."

Duncan takes his friend's advice. He enrols in a night school Spanish course. Never receptive to language courses in high school, for some reason he excels at night school, perhaps because he's now anticipating a defined purpose.

One night, during a break while performing jazz at The Cellar in Yorkville Village, Duncan is approached by a woman. "Can I share your table with you?" she asks. "It's busier than usual tonight."

"No problem," Duncan responds, extending the only vacant chair in the club to her."

"The band sounds great," she offers.

"Thanks." He sips some coffee. "These guys in the band are terrific to work with."

The woman is interrupted by a man whispering in her ear.

"Maybe later. I'll see you around midnight?" she tells him.

Several other men pass the table with greetings like, "Hey Cindy. Working tonight?"

Her answer is the same to them all. "All booked up guys. Maybe tomorrow."

Duncan's journalistic curiosity draws him into a direct question. "So, what's your story, Cindy? Are you a working girl? I've seen you in here before."

"Yeah. You found me out. Gotta make a living, you know. Pay the rent. Look after my daughter."

"Wow. That has to be a tough go. How old's your daughter?"

"She's just four. My sister helps look after her when I'm working. She's a real cutie too. I mean my daughter, not my sister. Well she's a looker too, but she has a respectable job in an office."

Duncan asks, "So how does it work? Are you a freelancer, or do have an agent?"

"Do you mean a pimp?"

"You said it, not me."

"I'm a freelancer. As long as I stay out of the other girls' territories, I'm safe." She gulps the last of her coffee. "Gotta go. I have a ten o'clock. Maybe see you around."

"Yeah. Take care Cindy."

"You too."

Cindy sits with Duncan the following week, mainly for the conversation. She asks, "How do you survive as a musician. It's pretty much the same as what I do, no?" she poses. "You gotta do what the customer wants. That kinda takes the art out if it, doesn't it?"

Duncan laughs. "Here I get to do pretty much what I want to do. The money isn't great but it helps the college expenses."

"Oh, a student, eh? What are you studying, Duncan?"

"Documentary photojournalism, mainly multiple picture stories on interesting things in life." All week, Duncan has considered asking

Cindy about doing a story on her. It seems that now would be the right moment to ask.

"What would you think about me taking photos and doing a story about you? Not while you're working per se, but photos of you in here, contacting clients, what you do for leisure, family life, etc. We'll do some interviews, and the written copy will cover the intimate details. The photos will provide the ambience to give the story some emotional qualities. You know, the late nights, the dim lighting, smoke, atmosphere, etc."

Cindy hesitates before answering. "Sure. Let's do that."

Duncan is gobsmacked. He was certain she'd turn him down.

For the next month, Duncan works diligently on the story. Initially, he shadows Cindy by capturing establishing shots around the club, taking cabs at night, and returning home later, even candid shots of clients talking her up and playing coy with her and sharing jokes. Duncan promises Cindy that the clients will be unrecognizable in the photos. Further along in the story, when they are both more at ease, he's invited to her apartment to take photos of her preparing herself for dates. She allows him to include some detail photos of tattoos in intimate locations.

Eventually, Duncan suggests including the normal activities in her day, the things every working person tends to: laundry, shopping, budgeting, spending time with her daughter.

The story becomes a vehicle for normalizing the otherwise stigmatized world of a sex worker. Jack Bryant praises Duncan for his sensitivity and his ability to avoid sensationalism. He publishes the story in Human Interest (HI) magazine. There are many positive letters to the editor. Of course, there are also the negative letters that threaten to cancel subscriptions for publishing 'filth,' but Jack gives Duncan his support.

Duncan continues his coverage documenting the elders in Manitoulin Island. During his visits with the elders, they share many of their ancient stories with him and include him in sweet grass ceremonies that reinforce the importance of the circle in their culture.

Upon graduation in May 1971, Jack Bryant offers Duncan a full-time position at the magazine as a photo editor's assistant. He encourages Duncan to continue shooting assignments for the magazine and allows him to freelance on the weekends for newspapers as long as the subjects don't conflict with their own material.

He's also able to continue playing piano in local clubs with various jazz groups and as a soloist. Life is good.

PART TWO
1948 – 1968

CHAPTER 04

THE ESTATE

Dos Rios, Nicaragua, 1948 – 1968:

Sister Hortencia prepares a carafe of dark coffee to prepare for the long day ahead of her. Doña Isabel, the young wife of Don Ricardo, is expecting her debut child. Her labour screams are already escaping through the open windows of the large white house on the hill, announcing to the citizens of Dos Rios, that there will soon be dancing and excitement in the streets. Everything celebrated by Don Ricardo is cause for a party of immense proportions, at least for the small village in the highlands.

Dos Rios was founded to accommodate the workers at the gold mine several kilometres away via a mountain road barely wide enough to handle the mining company's trucks. Many of the workers live in homemade shanties scattered throughout the mountains within an hour's walking distance from Dos Rios, where supplies are available at the company store for prices well exceeding those in the cities.

For many of the workers and their families, the only available transport is by mule-drawn wooden-wheeled wagons, on horseback, or by foot. Every Saturday, *campesino* vendors trod the distance toting heavily laden baskets on their heads to market with their homegrown and handmade products. They hawk their wares from temporary stalls surrounding the park where Don Ricardo operates his horse racing and cockfighting at dusk on Saturday nights. Wages are paid at the mine by the end of shift each Friday with most of it returning later the same weekend through gambling and profits from the company store.

Sister Hortencia has monitored the expansion of Doña Isabel's midriff over the months and fully expects the population of Dos Rios to increase by two at day's end, assuming of course, there are no deaths.

Don Ricardo recently turned 30, ten years senior to his wife. He oversees the operations at the gold mine for its Canadian owners.

Doña Isabel is the sole daughter of a wealthy German industrialist who, anticipating the onslaught of World War Two, escaped to Central America with his wife, his daughter, and his vast fortune. He, and Isabel's mother, died in a sailing accident, relinquishing his entire estate to his daughter. Doña Isabel and Don Ricardo met two years ago at a fancy soirée hosted by *el presidente* at his home in the capital, where Don Ricardo impressed her with his Latino charisma and his private informal tango lessons. They were married within six months.

The Doña's screaming episodes become more frequent as Sister Hortencia saunters, coffee in hand, down the hallway in the grand *hacienda* to the birthing room. She directs one of the nuns to inform Don Ricardo about his impending fatherhood. "Tell him to hurry or he'll miss the big event."

When Sister Hortencia arrives, the Doña is shouting obscenities to her assistant and threatening her to eternal damnation.

"Everything is all right, Doña Isabel," the nun promises her. "What you are experiencing is normal, especially for a first-time expectant."

The Doña shouts. "This will never happen again, I can assure you, Sister. I'll take steps to make sure it never happens again."

"Be careful what you promise when the good Lord is within hearing distance."

"If he can hear me now, then he should stop this immediately." the Doña shouts at the ceiling, "Can you hear me Lord? Pull the plug. Right now." Suddenly, another contraction. "Not that way. *Jesús Cristo!* Just finish it up. Let's get this over with."

Sister Hortencia ignores the Doña's blasphemy as a child emerges, safe and sound. "A boy, Doña. You have a boy."

No sooner had she issued her declaration than a second head appears. With a broad smile, Sister Hortencia issues, "And another beautiful baby boy. Congratulations. You will make Don Ricardo a very happy man. It looks like the good Lord has ignored your cursing."

Don Ricardo bursts into the room without knocking. Sister Hortencia hands the first-born to Don Ricardo; tears and a broad smile overtake him. "See, Don Ricardo, it's a healthy little boy, and he has a little brother as well, equally handsome."

All attention is focused on the *patrón* and his newborn princes when the assistant whispers to the nun. "Sister, I think we might have a problem."

Doña Isabel struggles for breath. She thrashes in pain while blood flows freely from her loins. Sister Hortencia crosses herself before taking charge of the situation.

Don Ricardo panics. "What the fuck is happening? Is she OK? What can I do?"

"Just get out of the room. Now!" Sister Hortencia chases him. "Out! We need our space to deal with this. You can stand right outside the door but get out. Now!"

Don Ricardo obeys the nun's urgent commands without question. From his vantage outside the door he can hear the muffled panic in his wife's breathing and the nun's curt orders to her assistant. He listens anxiously as they struggle to keep the Doña alive.

Sister Hortencia applies CPR to the new mother with little success. The Doña surrenders life just as she passes a third boy child into the light, but with blond wisps of hair and a red birthmark on his left buttock.

"Three new breaths in Dos Rios to one less," Sister Hortencia mumbles, as Don Ricardo breaks into the room.

Sister Hortencia struggles with the good news and the bad. "My dear Don Ricardo. The Lord has blessed you with three handsome healthy sons to carry on your name. The Lord has also blessed Doña Isabel with a place in his eternal heavenly garden."

"Fuck you, Sister. I have only two sons. That last one is not mine. He is the child of Satan. Look, he even has the stamp of the devil on his ass. He murdered my beautiful Isabel. I can never replace her."

"The Lord works in …"

"Fuck the Lord and his mysterious ways. He allowed this to happen. And you, the Lord's helper and messenger, have contributed to her demise; you're an accomplice to the crime."

The nun attempts to console the *patrón*, but he backs away.

"I will arrange for a nursing woman from the village to care for my two sons. The other one, who belongs to some other beast, is the bastard son of the devil as far as I'm concerned. You can dispose of him as you wish but get him out of my house before he condemns us to burn in everlasting Hell."

* * *

In addition to the *hacienda* at Dos Rios, Don Ricardo also maintains an impressive large acreage estate, *La Finca del Oro*, within an hour of the capital where he intends to raise the children, especially when they are ready to attend school. Education is a priority for the *patrón*.

His wife's legacy guarantees that he and his sons will live in luxury for their duration. Don Ricardo demands the very best for the twins, Jorge and Manuel, and that includes a tight relationship with the powerful, mainly the church and the state. Don Ricardo's business acumen places him in favourable connection with the political and religious leaders of the day.

For favours undetermined, the bishop extends permission for Don Ricardo to construct a family chapel on the site, dedicated to his departed wife, for the exclusive use of he and his children. His excellency, the bishop, personally delivers mass to the family in the chapel. Domestics and other service providers employed by Don Ricardo, are relegated to attend mass in nearby towns.

After the family mass, the bishop usually joins Don Ricardo in the parlour for brandies and discussions of business-related topics. They are often accompanied by *el presidente* himself. On such occasions the topics of discussion meander into political issues, of which the bishop is also deeply affected by.

"*Señor presidente,*" the bishop poses. "What is the latest situation with the rebels? Do you have them under control?" He sips brandy with an extended pinky while waiting for the president's response.

The president delays a tangible answer by clearing his throat in contemplation of what to say to the bishop. Before speaking he presses the tips of his fingers together.

Don Ricardo also eagerly awaits his response by topping up the president's snifter.

"Your Excellency, I am proud to tell you, and you too Don Ricardo, that the communist rebel bastards are on the verge of being eliminated. We currently have them surrounded in the mountains with no possibility of escape. I shall be announcing the outcome later in the week."

Don Ricardo asks, "*Señor presidente,* what will you do if ..."

"This is magnificent brandy Don Ricardo," the president interrupts, holding the snifter against the light. "Can you see to it that I receive a case?"

"Ditto that for me," the bishop adds, swallowing the remains of his snifter.

Both Don Ricardo and the bishop accept the president's answer without further probing, aware that nothing has changed since his last missive on the state of the rebellion.

The president addresses the bishop. "And you, Excellency. What successes are you having regarding the issue of those young radical priests that keep cropping up? Surely it's best to deal with them before they become too entrenched into the system."

"Unfortunately they don't always show their true colours while in the seminary, *señor*, any more than your young officers do," the bishop responds. "Like you, however, the Vatican has methods in place to address such concerns as they develop."

* * *

While Don Ricardo still retains his executive position and title, 'Vice-President of Nicaraguan Operations,' at the Canadian-owned gold mine in Dos Rios, his time is more efficiently served close to the capital. His investments, expanded by his late wife's legacy, now include an import/export empire, a chain of restaurants, and a European luxury car dealership in the capital.

La Finca del Oro is efficiently operated and maintained by a team of managers and domestics who all dwell in accommodations situated near the main house. A cadre of gardeners keep the landscaping verdant and healthy, and a special team of grooms work under the guidance of the stablemaster to care for, and train, Don Ricardo's prize race horses.

His sons, Jorge and Manuel, are privately educated by carefully selected professors and Jesuits from the university. They learn to speak and write fluently in Spanish, English and Latin, and are instructed from the early grades in economics, military procedures, political science, and religious studies. For leisure, the twins ride horseback and play baseball, a sport introduced by the U.S. advisors and military personnel stationed there between 1912 and 1933, until installing the current president's father as their puppet ruler.

Jorge and Manuel are identical in all respects. Each of them are the only ones capable of telling themselves apart. Jorge apparently, subtly exhibits a more serious demeanour than Manuel, more willing to obey the rules their father establishes. Manuel appears to be more gregarious and whimsical, often challenging the teachers, sometimes mimicking his brother's seriousness to confuse them. The tone and timbre of their voices are indistinguishable, regardless of which language they are speaking. With this knowledge, there is a continuing game played between them, the domestic help, and their own father.

Don Ricardo struggles to distinguish the twins to no avail. There are no identifying birthmarks nor any gestural features that reveal their uniqueness. When they were young, he attempted to dress the twins differently, but they merely exchanged clothing at the first opportunity.

To the twins, the act of exchanging identities is a childhood joke that continues as they enter their teens, constantly causing confusion and frustrations for their father, their teachers, and the domestic help at the estate. Most give up on any attempts to call the boys by their proper names.

Their teachers attempt to solve the problem by seating the twins separately at desks quite apart from each other. The boys simply sit at the other's desk and play the role of their brother for the day. They submit test papers in the other's name. The teachers, as a counter measure to the twins' games, grade the papers identically.

The issue of identification becomes more critical to Don Ricardo when the boys approach the age of fourteen. For centuries it has been tradition in his proud Spanish ancestry, that the eldest son pursues a career as an officer of the nation's military with ambitions of high office. The second son is to study theology with expectations of papal proportions; definitely nothing less than an archbishop will suffice.

The tradition assures the family of security with both levels of power, the church and the state. The boys were both born at the same time and no record or witness exists who could identify which of the two boys had arrived before the other. It's a dilemma that occupies Don Ricardo's attention night and day. After months of agonizing over the dilemma, Don Ricardo decides on a solution. On their fourteenth birthday, the *patrón* summons the twins to his study for a meeting. He tells them that he can wait no longer, that the time has arrived when they must take seriously, their functions in life. The boys listen attentively as their father explains.

"One of you will be trained in the military arts, wearing the uniform of a distinguished officer, so we can forge forth with this great nation, maybe someday you will be a Colonel. Who knows? You could even become President." His voice becomes excited at the thought.

Don Ricardo continues. "The other son will enter the seminary to wear the robes of the clergy. I expect the chosen one to be no less than a bishop someday, maybe even a cardinal."

The boys glance at each other, curious about where the meeting is going. In unison they ask their father. "Which one goes where? Who will be the President, and who will be the Pope?"

"That's where my plan comes in, a plan that will help me decide, through a series of challenging tests, which occupation you are each most suited for. You will both take the tests together without my presence because it is extremely important that the highest regard for honesty and integrity is maintained."

He pauses before adding, with his pointed finger alternating between the twins, "The process is not to be taken lightly. Our individual futures are at stake, and the outcome will also affect our family's future business interests and our position in the community."

Jorge asks where the tests are to be written and is informed that no writing is required. "These are tests of commitment to our traditions and to your family." After some hesitance, he continues. "We also shouldn't overlook your departed mother who invested her life in bringing you into this world." Don Ricardo points to the sky. "She will be watching every move you make from above."

Manuel inquires when the tests will begin and his father answers. "This very night, after midnight. You are to take your beloved pet Afghan dogs, Marta, and Max, for a walk. They must never return. You are to destroy them with one rifle shot each and leave their remains behind the woodshed for the *zopilotes*."

The boys are speechless until Manuel pleads with him. "Why? This is such a stupid act. Why? For what reason? This is insanity."

Jorge agrees. "We can't kill Marta and Max. This is stupid. They're our best friends. What purpose will this serve?"

Don Ricardo slaps both sons assertively across their cheeks.

"Don't you ever call me stupid. Remember that this is about commitment. If you are to serve the President as an officer in the military, there will be a time when you must follow an order to take the life of someone who is close to you, a neighbour perhaps, or a friend, not just an animal, but a human friend. You must obey that order when it's given."

When the chimes of midnight peal from the antique grandfather clock in the parlour, Don Ricardo issues the order. He informs the boys that he will listen for the sound of the shots. Sadly, Jorge and Manuel gather the Afghans, whispering sweet nothings in their ears, and petting them more softly and friendlier than ever before. They disappear into the darkness while Don Ricardo stations himself on the porch, sips his brandy, waits, and listens. Time passes. Finally, a single shot pierces the darkness. Minutes pass until a second shot breaks the night silence. An hour later the twins silently return to their rooms with heads hanging low. There is no conversation.

In the morning Don Ricardo peers toward the woodshed where a gathering of *zopilotes* is circling. He summons his sons to another meeting in the afternoon.

They arrive for the meeting, saddened by their actions the night before. Don Ricardo welcomes them into the study. "I understand how difficult it was for both of you. I promise that you will find the next test considerably more enjoyable. I have selected two very attractive young ladies who will visit you during the night in the guest room."

Manuel asks. "Will we have to kill them behind the woodshed as well?"

Don Ricardo outlines the plan to them. "Everything will be in total darkness, and you will wait in the guest room. The electrical fuses will be removed so no lights can be turned on."

At midnight, the boys enter the dark room as instructed. Although they can't see a thing, their other senses reveal that they aren't alone. A sweet perfume is detected and the shuffling of bare feet against the wooden floor is heard. Initially there is kissing and mild curiosity that seems to be enjoyed by all, but there is a sudden escalation that defies all boundaries. The boys' puberty-driven hormones assume control over them. The night passes with moans and cries, and the creaking of bed springs. The essence of perfumes, perspiration, and sex permeates the room. Neither Jorge nor Manuel had been with a woman before and had no knowledge of how to behave beyond sheer lust, and the expectations of old family privilege. In time, silence prevails as sleep overcomes them.

When early morning light penetrates the Venetian blinds of the guest room, Manuel awakens to see the naked torsos of the women sleeping next to them.

"Jorge, Jorge," Manuel calls in a whispering but panicked voice. "Wake up, Jorge." He shakes his brother.

Jorge peers at Manuel through slitted eyes. "What's happening?"

"Come with me Jorge," Manuel whispers with his forefinger across his lips. "Come."

They leave the room quietly, closing the door behind them.

Manuel explains. "The women … from last night … they're not women, Jorge."

"Of course they're women, Manuel. They're certainly not men."

"No. You don't understand. They're not women, they're girls … our age. And worse, they are our friends, Margarita and Cecilia. They're not whores, like we expected. They're our childhood friends, the daughters of *Señora* Clara, the domestic who helped raise us."

"Why would Papá play such a dirty trick on us?" Jorge asks, his face frowned in guilt, on the verge of crying.

"We must wake them and send them quietly back to their mother before anyone else sees them."

At breakfast, the boys confront Don Ricardo. "Papá, how could you allow this to happen? We didn't know who they were in the darkness. We thought you were sending in prostitutes from the capital, but they were two young girls, good friends of ours whom we've known all of our lives. Their mother changed our dirty diapers when we were babies. We had sex with them Papá. Why? For what insane purpose?"

"So, yesterday I was stupid, now today I'm insane? I am your father." His voice increases in volume. "Until you are adults you will do as I say. Besides, don't worry about *señora* Clara and her daughters, I have paid the girls handsomely."

"Oh, for Christ's sake," Manuel groans. "You paid them? Congratulations, Papá, you have just turned two innocent young girls into prostitutes. Why? Why?"

"Sit down! Now!" Don Ricardo orders in an agitated voice. "Don't ever talk to me that way again." He points his finger into the faces of each of the twins. "I will tell you why. One of you will join the priesthood. You will sit in a box and judge other anonymous people for their actions. Some of them will have committed sexual sins, others murder. You must serve their judgements from a position of humility and personal guilt. We are all guilty in this world. That's why we ask God for forgiveness."

He continues pointing. "The other one will be in a position of power as an officer of the military. There will be times in the heat of conflict when you, and the men serving under you, are tempted by desire. You must remember this experience to make a wise decision."

This time, Jorge challenges his father. "What would be a wise decision?"

Don Ricardo ignores his question and continues.

"Tomorrow, *el presidente* is invited to visit us. In the meantime, you are expected to prepare short summations of why you will each be valuable to his regime and to his cause, a cause of patriotism and obeyance. After presenting your summations you will be invited to join *el presidente* and myself, as men, for brandies in the library. By sundown we will decide who of you will be an officer in the military and who will be a priest."

Jorge and Manuel spend the entire afternoon preparing their statements of loyalty. After dinner, they visit the woodshed with shovels and flashlights to bury the remains of their beloved pets. For reasons of embarrassment and guilt, they avoid the shame of walking past the domestics' quarters for fear of encountering *señora* Clara and especially her daughters.

The following afternoon, *el presidente's* Mercedes, a personal gift from Don Ricardo, enters through the iron gates and past the sign of *La Finca del Oro*, proceeding directly to the mansion. He is met by a butler and directed into the library where Don Ricardo waits to greet him. Brandies are served as usual, while they discuss the recent disruptions by radicals in the mountains to the north. The President assures Don Ricardo that he has destroyed the communist radicals without any retaliation and guarantees that nothing more will ever come from them.

The boys are led into the library and greeted, with a smile and a firm handshake, by the President. They sit quietly and respectfully await their turn. Jorge draws the short straw to speak first."

He delivers his prepared speech with elegance. *"Señor Presidente, bienvenido a nuestra casa.* I am sincerely honoured and humbled by your presence. It has been my lifelong dream to serve you and our beloved nation in whatever capacity I am called upon to deliver. Military service is the highest honour you can bestow upon me. I will serve you with immense pride and dedication to our cause, and with my last drop of blood, I will protect our sovereignty." He bows to his superior and returns to his seat.

The President rises and applauds Jorge's commitment. *'Bravo, bravo,'* he states.

Manuel is called upon to speak. *"Señor Presidente.* I, Manuel, am sincerely proud of my country, and of the wonderful, caring people encompassed within her boundaries. We all need protection from foreign interests, especially from those who threaten to rape and pillage our resources, our coffee, our fruit, and the gold in our mines. I will defend and protect our sovereignty against such intruders and will share the resources with all the people, regardless of their poverty or their wealth, because I believe that the people of this great land are the most valuable natural resource we have. *Muchas Gracias, Señor Presidente.*" Unlike his brother, Manuel doesn't bow but returns directly to his seat.

Don Ricardo stands to face Manuel, his forefinger wagging. "You have insulted our beloved President to his face. I demand that you apologize immediately."

El presidente stands to interject, signalling with his arm for Don Ricardo to stand back.

"I disagree, Don Ricardo. The boy's words were delivered with integrity. Manuel has displayed magnificent courage in speaking them. Shall we all drink to the presentations?"

The butler serves brandies to all.

The following year, both boys leave home for the United States. Jorge attends a private military boy's school where he is prepped to complete his higher education. Through connections within the U.S. Embassy and a recommendation from *el presidente,* Jorge is finally accepted for enrolment as an international cadet at West Point.

Manuel begins his education at a private Jesuit-operated academy in preparation for entrance into the seminary.

When both sons return home as adults in 1968, Jorge is accepted into the National Guard as a Lieutenant. Due to his commitment and diligence, as well as honouring his father's privileged position, he quickly rises in rank. His talent in delivering decisive orders in difficult situations finally earn him the rank of Colonel. He is placed in charge of the country's security, with special attention on curtailing the increasing threat of rebel activity.

Father Manuel, assumes a position as a novice at a small parish in an inner-city barrio, not far from *Mercado Central,* where he serves the spiritual needs of its poorer citizens. He creates a shelter for the homeless and organizes the formation of a hot meals program. His concerns for the poor and oppressed places him in direct opposition to the interests of his brother and father, and subsequently, the political and religious elite.

CHAPTER 05

PALO DE MAYO

Bluefields, Nicaragua, 1953:

"Ouch! That hurts!" Lydia Sosa flinches as Aunt Flora sews the finishing alterations on her new dress.

"Hold still, girl," Aunt Flora warns, her lips tightened against a mouthful of straight pins. "These are sharp. You don't want me to draw blood, do you? I won't be too much longer."

Lydia has trouble standing still. She's been itching to start dancing for a month.

Palo de Mayo (Maypole Festival) doesn't start abruptly or at any specific time. It officially begins on the first day of May but, like the hurricanes that plague the Atlantic seaboard every year, the initial breezes start churning weeks before, slowly gathering enough momentum to be taken seriously. Someone down the street flips a radio on and a neighbour responds while sweeping off her front porch by swaying her backside left and right ... not too fast, not too slow ... just settling into a groove that excites the otherwise dormant hormones of a middle-aged fish vendor who just happens to be ambling by. The vendor inhales the pulse of the music from one house and the suggestive movement from another porch is expressed in a livelier step and an added afterbeat to his musical shouting, "Fish for sale, I got fish to sell."

The soul of the festival is carried through the streets, toward the central market, past small gatherings of men hovering over a sidewalk checker match, into the church where the congregation and choir vibrate their entire bodies and clap hands together. Someone on a street corner slaps his hardened palms against the stretched skin of a conga drum, another snaps syncopated rim shots on the edge of a bongo or timbale and the message passes into the very soul of the village. By the first of May the festival has begun.

Street corners come alive with bouncing, shaking, vibrating masses of black, brown, bronze and tan; generations of African, Indigenous, Asian, Mediterranean and European, blended together in one hypnotic month-long party.

Lydia Sosa's caramel skin contrasts the fresh lemon yellow of her dress, designed and hand-sewn for her by her favourite Aunt Flora, especially for this year's festival. At 16 years, Lydia's parents finally allow her to attend the street dancing without being chaperoned too closely, although they warn her repeatedly to stay clear from the alcohol and to avoid any seedy characters who are bent on taking advantage of her naïveté.

"You can be sure that Aunt Flora and your cousin Hubert will be keeping their eyes on you, so toe the line, do you hear?" her mother warns her. Aunt Flora nods her agreement from the other side of the room.

Quietly, in a whisper heard only by herself, Lydia mutters, "Sure they will, until they're too drunk to walk, let alone to see, and that'll only take an hour or two."

"And Flora," her mother warns, "you be careful you don't swallow none of those pins or we'll be rushing you off to the clinic."

Even as she's dressing for the evening's events, Lydia moves her hips to the music, admiring herself in the full-length mirror in the hallway of the family's small, but tidy, house. She has grown up considerably in the previous year and is convinced that the new dress will show her off well to the young boys she sees daily at school, the ones who usually ignore her.

"Are you really going to let her out in public wearing that dress?" her father asks in a worrying voice.

"Hmm," her mother ponders, realizing that she might have given Lydia too much leeway a year too soon.

"Ah, Mamá," Lydia pleads. "You said I was old enough."

"I never thought you were as old as you look in that dress," her mother answers. "Just look at you. My goodness, girl. You're going to catch a cold, or something even worse, dancing like that." She turns to her husband and laughs. He doesn't.

"Oh, Mamá. I'll be a good girl, you'll see." Lydia hugs her mother before starting out the front door. "Thank you, you're so good to me." She kisses her mother on the cheek, and then she turns to embrace Aunt Flora. "Thank you ever so much. The dress makes me look so beautiful."

From inside the house, her mother watches as the bright yellow dress sashays its way down the street toward the festivities.

"My oh my," she moans." You keep a real keen eye on that cousin of yours, do you hear me Hubert? She's going to crank up the motors of all of them little boys out there."

"Yes ma'am."

Weak rays from a lonely streetlamp create starry sparkles on the droplets of perspiration that roll down Lydia's face and shoulders. The same starry droplets provide the only outline of her body; otherwise only the yellow dress is seen as if it moves without any body in it at all.

Lydia has danced since she was old enough to stand on her own two feet. Before then, she was carried around in her mother's arms as she and her father danced. The pulse was born within her.

Her classmates take turns dancing with her, as if there's a contest between the boys as to who can dance the longest, and most intensely, with Lydia Sosa. She seems tireless; she dances with all who ask, sometimes with three or four at a time.

Those who aren't actively dancing with her, watch her move while she dances with others. They notice how much she has grown up since only yesterday at school. The more machismo of the young boys whisper lewd teenage comments to each other about what they would like to do if they could be alone with her. The lesser machismo just giggle as if they understand, hoping that they'll become more machismo in the process.

Lydia, however, is oblivious to everything but the dancing and to how wonderful it feels deep inside where the rhythms are embedded.

* * *

A tall, dapper man has been looking forward to the festival for weeks. He arrives in town from the capital with plans to celebrate, to get drunk, and to spend the night with a beautiful woman. Before he joins the dancing, he books himself into a hotel room where he bathes and cleans the travel dust from his bronzed muscle-toned body. He books the room for two nights so he will have a dry place to sleep the evenings away and, who knows, he ponders, maybe he'll get lucky.

He fastens the buttons down the front of his embroidered *guayabera*, leaving the golden mandala on his upper chest exposed, while staring at himself in the scratched hotel mirror. He runs a comb through his jet-black hair before slithering like a tomcat into the darkened street.

He dances with many women as he meanders through the vibrating streets. Some bolder women entice him to them with body language that suggests more than dancing. In a short time his body, like everyone else's, is consumed by the energy of the music as it passes from one dancer to the next like a virus. It's inescapable. It radiates through sound waves that penetrate the skin and it rises up from the earth and the hot pavement like an earthquake, forcing its magic through the feet and the legs until the torso can no longer resist.

It's inevitable that the man is attracted to the undulating yellow dress that glistens in the darkness. Lydia quickly becomes the focus of his intentions. He's fascinated as she teasingly ignores him, heightening his desire. Slinking closer and closer toward her, he wraps his strong arms around her bare golden shoulders, placing a beautiful flower, a white Madonna lily, in the glistening black hair above her left ear. He places his lips to her earlobe, whispering as he kisses her.

She senses his hunger and feels the warm air from his lips tickling her ear like the soft touch of a butterfly's wings in flight. The heat within her beckons him closer and he understands; her heart pounds with excitement.

With half-closed eyes Lydia notices the clockwork movement of the mandala vibrating against the man's perspiration-soaked chest through the plunging neckline of his *guayabera*. She responds by teasingly turning her back to him before turning again with her eyes staring into his.

The man watches as the shining beads of perspiration flow down around her thick full lips. They dance with intensity. The younger boys back away from the stronger competition.

He's at least 20 years her senior but the age difference is proportionally reduced by the excitement of the dancing, the sudden apparent increase in Lydia's age, and the freedom that each has been given for the evening. Both Aunt Flora and Cousin Hubert have long since ceded their chaperonal duties to pursue activities more to their own personal liking.

The man removes a flask from his pocket and draws a swig of *chicha* (a homemade fermented corn drink) before offering the flask to Lydia. Not to be excluded from the excitement, and to demonstrate her bravado, she draws a swig of her own and dances away from the man. He follows, sharing further drinks.

For the suitor and Lydia, they are alone with their desires. They exchange no words, and ask no questions, speaking to each other only through their movement.

* * *

Lydia wakes in the predawn; darkness prevails over the town while moonlight strays into the room. Her head spins blurred details of the previous night. The surroundings are foreign to her: a small room with a washstand, an outdated calendar picture of an unclad white woman, pungent odours of sweat and sex, torn and water-stained wallpaper. Beside her lies the exhausted body of a stranger. She vaguely remembers dancing with the man from the night before but failed to ask him his name; she wouldn't have remembered it anyway.

She lies naked in the bed, the sheets hot and damp beneath her. Her beautiful yellow dress, made lovingly by Aunt Flora, appears haphazardly in a ball on the dusty tile floor; her matching yellow lingerie is strewn across the room. A white Madonna lily, a symbol of purity, lays dying on the floor. She dresses quickly, escaping silently from the room before the stranger awakes.

She drills herself with questions as she wanders about town trying to find her bearings. 'What have I done? How did I get here? What time is it? What will Mamá be thinking?'

Her mother is much less than ecstatic when Lydia finally sneaks through the door of their humble home, her new shoes dangling from her fingertips. Her father succumbed early to the festivities and passed out in the hammock, but her mother kept herself awake throughout the night waiting for her precious Lydia to return. Her reaction to the girl's arrival, just as the first hint of daylight teases from beneath the eastern horizon, is mixed, at first elated that her daughter appears to be safe, but furious that she has disobeyed her curfew on her first night out alone. Some penalty is surely in order, but her mother agonizes over the method or the severity of it, so much so that she threatens her with her forefinger pointing into Lydia's eyes.

"Just wait until your father hears about this, young lady. He will be furious. I have no idea what his punishment will be, but I can guarantee that it will be the worst you've ever had."

During the morning, the steam gradually loses pressure from her mother's ire, as she tends to her normal chores of cleaning and cook-ing. She does manage to mumble her disapproval to Lydia at intervals between the chores, but somehow fails to confront her with the questions that are at the forefront of the 16-year-old's fears. 'Where have I been? What have I been doing? If I've been doing anything, who have I been doing it with?'

Her father dozes throughout most of the day and isn't of a keen mind even after waking. By then her mother has become totally occupied with nursing his headache and preparing supper. She has lost any desire to face another confrontation with her daughter. Besides, dear Aunt Flora and Cousin Hubert are also expected for supper, and they will need some tender healing care as well.

* * *

Months pass before Lydia can no longer conceal her condition; her mother's anger boils over.

"You have disgraced this entire family and all of the good Christian values you've been taught. How dare you violate those teachings? What will the neighbours think, and what about Aunt Flora? How will you explain all of this to her, after everything she did for you?"

The embarrassment is unrelenting, continuing through the next month as she experiences changes in her body. Her mother stops communicating with her and, because of the friction in the tiny house, her father spends more of his time away, usually drinking with his friends at the fishermen's bar.

One night, her well-lubricated father returns home to deliver the edict, as if responding to the questionable advice of his inebriated drinking buddies.

"You will not disgrace this family any longer," he warns, pointing his finger directly into her face. "You have until the end of the month to vacate this house. From this date forward, you are not a part of this family. Enough said."

Lydia's mother remains silent through her husband's tirade. She knows enough not to disagree or question his authority when he's been drinking.

Lydia concludes that she must immediately leave town and move to the capital, where she is unknown and where there are greater opportunities for earning an independent income. She vows to have the baby and to remain unattached to any man so her child will receive the loving attention that only she can provide.

* * *

Late one night, in her fourth month of pregnancy, Lydia quietly packs a small suitcase with practical clothing and a photograph of her family. The yellow dress is placed neatly across her bed. She attempts to secretly depart but is met by her mother at the front door.

"I have spent sleepless weeks knowing that early one morning you will pass from our lives into the darkness, never to be seen again. I want you to know that this is not my wish, nor is it my desire to be the unknown grandmother of the child you carry with you as you leave."

Lydia and her mother spread endless tears on each other's shoulders.

"I am so sorry," Lydia sobs. "This is not how I want it to be, but it is how it must be. I will write to you when I am settled and secure in the capital. It might take some time. Please don't worry about me. I will be a good mother … just like you, Mamá."

Her mother's voice remains silent during their departing embrace. The swelling in her chest and her tears prohibit words from passing, but the sadness in her eyes imbed an indelible image in Lydia's memory. She silently passes an envelope of money into her daughter's hand, stained and worn *córdobas* of various denominations culled from months of cleaning other people's homes and clandestine savings stolen from her meagre weekly food allowances.

CHAPTER 06

THE MARKET

Managua, Nicaragua, 1954 – 1968:

The hustle and bustle of the capital present Lydia with a cultural shock, confusing at first, but she welcomes the energy and the potential for her and her expected child. At *Mercado Central* she asks for work at every stall but is turned down. Although disappointed, she remains optimistic when she notices that some vendors don't work from stalls but as ambulatory vendors, wandering through the aisles shouting their wares, *"Hay sucre, maiz, granos, tortillas ... "*

Sacrificing a portion of her meagre savings, she invests in a package of 20 cigarettes, opens the package, and places several cigarettes along the brim of her straw hat.

"Hay cigarros, cigarros." Before reaching the end of the second row, the entire package is sold, one cigarette at a time. She invests the profits from the first package into two more packs and continues until, at days end, she saves enough for a meal. She repeats the process

again the following day, and the next, until she becomes a regular with customers waiting for her.

Accommodations are too expensive for Lydia, but she manages to sleep nights, sharing the space with bags of grains, under a tarpaulin protecting one of the stalls from the rain. Vendors start arriving at five each morning so Lydia must wake before they arrive.

One early morning during a heavy rainfall, Lydia is discovered by the owner of the tarpaulin. She's in the final pangs before giving birth. The vendor immediately calls for assistance. Sister Nadia, from a nearby convent, quickly arrives to help. She moves Lydia safely to the convent where she is cleaned and provided with a midwife. A baby girl is born later in the morning. Lydia names the girl Azucena, after the white Madonna lily, a symbol of purity, worn in her hair when the baby was conceived.

Sister Nadia arranges for a small room in the home of a parishioner to be available to Lydia and her daughter until they are able to afford something more suitable. Lydia wastes no time in returning to the market. She straps the baby around her bosom while continuing to sell her wares.

* * *

When Azucena starts to talk, she learns to shout, *"Cigarros, hay cigarros …"* in unison with her mother. Once able to walk steadily, she wears her own straw hat with individual cigarettes in the hat band. Often customers prefer to buy from the cute little girl instead of from her mother.

Lydia and Azucena struggle to survive in the capital but gradually, Lydia is able to establish a small business selling sundries like cigarettes, candy, flowers, anything she can buy in bulk and sell in smaller quantities.

Seven days a week, from daybreak at five in the morning to nightfall at five in the evening, the two wander the market corridors and laneways shouting the names of their wares, *"Cigarros, chicle, bonbon*

... " Lydia carries her wares in a large basket balanced on her head, Azucena does most of the shouting.

In time, Lydia is earning enough to lease a small stall on one of the market's busiest corridors. She posts a sign advertising her cigarettes and adds other wares of interest to her customers: matches, lighters, papers and loose tobacco, flowers, and gum. She also acquires a coffee maker, offering cups of hot java, and arranges for a contract to sell local newspapers.

Azucena, now six-years-old, is able to wander the aisles by herself shouting her wares, while Lydia handles the stall. Lydia isn't worried about Azucena's safety; most of the other vendors know the child and watch out for her.

Lydia is determined to do whatever it takes to create a better life for her and Azucena, but she refuses to sink so low as to satisfy the desires of some of the men who approach her at the market offering money for intimacies, unlike some of the other vendors who encourage it.

"Someday people will look to us with respect," she promises Azucena whenever things look grim. "We will have our own house to live in, maybe even with a garden where we can grow our own fresh food, some juicy red tomatoes, many beans, mangoes, everything we need to live."

Azucena loves the quiet times they're together, when Lydia talks to her about their wonderful future. The child asks, "Will we have a cow for fresh milk and some chickens for meat and eggs?" she asks her mother. "Sometimes it is also good to have meat with our beans and rice."

To keep the dream alive for her daughter, Lydia answers, "Yes, and those things too. Maybe we will even have a little farm in the country, our own land to work on, with chickens, cows, oxen and horses." Of course, Lydia realizes the futility of dreaming the unattainable, but she offers her daughter some hope. "We must always have dreams, my little Azucena."

A silent voice emanates from deep within, always steering Lydia back toward the reality she's accustomed to. 'Don't be so crazy, woman. You're a peasant, a *campesina*. You will never own land; not in this country for sure. Why give the little girl false hopes? She will only become disillusioned, and her stomach will crave for things she can never eat.'

"When will I go to school?" Azucena asks.

"Now is not the time to talk about school. We have things to sell."

It's toward the end of the day, the sun is hinting at its disappearance and Lydia and Azucena are almost sold out. Azucena calls out her list of products for the last few times.

One of their pastimes is for Lydia to tell her daughter about the dreams she had the night before. Azucena is mesmerized by the fantastical images presented by her mother. With a package of Crayons she receives as a Christmas gift, Azucena begins drawing, with limited colour, the dreams she envisions in her own child's imagination. When Lydia realizes the fascination that Azucena has with drawing she barters a package of cigarettes for a basic watercolour painting set at one of the other stalls.

Although still the obvious work of a child, the paintings improve steadily, and Lydia is so impressed that she posts the best ones around the stall to show off her daughter's talents. In no time, customers express their fondness of the paintings, even offering to buy some of them. Azucena's paintings from the dreams are not realistic, but they offer an image based upon her interpretations of the dreams; sometimes wildly fantasized.

With time, her paintings become more realistic, although still interpretive. That's when the public becomes more interested in her work. It's also when Lydia recognizes the commercial value of the paintings and starts posting prices alongside the artwork. One of the customers suggests that Azucena should start signing her work, so she develops a stylized image of a white Madonna lily as her identifying signature, a visual interpretation of her name.

* * *

Over several years, the paintings become more popular than the cigarettes, especially after the daily newspaper publishes an article about the 14-year-old Azucena and her art. It quotes her as saying that her ideas come from her mother's dreams, and she interprets them. Several photos of Azucena, her paintings, and Lydia appear alongside the article. The story attracts the attention of more customers, but particularly of Father Manuel, a priest at the local parish, who comes to visit them at the market.

"Hola señora y señorita. I am Father Manuel and I've come to see your paintings. I have heard many good things about them." He studies them closely with the eye of a serious art critic. "You have a wonderful talent," he tells Azucena. "Do you study art in school?"

"I don't go to school, Father. I work here all day at the market."

"But you speak eloquently. Where did you learn that?"

"From my mother. She teaches me lessons at night, and we speak in both Spanish and English. She is from the Atlantic coast where they speak English as well. She also teaches me mathematics and to be a nice person."

"I see. So, you are even more talented than I expected. How would you like to go to school, a school where they also teach fine art? Would you like that?"

Lydia interrupts. "Father, please don't put wild ideas into her head that she can never realize. We must continue working here at the market. We are poor. Education is not available for us. You're an educated man, you should know that."

"I do know that *señora.* I see it every day in my church. I want to change the way things are. I believe that every person deserves an education. That's why I want to help Azucena. It would be a tragedy for someone as talented as she is to be refused an education. Please allow me to help." He touches Lydia's arm.

"How will we survive, Father? Where will we live?" She spreads her arms, palms up. "What will we eat? I ask you that."

Father Manuel responds. "What if I offer you and Azucena a job that pays more than you make here and will provide your daughter with an education at the same time. Before you say no, I have the ability to make sure that can happen. My father owns an estate outside of the capital. You can both work and live there as domestics, except when Azucena is attending school during the weekdays. She appears to be a fast learner, so she could probably graduate to high school in a few years, where they have a fine arts program to prepare students for the university. Can you imagine her attending university while staying here at the market?"

Lydia chuckles and challenges the priest's wisdom. "Not to offend you Father, but I think you are smoking more than the cigarettes I sell."

"I appreciate your humour, *señora*, and I applaud your dedication to Azucena. I must assure you, however, that I am not smoking dope. I am very serious. You can start your new job within a week or two, and if, after one year, you decide against it, I will guarantee your stall back here at the market. But whatever you decide … it is important that your daughter continues to attend school. It would be a tragedy for her to miss out on that opportunity."

Lydia is sceptical of the priest's promises. Education in Nicaragua is limited to those with money, a position also supported by the church that operates most of the schools. While she was fortunate that her father earned an honest living as a self-employed fisherman in Bluefields, she was able to attend public school. That is how she learned to read and write, and to subsequently pass on her knowledge to Azucena. But she realizes that her daughter must learn much more than she did, and that her income will never be enough to provide a formal education.

Azucena draws her mother away from the stall for a private conversation. "I think he means what he's saying, Mamá. He may be a priest, but I think he's honest. I have a strong feeling about this. We shouldn't pass this opportunity up."

Lydia ponders the situation before approaching Father Manuel with a counter offer. "I won't be anybody's domestic. My father was a self-employed fisherman. He always told me to stand up for myself. 'Don't work for the other guy,' he used to say. Since I left my family home, I have learned to be independent. I now enjoy my freedom here, at the market. I will remain here."

Lydia walks in circles around her stall, agonizing about the decision she's about to make. For a brief moment she puts her hands together and closes her eyes in prayer. Finally she faces the priest.

"You are correct, Father. My daughter needs a proper education, the kind you are promising her. She will live and work at your family estate during the week so she can attend classes, but she must be here at the market with me on the weekends when it is busy. If that's a deal, then you must put it in writing and then we will shake hands."

PART THREE
1972 – 1973

CHAPTER 07

BASEBALL

Toronto, 1972:

"I'm going to Nicaragua, Jack … if that's OK with you."

"What?" Jack is stunned at Duncan's sudden declaration. "Why? What for?" he asks.

"As you know, Jack, I'm a baseball freak. The International World Series of Baseball is happening there in November, and I'd like to cover it. There'll be teams from all over the world. I think it would be an interesting assignment for the magazine, don't you?"

Jack rubs his chin before responding. "Well, it would be interesting for you, that's for sure. What about our readers?"

"I thought about all that, and I've written it all down in this proposal." Duncan hands four pages of story ideas to Jack.

Duncan's proposal reads, 'My plan is to cover the International World Series of Baseball from a sports perspective, but also to examine the cultural obsession with baseball in Nicaragua. I'll leave in early November to cover the tournament and remain in the country to photograph other stories with tourist interests, including a typical Nicaraguan Christmas and New Year's celebration before returning home.'

Within an hour, Jack calls Duncan. "My office, now!" He throws the proposal onto his desk in front of Duncan and waits for his reaction. Duncan is silent, unsure of how Jack will react.

"I love this," Jack shouts. "Let's do it." He laughs as Duncan's expression changes from a serious frown to elation.

"Whew! I didn't see that coming." Duncan takes a deep breath. "I thought you were going to fire me."

"This is what I think, Duncan." Jack says, staring at Duncan from across the desk. "We don't need a written contract, do we?"

Duncan remains stunned.

"Here's how it's going to work," Jack continues. "I'll agree to give you an unpaid leave of absence while you're not here, but I'll pay you freelance rates for any photos and stories the magazine publishes. You'll retain all copyright to your work and you can freelance it to other outlets after we've published it under first rights. Got it?"

"Yeah," Duncan agrees, otherwise speechless.

Days before his departure, Jack throws a staff 'going-away' party for Duncan at the local bar and presents him with a gift of 100 rolls of Tri-X and 40 rolls of Kodachrome, worth more than the salary he'll be giving up while away. The magazine also provides him with press accreditation.

A college classmate of Duncan's arrives at the party.

"Hey Willa. What are you doing here?" Duncan asks.

She answers, "I'm your replacement until you get back. I used you for my reference."

Jack interrupts their conversation. "I didn't bother to check her references, Duncan. I figured that if she knew you she'll be perfect for the job. Besides, I told her that, if you don't come back from Nicaragua, she can have your job fulltime."

Duncan is ecstatic; it's his first major assignment. 'What could be better than this? An international assignment, baseball, photography, leisure, free film? Life is good.'

* * *

The first leg of his trip is a five-hour flight to Costa Rica, followed by a two-hour layover before connecting with his flight for the short hop to Managua.

In-flight breakfast arrives just as first light radiates a blanket of soft warmth through his east-facing window seat. The pilot announces their pass over Miami and introduces the passengers to the white beach-ringed island of Cuba. It seems much larger than Duncan had imagined.

Far below, minuscule vessels in full sail dot the azure beauty of the Caribbean, reminding Duncan of the toy boats of his childhood. Suddenly, the sharp oblique rays of the rising sun pierce the water, lighting the textures and colours beneath the surface. From 30,000 feet Duncan imagines details and moving life forms from the ocean bottom. He attempts to read the morning edition of the Star with his second coffee but the steady vibrations of the L-1011 aircraft summon him to much-needed sleep.

In a dream Duncan hears Jack's voice telling Willa, *"If he doesn't come back from Nicaragua, you can have his job fulltime."*

Duncan's dream continues.

He zooms downward from the plane to the deck of a large sailing yacht where he sunbathes on his back peering skyward. A tiny L-1011 airliner soars silently across the deep blue sky leaving contrails in its wake. Suddenly an invisible force vaults him back toward the aircraft until gravity reclaims him, drawing him toward the sea below. Several times he's trampolined as if being rejected by both extremes before finally returning to his window seat.

Duncan's eyes open as slits to confirm his location until the steady hum and vibration return him to sleep.

Outside his east-facing window, sparks appear, quickly escalating to smoke and flames that trail behind the engine. 'Why am I so calm when the other passengers are screaming?' he wonders. 'Will you all please shut up?' When smoke seeps into the cabin it veils the brilliant azure of the sea. Duncan is thrown from the aircraft to the ocean with the jagged rapidity of a silent movie. Treading water to save his life and surrounded by sharks, he witnesses the spiralling L-1011 plunge toward its demise and he's abruptly relocated into his window seat moments before impact, shouting with the others.

"Is everything alright, sir? Can I help?" A flight attendant hovers over Duncan.

He stares up at her, perspiration flowing. He glances out the window at the clear blue of the sky and the sea. "No … I'm OK. I guess I was dreaming. Sorry."

"Is there anything I can get for you?"

"A drink would go well right now. Jack Daniels, please."

* * *

Managua, Nicaragua, 1972:

Accommodations in the capital are scarce, but Duncan locates a small pension two blocks from the Inter-Continental hotel, where most of the international press reporters and photographers are gathered. At least he'll be able to socialize with them in the hotel bar.

Duncan photographs the events of each game during the International World Series, with excellent access to the players and to the action of the major games. He's excited by the diversity; a United Nations of cultures and languages. Teams from Latin America share the diamonds with Japanese, European, and North American players. Crowds cheer for their favourites in their own languages while sharing their common passions for the game.

Duncan approaches his idol, Roberto Clemente, who is managing the Puerto Rican national team at the tournament. Clemente remembers him from the Florida training camp and agrees to sit for a series of portraits.

'I can't believe how this is all turning out,' Duncan ponders in his pension while trying to get some sleep. Clemente actually remembers me. How can this happen? I'm just a nobody after all.'

Two days later, Clemente invites Duncan to join him for lunch. At *Los Antojitos*, they share a *Plata Tipica* consisting of rice, beans, chicken, and tortilla with salsa. Clemente shows Duncan how to load and eat a tortilla and talks about the similarities of his Puerta Rican roots to the food and environment in Nicaragua.

Reiterating what his Nicaraguan friend from college said, Clemente also explains how baseball became the sport of choice for certain Latin American countries, especially where there were influences from the United States: Cuba, Dominican Republic, Puerto Rico, Nicaragua, even Japan. All where the surrounding countries are obsessed with soccer.

Before leaving the restaurant, Duncan hands their waiter his camera. "*Señor,* please take a few photos of *señor* Clemente and me together."

Duncan makes a special 'asterisked' entry in his note book: *** Roll #15, Frames #13 – 20, Clemente and me.

As Clemente leaves the restaurant, they promise to meet again soon.

"*Hasta la próxima,*" Clemente promises, explaining that it's a Spanish promise to meet again later in the future.

"*Hasta la próxima,*" Duncan counters.

With the afternoon free, Duncan explores alternate routes away from the main avenues to familiarize himself with the city.

Passing through a barrio on his route back to the pension, Duncan stops to photograph some young kids playing baseball on the street. They're playing with gloves home-crafted from pieces of cardboard and tape, bats carved from 4 x 4 lumber smoothed on the corners, and a baseball wrapped in an old sock, probably sewn together by one of the kid's mothers. No Louisville Sluggers here.

The tournament ends with Cuba taking gold, the United States finishing with silver, and the host, Nicaragua taking bronze. Duncan notes that Canada finishes in ninth place.

'Who cares who wins?' he mulls around in his head. 'Canada, after all, has hockey, and we haven't been taken over by the U.S. Not yet anyway. Besides, we still love baseball. At least we have the Expos, our first major league team.'

In the weeks after the tournament, Duncan follows his heart, spending his days wandering through one barrio after another; a few with wealthy looking homes protected by gates and barbed wire, but many others revealing varying degrees of poverty. It's in the poorer barrios where he's met with exuberant hospitality, welcomed by children and parents alike.

Children approach him in the streets shouting, *"Tomo foto,"* while acting out in imitation of Duncan's photography stance.

One morning Duncan is approached by a young boy he guesses to be six or seven. The boy takes Duncan by the hand pulling him toward an alleyway leading into a series of small adjoining *casitas* where he's met by a mother and five other children. The woman signals to Duncan with a waving hand to come closer. As he obeys, she assembles the children in a formalized group in front of their humble home.

"Por favor señor, toma una foto de mi familia," she says, requesting a family photo. She holds her hand to her eye and tweaks her forefinger to indicate a camera. Duncan obliges.

"Lupita, agua." The mother orders her daughter into their *casita* to fetch Duncan some water.

"Gracias, señora, gracias," he thanks her.

Duncan agonizes over the reality that he can't provide an immediate print for the woman, nor can he even show her an example of how the photo appears. In his broken Spanish he attempts to explain the difficulty to her but she totally understands, waving her hand. *"No problema, señor."*

Realizing that Duncan is making an honest attempt to speak her language, however crude it is, the woman resorts to mixing her Spanish with snippets of English she has heard. Together they manage a level of understanding.

"*Señor*, you are *periodista*, no?" she asks, speaking slowly. "*El beisbol esta terminado. Por qué* you are still *aqui, en Nicaragua?*"

"I want to be *un turista, ahora.*" Duncan answers.

"*De donde esta?* Where are you from?" she asks, using both languages.

"Canada."

"*Ah. Canadiense. Bueno.*"

Duncan explains in English, using waving arms and pointing fingers for emphasis, that the film must be developed in Canada. He promises that if he ever returns to Nicaragua, he will deliver a print to her."

"*Si. Entiendo,*" she nods and smiles, confirming that she understands."

"*Como se llama?*" Duncan asks her name.

"Maria Gutierrez."

"*Me llamo* Duncan. *Mucho gusto.*"

When Duncan turns to leave, *Señora* Gutierrez touches his arm. She points at a Canadian flag pin attached to his shirt and points her finger back to her. Duncan, the tourist, pulls some pins from his gadget bag and gives her one.

"*Cinco mas,*" she adds, holding five fingers up. "*Para los niños.*"

While Duncan counts out five more pins for the children, Maria places her pin through the piercing on her ear. Duncan takes another photo of her with her new jewelry.

On his return walk to the pension, reality strikes Duncan. 'The mother understood from the beginning there would be no print for her. She intended the photo opportunity as a gift to me, a total stranger, not the other way around as I had agonized over. She viewed it as a record of her family and her home for some kind of posterity, as if she recognized the historical value of the photographic image.'

Fortunately, Duncan's journalism education trained him to record the names of his subjects whenever possible. In a well-worn notebook, his constant companion, he records, '*Señora* Maria Gutierrez and family.'

CHAPTER 08

CIRCLES

Christmas looms on the horizon and some of the locals from the barrio around the pension invite Duncan to celebrate with them. He contributes two bottles of rum and joins his new friends at *'Bar J-J,'* a local bar owned by Juanita and her husband, Julio. It's a simple place with a homemade patio and a variety of mismatched chairs adjacent to a *casita* where the owner's family lives. Strings of multi-coloured lights line the perimeter of the patio, waving in the evening breeze. A party atmosphere evolves into singing and dancing when a traditional band of travelling musicians arrives to perform.

Juanita hauls Duncan onto the dance floor and together they move to the fast-paced salsa music although he has no idea what he's doing. Suddenly, Duncan trips and falls when he feels the floor moving beneath him. Everyone laughs at the crazy *gringo*, telling him not to worry.

"It's just Mother Earth warning you about drinking too much," one of the locals says, laughing.

Duncan quickly applies a lesson learned in Manitoulin. When people of another culture and language laugh at you for stumbling around or saying something stupid in their language, the best reaction is to laugh as well; acknowledge their humour and join with them. In a mere few minutes, they are all friends, celebrating a universal *fiesta*.

Shortly after midnight the ground rumbles and swells. All hell breaks loose as the floors and walls of the building crack and shake violently. The partygoers escape to the open street while the bar and home are twisted to rubble. Chairs and tables are tossed airborne, scattered not only by the vibrations that rattle the foundations of the city, but by the unsettled airwaves between the structures as well.

People from around the barrio scream to God for protection. Bodies eject from their homes into the streets by unseen forces, only to be crushed by flying objects ranging from bottles to Toyotas. Maintaining balance is rendered impossible as the roads crack and rumble underfoot. Darkness is sporadically interrupted by flashes of sparking from live electrical wires and broken poles and the flames that surge from fractured fuel lines. It's difficult to determine how much damage is occurring, but the shouts and screams of people in distress are indications that it's widespread.

Duncan's camera gear is always at his side but any attempts to photograph in the midnight darkness, especially with the continuous movement, are difficult. He manages to take random exposures during flashes and outbursts of fire.

"Tiene cuidado," a passerby cautions Duncan, pointing to live wires jumping and snapping in his path.

Traffic ceases to move on the uneven pavement but anxious and desperate drivers insist on manipulating their family-crammed cars and *camionetas* through the chaos. People scramble to locate family, friends, and belongings trapped in their homes.

After checking the welfare of his new friends from the bar, Duncan begins trekking slowly through other barrios toward the centre of the city.

'I can't believe it,' Duncan's mind turns his thoughts in circles. 'I came here because I love baseball. And what am I doing now? Maybe Willa gets my job after all.'

He's faced with scenes of ruin, broken bodies, and comatose individuals who wander aimlessly through the rubble. People scream from buildings and shout names of the missing.

"They didn't teach any of this shit in journalism school," Duncan reflects aloud. "Of course, how could they? This is an exercise in learning by the ass of my pants."

It suddenly strikes him. 'I'm just lucky to be alive. It's my job, as difficult and as callous as it seems. Baseball yesterday, and then this ... this fucking Armageddon today. I have a camera, and I'm surrounded by the biggest world news of the day. Somehow, I have to get through this, and get the evidence at the same time as helping these poor bastards whenever I can. I can't ask myself whether I'm doing the right or the wrong thing. I just have to jump in and do whatever seems right for the moment. I can't worry about yesterday or tomorrow ... it's all about right now, the present. Time alone will dictate what happens next.'

Within an hour, two significant aftershocks add more death and damage. The entire electrical system is shut down and fresh water pipes are broken and blending with waste systems. Two newer structures, the Intercontinental Hotel and the Bank of America, escape major damage. The remainder of downtown Managua is levelled.

As the first light of dawn creeps over the city, the magnitude of the disaster emerges. People wander dazed, weeping, bloodied from injuries, searching for loved ones. The entire infrastructure is grounded to a halt. Fires burn with no hope of being extinguished. Acrid smells invade Duncan's nostrils: smoke, gas, burning refuse, human waste, death, all blended into a single sickening scent.

The new light is ominous light, the sun prohibited from casting shadows by airborne dust and debris. Bodies, body parts, and suggestions of human remains litter the streets and open doorways of partially-standing buildings and homes.

Duncan's brain rattles with intense confusion, attempting to resolve the rights and the wrongs of his chosen occupation.

A voice inside continues to haunt Duncan. 'I came here to photograph a simple baseball tournament, a joyful, healthy activity that brings happiness and satisfaction to so many. Today, I'm faced with death and destruction. I can't just pack my cameras away and close my eyes as if this isn't happening.'

'Why the fuck do I take photographs anyway?' Duncan ponders, suddenly recalling photographs he'd taken a few days before. 'For the same reason the mother, Maria Gutierrez, wanted her photo taken with her family; posterity, the need to remember. That's why.'

Duncan sidesteps into the small alleyway where the Gutierrez child led him. The poorly-constructed *casitas* are levelled, as he expected. The background to his family portrait no longer exists. 'What about the mother, the kids, the little girl who brought me water, where are they? Already, my photos are history.'

Emotions grab Duncan by the gut. He crumbles into a ball on the ground, weeping like a child over a broken toy, or like he reacted as a child to the unexpected demise of his pet budgie, Quackers.

He drags himself back up, only to face the *casita* that is no longer standing.

"Gutierrez! Gutierrez!" Duncan shouts the family's name frantically; his voice echoes amid the debris and remainders of flimsy wall structures that once formed a community. He waits for signs of life, hopefully a response from one of the children, but ideally an appearance in the courtyard by the entire family. He searches through the rubble: a child's doll, dirty and armless, a dented pot, a ladle, broken glass, a soiled pillow emblazoned with a Mickey Mouse motif.

"Gutierrez! He shouts again. Where the fuck are you?"

From the barrio, Duncan moves further into the bowels of the downtown commercial sector. He approaches a large cathedral. A rescue crew attempts to move a section of the stone wall that has tumbled to the ground. Duncan slowly eases toward them, taking several photos on the move before joining the crew to aid in the rescue.

A person is trapped beneath the boulders and, in a weakened voice, a woman calls out for help. With their concentrated effort and several lengths of broken timber as levers, the men shift one of the boulders aside, revealing a young woman's face and arm. It soon becomes evident that the woman is pregnant and in the process of giving birth.

The assumed leader of the rescue team asks for calm. The scene quietens to an eerie silence, despite the gloomy backdrop of sirens and human suffering. Gradually, they ease the woman from the wreckage and carry her away from immediate danger. She screams and calls out, "Mamá, Mamá … "

The rescuers relocate the woman across the street to a temporary shelter covered by a tarpaulin, where she can be protected from the elements. Duncan watches from a distance, hearing the woman's haunting screams. Two rescuers assume the role of midwives as the baby is brought safely into the world. After hearing the child's first cries, the young mother collapses.

Duncan turns to leave but notices another rescue attempt occurring at the cathedral. A woman, this time older, is pulled from the wreckage but sadly, she succumbs to her injuries. It is soon learned that the victim is the mother of the younger woman; the grandmother who will never know her grandchild.

Duncan's cameras capture the entire event: the rescue, the birth, the relocation to the shelter, and sadly, the unsuccessful rescue attempt of the older woman. Duncan understands the importance of what he has just witnessed and documented: life and death amid the ruins; an ominous circle that has been completed.

Duncan's mind has remained extremely calm throughout, but his stomach issues an early warning. He sets his camera gear on the ground and allows his eyes to swell with tears. His body trembles uncontrollably and his gut empties. He's read about the phenomenon and heard about it from his more experienced peers, a reaction to trauma commonly referred to as 'delayed emotion.'

For some bizarre reason, photojournalists (and others dealing with stress) are able to maintain a level of calm while facing the horrors and tragedies of extreme events: death, sickness, and war-ravaged bodies. Reality sets in once the job is completed, or sometimes as delayed as days, months, or even years. It's a form of PTSD. Duncan personally believes that it's healthier to experience delayed emotion as soon as possible after the event. 'Let the tears flow, and then move on.'

In the midst of the chaos, Duncan's thoughts wander briefly back to the bandstand in New Orleans. The pulse of jazz fills him with warmth and, for a moment, cancels out the smells and cacophony of reality. He is grateful that he can transfer his emotions to another passion, a much-needed diversion from the gritty reality of his profession.

Duncan explores further through the rubble of the commercial district, photographing the destruction and other rescue operations. He witnesses an altercation between several national guards and a family. One of the guards attacks a man whom they accuse of stealing food from a market stand. The man protests but is beaten with a rifle butt. When his wife intervenes to stop the attack, she's pushed to the sidewalk while their children watch helplessly. The guard seizes the allegedly stolen food and throws it to a pack of dogs.

While Duncan records photos of the altercation, one of the guards notices him; he shouts and aims his rifle toward him. Duncan immediately releases the camera and raises his hands in the air.

"Soy periodista. No tomo mas fotos," he pleads, declaring himself as a journalist and that he won't take any more photos, fully aware that he has already secured the essential images that tell the story. The guard kicks at the man and tells him to go. Duncan seizes the opportunity to disappear from the scene as well.

Further into the downtown sector, Duncan encounters a Baldwin piano dealer's sign hanging askew from a concrete building. Inside, a grand piano sits, covered in dust and broken glass where a showroom used to be. He enters the showroom carefully, sweeps debris from the bench, and strikes a few dissonant chords on the keyboard. As can be expected, the piano is in dire need of tuning, however, Duncan exercises his musical diversion by pounding out some Oscar Peterson phrases that lead to an impromptu version of 'Hymn to Freedom.'

While playing, Duncan detects the brassy strains of a trumpet behind him. He turns to face a middle-aged man smiling with his eyes as he enters the showroom. As a point of darkened humour, Duncan utters, "Ah … it's the horn of Gabriel." The man laughs, then quickly weeps as he stumbles forward to embrace Duncan, a kindred spirit brought together by music, the universal language.

The trumpeter introduces himself as Pablo, who plays in a jazz group at one of the city's hotels. His horn is the only item he was able to salvage from his ruined home. "It's my bread and butter," Pablo says in broken English, adding, "it's my body and my soul." He breaks down, crying. "My horn is all I have now."

Duncan is reduced to tears. He embraces Pablo, introducing himself.

"Sometimes music is just what we need," Duncan tells Pablo.

Duncan returns to the keyboard and lays down some blues chords; Pablo joins him on trumpet. After several jazz classics, Pablo plays the melody to 'Silent Night.' Instinctively, Duncan removes a tape recorder from his photo vest and records the session, one Christmas carol after another. Suddenly, during *Adeste Fidelis*, a loud cracking sound thunders above them. They scamper for the open street moments before a massive slab of concrete collapses, crushing the Baldwin grand piano into kindling.

Pablo turns to Duncan. *"Gabriel no. Joshua, si,"* and blows a short quote on his horn from, 'Joshua Fit the Battle of Jericho,' in which the trumpet caused the walls to tumble.

For a while they meander together through the streets trading stories about music, alternating between English and Spanish.

"Miles Davis, *mi héroe*," Pablo declares.

"Mine too," Duncan replies.

"I must go soon," Pablo says, "I have friends to find."

The two musicians embrace with the knowledge that they have shared something truly important, a small glimmer of hope among the destruction; a powerful memory of friendship they will cherish for the remainder of their lives.

Duncan is reminded of the moments in his life when music has calmed the waters for him, complex emotional moments like when he instinctively performed the piano at his grandfather's funeral, and when, following a serious disagreement between he and Penny, he proceeded to compose a love ballad for her.

He understands how important this moment must be for Pablo. 'The poor bastard has lost his home and possibly some family members. He's thrown out into the street in a daze with his only remaining possession, the trumpet that he not only makes his living with, but the instrument that can calm his soul.'

Duncan takes some photos of Pablo as mementos of the occasion. They promise to meet again someday.

"Hasta la próxima," Duncan tells him.

At Pablo's request, a passerby agrees to take a photo of them together with Duncan's camera against the backdrop of the dilapidated Baldwin sign. Pablo produces a damp musty business card from the Inter-Continental Hotel.

"They know me there. You send me the photo and letters there. I will receive them."

Duncan reciprocates with his business card.

As they depart, Pablo gives a thumbs up and shouts, "Miles Davis!" His voice echoes through the shells of broken buildings.

When Duncan returns to the temporary shelter, he replays the taped music for the workers and patients. There are tears of every emotion and choking voices as they sing along in hopeless intonation, but with a dampened spirit of Christmas.

Duncan notices a priest standing over the new mother. "Hello Father. How is the woman doing?"

"Oh." The priest stands and faces Duncan. "And you are …?"

"I'm Duncan. I was here when the woman and the baby were rescued."

The priest shakes Duncan's hand. "I'm Father Manuel." He surveys the cameras around Duncan's neck. "Oh. Are you the photographer who rescued Azucena?"

Duncan responds. "Correction, Father. I was only one of several people involved. The others did most of the work."

"As the photographer you will then want the mother's name for your information. She is called Azucena, after the white Madonna Lily. She has chosen to call the child Tomás Jesús … like the Christ child, Jesús. It's a very popular name in Latin America."

"Thank you Father. I don't want to bother her at this time. I'm sure you will understand."

"I think she would like to talk to you, *señor,* to thank you for your help. She is groggy but able to communicate. Don't worry, she speaks some English."

"So we will resort to speaking *Spanglish* together," Duncan smiles to the priest.

Azucena peers up from her cot. Duncan surmises that she is younger than she appears after her ordeal. They exchange short fragments of conversation.

"Muchas gracias, señor," she thanks him.

Duncan wishes her and Tomás, good health.

She notices the maple leaf on his camera bag. *"Canadiense?"* she inquires.

"Si, Canadiense," Duncan confirms.

They shake hands before Duncan turns to depart. *"Hasta la próxima,"* she says, a promise to meet again.

"I could take a break for a few minutes, *señor,*" the priest says, extending his hand to the side. "Shall we take a stroll across the avenue toward the cathedral."

While walking, Father Manuel states that he is a long-time friend of Azucena and her late mother, whose name was Lydia.

"Lydia worked at the market and Azucena has lived and worked at my father's estate for several years while she attended school."

"You speak English very well," Duncan comments, "I detect only a slight accent."

"Thank you. I attended seminary in the United States. That's where I really started to use it, although my father demanded that I learn to speak English from the time I was a child."

The priest redirects the conversation back to Azucena.

"They are very special people. Lydia is … I mean … was, a very diligent hard-working woman." He wipes a tear from his eye. "Azucena is a wonderful artist, a painter with exceptional talent. One of these days she will become famous."

After some delay, the kind of silent pause one often uses before revealing a secret, Father Manuel adds, "She paints visions of events yet to happen."

"How is that possible?" Duncan asks in disbelief.

"When she was just a child working at the market, her mother described her dreams to her. Azucena started painting her mother's dreams, and many of the events she painted came to pass, sometimes the next day, at other times a month, maybe even a year later. Even when she and her mother were separated, Azucena received her mother's dreams through some kind of telepathy. I can't imagine how she will continue to function without her mother's dreams."

"That sounds like something out of a science fiction novel," Duncan suggests.

"Let me show you something, Duncan." The priest leads Duncan by the arm. "Azucena completed her last painting two weeks ago. It's hanging at the convent where she and her mother were staying while waiting for the arrival of her child. It's a realistic depiction of the plaza where we are walking right now. The cathedral is in the painting and she positioned the clock of the cathedral at 12:35. I want you to look at the real clock up there."

He points toward the spire of the ruined cathedral. "The clock has stopped at 12:35, the precise time the earthquake shook the cathedral." He turns to Duncan with a questioning face, his arms outstretched, the palms of his hands facing the sky.

Duncan asks, in wonderment, "How can such a thing happen? How, as a priest, can you explain Azucena's gift?"

"My answer, as a priest, would be that God is sending her the visions," Father Manuel answers, raising his forefinger as a pause. "However, a wise man once told me that there are some things that are not intended to be explained. They just are." He hesitates. "Like for instance, why the cathedral clock stopped at 12:35, when the earthquake really struck at 12:30. Considering the magnitude of the event, a clock that runs five minutes fast is of little consequence."

Duncan responds. "An Indigenous elder from northern Ontario shared the same wisdom with me. There is no word in their language for coincidence, suggesting there are some things we aren't meant to understand."

"Isn't that a coincidence," Father Manuel offers, smiling.

"No, it's not a coincidence, it just is," Duncan replies, grinning.

He senses similarities between his experiences in Nicaragua and what he encountered during his first trip to Manitoulin. Somehow he is only scratching the surface of a much greater and more complex story. He wants to learn more about Azucena and her mystical talents. He also wants to keep in touch with Father Manuel, who seems to be a storehouse of information.

Duncan is eager to process his work and decides to leave for Canada as soon as a flight can be arranged. At the moment, the airport is only cleared for relief flights, but he opts to camp out at the airport and hope for a seat on any flight returning to North America.

At the airport, news is passed around that Roberto Clemente will be arriving on New Year's Day with a planeload of aid for the victims. The baseball icon chose to accompany the flight personally to guarantee that the aid is distributed directly to the people in need, and not hoarded by the Somoza dictatorship as rumoured.

Duncan reasons. 'My entire story here will have completed another circle, from baseball to earthquake, from life to death, and from earthquake back to baseball.' He had photographed Clemente only a month before at the tournament.

On New Year's Eve, Clemente's flight crashes shortly after takeoff; Duncan's idol dies in the crash.

CHAPTER 09

PENNY

Toronto, 1973:

Jack Bryant meets Duncan's flight when he arrives in Toronto late Thursday, following three connections in Costa Rica, Mexico City, and Miami.

"God, it's great to see you safe and sound, Duncan." Jack smiles as he hugs his star photographer.

"I'm just glad to be here," Duncan answers in a weary voice. "The last month has been a roller coaster."

"I'll bet. From what I heard you've been through hell. Let me take you home." Jack picks up Duncan's luggage but leaves the camera gear and the film for Duncan to carry. Jack already knows how photographers can be so fussy about their film, especially the obsessive Duncan. "Get some sleep, and we'll meet on Monday to go over everything. You look like shit, by the way."

"Thanks, Jack. You're not looking so bad either."

Once in the car, Duncan starts to doze off.

"Have you eaten anything? Jack asks. "You must have lost 20 pounds. Should I stop somewhere for a bite?"

"Hell no. Just get me home so I can catch up on sleep."

"Good. Take the time to rest, get cleaned up, and then be prepared for some late nights."

"I have to process my film."

"I know you're exhausted, Duncan, but we have a two-week deadline for this story. Can you make it?"

"I'll sleep tonight, no problem, Jack, but I can't rest until I can see the results. Let me work the weekend. I'll pull some overnighters and have all 100 films processed with contact sheets by Monday. Then I'll rest. You know me. I can't sit on undeveloped film until I know exactly what I've got."

"OK, Duncan. There's no sense in arguing with you. I'll make sure the chemistry's all fresh for you. Willa, your friend from college, did a great job while you were away. She does nice work. I'll have her mix the chemistry and she can help you process film on the weekend."

"Willa? Great. She's a good photographer. Duncan hesitates before joking, "She must be disappointed that I made it back safely. She'll miss out on a fulltime job."

"I gave her the job anyway, Duncan. She'll start out as a darkroom tech and fill in whenever you're away on assignment."

On Monday, Duncan and Willa present contact proof sheets to Jack as promised.

* * *

Jack is ecstatic about Duncan's work. Unfortunately, Human Interest can only use some of the material. On Duncan's behalf, Jack calls several larger magazines that might be interested in publishing his earthquake story from a news perspective.

Human Interest publishes the International World Series story with a sidebar on baseball culture in Nicaragua. They run a 'rest-in-peace' sidebar on Roberto Clemente along with a colour cover shot from the tournament material. There's also a few pages with overall views of the earthquake damage. Combined, Duncan's work is spread over 12 pages, the largest coverage on a single topic in the magazine's history. Jack dedicates an entire page for a profile of the magazine's star photographer, Duncan MacGregor.

InterNews, an American news magazine buys first rights and publishes the photo essay titled, 'Birth and Death Amid the Ruins,' which ultimately wins two major awards for Duncan, 'Photo Essay of the Year' and 'News Photo of the Year.' InterNews places Duncan on their freelancers Rolodex file with a promise to contact him for future Nicaraguan assignments. In the meantime, they feed Duncan several localized Canadian assignments.

Duncan already knows that he'll be returning to Nicaragua sooner or later. After the magazine is published, he re-enrolls in Spanish lessons and contacts some new Canadians from Central and South America through Latino cultural groups. He starts reading about Latin American history and embraces the contemporary literature of the region. Over time, his new Latino friends invite him to their festivals and house parties, where he's encouraged to speak in Spanish.

* * *

One Sunday afternoon in mid-February, Duncan is in a laundromat waiting for the dryer cycle to finish.

'Oh shit,' Duncan utters to himself, squinting his eyes to sharpen the focus. 'It can't be. Is that really her? What the fuck is she doing here?'

Penny enters the laundromat with a load of laundry.

'Christ, what do I do now?' he agonizes, staring at her from a distance. She loads her laundry into the machine.

'I haven't laid eyes on her since she left for England. I've been so busy that I haven't even thought about her.'

"Duncan? … Duncan, is that you? Is that really you?"

Their eyes connect. It's an awkward encounter for both of them. They stare, both attempting to find the proper facial expression for the occasion.

Duncan fakes his surprise, "Holy shit. Penny? What are you doing here?"

"I don't know. Laundry, I guess." She points her finger at the side of her head. "What else would I be doing in a laundromat?"

"This is weird," Duncan says, bending to pull his clothes from the dryer. "I mean, it's been a long time, eh?"

"Wow, a long time; a lot of water under the bridge, eh Duncan?"

The conversation is going nowhere. Neither wants to delve too deeply. Duncan concentrates on pulling a shirt from the dryer. Penny bites her lip as if there's something she should say. Finally, she avoids anything important.

"So, what are you up to these days, Duncan?"

Duncan avoids any mention of his photography. It's not part of their life together.

"I'm playing a solo gig every Wednesday at Quixote's, a jazz club down in the Village." Duncan fumbles with his fingers, not sure of what he should say next. "How about you? What are you up to?"

"I have a lecturing job at the university … in the arts faculty."

"Great."

Duncan's anxiety kicks in, recalling why he hasn't bothered thinking about Penny. He finally breaks the stalemate. "I should get moving, I have a lot to catch up on. Take care, eh?"

He moves toward the exit without making further eye contact.

"Yeah. You too," Penny offers to the back of Duncan's head.

* * *

A month passes. It's Wednesday, and Duncan is at Quixote's laying down some challenging chord changes in 'Round Midnight, one of his favourite Monk tunes, when he sees Penny enter. She gazes around the club before occupying a table near the piano and orders a Chardonnay. Duncan has no choice but to join her during his break. Conversation is stifled.

"What's up?" he asks.

She hesitates, sips some wine. Her face displays a serious intensity.

"I want to tell you something, Duncan It's something that needs some explanation. I couldn't tell you at the laundromat and it's been haunting me ever since."

"Look Penny," Duncan jumps to conclusions. "If you're going to try to explain why you never answered my letters, don't bother. I'm getting on with my life now, and I really don't need to go backwards."

"But this is important, and you should know." Frown lines strengthen across her forehead.

"Like I said. I don't need to know the details. You obviously met some other guy, and I can understand that. Let's just leave it at that. It's probably better that it worked out this way."

"I can't leave it unsaid. It's something that involves you, and I feel compelled to tell you about it. Otherwise, it will tear me apart."

She hesitates and sips more wine for reinforcement. "I was pregnant. I had a son." More hesitation. "You're the father. There, I've said it. Now you know."

"What?" Duncan's in shock. "How can that be?"

"The traditional way," Penny answers with a forced smile. "By my calculations, he was conceived just before I left for university. I couldn't tell you this when I was pregnant."

"For Christ's sake, why not? I thought we were in love. Hell, we even talked about getting married when school was finished."

"It would have screwed up your music studies at Berklee, and probably your entire career. I couldn't do that to you."

Duncan gets up from his chair and stumbles around in circles for a minute. Suddenly he pounds his fist on the table.

"Fuck that. I screwed that all up on my own. I quit Berklee right after you stopped answering my letters. I was so pissed off and depressed that I let everything slide. I stopped attending classes. I just sat in my room with the rats and the cockroaches until I couldn't stand the loneliness anymore. I didn't take any more gigs. Finally, I returned to Hamilton and moved in with my parents. The only good thing was that Berklee refunded half of my tuition."

"I'm so sorry, Duncan." Penny places her hand on his arm.

Duncan pulls his arm away. "What about your studies in England? Did you have to quit?"

"I was able to complete my first year while I was pregnant. Then I returned to Canada and finished my degree at U of T."

"That must have been a struggle for you. Why didn't you call me?"

"Hell Duncan. I thought you were still in Boston, or maybe you were on the road with some band. Wherever you were, I didn't want to screw things up for you."

"I never finished my studies at Berklee. When your father said you didn't want to see me anymore I was depressed and quit college. I originally planned to head to England to confront you face-to-face. I thought you had just found some other guy. Then, reality sunk in. How stupid of me to travel all that way just to be rejected."

"That wouldn't have been a great idea. It's a good thing that you didn't go." Penny sips some Chardonnay.

"I should have gone. At least I would have found out the truth. I would have married you Penny, you know that. Hell, I would have even stayed in London with you. They have a great jazz scene there."

"That's exactly what I wanted to avoid. It wouldn't have lasted, you know that."

"What about the baby, Penny?" Duncan probes, unsure of what comes next. "When do I get to see my son?"

Penny redirects the subject. "So, what have you been doing all this time, after quitting at Berklee?"

"Before we get into that, I want to know more about our son? What's his name anyway? When will I get to meet him? Tell me about him. Is he chubby, is he dark or fair haired? Does he laugh a lot? What colour are his eyes? Anything. Tell me anything."

Penny stares down at the table. Her fingers follow the patterned outlines on the tablecloth.

She looks toward Duncan but avoids direct contact with his eyes. "So, you must be doing something besides these jazz gigs. Otherwise you're starving."

"What about the baby, Penny?"

"I just need time, Duncan. Can you at least give me some time?"

Duncan backs off, before continuing.

"Since Berklee? Hmm." He strokes his chin. "Where do I start? I travelled for a few months to rediscover myself. What I realized was that I loved photography. I also discovered how curious I am about different cultures and that I can use photography to express my concerns for the human condition. When I returned from travelling, I enrolled in photographic arts at college with a major in documentary photojournalism. That's what I'm doing now. I work full-time for a magazine and freelance work to others."

"Do you get any interesting assignments?"

"Hmm. Funny you should ask. I just returned from Nicaragua after covering the earthquake. Obviously, I still play music when I get the chance. I write a bit as well. So, how about you? Are you married, hooked up with someone? There better not be some other guy raising my son."

"No. There's nobody else," Penny responds carefully. "I've managed well on my own, and I'm lucky to have a good education. I have a wonderful job at the university and my parents have been very supportive." She shrugs, "What do I need a man for anyway? How about you Duncan? Are you with someone?"

"No. Like you said earlier, it wouldn't work out, especially with all the travelling I have to do. No, let me rephrase that, with all the travelling I *want* to do."

Penny chuckles. "Exactly."

Duncan finally steers the conversation back to more pressing matters. "What's his name anyway? Your son. My son. Our son. I want to meet him?"

Penny frowns. "That's the most difficult part of the story, Duncan. I don't quite know how I can tell you this."

"What are you trying to tell me, Penny? If I have a son, then I have a right to know." He stammers to allow a sudden new thought to materialize before asking the question. "Wait … did you have an abortion?"

"Oh, I thought about it, seriously. In fact, I spent so much time agonizing about making the decision, that it was too late; I was too far along. I gave birth to a healthy baby boy in May."

"How old is he now?" Duncan asks, pausing to do some mental calculations. "So, he must be four, right? He must already be curious about why there's no father around. Did you tell him who I am?"

Penny drops the bombshell. "He was adopted. I'm listed as his birth mother, but he won't have access to that information unless I sign a waiver to allow the adoption agency to provide it, and only if they receive a request directly from him."

"Who did you list as the father?"

Penny returns to running her finger along the patterned tablecloth, hesitating an embarrassingly long moment before responding. "Unknown."

"Christ Almighty." Duncan shakes his head. "When you wake up in the morning, you have no fucking idea what the day will bring. Today has turned out to be one disastrous, fucked up day."

There's silence. Duncan checks his watch.

"I have to get back on the stand, Penny. Can you and I can get together sometime soon, maybe have dinner? There's still a lot to discuss."

"I'll have to let you know, Duncan. This has been very stressful for me, just finding the courage to tell you. I'm not totally convinced I made the right decision. Time will tell."

"It's been a bit of a fucking shock for me too, you know, but I'm glad you finally told me. I won't get much sleep tonight however."

Penny drains her glass and stands up. She looks at Duncan for a moment until he moves closer. She gives him a polite, but non-committal, hug. "I have to go."

PART FOUR
1974 – 1975

CHAPTER 10

UNREST

Toronto, Friday, December 27, 1974:

"Urgent! This is InterNews magazine calling for Duncan MacGregor."
The voicemail message has already started when Duncan finally reaches
his phone. His clock reads 11:48 pm.

"Hello, Hello, this is Duncan. What's up?"

"Leave immediately for Managua, Nicaragua. There's been a kid-
napping and there are bodies. What we know at the moment is that
armed guerrillas raided a Christmas party and kidnapped 13 business
and political leaders. The country is at a standstill. Get us everything
you can. Send raw film. Colour only."

Duncan quickly grabs some light clothing, his passport, film, and
camera gear. At the last minute he throws a package of images from his
previous visit into his bag. If there's any free time, he hopes to revisit
some of the people he photographed and give them prints. It's a policy
he's continued since his first experience in Manitoulin.

He manages to secure a flight to Miami on short notice, with a brief layover before catching a direct hop to Managua.

*　*　*

Managua, Nicaragua:

Chaos meets him upon arrival at Managua airport. Armed guards surround the entrances and exits, and luggage is critically examined. Oddly, he's passed through customs without incident and an unexpectedly polite welcome. *"Bienvenido a Nicaragua, señor."*

Duncan secures a third-floor room at the Inter-Continental and heads directly to the bar where journalists shuffle to file stories and wheedle information from other reporters. He orders a Heineken and introduces himself to a cadre of AP reporters. His credentials from InterNews improve his access.

One of the reporters updates the situation for Duncan. "Currently, the country's on high alert. There's already been four killed. The home of the agriculture minister is locked down, surrounded by the army and National Guard, all heavily armed. The press is being kept at a distance, but we understand there may be an announcement from the President at any time. We're heading to the scene right now, if you want to join us, Duncan; we have a car."

Conversation bounces amongst the journalists in the car revealing the level of their anxiety and excitement of covering an international story that could lead to major confrontation. They all expect that a revolution on the scale of Cuba could be in the works.

"The President is going to massacre those bastards, don't you think?"

"I heard he wanted to blow the bloody place up with the hostages and rebels inside, until he found out that his sister, who's married to Nicaragua's Ambassador to Washington, is among the hostages."

"What are their demands? What do they want?"

"I heard five million is the amount. They also want the press to print their manifesto."

"Like that'll ever happen."

"Do you think President Ford will send in the troops?"

"Not a chance. Shit, they just got rid of Nixon and the legacy of Vietnam is still in the public's mind. No way."

Waiting outside the mansion challenges Duncan's need for sleep. Fortunately, the journalists take turns grabbing short naps in the car. There isn't much to photograph at the mansion where the hostages are being held. Duncan manages some overall shots that show armed guards and the mansion from a distance.

Finally, on December 31, an agreement is reached. The President agrees to pay one million dollars in ransom and to release 14 political prisoners and fly them and the kidnappers to Cuba. He also allows them to broadcast the FSLN manifesto to the people on public radio.

Crowds of supporters and curiosity seekers gather along the route toward the airport to witness the entourage as it passes. Duncan gets good photo coverage of the masses of people cheering the guerillas as they pass, the FSLN red and black banner flying from a window. It is a turning point for the rebels, evidence of their increasing popularity.

Duncan files his story with InterNews and couriers his film from the hotel. He sucks back a quick beer to celebrate the new year and retires to his room.

In the morning he takes coffee on the balcony, surveying the city centre with enough altitude for him to quietly assess the effects from the earthquake two years before. Much of the destruction remains; shells of buildings yet unrepaired, many side streets still cracked and pot-holed, poorly constructed *casitas* cropping up in barrios.

For lunch, Duncan walks across *Avenida Bolívar* to *Los Antojitos*. Bill Haley and the Comets spew classic rock through tinny speakers into the patio. Afterward, he strolls through the barrio that he remembers from his first visit. Much of the rubble has been removed or, in some cases recycled, in attempts at reconstruction. The new structures exist as temporary, but expedient, solutions for protection from the elements, in the hope that the future may provide more permanent housing.

Duncan's stroll takes him past *'Bar J-J,'* the bar that he escaped from on the night of the earthquake. There is still a bar, opening onto a small patio area. A makeshift cover fabricated from a metal sign advertising *'salsa ingles'* (ketchup), hangs precariously above the bar protecting three stools of various heights and origins. The patio, where dancing is encouraged, is cracked and uneven with weeds emerging. He raps his knuckles on the bar. *"Hola,"* he calls out. A woman appears from the attached *casita*.

"Hola, señor. Quiere cerveza?"

"Si por favor," he responds, accepting the offer.

The woman turns around, grabs a beer from the fridge, and snaps off the cap. She hands it to Duncan.

"Do you remember me, Juanita?" Duncan asks, accepting the bottle.

She studies Duncan for a minute. *"Ahh, si. El canadiense."* She rounds the bar and greets him with an embrace. *"Como estás?"*

"Muy bien, gracias," Duncan answers. *"Y tu?"*

Juanita tilts her head from side to side. *"Más o menos,"* (so-so).

After their embrace, Duncan reaches into his bag and pulls out a black and white print. He hands the woman a photograph he took of her and her husband, Julio, dancing at the Christmas party from the last time he was there. She stares at the photo for a moment, moving her fingers across the surface until tears appear.

Duncan asks, "Is Julio, your husband, at home?"

Her face saddens. *"No. Julio es con Dios. Está muerto."*

Duncan is shocked to hear of the passing of Julio and offers his sincere condolences.

"Qué Pasó?" Duncan asks. "He was still a healthy young man, no?"

She confides, "My husband attempted to get assistance from the government to repair the house and the bar after the earthquake but he was refused, *tres veces.*" She displays three fingers. "So, he organized some of the neighbours from the barrio to appeal the decision. Soon afterward, some thugs arrived at night and dragged him out onto the street, where they beat him to death with baseball bats."

Juanita starts weeping. "They called him a communist organizer.

Julio was no communist. He just wanted to get his business started again. I sincerely believe they were from the national guard, but they were out of uniform."

Duncan is stunned by the news. His brief friendship with her husband, Julio, recalls fond memories, despite the tragedy of the night they shared.

"I remember Julio as a kind, gentle man," Duncan recalls.

"Si. Un buen caballero." Juanita agrees. "I miss him."

She lowers her head in silence before continuing. "So, I keep the bar open just the way it is. It's the only income I have, although I also have a sewing machine that I use to repair people's clothes. Not too many people in this barrio can afford new clothes these days. So ..." she smiles and shrugs her shoulders, "repairing old clothes is a growing business, no?"

Duncan drains his beer and hugs Juanita. *"Hasta la próxima."*

He turns from the bar to explore further into the barrio. Small wooden *casitas* line the alleyway leading to where the Gutierrez family lived. Several children play in the courtyard surrounded by newer, but equally humble dwellings as before.

Duncan approaches the children. "Gutierrez?" he asks.

One of the boys runs away, returning moments later, holding the hand of a woman.

Duncan repeats. "Gutierrez?"

The woman questions, *"Si? Me llamo Gutierrez."*

Duncan produces a photo of the family grouping taken during his previous visit.

The woman sighs, *"Ah-h-h."* She explains to Duncan that the photo is of her sister's family, adding that only three of the children remain alive.

Duncan places his hand on the woman's shoulder, offering his condolences. *"Y su hermana?"* Duncan asks, about her sister.

"Maria? Está muerta," she replies shaking her head. "Gone." She gestures with a wave of her hand and explains that the remaining children live with her.

Duncan wipes tears away with the back of his hand.

The woman consoles him and offers to return the photo to Duncan.

"It's for you, and the children," Duncan responds, turning to leave.

The woman touches his arm. *"Por favor, señor ... toma una foto,"* she says, asking for another photo to be taken. *"Como la otra,"* (like the other one).

The woman looks over her shoulder and shouts several names, and soon numerous children of varying ages appear, posing themselves as a group before their haphazardly reconstructed *casita.* Two of the children are wearing Canadian flag pins as earrings.

Before going to the hotel, Duncan returns to '*Bar J-J.*' He orders a beer and shares more tears with Julio's widow, Juanita.

* * *

Upon Duncan's return to the hotel, a commotion among the journalists signals a newsworthy event is unfolding.

"There's a standoff over by the university," an AP reporter shouts to Duncan, hailing a taxi at the same time.

He and Duncan share a taxi that drops them off a block from the university. A crowd of students has occupied an area of the campus and is marching, carrying placards demanding rights for the poor and for the resignation of the president. Some students carry hand scrawled FSLN signs, the designation for the revolutionary group, *Frente Sandinista Liberación Nacional.*

Duncan starts photographing from a distance and gradually moves closer until instinct and experience draw him and his cameras inside the peaceful crowd of demonstrators to capture their expressions and gestures on film. Their shouting follows a familiar rhythmic pattern, having the same pulse as used by the civil rights and the anti-war demonstrators in the U.S. The language is, of course, different, but the zeal and urgency for change feels the same. As they march, many citizens cheer them on from the sidelines and raise their fists in solidarity. Others join their ranks, and the numbers swell.

National Guards are erecting barricades several blocks ahead. The demonstrators must see them too, but their pace remains steady and determined.

Duncan breaks from the crowd and jogs ahead of the marchers until he's strategically placed between the two factions, within a city block of the barricade. His gut tells him that the demonstrators are so determined they won't stop but will clash with the guards at the barricade.

Suddenly from behind him, the guards advance, swinging batons wildly. Duncan is knocked to the pavement and hears the heavy clunking of military boots passing his head. Rolling to the side, he avoids being trampled, while pointing his camera in the general direction of the demonstrators. The two factions collide before his lens, batons smashing at unprotected skulls, blood-spurting bodies hitting the pavement. Some demonstrators escape to side streets, but many dedicated ones maintain the pulse of the march, chanting, until they too, join the wounded.

Duncan continues to photograph while dozens of demonstrators are rounded up and thrown into waiting trucks with barred windows. The beatings continue after they're captured. Chanting turns to screams, while the guards shout 'comunista,' with hatred in their eyes.

In the corner of his vision, Duncan notices Father Manuel in the march. He's approaching the bloodbath zone when suddenly, a guard's baton strikes the woman next to him on the side of her head; she falls, dazed and bleeding. Duncan quickly realizes that it's Azucena who's been hit. He runs toward her during the melee, but a guard forces him back with his boot and stands over him, threatening with his baton. Duncan sees the woman being hauled away to a waiting truck with the others.

Suddenly, Father Manuel forces himself between Duncan and the guard, pushing Duncan off to the side of the street.

"Are you OK?" the priest asks, pulling Duncan up. "What the hell are you doing here? You almost got killed. These bastards are vicious."

"Was that Azucena I saw? What will happen to her?"

"Now that she's in the truck, she'll be safe until they start interrogating her at the holding cells. That's when it could get very rough. Some don't survive."

Duncan asks in a desperate voice, "What can we do? Where are they taking her? Can we go there and plead her case?"

"That's exactly what I'm going to do," Father Manuel insists. "I know where they're taking them. Come with me."

Father Manuel and Duncan run to the next street and hail a taxi. The priest rattles directions to the cabbie, and they soon arrive at the prison.

"You wait here, *amigo*," he tells Duncan. They won't let a journalist inside anyway. Stay out here, away from the gates, and take lots of photos. People will be coming and going here all night; I'm sure they'll have stories for you. I'm going inside. They'll let me in to console the prisoners; so far, they haven't started killing priests." He feigns praying to God. "Don't worry. I will find Azucena. I think I know how to get her out safely. Just wait for me, I might be a few hours."

Duncan watches people arriving, hopeful to free their loved ones. Only a few succeed in getting past the guards at the front gate. He analyzes the overall situation in terms of how he might capture some of the moments on film. The guards are watching him closely but recognize that he's a member of the foreign press. Some may even have seen him arrive with Father Manuel. Duncan surmises that they probably have orders to back off, especially when it's the U.S.-based press. InterNews, his employer, is an American news magazine with leftist sensibilities, and would most certainly use photos that could be critical of the regime. He takes advantage of the benefit to snap some candids, and to talk to some of the families waiting outside the prison. As he assumed, the guards study his actions closely but remain at a distance.

Rather than putting the camera to his eyes, Duncan resorts to the 'shooting-from-the-hip' technique to avoid any problems. The technique makes it difficult for him to compose as carefully as he likes, but it's the difference between getting photos or not. Some of the results, Duncan knows, will be useful, and he hopes that a few will be stupendous.

"How long have you been waiting?" Duncan asks one couple, whose worry shows in their faces.

"We will wait as long as we must," the man answers. "Our daughter is inside. She has been there before. We can only wait … and hope."

"And pray," the mother adds."

The father tells Duncan that the first offenders will be allowed to leave after the guards scare the shit out of them. "Unless," he adds, "they are from a family known to them already … or, if someone has ratted on them, like a teacher, or even a priest."

The man's last statement worries Duncan, as darkness falls. Finally, at six-thirty, Father Manuel and Azucena exit through the prison gates. His arm is placed around her shoulder and her head is bowed.

The man he was talking to earlier leans over to Duncan. "Except for Father Manuel. He is one of the few good priests. Father Manuel helps the poor … unlike his brother, the tyrant, Col. Jorge, who kills the poor."

Duncan wishes the couple good luck with their daughter's release.

A taxi arrives and is instructed to take them to Father Manuel's church in the barrio. There is minimal conversation in the taxi. Azucena keeps her head bowed the entire time.

When they arrive, Azucena takes a quick shower at the nun's quarters, and they tend to her wounds. Luckily, the wounds are superficial, some bruising and one minor laceration. The nuns assist Azucena in applying some makeup to hide the visible marks on her face and neck. She emerges bubbly and smiling as if it's just another day at the office.

"Now I look like a movie star," she shouts.

Father Manuel asks Azucena if she remembers Duncan.

"Of course," she says. He's the handsome man who saved my life. *Hola señor.*" She offers her hand.

"Please call me Duncan."

"*Está bien, Dooncan.*" Azucena agrees. "I'm famished," she says. "Let's eat."

They arrive at *Los Antojitos* by taxi and order *biftec* dinners all around on Duncan's expense account. He'll include it in his invoice to InterNews. When the food arrives, it occurs to Duncan that restaurants heap enormous piles of food on the plates while so many people struggle to survive. Regardless, Duncan orders a bottle of *Ron Oro* for the table.

Azucena is talkative beyond belief for someone who has experienced such trauma only hours before. He suspects she might be experiencing a level of shock, but Father Manuel assures Duncan that this is her normal demeanor. By the second glass of rum, she becomes very talkative, expressive, and outgoing.

"So *Dooncan*, tell me about yourself. What is your wife like?"

"Umm, I'm not married. I don't have a wife."

Recognizing Duncan's discomfort at Azucena's question, Father Manuel introduces a new topic.

"Azucena started studying fine arts at the university this year," he tells Duncan. "She's a very attentive student."

"I want to be a teacher someday," Azucena says.

Father Manuel adds, "She's a very talented artist. People think she possesses special powers."

Duncan offers, "I'd like to see your paintings sometime?"

"Of course," she replies, "Tomorrow. I will come by the hotel, and we can walk to the gallery from there. I have a show ongoing."

"Wonderful," Duncan agrees.

CHAPTER 11

A QUIET DAY

Managua, Nicaragua, 1975:

Early in the morning, the phone rings in Duncan's room. It's 8:35 am. The voice announces that someone is waiting to see him in the lobby. He dresses quickly and hurries to the lobby.

Azucena, dressed fashionably chic, waits for him while fingering through an arts magazine at the newsstand. He mentions his surprise at the early hour of her arrival and suggests breakfast before they leave the hotel. They have coffee and croissants in the hotel cafeteria.

The journalist from AP, who shared the taxi with Duncan yesterday, recognizes him in the cafeteria. "Did you get anything decent from that demonstration?" he asks.

"I don't know," Duncan responds, "I'll have to see."

"Here's my card. Let me know if you can share anything."

"Will do," Duncan promises.

Azucena speaks between sips of coffee and a bite from the croissant. "You have such a wonderful life, *Dooncan*. You see all kinds of exciting things and get to travel. I envy you."

"It's better than getting beat up and locked up in prison, Azucena," he jests, "although there are certainly some of those challenges in my profession too."

"Now," she says, "it's time for you to learn my name. It is pronounced, *Athucena*. The Z is pronounced like a *TH* and the C is softer, like trying to say S and *th* at the same time. Try it. Of course, if you are somewhere else, like in Mexico, Cuba, or Barcelona, it would sound slightly different."

Duncan succeeds after several attempts.

In turn, Duncan instructs Azucena how to say his Scottish name correctly. After repeating Duncan several times, she gets it under control. He tells Azucena, "If you were in Scotland, my name would sound different as well, more like you are already saying it as *Dooncan*."

"So, I was correct all along," she says laughing, "and it is you who is wrong." She pushes herself against his arm.

It's a fresh crisp morning, perfect for walking. Azucena leads Duncan through a well-treed barrio, an area that escaped major damage during the earthquake. There is greenery everywhere. The gallery is located several blocks away in a suburban park setting. Adjacent to the gallery is a bistro.

"So, my show is in this gallery, I hope you like it. They have live jazz music in the bistro at nights. Do you like jazz music, Duncan?"

Duncan chuckles. "You have no idea. It's my passion."

As they move through the show, Duncan takes photos of her and her work. He asks, "I've heard that you used to paint from visions you received from your mother. Can you explain that process to me?"

Azucena avoids answering directly by joking, "If it wasn't for my mother, I wouldn't have any talent whatsoever." She adds, "I still receive visions from her, in my dreams, even though she is …"

"How is that possible?"

"I have no explanation except that they just come to me while I'm sleeping. Sometimes they are visions of things that haven't yet happened."

"Receiving the visions from your deceased mother is amazing enough, but foreseeing the future is beyond my imagination, in fact it's beyond any scientific explanation."

Duncan points to a large canvas depicting a fiery battle in a forested mountainous area. There are corpses lying among the trees. "Where is this, and what is happening?"

She replies, "It's a battle. I don't know where it is, maybe in the north of the country, near Matagalpa perhaps. Or ... maybe it's not even in Nicaragua."

"When did it happen?" Duncan quickly rephrases his question into the future tense. "I mean, when *will* this happen?"

"I don't know such things, I only paint what I'm compelled to. When it does happen, maybe it will be important enough to change history." She hesitates to ponder, and then shrugs, "And maybe not."

"It's unfortunate that you can't predict when and where. It would be a wonderful talent for a journalist to have."

She smiles. "Let me show you around the city this afternoon. And tonight, we will have something to eat and drink at the bistro while listening to live jazz."

"Sounds fantastic, but are you sure you're up to it after your ordeal yesterday?"

"If I fall asleep in the middle of our conversations, call me a taxi. But, if I stop breathing, call me a priest."

"Not a doctor?" Duncan asks.

"In this country there are more priests than doctors and they're all willing to steal your money and your soul ... except Father Manuel, that is."

Duncan holds onto Azucena's words, wondering if what she says is indeed true.

They walk toward the waterfront, through the streets of dilapidated buildings and past the former Baldwin store where Duncan played the grand piano with Pablo. 'What ever happened to Pablo?'

he ponders. The piano has been removed but the sign remains affixed to the wall.

As they walk, Azucena identifies the businesses that previously occupied the premises.

When they reach the edge of the plaza, she points toward a magnificent white structure surrounded by open space.

"That is the *Teatro Nacional Rubén Darío*, named after our nation's most famous poet. As you can see, the theatre has survived the earthquake intact, just as his writings have survived over the years. Greatness cannot be destroyed. Do you agree?" She looks directly into Duncan's eyes, a characteristic that makes Duncan uncomfortable but welcoming at the same time.

"You must read Darío's, *'A Roosevelt,'* Azucena adds. It's a powerful address to then-president Theodore Roosevelt."

"I will," Duncan promises." He makes a note of it in his book.

"Nicaragua is well-known as a nation of poets," Azucena tells him. "Everyone who can, writes poetry. Unfortunately, a large percentage of our population is illiterate, because education is reserved for the rich. This situation must be changed if Nicaragua is to survive. It is the main reason I support the FSLN. I believe that education should be a right and not a privilege, and it should be provided free to all the people, rich and poor, men and women."

"That's how it is in my country, Canada," Duncan offers.

Azucena reveals, "I would be illiterate if it wasn't for Mamá, but I would be uneducated if it wasn't for Father Manuel."

"You are living proof of the potential of Nicaragua," Duncan offers. You're a university student, well read, and speaking two languages. Very impressive."

"Flattery will get you everywhere," Azucena jokes, placing her arm around Duncan's. "Someday, I will tell you all about my family history, but not today."

Duncan is surprised at Azucena's outgoing attitude. "Has anybody told you that you're a flirt?"

"I am a Nicaraguan. We are friendly outgoing people; we laugh, we joke, we embrace, and we love music, the arts, and dance … and yes, we flirt."

She hesitates before continuing.

"In these difficult times, it is important to immediately identify people as either friends or as foes. As you discovered the other day, there are differences of opinion in our country as to how we should live our lives, and who should be running things. We, the FSLN, are struggling to provide a better life for our children: access to education and health care, and improvements for women."

"That's a tall order. It appears that the President doesn't agree with those changes you want to happen … and he has the army."

"There are both kinds here, friends and foes, as everywhere else, I suppose. I have identified you as a friend. Father Manuel has, also. You must be a friend, because you helped save my life. We have many other friends on our side. We even have friends in the military. Change takes time. You will see."

"So tell me, Azucena," Duncan asks. "What exactly is the FSLN? Who do they represent?"

"The FSLN isn't a single entity. For many years there have been various groups opposed to the Somoza dynasty. Finally, in 1961, three of the groups agreed to work together toward a final push to overthrow the government. They formed the *Frente Sandinista de Liberación Nacional.*"

"Do the three groups always agree on the same principles?" Duncan probes.

"Not likely," Azucena responds with a grin. "Each of the groups represent a variety of ideologies. There are Marxists and moderate socialists, some are merely disgruntled capitalists. In other words, they represent the entire spectrum of *nicaragüenses*. We can't fail."

From the theatre, they walk across the open plaza to ruins of the Cathedral, where Duncan first encountered Azucena. She remains silent, her eyes closed, in remembrance to her mother. The clock still reads 12:35.

"This place is always very confusing to me," she says. "It's a mixed blessing. It is where God took my mother from me and gave me Tomás. Life and death in one fleeting moment. You were there, Duncan. You remember." She places her hand in his and squeezes.

'Is she hitting on me, or is she just being friendly?' Duncan ponders. He consoles her by squeezing back.

"I see that as a circle being completed," Duncan explains. "This is a concept I learned from a wise Indigenous medicine man in northern Canada. Life is a circle, and people and occurrences form circles and complete themselves to us. They are to remind us that we should recognize and cherish these things. I believe it was the elder's way of telling me that there is no end to life."

Azucena stares into Duncan's eyes. "So, Duncan, do you believe in the afterlife?"

"Not necessarily in the biblical sense, but definitely in a philosophical sense. I am not what you would call a religious man, but a spirit lives within me, one that drives me to create. My afterlife is a compendium of what I create and accomplish while I'm here … alive … and what I leave to others as a form of legacy."

"Legacy is one thing, Duncan, but do you have a soul?"

Duncan rubs his chin. "A soul … hmm." I'll have to think about that."

Before Azucena can continue, Duncan adds an afterthought. "Yes." He pauses to contemplate his thoughts. "Yes. I have a soul. Memories, they're my soul. They provide the proof that I once existed. They're also my afterlife … and my legacy."

Azucena offers an opinion. "You never mentioned God. Where is He in your life?"

Duncan hesitates before offering an answer. "I think that my beliefs closely relate to those of Buddhism, although I am not a practising Buddhist. I often consider the existence of an afterlife in the form of reincarnation, where I would reappear after death in another lifeform."

Azucena laughs. "So ... then you could come back as a chicken ... or an iguana, or even a tapeworm."

"Possibly," Duncan agrees, "but think of the stories I could tell."

While Azucena laughs, Duncan reflects the conversation back to her.

"And you Azucena, are you a believer in the afterlife?"

"I believe in Heaven, where my mother is living now. I cannot, however, subscribe to a Hell, because it is here with us now, all the time. This week I was introduced to Hell in that prison, and I fully expect to return there during my lifetime. If I should die in there, I am confident that my soul will be transported by God, to be with my mother, and with many others with whom I have shared my life on earth. Maybe we will meet again there."

Duncan chuckles. "What about your legacy?" he asks. "Of course you will leave the world your paintings, but what about your thoughts and philosophies?"

"Then maybe I too, believe in reincarnation. How else could I pass on my dreams and visions, like Mamá? Maybe I could be a Buddhist."

Duncan offers, "Everyone should have dreams and ambitions for their life. Some follow a god and some put their faith in themselves. Either way, I never judge anybody for what they believe, only for how they conduct themselves while they're here."

Azucena strokes his arm. "That's a very honourable code, Duncan. I just wish the rest of the world felt the same way."

Azucena turns her eyes into Duncan's. "One of my desires is to paint in our own beautiful Garden of Eden located in the south of Nicaragua. One day I will go there to paint. It is said to be a powerful experience." She smiles, her brown eyes brighten and continue to focus on Duncan's. "Maybe you should visit there."

"I'd love to see that."

Azucena adds with a smile, "Maybe you will find your God there."

"I never said my god was missing," Duncan adds with a responsive chuckle. To change the subject, Duncan asks, "How is little Tomás doing? I think of him often. He must be growing quickly these days.

"Thank you for asking. He is doing very well, a toddler now, and very active. I considered bringing him with us today, but he would tire too easily with all this walking. He is spending the day with Father Manuel, who is teaching Tomás to play baseball. There are other children there to play with, many are orphans, so he doesn't become lonely, and he is learning to be sociable."

"Maybe I could play baseball with Tomás someday. It's one of my passions … along with jazz, of course."

"You have many passions, Duncan." How do you keep up with them?"

"It's difficult sometimes," Duncan answers. He adds, "Maybe, when Tomás is older, I could teach him to play the piano."

Azucena stares into Duncan's eyes with an intensity that demands Duncan's attention. "Does that mean that you will be returning to Nicaragua, Duncan?"

"I never know where my job will take me."

* * *

The tropical heat and humidity increase as their sightseeing continues into the noon hour. Duncan suggests a refreshment break, "a beer perhaps."

Azucena recommends coffee. "My mother always insisted that when it's hot, you should drink hot."

"That wouldn't work in Canada; we do the opposite. This is cold beer weather. In the winter, when the blustery cold winds blow the snow around, we drink coffee and hot chocolate, or a warming alcohol like Rum Toddies."

"When in Rome …" Azucena quotes, leading Duncan to a café patio overlooking a small *laguna*. They locate an umbrella-protected bistro table. A slight breeze passes over the *laguna*, not cooling but sufficient to dry the excess perspiration from their skins.

"So," Duncan quizzes, "what's in store for us this afternoon?"

"Something very special, something that will awaken your senses to our country. They will convince you to return here often, to Nicaragua."

"It sounds mysterious and secretive. I can't wait."

Soon they're back out on the street, a raucous busy avenue. Azucena flags a taxi and provides directions.

"*Un taxi por el día,*" she tells the driver that they'll hire the cab for the day.

"Let me pay for this. I have an expense account," Duncan offers, removing some money from his wallet.

"Not yet." Azucena jumps between Duncan and the cabbie. "Put your money away Duncan, until later. Otherwise the driver will just take your money and won't wait for us."

They travel south, past the city limits. It's a leisurely ride. Occasionally they pass a gathering of vendors where cars stop. Other vendors, mainly women, walk with perfect posture along the roadside, balancing their wares on their heads, some even with babies wrapped to their breasts.

The taxi turns off the highway, following a twisting road up a gradual incline. They leave the taxi to walk. Duncan senses a strong sulphurous odour, almost painful to his nostrils.

"Are these the senses you wanted me to awaken to?"

"They can definitely awaken the senses, but they are not the ones I was referring to. It occurred to me that you might never have experienced a live volcano before. I will take you to the edge of the Santiago crater."

Azucena leads Duncan toward the crater. A steady plume of acidic smoke rises from deep inside the earth. In an effort to conceal his chronic acrophobia, Duncan follows Azucena, daring to advance toward the edge. With each step he carefully considers his footing on the loose gravel.

"You walk like a *mula*," Azucena laughs.

"A what?" Duncan reacts.

"A *mula* ... a mule, you would say in English. They are sure-footed. That's why they are used in the mountains. They are much more reliable than horses."

"Is that why they call them pack mules, then?" Duncan asks.

"*Exactamente*," Azucena nods. "Do you know that mules can't reproduce; two mules can't make baby mules. Mules can only be made by a female horse and a male donkey."

"And I thought I knew everything," Duncan laughs.

Deep in the bowels of the earth, between bellows of smoke, a red boiling glow is visible. Duncan slowly retreats.

"The rumour is that the National Guard drops political prisoners into the volcano from helicopters." Azucena adds, "while they are still alive."

"Shit," Duncan shivers. "That sounds to me like a good reason to vote for the President," he says with a weightbearing smirk, as he looks from the volcano back at Azucena. "That's a joke by the way."

Azucena frowns. "That may be a joke, Duncan, but under the current political situation, it isn't very funny."

"Sorry," Duncan apologizes, faking a sad face.

Azucena squeezes his hand. "Please don't be offended by my response, Duncan." She laughs. "It is a funny joke. It's just that things are very tense in Nicaragua these days." To atone for her criticism, Azucena slides her arm between his and they return to the taxi.

A short drive later, they arrive at a thriving community. The taxi parks near the main market.

Azucena assumes the role of a tourist guide. "We have arrived at the city of Masaya. It existed long before the Spanish arrived. Many of the people living here today are direct descendants of the Indigenous people of old, the *Niquiranos* and the *Chorotegas*. This market is their commercial centre, where you can find almost anything, but especially the Indigenous handicrafts and foods."

Duncan quickly enters the marketplace, loading one of his cameras with his favoured Kodachrome film. The brilliant, saturated hues of textiles; woven mats, clothing, and hammocks, accompanied by unlimited odours of food and spices, and the cacophonous orchestra of bartering vendors assault his senses as Azucena had promised.

'I could live here,' Duncan ponders.

Azucena strolls calmly behind him, chatting to people and watching Duncan dance wildly and excitedly through the crowded aisles snapping images, issuing snippets of conversation with total strangers, and waiting for their responses. Duncan smiles at people and darts among them like a child at a circus. His cameras, one loaded with colour and the other with black and white, click rapidly with sequences of images while the corners of his eyes anticipate where his camera will follow.

Some of the vendors are curious about the *gringo* with the cameras. Azucena explains to them about Duncan and his occupation, *"Un fotoperiodista de Canada."*

After leaving the Masaya market, their taxi continues to a community of modest dwellings, not unlike the temporarily restructured ones in the barrio where Duncan stayed during the earthquake.

Azucena announces their arrival in the small village of *Niquinohomo*, a primarily Indigenous settlement where many of the colourful crafts Duncan saw at the market are made.

"This is the birthplace of Augusto C. Sandino," Azucena informs. "To many of us, he is a national hero. The movement, which I represented yesterday, is based on his name, *Los Sandinistas*. This is a name you will be hearing much about in the very near future."

"Since I was in Nicaragua the last time, I have read a bit about the country's history," Duncan tells Azucena. "Sandino was an early revolutionary in the 1930s who was tricked by the Americans and subsequently assassinated, right?"

"Exactamente, Duncan." Azucena squeezes his arm. "Congratulations. You already know more than most foreigners. "That's when they installed the first Somoza as President. The current dictator was

preceded by his father and his brother. The family has ruled Nicaragua with an iron fist since 1936, always with the assistance and blessings of the U.S. government."

Duncan adds an anecdote. "Apparently, in 1939, President Franklin Roosevelt said, 'Somoza may be a son of a bitch, but he's our son of a bitch,' according to news sources I've read."

"That would have been the father of our current president," Azucena explains. "Like father, like son."

Duncan adds, "It's all in the family."

They approach a small *casita* and are welcomed into the humble home by a frail woman who appears to be in her late-60s. There are three chairs in the room and a table used for eating and making crafts. Four children of various ages from approximately three to early-teens, stare at Duncan with his cameras hanging from his neck. They seem to know Azucena, who talks to the children by name. They give her hugs. Duncan assumes the woman must be their grandmother, but discovers, when introduced to her, that she is their mother; obviously not as old as Duncan originally surmised.

While the mother is speaking with Azucena, another woman, much older with hunched over shoulders and arthritic hands appears from another room. She silently gathers the last remnants of corn flour in a bowl from an otherwise empty cupboard and disappears through a rear door.

'She must be the grandmother,' Duncan assumes.

The mother opens a box on the floor and removes some craft materials, patterned cloth, some straw, an Exacto knife, and a pair of scissors. Azucena tells Duncan that it's OK for him to take photos of the woman working.

Azucena explains, "This is an ancient craft from pre-Columbian times. Each generation of the Indigenous people are taught, as young children, to carry on the tradition of making figures from straw. The original purpose was for spiritual reasons, but when they were

Christianized by the colonizers, they were forced to abandon their traditional beliefs."

Duncan assures Azucena that the Spanish colonizers were no different than the British, who forced the Indigenous people of Canada and the U.S. to abandon their languages and their unique cultures, and forcibly removed their children, placing them into residential schools run by churches under government contracts.

As he takes photos, the grandmother reappears with two tortillas on banana leaves. She extends them toward Azucena and Duncan. The grandmother's face lights up with a smile, exposing three lonely teeth. With only her gestures she encourages them to eat. Azucena offers her thanks to the old woman by bowing to her. Duncan copies Azucena's gesture.

Quietly, as an aside, Duncan whispers to Azucena. "I'm uncomfortable about eating this. There's nothing else left in the house for them to eat. We're taking their only food."

Azucena whispers an answer. "Eat. You must. Otherwise, you are rejecting their hospitality. It's like slapping them in the face. You must eat what they provide."

Duncan obeys what he's told.

When leaving, Duncan and Azucena thank the family for their hospitality. Azucena instructs their taxi driver to meet them at the upscale restaurant across the plaza and invites him to join she and Duncan for lunch. It's a pleasant walk through the plaza under an umbrella of greenery. The driver joins them at their patio table.

Duncan orders a meal of steak and rice, Azucena orders *lengua* (tongue). After ordering, Azucena strolls into the kitchen and talks with the chef. When their meals arrive, Duncan watches as the chef and his helper personally walk across the plaza with silver platters, to deliver a similar meal as Duncan and Azucena are now enjoying, to the house they had just visited.

Azucena notices Duncan watching the chef. She smiles. "They will eat now. Maybe for them, this is like the circle you talked about."

Duncan chokes and turns away, shielding his face with his napkin, while salty tears sting his eyes. "This has been a circle for me as well," he admits.

He goes on to explain to Azucena about meeting the elders in Manitoulin and the similarities between the elder's wife making apple pies and the grandmother making the tortillas. Quietly, he thinks about Azucena's compassion to the poor and unfortunate and feels honoured to be in her presence.

Azucena places her hand on Duncan's arm. "You don't have to hide your face from me when you cry, Duncan. There is no embarrassment in showing your emotion. It is not a weakness, but a strength, a quality that I admire in you. I first witnessed it when you played the tape of Christmas carols during the earthquake. You were overcome by the irony of the situation of course, but more importantly, by the emotion we all shared. You are a compassionate man, Duncan."

Duncan wipes his eyes with the back of his hand. "You really care about people, Azucena. You have a gift. I admire that about you."

Azucena responds. "There are many of us in Nicaragua who have the same gift. We want everybody to have food, and to share the same benefits as the rich and powerful."

* * *

In the evening, they arrive at the bistro next to the art gallery. Duncan invites the taxi driver to join them.

"*Si. Gracias, señor.*"

Azucena and Duncan choose a table near the bandstand and order a bottle of *Ron Oro*.

Suddenly, a voice shouts from behind them. "Miles Davis!"

Duncan turns and is confronted face-to-face with Pablo, the trumpet player he met during the earthquake.

"*Pablo, amigo.*" Duncan stands and wraps his arms around his friend. "You survived."

"They can't kill Miles Davis; he lives forever, no?" Pablo responds, sporting a huge smile.

Duncan introduces Pablo to Azucena. "This is my dear friend, Pablo. I met him only an hour after I first met you. He plays the trumpet on the tape you listened to when Tomás was born. I call him Miles Davis after a great jazz musician we both idolize." He pats Pablo on the shoulder as he speaks.

Azucena shakes Pablo's hand. "If you are a friend of Duncan, then we are friends too."

"*Mucha gusto, señorita.*" Pablo embraces Azucena.

"*Venga.* Join us in the band, *amigo*," Pablo invites Duncan.

Duncan turns to Azucena, raising his eyebrows for her approval. She applauds.

He joins the band for a set. For their reunion, the band performs a medley of Miles Davis' classic tunes. During the set break the entire band joins Azucena and Duncan at the table, where she's treated to uninterrupted musician stories and jokes.

When the taxi delivers Duncan to the hotel, he pays the driver adding a generous tip.

"Take this lovely woman home," he tells the driver.

"*Si, señor, Muchas gracias,*" the taxi driver responds.

Azucena embraces Duncan before he leaves.

"You should live here, Duncan, here in Managua. You would have so much fun and such a great life."

"It sounds idyllic."

PART FIVE
1975 – 1979

CHAPTER 12

DINNER WITH PENNY

Toronto, 1975 – 1977:

Dozens of messages await Duncan upon his return home. The first is from Penny. "Call me back when you get this message. I think it's time."

'Time for what?' Duncan wonders.

Before returning Penny's call, he scans through the other messages. "Hey Duncan, it's Freddy. Can you sub for me at George's next week?"

Duncan is eager to work with Freddy's band. He always has a stellar lineup of musicians and great tunes.

He returns the call, leaving a message. "Hi Freddy, it's Duncan. I accept. Get back to me with details."

The following morning, Duncan returns to his normal routine, editing and freelancing for the magazine. His assignment for InterNews was shipped directly from the hotel before leaving Nicaragua, but he must still process and edit his personal work.

Later in the evening, while in the darkroom processing 16 rolls of Tri-X, the phone rings. Unable to answer, he lets the message record.

"Hey man, it's Freddy. Glad you can help us out at George's. I also have some other gigs for you around town. I'll see you next week. Gotta run. Cheers."

Two days pass before Duncan finally calls Penny.

"Hi Penny. What's up?" he begins.

"I think it's about time you and I go out on a date. What do you think?"

Duncan recalls how Penny was always blunt and to the point. It was one of the features that, strangely, attracted him to her.

"Sure, I guess that can work. How about dinner? You choose the spot. Can I suggest next Sunday? It's the only day I have open. I'll pick you up."

"Yeah, that'll work. OK." She spells out her address and they agree on a time.

Penny's choice is a quaint Mediterranean bistro near St. Lawrence Market offering a menu of Arab and Greek dishes. Penny opts for fish, Duncan orders lamb; they agree on a Chardonnay.

Conversation is explorative at first, foraging through topics of work and other non-committal niceties about their interests, theatre and music, until Penny's directness breaks the banality.

"So, Duncan. Are you at all curious about women these days, or have you joined a monastery?"

"Yeah right," Duncan answers with a grin. "I'm embarrassed to say, Penny. I'm curious, but there's nobody in my black book and my schedule is so erratic."

Penny snickers. "I thought you said that your schedule is so 'erotic.' Let me guess, your 'black book' is really a Rolodex of clients and musicians."

"That's it, I'm embarrassed to admit. So, what about your life, Penny? Do you share it with anyone?"

"Well … I'll be straight up with you, Duncan." Penny blankly stares at her finger drawing patterns across the tablecloth.

"There was a man in my life for a short time, a history professor at the university. He was a bit older than me." She pauses. "Actually, he was a *lot* older than me," she admits, laughing. "We met at the faculty club and I dated him for a few months."

"What happened?" Duncan prods, sipping some wine. "Who left who?"

"One day I met his wife through another acquaintance, and he became history." She giggles, tipping her glass. "Ironic, isn't it?"

Penny turns to Duncan. "It's your turn."

"OK. I'll be straight up with you too. I had a weekend fling with a woman in a New Orleans hotel room, a beautiful blonde southern belle with a long slow drawl."

"And big boobs, right?"

"Well, that too. She told me she just wanted me for my body."

Penny sputters, choking on her wine. "Was she desperate?"

"Good one. No. She had just discovered that her husband, a marine, was screwing her younger sister. I was her revenge."

"When was that?"

"Oh … it was a while ago …" He hesitates. "I hate to admit it; 1968, to be precise. Her husband had just shipped out to Vietnam."

"Wow. You do live in a monastery."

Duncan orders desserts and coffees, adding a cognac for himself and a B&B for Penny.

"This has been an enjoyable evening, Duncan. We've had some laughs. I haven't laughed much lately. I haven't done much of anything lately. To be honest …"

"I thought we were already being honest."

"That was for laughs. Now I'm being dead serious, OK?"

She stares at Duncan, waiting for approval. He nods. She continues, "Good. I'm lonely, and I'd like it if we could start seeing each other again. Can you fit me into your busy schedule? Of course, only if you want to."

"You're right Penny. I do have a busy schedule. That's the way I like it. I don't want to jeopardize it with a complicated relationship. Can you understand that? My life has become my passion."

"Let me ask you something Duncan. Do you miss me? Do you miss being with me?"

"Of course, I do, but I have to admit, Penny, I was fucking angry with you about how you handled your pregnancy, and how you didn't include me in your life back then. I went through hell trying to sort it all out. I'm not sure I can ever forgive you for that."

"I've thought a lot about that since we met at the laundromat," Penny attempts to defend her actions, "but I couldn't handle it in any other way."

"What's done is done," Duncan tells her. "Let's just deal with the present."

"OK," Penny agrees. "In that case, right now, in the present, what do you want?"

"What do I want?" Duncan repeats. "Right now?"

"Right now," Penny repeats, emphasizing by tapping her forefinger against the table.

"OK. Here goes." Duncan leans toward Penny and whispers. "Right now I can only listen to what my hard-on is telling me. That's all I want right now."

Penny places her hand over his and strokes it. "Take me home Duncan. Let's do some make up sex."

Duncan smiles with anticipation. "That's a lot of sex to make up."

He wants to tell Penny that it's just sex, a no-relationship one-timer, but he doesn't.

* * *

Over the following weeks and months, Penny and Duncan manage to squeeze occasional dinner dates between Duncan's heavy schedule. There is no mention of Penny's pregnancy and their unknown child, until one day, while they're walking past some children playing in the park, Duncan refers to being a father and regrets being unable to play baseball with the child he never knew, or to teach him to play the piano.

Penny becomes agitated at Duncan for bringing up the past. Her aggressive side kicks in.

"What if you're not really his father? What if I was fucking somebody else that summer besides you? Maybe I was fucking that overfed cook at the White Spot Diner, or maybe I had a quickie with the pissed-up bartender at the Brass Rail while you were in the washroom. What about that possibility?"

Duncan looks straight into her eyes. "Then I would never have known about it, would I?"

Penny suddenly explodes. "I don't care anymore. I should have gone for the abortion. What kind of parents would we have been anyway? You have your career, I have mine. We get to have dinner dates and fuck each other on Sundays. To me, that sounds like an ideal arrangement for both of us. What more could we want?"

"It *is* the ideal arrangement," Duncan agrees. "I should have told you at the beginning, I don't want to get involved in any relationship but that's what's happening, isn't it?"

Penny plunges into a crying jag. Duncan attempts to console her, but she shrugs him away.

She blurts, "Why don't you go back to your 'southern belle?' You can fuck her brains out all weekend, wherever you are in this world. It won't be any of my business. I won't even care."

Duncan adds sarcastically, "Of course you won't care. You'll have your ancient history professor on the sly. Maybe he can sire your next child. Maybe you could make it into the history books. What the hell, make it into the Guinness Book of Records."

Realizing they've both stepped over boundaries, they retreat into silence while Duncan drives to Penny's house. They embrace before Duncan returns home.

Despite Duncan's wishes to keep everything at arm's length, he and Penny continue meeting whenever Duncan's schedule permits, avoiding discussions about a more permanent relationship. It's revealed however, that Duncan's unpredictable scheduling is a problem for Penny. She finally admits that his travel to dangerous hot spots would add undue pressure on his role as her potential partner.

"What if you never come home again? What if I read in the paper that you've been killed in some foreign shithole? What if ..." Her voice breaks before continuing. "What if we were to move in together, or get married? What then? And what if we were to have children? I can't handle that."

"Hold it, Penny." Duncan raises his arms to place some distance between them. "What's all this marriage shit? Jesus Christ. Where does that come from?"

"Isn't that what we always wanted, Duncan? Right from the beginning. We talked about marriage way back then, when we were in school."

"We're not way back then, Penny. Give your head a shake." Duncan silently walks around in circles with his hands enveloping his head trying to decide what to say next.

"So, let me get this right," Duncan continues. "From what you're saying, it's between us having a family or me pursuing my interests in life, right? One or the other?"

Penny stammers in an attempt to clarify her position but Duncan steams ahead.

"When you decided to put our son up for adoption ... that's right, *our* son ... you used my passion for music as the reason you failed to even tell me about him."

"Now just a minute, Duncan. I chose to ..."

Duncan lifts his hand. "I'm not finished Penny, for Christ's sake."

Penny places her hands on her hips. "I'm waiting."

Duncan carves ahead to make his point heard.

"Now you're talking about having a baby ... without even talking to me about it, I might add. And, to add insult to injury, you use my occupation as a photojournalist ... my passion for what I do ... as the reason not to have the baby. Do you even listen to yourself? Have you been thinking of this all along, or is it just something that popped up in your head to aggravate me ... to stick pins into me like a voodoo doll?"

Penny turns and walks away.

***

In November 1976, Duncan reads in the newspaper that Carlos Fonseca, one of the founders of the FSLN has been killed during a battle in the mountains east of Matagalpa. He immediately recalls Azucena's painting of the battle scene hanging in the gallery, and her comment about history being changed. He attempts to rearrange his busy schedule so he can travel to Nicaragua but previously-booked freelance assignments get in the way.

There's a critical election in Quebec that brings René Lévesque and the Parti Québécois to power, the first time a party promising separation has won an election. Duncan is hired to cover the events during the campaign, and especially the follow-up afterward. InterNews hires him for their international readers and Duncan freelances photos to Jack at Human Interest as well.

To complicate matters even further, he's in the middle of purchasing a new townhouse close to St. Lawrence Market, a place he can finally call home. The freelance business has been bountiful lately, and he decides that now is the time to make the investment.

Finally, in July 1977, there's an opening in his calendar. He immediately books a flight, and calls Penny to let her know that he'll be leaving within the week. "I should only be a couple of weeks."

"Here we go again," she starts. "This is what I was talking about. As soon as you get a break from work, you book another trip. We could have arranged a vacation for ourselves, but no, you fly off to your little tropical paradise. I'm beginning to think you have a little 'chiquita' down there. This is why we can't be ..." She stops herself in mid-sentence. "Never mind. I'm sorry for ranting Duncan. It's your job and it's not my place to criticize you. Bon voyage. I'll see you when you return."

CHAPTER 13

REALITIES

Nicaragua, 1977:

There's tension in the air when Duncan arrives in Managua, similar to when he was there covering the hostage taking. From his taxi window he notices the massive amount of hand-painted anti-government graffiti on homes and buildings. He books a room at a pension, *Casa de Fiedler* and arranges to meet Father Manuel at *Los Antojitos*. After some small talk, Duncan asks about Azucena.

"Azucena is away from the capital," the priest says, "I can't reveal any information to you about where she is."

"How is Azucena doing at university? Duncan inquires.

Father Manuel delays his response.

"What's with all the cloak and dagger, Father?"

"I'm sorry. I'm afraid that Azucena's university classes are on hold for the moment. Many young people are joining the revolution. To do that, they must leave their families and their friends. They leave school and their jobs behind, and they go to the mountains or to the jungle.

Some leave the country and go to Costa Rica, north to Mexico, even to the U.S. As you know, everything is in a turmoil here. People disappear. People die."

"At least tell me if you know that Azucena is safe. Is she out of the country? Did she run off to join FSLN? What?"

Father Manuel hesitates, pulls a hefty drag on his cigarette and exhales toward the sky while the wheels of his mind churn.

"So, Duncan. How is life treating you up there in Canada? Up there in the snow?" the priest asks, avoiding Duncan's questions about Azucena. "What do the young people do there, in Canada? Do they play hockey? Do they go out on dates? To parties? To dance together and get drunk? Do they make love with each other? Do they attend university? Do they marry and have children and buy nice cars and homes in the suburbs? Do they settle into well-paying office jobs and live the good life? Do they retire early to spend their winters in the sunny south, in Florida, in Mexico? Of course that's what they do."

Tears flow freely down the priest's face as he speaks emotionally. He stops to wipe his eyes and gather himself together. His voice quivers.

"The good life. That's what you call it, right? What the fuck is the good life anyway, Duncan? I never understood that concept. What is it good for anyway?"

Duncan attempts to console him, but the priest regains his composure, and continues.

"Your good life is only possible through the sweat of our Latino labour, our poverty-stricken, uneducated peasantry, and the riches of our corrupt leaders who rape and pillage their own people so rich *gringos* can live the good life. Where do you think the coffee for your lattes and espressos come from? The rum for your daiquiris? The gold for your jewelry? The bananas for your ... how do you call them ... splits? The tobacco for your cigars, and I might add, for your cancers? While your children are attending university, ours are dying in the streets and eating snakes in the mountains, trying to have a life, not even dreaming about the *good* life, just trying to stay alive."

"I'm terribly sorry Father," Duncan interrupts. "I didn't want to upset you. I understand your ..."

"No!" he stops him, raising his forefinger. "I don't think it's possible for you to fully understand our situation. I do, however, believe that you, Duncan, *mi amigo*, would sincerely *like* to understand how it is."

"Then allow me to learn more Father, please. Allow me to discover how your situation is. Allow me to tell this story, otherwise the world will accept, without question, the press releases from your corrupt government, and from the American propaganda. Believe in me. Have some faith in my integrity as a journalist and lead me in the direction I must go. Please."

Father Manuel chuckles. "So much for journalistic objectivity, *mi amigo*." He waves his hand at the waiter, *"S-s-s-t, señor,* he hisses. *"Ron Oro por favor, y la Plata Tipica."*

Duncan continues. "Regarding the issue of objectivity in journalism, the only truth I can tell is the truth of what I see and what I experience; in other words, what I know. I must be exposed to many truths, but if you hide this truth from me, there's no way I can deliver the story truthfully. Therefore, I wouldn't be objective, would I?"

"How can I trust you, *amigo*? There are many untrustworthy people in my country at this time."

Their meals arrive with a bottle of Golden Rum as ordered.

Duncan offers a peaceful solution. "For now, let's agree that tonight we will just eat and drink. Will it be too difficult to avoid discussing politics?"

"I will always agree to eating and drinking *amigo*." Father Manuel raises his glass to toast. They discuss baseball, family, and the arts.

While eating their dinners, a thin, raggedly dressed young girl, possibly 10 years old, shyly approaches their table. She gestures with her hand toward her mouth, and utters in a weakened voice, *"Comida por favor."*

Duncan gestures for her to sit at their table and beckons the waiter. "Some food and Coca Cola for the girl, *por favor."*

The waiter resists, but Duncan insists. *"Gallo pinto, para la niña, por favor."*

Father Manuel remains quiet, scrutinizing the situation with interest as it unfolds. When the girl's food arrives, Duncan pays for it and gives the waiter a generous tip. The girl consumes the food enthusiastically, as if this is her first meal in days.

Duncan talks to the girl with respect, introducing himself and Father Manuel. *"Como se llama?"* he asks her.

"María," she answers softly, her eyes looking downward.

Duncan summons the waiter again and orders three ice creams for the table. When María finishes eating hers, she rises and hugs Duncan with tears of gratitude in her eyes that smear down her cheeks. She thanks Duncan, *"Muchas gracias, señor."*

She turns to Father Manuel, curtsies slightly, and crosses herself before disappearing between the palm trees and up the boulevard.

There is silence between Father Manuel and Duncan. They drink and ponder, each with their own thoughts. Manuel, emotion-struck, looks toward Duncan.

"She's gone to the Garden of Eden," he says, "to the place we call *Paraíso.*"

Duncan is confused. "Who's gone to the Garden of Eden? The little girl, María?"

"Azucena," Manuel answers. *"Compañera* Azucena."

"What Garden of Eden, and why?"

"For further study of her art," Manuel replies, adding, "and to be with her *compañeros.* They are in the process of organizing the final assault. Of course, you don't know that because I never said a word."

Duncan recalls Azucena mentioning a special place she called Nicaragua's Garden of Eden.

"Where is that place, and why should that have been so secretive?"

"You will have to discover that for yourself."

"So that's the secret you kept from me before? Why tell me now?"

"I have just witnessed that you have the heart of a revolutionary.

You want to understand the plight of the poor. I now know that I can trust you."

"Wonderful. Let's drink to trust." Duncan pours the last drops of their rum.

"Where are you staying, *amigo*?" the priest inquires.

"At *Casa de Fiedler*, just two blocks away from here."

The priest instructs. "Say nothing to anyone about your plans. In the morning, quietly leave the pension and take your belongings with you. There will be a taxi waiting for you down the street. It will have a small blue ribbon attached to the antenna. Don't ask the driver any questions, just go where he takes you."

"*Gracias* Father," Duncan offers, extending his hand.

The handshake gesture is not countered.

"I will leave you now with no fuss," Father Manuel says, downing the remainder of his drink before standing. "We will meet again when we must. *A Dios, amigo*."

CHAPTER 14

PARADISE

Duncan enters the promised taxi with a blue ribbon. It takes him through the capital to another barrio and parks close to a small *casita*. He's informed that the house also serves as a café, where he must order a coffee and a chocolate croissant.

Two uniformed men are seated on chairs along the wall. The woman serving Duncan waits until the men leave before leading him out a rear door where he enters a waiting, and well-worn, Toyota *camioneta*, driven by a young man named Sergio. Concerned about the cloak and dagger secrecy, Duncan pays close attention to their route and mentally records the truck's odometer readings, in case he must find his way back if things turn bad.

Sergio steers the vehicle south through Masaya and continues through the colonial city of Granada, where they purchase supplies of food and water. Leaving Granada, they travel on a series of secondary roads for close to an hour. They arrive at a highway and pass through a village before veering right on another secondary road south that seems to be unending, surrounded by rainforest and lush jungle habitation. The *camioneta* is on an obstacle course, veering from side to side to avoid potholes and wayward tree branches. The constant motion jostles Duncan to sleep … and to dream.

Azucena and her compañeros appear on the road in front of the camioneta. They're dressed in camouflage and sport berets and red and black bandanas around their necks, the colours of the FSLN. Fully loaded bandoleer belts cross their chests. Azucena signals the driver to stop, firing an automatic rifle into the air. She orders him to get out. Her armed compañeros load into the bed of the camioneta and Azucena takes over behind the wheel. As she drives there is no communication between them. Suddenly there's rapid gunfire. The camioneta stops abruptly and everyone except Duncan escapes into the forest. A barrage of gunfire continues from all directions until interrupted by a sudden loud explosion. The camioneta vibrates erratically.

"*Mierda,*" Sergio curses, waking Duncan abruptly. Outside the vehicle, Sergio points downward. "*Reventón,*" he complains, repeating "flat tire" in English for Duncan's sake. Within minutes Duncan and Sergio install a spare and continue their journey.

Finally, they enter a small village at the end of the road. The odometer has increased by more than 300 km. Darkness settles in. The driver locates an *hospidaje* where they book a room for the night.

Early in the morning, Sergio tops up with gas and leaves for the capital. Duncan walks to a rustic wharf, where a fisherman waves him into a boat sporting a blue ribbon. They motor out onto the lake, eventually disembarking at a large island. He's convinced that he has indeed arrived in paradise, a living, breathing Garden of Eden.

"*Hola Duncan. Bienvenido al Paraíso de los Redespiertos.*" Azucena welcomes Duncan with a smile and embrace, as if she's been expecting him all along.

He's relieved that she's dressed in a traditional cotton dress instead of the expected camouflage. "Whoa. What did you just invite me to?" Duncan asks. "My Spanish is too rusty for so many words at once."

"It means the Paradise of the Reawakened. You can just call it

Paraíso, or Paradise. It's similar to the Garden of Eden, but this special place is for those who want to change and be changed, and to alter the way things already are. Here, in *Paraíso*, you will experience fresh thoughts and new ways of doing things, like art for example, but also in politics, religion, and philosophy."

She introduces Duncan to the community of Indigenous locals, visiting artists, poets, activists, and theologians who have gathered in search of artistic renewal, harmony, and fresh truths, some faith-based, others secular.

Duncan learns that, because of their focus on the oppressed poor, their ideologies are challenged by the current government as communistic in structure, and therefore suspected of collaborating with the revolutionaries.

After some discussion with the others, Azucena instructs Duncan. "You are free to take photos as you wish, but there are some concerns about who will see the images. Some of these people are already known to the police and to the military. Others are not yet known, but their safety is paramount. Otherwise, their lives will be in danger, and they are all important to our cause. We cannot jeopardize their well-being, or the community's, especially at this crucial time. For this reason, we request that you don't publish the photographs for a while."

"For how long?" Duncan asks.

"You will know when the time comes. Soon, we expect."

Duncan is allowed to photograph freely and manages to construct a comprehensive photo essay plan in his mind, and subsequently, on film. Of course, it must show the art, the music, and the camaraderie, but the faith and the politics are also essential to the story. Symbolic photographs may be necessary to represent the latter without revealing any critical information.

Much of the activity is informal, often among friends during the evenings. Duncan works with a small kit, limited to three lenses, allowing him to utilize a quiet unobtrusive approach to his photography. He pre-composes the images in his mind before raising the camera to his eye, pushing the shutter button when gestures express a peak moment or activity.

As permission was granted when he arrived and his presence in the community was announced, Duncan is able to work without fanfare. Many of his subjects are no longer concerned that he's even among them. The onus is on Duncan, of course, to honour the conditions placed upon him about publishing the images, until such time as it becomes obvious.

'I have no idea how it will become obvious,' Duncan wonders. 'I'll just keep working and take their word for it.'

When Azucena isn't painting, she interacts with other members of the community. Through his association with her, Duncan is able to include others in his images. The discussions are emblazoned with passion, whether it's politics, religion, or their respective arts.

'Is this a Latino thing?' he wonders. 'Is there a passion gene that prevails? No matter what the subject, there is excitement and intense commitment.'

Duncan realizes that this is becoming the focus of his photo essay. It's expressed in the faces and the hands, in the hugging and the closeness, and in the life that shows through whether dancing to the music or performing a work of poetry.

"I've never heard so much poetry in my life," Duncan tells Azucena. "It's contagious. I might even try writing some myself."

"You should do that, Duncan," Azucena encourages. "It will help open your soul."

"Does my soul need opening?" Duncan asks.

"Hmm," Azucena nods, without words. Instead, she grins and wraps her arms around him.

Duncan expected his visit to the community to be short, but it continues over several weeks. It's a slower moving environment and Azucena's presence makes it even more difficult to leave. He manages to watch and photograph her while she paints and, through this focus, he gains more insight into her commitments and attitudes toward her faith and the revolutionary politics.

Some of her brush work is quiet and meticulous, pondering every small detail, but suddenly, she attacks the painting with an unbridled passion as if overcome by some inner spirit. Colours scream off the canvas leaving trails of texture in their strokes, sometimes extending beyond the perimeters of the canvas, very unlike the realist style of her earlier work.

At times her eyes focus, Zen-like, at a point located well beyond the surface of the canvas. At other times her eyelids close for minutes while her brushes and knives continue with an apparent life of their own. She moans and mumbles obscure phrases. Finally, as suddenly as it starts, she returns to a calmness and quietly backs away from the completed painting.

In the beginning Duncan avoids questioning Azucena about the meaning of her latest work. Having watched and photographed her, he understands that whatever is going on during her creative process, it is immensely personal. The final results appear abstract, not revealing any subjective purpose, but demanding long concentrated viewing and searching.

There are many opportunities in *Paraíso* for them to relax and pursue the philosophical conversations that Duncan enjoyed so much during his previous visit. It's the discussions that attract him to Azucena, a magnetic blend of extreme intelligence, commitment to a cause, compassion with the less fortunate, and her adventurous artistry. Of course, he can't ignore her natural beauty.

"Your approach to painting has changed drastically," Duncan comments. "How is that possible?"

Azucena explains her process to Duncan, waving her arms about as she talks. Her voice is calm at the beginning but builds momentum as her excitement increases.

"There's something about this place, Duncan, this *Paraíso*, that encourages me to explore life freely without restrictions and rules. It's like being born again, but not in the usual religious context, although there is definitely a neo-Catholic presence here. It's a freedom that offers us the opportunity to re-interpret the gospels in more personal and interactive ways. It's so unlike the traditional masses at church as we've always experienced them, where the priest tells the congregation what to believe and how to think."

Duncan asks, his face displaying an inquisitiveness. "How does this freedom, this rebirth, affect your art?"

She continues. "It's not only the religious component that is being reborn. For me, it's also my very soul: my outlook to painting, my political attitudes, my love of life, and my openness to loving others. These things are all connected, Duncan."

Her arms form an arc, creating a large circle coming together. "We're a community of people committed to experiencing life in a more holistic manner. Don't confuse *Paraíso* as some kind of cult, Duncan. We are free, indeed encouraged, to believe in our own way, think our own thoughts, and come and go as we please. There are atheists and other non-Christian faiths; vegans and meat-eaters. We all eat at the same table, so to speak."

"When I arrived here, you seemed as if you already expected to see me," Duncan guesses. "How could that be?"

"When I saw you arrive on the island I was overtaken by a beautiful warmth. I haven't stopped thinking about you since we spent that wonderful day together. When I dropped you off at the hotel, I was prepared for the possibility that you would never return to Nicaragua. It wasn't until several days ago, when your image reappeared to me, that I knew you were coming back. Do you find that weird, Duncan?"

"In my usual analytical mind, I do, but I will try to understand. I didn't even know I was coming here myself until the day before I arrived."

"Welcome to *Paraíso*, Duncan. By the time you leave here, you will lose your analytical mind, nothing will seem weird, ever again."

Azucena grabs Duncan's hand. "Come with me now. Join me in meditation. There is no need to express yourself in religious terms.

This has nothing to do with the teachings here, but of the environment in which we work, this island, this paradise. Just join me in meditation. You'll travel to another zone, from where you'll experience fresh thoughts and new, innovative ways to express them. You will realize your deepest wants."

Duncan sits beside Azucena in a lotus position, curious to see if her special talents are capable of reading his mind.

They sit quietly together in a clearing among the trees. Duncan notices an entire community of ants, perhaps thousands, marching in a tight single file down the trunk of a nearby tree, passing over from one leaf to the next on an endless quest. He watches their journey with focused interest. 'Where are they going and why? A search for food? A fertility rite? Heading to battle? Relocating their home? Escaping from an unseen enemy? An ancient genetically imprinted ritual perhaps?'

"Hold my hand, Duncan." Azucena speaks in a calm voice. "Allow us to become one spirit. Allow our thoughts to travel between us. Close your eyes and look inward. Feel the movement of your thoughts as they blend with mine."

Duncan feels her soft hand in his. Her fingers move delicately in his palms. His attempts to cleanse his mind of extraneous thoughts are challenged by Azucena's beauty and sensuality.

"Breathe slowly, Duncan," Azucena whispers. "I sense your breathing is uneven. Calm down. Be quiet. Focus on the breath as the old traditional thoughts are distilled and exhaled. Inhale the freshness of *Paraíso* to replace them. Allow your mind to become quiet. Remain silent. Relax all your muscles and concentrate on the breathing, quietly and steadily in harmony with the environment. Only when your mind is clear can you allow new thoughts to enter."

Their collaborating senses absorb the natural voices of animals and the soft swaying leaves of the rain forest as they blend with the steady uncomplicated rhythms of their breathing and the pulsing of their hearts.

Azucena continues in her soft meditative voice. "There is a belief from ancient folklore that whatever age a person is when they discover the beauty and love of this paradise, their life will start again with the fresh naïveté of a newly born child. They will see the world with new eyes, their senses will relearn the joys of exploration, their art will change forever, the rules abandoned, and they will discover new love as fresh as their first kiss.

They spend many hours together in meditation. Duncan loses track of the boundaries of time. Being with Azucena is what he looks forward to each morning, recognizing of course that they each need their private time to create.

"Why does everything here feel so free and easy going?" Duncan asks Azucena, taking his first sip from his morning coffee.

"You feel free because you're allowed to be free," Azucena tells him. "Here, there is nothing expected from you: no deadlines, no bosses, no contracts. You are whatever you want to be. You're only limited by your own expectations of yourself."

"I understand that," Duncan acknowledges with a nod. "I usually have high expectations when I'm working on assignments, and I still have the same expectations here. The difference for me is that I don't know what the hell to expect."

"That's the best part, Duncan ... expect the unknown. If you don't know where it's all going, you can choose one of many ways ... or choose them all if you wish."

Duncan adds, "Or choose none of the above, right?"

"Exactamente."

Azucena places her hands on Duncan's shoulders. "Look at me Duncan. Look into my eyes and listen. If you freeze up with anxiety and fear of the unknown, you won't go anywhere. You stop creating and thinking. In other words you stop dreaming. If you allow the freedom to fill you with dreams and hope, it will take you wherever it takes you ... into the unknown. You can go anywhere from there."

Duncan is mesmerized by the intensity of Azucena's brown eyes staring directly through his own.

Fragments of pictures never previously imagined dance openly within the space behind Duncan's retinas, a space void of commitments or structures. With each blink of his eyes, a new image appears. His own voice tells him, 'I am the camera.' Azucena's voice accompanies the images like a musical backdrop.

"Duncan. Did you hear what I said?"

"Huh? What?" Duncan blinks rapidly; his eyes scan the environment before returning to Azucena's stare. "Oh, yeah. I heard you. Follow the unknown, right?"

Azucena continues. "Right now, we are in the unknown. This *is* a dream, Duncan. An empty place to explore our potential without restrictions or rules. This is freedom. It is a freedom we must take with us when we leave *Paraíso*."

With each new morning, Duncan experiences a renewal in the way he approaches his photography; it's a looser, less rigid acceptance of his compositions and of the subjects he chooses. Of course, the people are still his main interest, but he's seeing them differently. They jog in and out of his frames, less as individuals and more as components in the overall natural environment.

He reserves his black and white film for more serious documentary images, switching to his second camera loaded with Kodachrome, his favourite colour film, to fully explore the diverse saturations of greenery, and to photograph the artists and their work.

During mealtimes, conversations about the pending revolution are common. Azucena is an active participant, especially concerning the roles of her fellow *compañeras*, the women who are as active in the movement as their male counterparts. There are worries about the nearby military buildup and whether the island community is in danger of being attacked.

"We are poets and painters," one man states. "What threat are we to the government?"

A woman counters, raising her fist above her. "Then we are more dangerous than if we had the atom bomb."

The conversation is met with laughter but tempered with an unspoken air of acceptance.

Azucena and Duncan's meditation sessions are gradually becoming more intimate. There is increasing contact between them and the nature of their discussions become personalized, focusing more on sensual concerns than mindfulness.

Duncan is torn between his increasing fondness for Azucena and the reality that he must return to Canada when his sojourn in *Paraíso* is finished, back to the rigidity of a working life, and of course, Penny.

Since his arrival, Duncan has gradually accepted Azucena into his heart. Her beauty and her passions for life and art are so different from Penny's outlooks. Azucena's sensuality is natural and compatible with Duncan's approach to life. Penny's is forced and competitive, always attempting to fit their relationship into a set of rules: marriage, children, commitment, and job security.

One late afternoon, Azucena invites Duncan to join her at her favourite meditation clearing deep in the forest. She leads him by the hand along a narrow pathway. A soft breeze creates a melody as it filters through the trees, broken only by the percussive calls of toucans.

They stop at the clearing and assume their lotus positions as usual, committing to breathing and finding their quiet zones. Azucena takes Duncan's hand and rests it on her lap. In her calm, quiet whispering voice she says, "When you are comfortable, I want you to share this time and space with me. I want to remember us together, accepting all the beauty that nature has to offer. Let us join our bodies and spirits together … as one."

Duncan and Azucena pass through a threshold, a point beyond which they can never ignore. Azucena's place in Duncan's heart is secured forever. Even if they never see each other again, the importance of their intercourse here, in this beautiful paradise, is infinite.

'How will I deal with Penny?' Duncan agonizes. 'Should I tell her? Why? We're not a couple, we're not committed to anything? Are we?'

His thoughts reverse from his concerns about Penny to his feelings for Azucena.

'I should move here. What the hell. We could live here, in *Paraíso*.

We'd make a wonderful couple, Azucena and me. I could help raise Tomás; maybe I could even adopt him as my son.'

Duncan briefly considers the impossible. 'Fuck it. I could live in two different worlds. I'll date Penny as usual when I'm in Canada and be with Azucena when I'm here. Yeah, as if that would last. My conscience and guilt would destroy both worlds.'

Finally, Duncan accepts the occasion to celebrate the unknown. '*Que sera, sera*! Whatever happens, happens. If I've learned anything here, I'll follow my dreams to the unknown.'

On their return to the community, Azucena confides that they will be leaving *Paraíso* in the darkness of night. As they prepare to leave, she gives Duncan a painting, wrapped securely for protection.

"It is a gift from me to you, Duncan. Don't unwrap it until you arrive home in Canada. Hang it in a special place where you can always see it, and where you can contemplate what you feel and remember."

"I will never forget what has happened here, Azucena," Duncan promises, "to me … and to us," He embraces Azucena, stroking her back with curious hands. They settle on her lower back and draw her pelvis tight to his. "I wish this could last forever," Duncan whispers.

Their departure has been totally arranged for them. Azucena, Duncan, and other members of the community, travel by boats down the river into Costa Rica where they disembark.

On the shore, Duncan bids farewell to Azucena. They embrace once more with passionate kisses. *"Hasta la próxima,"* she whispers, touching Duncan's lips with the tips of her fingers.

"Until the next time," Duncan repeats.

Duncan is led to a vehicle that transports him, with his film, camera gear, and the wrapped painting, to the San José airport for his safe return to Toronto.

CHAPTER 15

TRIUMPH

Toronto, 1977 – 1979:

Duncan unwraps Azucena's painting and hangs it on a north-facing wall. The diffused natural window light illuminates the entire painting evenly without direct sunlight that would fade the brilliance of Azucena's colours. He pours a Merlot and stares into the painting, hoping to relive the same magic of Azucena's passion as he experienced when she painted in *Paraíso*, and of course, when they communed with nature so connected. He hadn't seen this painting while he was there, but it displays the wonderful vitality that she exhibited in her new approach to painting.

At first glance, his vision is limited to the abstraction, red and orange flashes of heavy knife strokes across a variety of soft greens and yellows. The longer he gazes, his focus relaxes and the closer her intent appears to him.

"It's *Paraíso*, no doubt about it, but it's on fire," Duncan states aloud. Further exploration reveals two small shapes hidden amongst the foreground greenery: one, a golden cinnamon hue, the other, a paler magenta-toned figure. The shapes are bound to each other as lovers.

His memory recalls his conversations with the elders in Manitoulin, how the fires they set allowed their island paradise to regrow and to provide future generations of their people to experience new life.

Duncan listens to Miles Davis' 'Kind of Blue' album and settles into a second glass of wine. He closes his eyes to soak up the muted sounds of 'Blue in Green' that transport him into his quiet space and returns him to the paradise he had left only days before. It seems appropriate for Duncan to be consumed by the music that created a new awakening for Miles, and for jazz, at the same time as he's sharing Azucena's renewal as an artist, and most certainly, his own.

A week later, his exposed Kodachrome films are processed. He opens the boxes and sets the transparencies onto the light table. There is nothing more satisfying to a photographer than peering into a light table covered with 2 x 2-inch slide mounts and hundreds of backlit multi-coloured rectangles staring back. At first glance they present a mosaic of random tiles in unrelated abstraction until, with a magnifying loupe, Duncan's eyes begin to search into the subtle details of each one.

Initially, he reacts with disappointment, 'These aren't mine. Shit, Kodak fucked things up,' he reacts, angrily smacking his loupe on the desk. 'They gave me somebody else's slides.'

On further examination he discovers that they are, in fact, his images from *Paraíso*. Colours and contrasts he doesn't remember seeing before; sweeping compositions that spread randomly over the edges of the frames with dashes of sharp and unsharp fragments. He's drawn into each image with increasing excitement. People sweep across the frames in flurried motion and their eyes peer from corners, body language caught in mid-gesture, laughing, crying, loving, praying.

Upon opening the final two boxes of slides and laying them on the light table, he sees Azucena painting. Her passion for rediscovery is expressed through slashes of blazing movement, continuous surges of energy sweeping across the surface while her long black hair soars about her. Rather than attempting to fix the action in frozen segments of realism, as he would have done previously, Duncan has allowed his images to share her enthusiasm, moving both himself and the camera, with and against her actions.

"They're alive!" he shouts aloud to himself, twisting in circles about his workroom. "Yes! Yes! Yes! They're living, breathing slices of reality, without being bound by the phoniness and restrictions of perfection."

* * *

In November, Duncan receives a letter from Father Manuel relaying disturbing news that *Paraíso* was destroyed by the military during an attack on the locals. People were killed. They turned the church into a prison and burned everything else: the buildings, the paintings and the treasured library, all gone. The surviving inhabitants, including Azucena, are now listed as wanted by the military for crimes against the state. It is assumed that they escaped down the river to Costa Rica and are preparing an assault on Nicaragua from there.

It suddenly strikes Duncan that he was part of the escape when they departed from the island. He's extremely concerned for Azucena's well-being and considers writing back to Father Manuel, but he worries that, should his letter be intercepted by the authorities, it could endanger Azucena and the others.

Within a few days, another letter arrives in his mail from Costa Rica, a simple message enclosed, 'Looking forward with love to our next encounter,' followed by a white lily monogram.

Azucena is constantly at the forefront of Duncan's thoughts. He can't erase the precious moments they shared in *Paraíso*, not that he wants to. In spite of his feelings, life back in Toronto returns to a semblance of normality. Duncan continues to see Penny, always with the veil of secrecy haunting his conscience. He carefully chooses his words during conversation, and the guilt continues to build.

While alone, Duncan rationalizes his actions. 'What the hell. It was just a one off. What are the odds of it being repeated? I may never see Azucena again.'

But when confronted by the painting, accompanied by a glass of Merlot, he yearns for Azucena's touch and her beautiful words.

Occasionally, during Duncan's time with Penny, the subject of their son arises, usually causing anxiety for them both, and creating further dents in their relationship, such as it exists.

In the spring of 1979, Duncan is offered a full-time faculty position teaching photojournalism at the college. He accepts the offer and is scheduled to begin his teaching duties in September.

Two weeks after receiving the confirmation of his new appointment, he receives an envelope anonymously slid under his front door. It contains an airline ticket direct from Toronto to San José, Costa Rica, a message reading, 'Take this flight,' and a small 4x6 inch photo of a painting. The signature on the painting represents a white lily. Without questioning, Duncan quickly packs his bag, calls Penny, and leaves immediately. Penny is not amused.

* * *

Costa Rica & Nicaragua, 1979:

Upon disembarking at the San José airport Duncan is approached by a young woman who, without conversation, presents him with an identical photo as the one slid under his door. He shows her his own print and is escorted to a waiting vehicle that transports them to a modest suburban home on the edge of the city.

Once inside, he's introduced to several of the *compañeros*, some only sharing their assumed name, their *'nom de guerre.'* Father Manuel is among them but Azucena is nowhere to be seen. Throughout the entire flight, Duncan has anticipated this moment, when he can hold Azucena in his arms once again. Absence has truly made his heart grow fonder.

The apparent leader of the group, a *comandante*, welcomes Duncan. "We are aware of your talent, *señor*. Based on recommendations from *compañeros* Manuel and Azucena, I believe we can trust you. Can we count on that? It is extremely critical that we can."

Realizing that his commitment to objectivity is being challenged, Duncan responds. "I always photograph what I see and what I deem as important to the truth. I view my position here just as I would if I were to be embedded within the Canadian troops. You will no doubt, be watching me carefully as I work. I can accept that. Considering that I still know nothing about what I'm here for, I can make no other promises but to guarantee that my photo coverage will be honest and truthful, based upon what happens before my eyes and my cameras."

"Fair enough, *señor*," the *comandante* agrees, a tentative smile on his lips. He places his hand on Duncan's shoulder, grins, adding, "However, sometimes, our truths may be different from yours, *señor*."

"That is always the way it is, *comandante*," Duncan responds with a similar grin.

The *comandante* continues. "You are invited to accompany us into Nicaragua on a historical journey. It will begin very soon. Our first intent is to retake the city of Rivas and then proceed to Granada. I have no idea how long it will take. There will be discomfort, confrontation, and most certainly injuries and death, depending on who we encounter. You will be recording history as it unfolds, *señor*. We view this as the final act of the revolution. Most of the country is already under our control. There is no turning back. *Entiende, señor?*"

"*Si comandante.* I understand," Duncan replies, mentally considering the consequences of his commitment. "When do we leave?"

"You will know when it's time."

During the night, Duncan's mind throws curves at him.

'Why am I here at all? Is it because of my feelings for Azucena? Is that the only reason? Or, have I become committed to the cause? What cause? Is it a cause for justice? Where does my journalistic objectivity fit into this? What kind of a fucking romantic have I become?"

In the morning, Duncan seems to have resolved any confusion. He showers and steps into the kitchen for breakfast. Azucena runs and attaches herself to Duncan. Their lips meet but with discretion, considering the other *compañeros* at the kitchen table.

"I'm so sorry I wasn't here for your arrival, Duncan," Azucena apologizes, caressing her hand along Duncan's arm. It's a simple gesture that sends a tingle through Duncan's bones. He reads far more into the touch than is evident to others.

Azucena adds, "I was on a mission that took me away from here for a few days. I only returned early this morning. I'm so happy you came."

Realizing that the call to action could occur at a moment's notice, Duncan prepares for the journey ahead by checking and cleaning his camera gear and organizing his film pouches.

It's difficult for Azucena and Duncan to spend any time alone. There are so many concerns he wants to discuss with her, mainly about their mutual artistic reawakening, but also the realization of their feelings.

Late one evening, they find themselves alone in the back yard under the stars. They grasp each other like hungry animals, groping, their kisses deep, their hearts pounding with desire.

They quickly succumb to each other, folding together in the afterglow as lovers.

Azucena whispers into Duncan's ear. "I needed you so much Duncan, but more than that, I want you always."

"I love you Azucena. I will always love you."

They sit on a garden bench, touching and nuzzling their perspiration-soaked bodies together. Duncan tells her how he can't think straight when he's away from her.

Azucena, considering the impending military raid, and equipped with the knowledge that Duncan loves her the same as she loves him, feels compelled to reveal her life story.

"There are things that you should know about my life," Duncan. "Things I have previously kept private. I want you to know everything about me before we depart on this dangerous mission. Please don't stop loving me after what I tell you."

Duncan embraces her as confirmation.

Azucena begins by explaining where her mother originated from.

"My mother, Lydia, was from the Atlantic coastal town of Blue-fields. She was a beautiful woman of mixed race, blended from a black Caribbean mother and a Latino father, both mixed with Indigenous ancestry. Her skin had a golden caramel appearance, especially when the sun reflected from her. I am fortunate to have acquired her skin tone."

"Your skin is beautiful," Duncan compliments, stroking her cheek with the back of his hand. Azucena blushes. He adds, "It's even more gorgeous when you blush."

"When my mother was 16, she attended her first *Palo de Mayo* Festival, on her own. She wore a bright yellow dress made for her by her Aunt Flora, especially for the occasion. That dress, and her natural beauty of course, is the reason I exist. She attracted the attention of a man from the capital who took advantage of her innocence. Her parents, my grandparents whom I have never met, banished her from the house when they realized she was pregnant, so she relocated to the capital."

Duncan cringes at the severity of the punishment. It occurs to Azucena that he may be shocked by what she's telling him.

"You may find that to be an extreme punishment, Duncan, but that's how things used to be; they still are in some communities."

Azucena presses on, her face holding a proud and powerful emotion as she speaks of her beloved mother. "My mother found accommodations under a tarpaulin at *Mercado Central* in Managua, which is where I was born. Fortunately, the woman who found us, a nun named Sister Nadia, helped us find a small room. My mother worked at the market as an ambulatory vendor, selling cigarettes one-by-one. Somehow we survived those early years together."

Duncan is personally moved as Azucena speaks passionately from the heart.

"At nights, my mother and I held hands together and she told me about her dreams, images that I received as visions to be interpreted. I used to believe that the dreams were transferred to my imagination through our hands." Azucena smiles softly. "Mamá gave me some watercolour paints so I could paint my interpretations of those dreams. In time, I became quite good at painting. People at the market even wanted to buy some of them. Eventually, after some years, Father Manuel arrived at the market and saw the paintings. He thought I had some talent. He offered my mother a job at his family's estate, as a domestic, but she turned him down. Instead, she proposed that I should go to the estate alone so I could receive a proper education as he promised. He also encouraged my interest in art and education. I was a good student and received excellent grades. I went to high school and continued to do well."

"How did it work out for you, living at the estate?" Duncan asks. "Weren't you lonely?"

"Not usually. There were other domestics my age, and I kept busy with my studies and painting. I also had chores to do and I helped Mamá at the market on weekends."

"That must have kept you busy, coming and going," Duncan assumes. "Was somebody driving you."

"Always. Either Father Manuel or one of Don Ricardo's helpers."

"Where did you get your ideas for paintings, especially being separated from your mother all week?"

"This is the weird thing, Duncan. "Even when I was alone at the estate, and Mamá was working at the market, I continued receiving her dreams, which I interpreted and made paintings from. That's when I realized there was more to it than holding hands. Our minds and imaginations were somehow synchronized. What I received were more like visions than merely dreams. Sometimes, they arrived as finished images, at other times only fragments, left to be organized and assembled in my imagination like puzzles."

Duncan wants to comment but is interrupted.

"Wait, Duncan, please. There's more I must tell you before it's too late. It turned out that I received a broader education at the estate than intended. As a teenager, I was invited to work in the main house as a domestic, providing I maintained my grades at school. I was given my own room in the main house, and on special occasions, I helped to serve meals to the dinner guests and to Don Ricardo's family, even to the president on occasion."

"The President himself. Wow!" Duncan reacts.

"It is important to tell you that Father Manuel and his brother are twins, identical in every respect. I didn't know that when I first moved into the main house. One evening a man came to my door and watched me from the hallway. I thought it was Father Manuel, but he was wearing the uniform of a National Guard officer. At first, I thought it was a joke and I laughed. But it was Col. Jorge, Father Manuel's twin brother, whom I had never met before. I felt uncomfortable at first, but he was very kind to me."

"In what way?" Duncan asks.

"Well, whenever he visited the house, which wasn't often, he brought presents. One day, he brought me a chic black dress with spaghetti straps. I looked very smart wearing it. He asked me to model it for him and commented how beautiful I looked. He even helped me fasten the zipper. It fit me snugly and I felt like a beautiful woman. Sometimes, in the evenings when I was all alone in my room, I would wear the dress, just to see myself in the mirror. I posed like a model, tousled my hair, exaggerated my bosom, just like I saw in the magazines."

"Weren't you suspicious about the gifts?" Duncan asks.

"Not at first. You must understand that I was a naïve teenager and it was the first time any man showed interest in me. I was flattered. One night, while I was posing, Col. Jorge arrived at my door. He watched as I posed and said sweet things to me. Before I knew what was happening, we were together in my bed. In the weeks that followed, he visited my room and asked me to put on the dress, while he watched. He used to call it our secret dress. He liked me posing like a model. Then he would start to undress me. I admit that I was flattered by his attention at first, and I welcomed him into my bed. When he wasn't there, I fantasized that he was. I imagined that I could be Col. Jorge's wife and bear him many children."

Anger distorts Duncan's face.

"How old were you at the time, Azucena?"

"Sixteen."

"You do realize that he was taking advantage of you, don't you? It doesn't matter that you were enjoying the attention and the sex. You were only 16, a child. He used his power over you. He was a Colonel in the army for fuck sake."

"I know that now," Azucena says, calming Duncan with her touch. "But when it happened, I didn't think of it that way. After I became pregnant, Col. Jorge never returned to see me. He was always out doing military manoeuvres, up in the mountains fighting the *guerrilleros*. It was Father Manuel who came to my assistance when I needed help. He didn't even ask me who the father was. He made sure my education didn't suffer and he eventually moved me to the capital, where my mother and I lived together with the nuns, until my due date was near.

"Several weeks before Christmas, I received a vision from Mamá. It included the plaza and the cathedral. I wanted to have my baby blessed by the Bishop in the cathedral. I had met him at some of the dinners I served for Don Ricardo and he promised to bless my child. When I painted the vision, something compelled me to paint the clock at 12:35. I took that as a sign from God that my baby would arrive at that time."

Duncan reveals, "Father Manuel told me about that painting and how strange it was that you foresaw the time of the earthquake."

"On the evening before Christmas, Mamá and I went to the cathedral where I hoped to have God bless the birth of my child. Instead, God took my mother. You know all about that. You were there, Duncan."

Duncan feels his chest tighten; he remembers the day well.

"Soon after Mamá died, while I was still with the rescuers, I received more of her visions, and I continue receiving them. Her visions are the inspirations for my paintings to this day."

Duncan embraces Azucena and pulls her close. She senses his excitement return and caresses him as acceptance of their shared desire. Their explorations toward pleasure are slow, unhurried, and gentle, as lovers.

While laying together, with nothing ahead of them but the unknown, Azucena asks for Duncan's promise.

"Please don't tell anyone that Col. Jorge is the father of Tomás. Tomás doesn't know. Father Manuel has never asked, and I have never told him, although he probably has his suspicions. I just want you to know before we set out on this campaign, just in case something happens. I want you to look after Tomás. Make sure he is safe from harm. Right now, he is in safe hands with the nuns in Managua."

Duncan consoles her. "Nothing will happen to either of us. We have so much to live for."

"I have one other request, Duncan. If I should die, I don't want a funeral. It is too final. I only wish to be surrounded by my friends, family, and *compañeros*. Understood?"

"*Claro*, my dear. And I wish the same for myself."

Before dawn, they are called to join the *guerrilleros* at the border. Much of Nicaragua is now controlled by the FSLN, especially in the north and around the urban centres of Estelí, Matagalpa and Leon. International support arrives from Panama and Costa Rica. Duncan is embedded with the southern flank of 300 armed *guerrilleros* entering from Costa Rica on their push north toward the capital.

News that the president has abandoned the country and flown to Miami is received with enthusiasm by the *guerrilleros*; a renewed energy pushes them forward. Everyone except Duncan and Father Manuel carries a weapon, including Azucena. Father Manuel's weapon is his cross and Bible, and Duncan's weapons of choice are his cameras.

Despite the encouragement of ultimate success, they still meet resistance and there are violent skirmishes and deaths, especially in Rivas, but the *guerrilleros* outnumber the National Guards. With the news of the president's abandonment, many Guards give up the struggle, either running into hiding or joining forces with the FSLN. Citizens along the way, some only armed with machetes, join the march, strengthening the *guerrilleros'* numbers.

In the historical colonial city of Granada, located on the north shore of Lake Nicaragua, the *guerrilleros* meet stronger opposition. To the government forces it represents the last stronghold before the capital. The fighting moves from street to street, and from rooftop to rooftop. Duncan follows the action unfold as he recalls the cowboy shootouts from the movie theatres of his childhood. This time, the blood is real, and when someone falls in battle, they often don't rise again.

As a group of *guerrilleros* move stealthily toward the entrance of a hotel, Duncan trains his camera on the perceived destination. Unknown to the *guerrilleros* are several army snipers positioned on the roof above the main entrance. Duncan, seeing the snipers through his camera, steps out from his own cover and shouts, *"Cuidado,"* to his *compañeros* in an attempt to warn them of the danger. The snipers open fire. The *guerrilleros* take immediate cover and return the gunfire. None of them are injured, but Duncan is hit in the left shoulder by a bullet ricocheting from a building.

He falls to the ground, blood spurts from his shoulder. He's quickly dragged toward cover and cared for by one of the *compañeros*. His arm is haphazardly bound with a rag, and his movement limited by an improvised sling fashioned from a red and black FSLN bandana.

Feeling like the proverbial 'one-armed paper hanger,' Duncan resorts to shooting photos with only his right hand until his mind becomes woozy from the pain. He's guided away from the fighting and laid down on a grassy patch in the central plaza.

He calls out for Azucena and prays that she is safe.

Azucena is several buildings away when Duncan receives the injury and is unaware of his condition until later in the day when the *guerrilleros* finally secure the main section of the city. In his haziness, Duncan calls out her name with a weakening voice. "Azucena, my darling. Azucena ... come to me."

Azucena retraces her steps through the city, searching everywhere for Duncan, fearing the worst. When she discovers him laid out on the ground with a bloodied bandana covering his arm, she panics.

"Duncan," she shouts, tears covering her face. She embraces him and covers him with kisses. "Please speak to me."

Duncan's good right arm caresses her back. "I'll be fine, my dearest Azucena," he groans in a weak gravelly voice. "It's just a fender-bender." Fortunately, the bullet merely grazed his shoulder, causing a mild but painful laceration.

On July 19, the *compañeros* enter the capital victorious, meeting the other factions at *Plaza de la República*. There is exuberance, music, dancing, and celebration at their success. The revolution is triumphant.

Duncan remains in the capital for several more weeks, recording the aftermath, the excitement, and the speeches. On the night before he leaves, he treats Azucena to a special dinner. They raise their glasses to toast Nicaragua's liberation. The dinner is quiet with minimal conversation between them.

Azucena breaks the silence. "I don't want you to leave, Duncan. I will miss you." She places his hand between hers and strokes his fingers. "Can we go somewhere to be alone for the night? Ever since the night the campaign began, when we left San José, I've waited patiently for an opportunity to share myself with you. If we never see each other again, I want to remember you as my lover. I want to perform magic with you. Let us celebrate *el triunfo* with love."

Azucena joins Duncan in his hotel room where the night passes, alternating between intelligent philosophical conversation and playful ecstasy.

While Azucena sleeps, cuddled tightly against him, Duncan stares upward, watching stray lights from passing vehicles scan across the ceiling. His mind and conscience twist the realities of life against his dreams and fantasies.

'How can my life be so beautiful, so full of wonderment and love but, at the same time, I'm confused with anxiety and guilt about what awaits me at home. Why can't this be my home? Why can't I live here with the woman I've fallen deeply in love with, the woman who challenges my mind and soothes my desires?'

In the morning Azucena, now awake, still clings to Duncan. Her face glows as if surrounded by a halo. She kisses Duncan, stroking her hand softly across his chest.

"I love you, Duncan," she whispers into his ear.

Duncan feels the warmth of her breath as she speaks. He rolls toward her face. Their eyes gaze into each other's for minutes; no words are spoken. Duncan weaves his fingers through her black wispy hair.

"I love you too, my dear, beautiful Azucena."

Following breakfast, Duncan's entire being weighs heavily as he sadly declares to Azucena that he doesn't know when, or even if, he'll be able to return. "So much depends on what awaits me back in Canada." He hesitates, adding, "I am starting a new teaching job at the college in September. It's difficult to predict what free time I'll have to visit again."

Azucena embraces him, pulls him tight against her, and kisses him warmly on the lips. With tears in her eyes, she stares directly into his. Her voice cracks, "We never say goodbye in Spanish. *Hasta luego*, or *hasta la próxima*, never goodbye. I already know that you will return to me. Trust me, I know. I just don't know when. I will live in haunting agony until you return, my dear. Never forget me, my dearest *compañero* Duncan."

PART SIX
1979 – 1986

CHAPTER 16

CANADA

Toronto, 1979 – 1986:

"Holy shit! What happened to you?" Penny greets Duncan after he returns to Toronto. She points at the bandage on his arm. "That can't be good."

"It's nothing, I'm OK." Duncan assures her. "I was shot, but it's not serious."

"What do you mean you were shot? Was somebody trying to kill you?"

"No, no. Nothing like that," Duncan underplays the situation. "They were shooting at somebody else and it ricocheted off a wall. It's just a surface wound. Don't worry. I'll take the bandage off tomorrow."

With the revolution successfully over, and Duncan safe at home, he's prepared to begin his new teaching career. Although he has mixed feelings about the changes in his life, he's happy that there's finally a steady job with a predictable income, a health plan, and, two months off each summer.

'With any luck, I'll be able to pursue freelance assignments or work on personal documentary projects,' he imagines. What he secretly hopes for is to return to Nicaragua.

Duncan is also happy for the people of Nicaragua, and particularly for his dearest friend, Azucena, who has put her life on the line for something she believes so strongly about and can finally enjoy a normal life with Tomás. He is saddened, however, that his own role as a photojournalist covering the changing developments in Central America has come to an end.

InterNews includes many of Duncan's photographs in their overall coverage of the Nicaraguan revolution and, through the wire services, his images appear in magazines and newspapers around the world.

His new responsibilities of preparing and grading course work, and endless faculty meetings, all serve to alleviate the void that Duncan experiences at missing the more active life of a photojournalist, but he is able to communicate his passion for the medium to his students.

Penny is ecstatic about Duncan's new position at the college. She'll see more of him, and he won't be off tempting danger in some foreign hot spot. His injury is, to Penny, a precursor for all the worries she experiences whenever he's away on assignment. She dreads the thought of reading Duncan's name in the headlines instead of under each of his published photos.

Duncan settles into a new scheduled life, a life that he, as a photojournalist, is unaccustomed to, but he finds living within a distinct pattern strangely comfortable.

There are moments when Duncan's thoughts return him to Azucena and to the paradise he has learned to love. Faced with the realities and responsibilities of his new job, however, he starts discounting those special moments as fantasies only to be revisited in his mind.

Penny's presence in Duncan's new life becomes a weekly affair. She often stays at his townhouse for the weekend following a Friday night date. Occasionally, they meet during the week after work for drinks. By Christmas, Penny and Duncan are cohabiting in his townhouse and steering their lives toward domestic normality.

They discover new enjoyments in family activities: walking in the park, attending gallery openings, going to the theatre and concerts.

Penny is aware that Duncan still needs to dabble at his art, and even encourages him to accept the occasional domestic assignment providing that it's interesting and stimulating for him. Duncan continues playing music but limits his involvement to short-term jazz gigs and the occasional concert, as long as they challenge his musical curiosity.

Duncan's new teaching position provides him with ample opportunities to see, and judge, other people's photographs, but his personal photographic activity is limited to editing and organizing work that he's already done, except of course, taking occasional photos of Penny or asking passersby to take photos of the two of them smiling together.

He considers the possibility of publishing a book of his photographs from Nicaragua but discovers that publishers are no longer interested.

"Nobody gives a shit about Nicaragua anymore," one editor tells him. "The revolution is over. It's finished. There are new fish to fry. What about some of those young students of yours, Duncan? They must be eager to taste the fish, right?"

"Eager, oh yeah. Some of them will leap off a bridge for a picture and won't even send you an invoice. But they lack the experience that can get them inside the situation. They're full of piss and vinegar, but they're short of sugar. Sure, they can get a peak moment, like a flying footballer, but they don't get the nuances yet."

"How do you mean that, Duncan?" the editor probes.

"It takes time to learn how to work the room, the room just being the scene," Duncan tells him, his eyebrows rising, as if he's about to reveal the long lost secrets of his profession.

"What advice do you tell your students?" the editor asks.

"If it's practical, try to dress the same way as your subjects so you won't stand out in the crowd. Then, start by moving around as discreetly as possible." Duncan assumes a crouching position to demonstrate. "It's like a cheetah checking out its prey by sniffing the wind direction and culling the best subjects from the herd. You take a few quiet shots without disturbing anyone or interrupting whatever's going on. Become part of the landscape. Study people's faces and their expressions. Watch how they interact with the other people; one person is never as interesting as two or three. Some of the best shots can come from this stage."

The editor infuses some levity. "When do you know when to attack?"

"Forget the cheetah now. You don't attack; you're not going to eat them. Just continue to maintain a low profile as long as possible." Duncan pauses and draws attention by raising his forefinger. "I was given good advice when I was starting out. If there was ever a secret, this is it. 'Shoot Around It.' It's a simple phrase that I use to this day."

"Explain that Duncan. I'm just a dumb photo editor."

"Explore the room and exploit the scene, wherever it is, by taking shots from as many angles and distances as possible. Shoot both vertical and horizontal frames of each situation because you never know how an editor, like yourself, will see the pages unfold. Constantly be aware of your composition, like where the subjects are situated in relation to their surroundings. Stay away from those big telephoto or zoom lenses; stick to the short and wide angles. Work close and quietly. Every time someone moves, take a picture. If they flinch, rub their eye, pull their ear, use their hands as they speak, push the button. Step back and try it again. Keep yourself in motion. We call it the dance."

"What if you get caught taking someone's photo?"

"Acknowledge them. Smile. Talk to them. Introduce yourself. Excuse yourself and move on. Every situation requires some customizing, but you get to know which technique to use. Let them think you've been distracted by another interesting photo opportunity, but always ... always be cordial."

"So, you're a dancing chameleon."

"Yeah, I suppose. That's a great analogy. I'll use that. Thanks." Duncan accepts the editor's comment as a gift before continuing.

"Students take a while to catch on to the ethics and the politeness factor. There are two kinds of students: the shy timid ones, afraid to approach their subjects, and the barnstormers, the ones who just barge in with both cameras blazing. I prefer the shy ones because they already possess a level of respect for the subject. Their only problem is to develop some respect for themselves; to believe in their own capabilities.

"And the barnstormers?"

"They don't understand how the reader responds to a photo. They think it's all about peak action, blood and guts. It's difficult for them to learn about softer elements: the compassionate tenderness between people who are suffering and the smiles on the faces of lovers; those are moments too."

"But your students are still young, right? They can learn."

"Shit yeah, they are young. Weren't we all? Many of them still don't know how to talk to people on the phone, or to comfort them when it's needed. That's the only way you can get the kind of photos I take. You have to respect the subjects. It's all part of paying the dues."

The editor asks, "How did you pay your dues, Duncan?"

"Mainly by just getting out and taking photos but," he hesitates, "I soon learned to do some research before walking into an assignment. Learn as much as possible about the people, the place, and the circumstances surrounding the subjects' lives."

"Research? What and how?"

Duncan scratches the side of his head. "Well ... after my first visit to Nicaragua, I planned ahead for my next by studying more Spanish at night school and meeting new Canadians from the region. They taught me about the suffering, the desire for decent lives, the poverty and the pride, and the need for independence and equality. They showed me, and included me, in their humour. I also read Latin American literature and history. That helped me understand how people of a different culture think. My experiences in Manitoulin taught me to shut up and listen."

The editor injects more humour. "That must have been the toughest thing for you, Duncan."

Duncan zips his fingers across his lips.

"You haven't mentioned the paparazzi, the ones who chase down celebrities? Where do they fit into all of this?"

Assuming a face of distaste, Duncan fakes a dry spit. "They're just fucking bounty hunters, that's all … and most of them are assholes."

Duncan chuckles before adding, "I know that editors will feed the fresh fish to younger, naïve photojournalists like my students. They need to start somewhere, just like we all had to. I just get the feeling that I'm being eased out to pasture, and I'm much too young for that. I guess the glue factory is just around the corner for me."

* * *

In August 1985, one week before Duncan is scheduled to return to the classroom, he surprises Penny with an unplanned mystery vacation.

"Hey Penny. Don't you think it's time we got out of the city? We've never taken a real holiday."

"Where can we go? Classes start soon. We only have a week left."

"Perfect. Why don't we just start driving north and see where it takes us. We'll leave in the morning."

From Toronto they drive northwest. A few hours later they arrive at Kincardine, on the shores of Lake Huron. They book into a modest motel before exploring the town and the wharf, where hundreds of summer boaters are docked before heading back to the city for Labour Day. In the evening they dine on local fish and chips at a roadside stand.

Sunsets across Lake Huron are magnificent and Duncan and Penny are treated to an intense red sky. Later, in the darkness, they are treated to a glorious display from the Aurora Borealis on their first night away from the neon brightness of Toronto. As the colour-shifting light bounces across the northern sky they walk together, arm-in-arm along the wharf, stopping to share conversation with the summer mariners who are always eager to brag about their expensive diversions.

At the motel, they open a bottle of Merlot and proceed to make love. The bed springs creak and scrape with every move.

Duncan asks, "I wonder what the people next door think we're doing in here?"

Penny laughs and answers, "Oh they know. Just wait until morning. They'll be sitting out front in their lawn chairs waiting to see who was next door fucking their brains out."

Laughter delays any possibility of an immediate climax.

"Jesus Christ, Penny," Duncan jokes. "Can we make any more noise?"

"Let's get it on. I'll show our neighbours what having good sex sounds like."

They laugh some more, until Penny draws Duncan inside. There's silence as they slowly enjoy each other. As the moment of collaborative ecstasy seems inevitable, Penny shrieks a barrage of moans and cries, and grinds her pelvis against the creaking mattress.

Duncan adds his excitement to the cacophony with a series of screaming satisfactions.

While still connected, Duncan observes, "We sound like a fucking symphony orchestra during a pre-concert tune up."

Penny shouts, "Ta-da-da-Dum-m-m," replicating the opening motif of Beethoven's Fifth Symphony. They both choke with laughter.

"Oh God," Penny says, placing her hand over her mouth. "That was amazing. I'll never be able to listen to Beethoven without laughing."

"Maybe we should play the Fifth while having sex from now on," Duncan suggests with a grin on his lips.

Afterward, laying exhausted on their backs, Penny points to the ceiling.

"Check out that light fixture above us, Duncan. It's full of dead flies. Doesn't anybody clean these rooms?"

Duncan jokes. "That's breakfast up there. If we keep the lights on all night, we'll have warm raisins on our oatmeal."

More uncontrolled giddiness fills the room, and probably the neighbour's room as well. An after-sex glass of wine becomes a pre-sex encore performance.

Their vacation revelry repeats itself at motels in Southampton, Tobermory, and in the Blue Mountains.

During one of their late night performances, Duncan laughingly suggests that they might take their show on a road tour.

From Collingwood they travel north-east into Muskoka. Eventually they arrive at the same Muskoka lodge where Duncan intends for them to relive their early days as students, years before.

"Ta-da," he shouts upon their arrival, his arms outstretched toward the main lodge. "Well, well. Look where we are."

Penny stares at the building for a few moments before losing it.

"How dare you bring me here? This is where our problems all began. How dare you?" Penny loses her cool as she releases a torrent of anger at Duncan. "This is the most inconsiderate thing you've ever done. There is nothing for us here but bad memories. Take me home."

"Ah, come on, Penny," Duncan pleads, dumbfounded at her reaction. "I thought you'd love this. I wanted us to relive our great times together."

Penny folds her arms and stares aimlessly out the opposite window. "Take me home, now!"

* * *

Upon their arrival home, Duncan hauls in their travel bags while Penny picks up several pieces of mail that await them. There are some pizza flyers, a phone and cable bill, and a bank statement. An envelope, addressed to Duncan, is from Nicaragua.

"This one's obviously for you," Penny says in a cold voice. She tosses the envelope onto the kitchen table.

Duncan picks the envelope up and opens it. It contains a letter, some press clippings, and a photo. While Penny opens the bills and bank statement, Duncan quietly reads the Nicaragua letter to himself.

My Dearest Duncan:

How is life treating you? Everything here was in turmoil immediately following the triumph. There were meetings to attend, speeches to deliver, budgets to sort out with no funds to work with. As you probably heard, Somoza emptied the banks when he left the country so we must do the best we can with what's left.

I became an organizer with the Literacy Brigade, travelling around the country teaching people to read and write. I find it so rewarding. The program has been very successful, even receiving accolades from the United Nations. When that was completed, I started working with the Ministry of Culture. I also began teaching fine arts part-time at the university. In my spare time I teach some classes at the School of Monumental Art. All things considered; I am kept very busy. Unfortunately, it leaves very little time for my own artistic quests. How is your teaching going? Are you enjoying it as much as I do?

I am enclosing a pamphlet from one of my presentations at Teatro Rubén Darío where I lectured about painting from dreams. Did you ever read, 'A Roosevelt,' the poem by Rubén Darío I recommended to you on our first visit together? It's just as relevant today as it was when he wrote it.

Also enclosed is a photo of my beloved Tomás performing in a school play. He is almost 13 years old now, can you believe that? I miss you and our wonderful conversations over dinner. There is so much more to talk about. I look forward to your next visit. Maybe we can return to Paraíso. Hasta la próxima, amigo.

Abrazos y Besos

Azucena.

Penny is curious about the contents of the letter but chooses to wait before saying anything. Instead, she watches Duncan's reaction to what he's reading. He smiles when he looks at the photo.

"It's amazing how time passes," he says, before offering the letter to Penny. "Want to read it?"

Penny shakes her head without saying a word.

After reading the letter a second time, Duncan places it in his briefcase.

Penny's curiosity is tweaked. She waits until Duncan settles in for an evening of TV. In the guise of unpacking her travel case, Penny locates the letter in his case and reads it.

The letter ignites Penny's fury. With the letter waving between her fingers, she fires at Duncan with both barrels.

"Are you having an affair with that Latina tart? She has a son that she loves while I can only imagine my son who I don't even know, and it pisses me off that you now have a photo of her kid but none of ours."

"So," Duncan counters. "All of a sudden he's *our* son? When did that happen? I thought he was just *yours*. My name isn't even mentioned on the fucking birth certificate."

"What good would that have done? You're never here to be a father. You're always off playing with your toys in some godforsaken place."

Duncan feels himself retreating into his private zone of silence in an attempt to erase the chaos. An image of Azucena dominates his empty space.

Duncan's silence only increases Penny's aggravation. Her shouting escalates despite Duncan's refusal to participate.

At the peak of her rage, Penny screams, "I insist that you destroy that fucking ugly painting that I never liked in the first place. Is that your beloved 'paradise' she wrote about? It looks uglier than hell if you ask me."

Duncan breaks his silence and blasts back into the fray. "Fuck off Penny. Pull yourself together, for Christ's sake. This painting isn't the cause of your anger. You need help."

Penny refuses to back down. "If you won't destroy it, I will." She grabs a knife from the kitchen and approaches the painting. Duncan reaches out to stop her when the knife gashes his arm, just inches from his previous war wound.

"Oh shit." Penny shouts with sudden panic upon seeing the blood surging from his arm. She immediately apologizes, wraps a towel around his arm, and rushes him to the hospital ER for stitches.

"You must be a bear for punishment," the doctor jokes after seeing the two wounds. "What happened?" the doctor asks.

"Which one?" Duncan responds, with a smile.

"Let's just talk about the one that's bleeding right now."

"Yeah ... well, it was just a stupid accident in the kitchen, Doc," Duncan explains. "I shouldn't be allowed to play with anything sharp, I guess."

As the doctor applies bandages, he enquires about the previous injury. "That one looks more serious. It came very close to the tendon. You should have had a real doctor patch that up. It looks to me like a gun was involved. You do know that we're supposed to report gunshot wounds to the police, don't you?"

"Not this one," Duncan explains before describing his war story.

* * *

Duncan's and Penny's relationship continues to wane. Most conversations result in conflict. They tolerate each other but life between them becomes challenging. During a dinner out, Penny drops a bomb.

"I've been doing some serious thinking, Duncan. We should try to have a child. I'd love to be pregnant again. I've done a lot of research. There are many women in their late 30s and 40s having families these days. What do you think?"

It comes as a shock to Duncan. He has missed the opportunities of parenthood as much as she has. He regrets with sadness, all the years he could have been playing baseball in the park, and teaching piano to his son, not to mention the absence of progeny in his family photos. While Penny has been vocal on the subject over the years, Duncan has suppressed his emotions, mainly to avoid further conflict. Now, while they're going through a period of upheaval, Penny suggests that a baby would be the solution to their woes.

'How do I answer her?' Duncan agonizes in silence.

"I'm waiting," she says, her wine glass balancing against her lower lip and her eyes fixed on his. "So, what do you think about my idea?" She sips more wine without sacrificing eye contact.

Duncan is at a loss for an answer … silent … until he blurts, "You'd have to stop drinking you know."

"That's not an answer, Duncan." She takes another sip. "Of course I would stop drinking."

Duncan tries everything to express his disagreement with her suggestion, without saying a defining, 'No!' He isn't even convinced that she wants to have a child. 'All she wants to hear from me is that I agree with her. I can't do that.'

Throughout dinner, he manages to divert attention from the topic, but he knows it's sitting just below a thin layer of iciness that prevails for weeks afterward.

Part of Duncan's reluctance to commit to having a child with Penny — another child — are the feelings he secretly holds for Azucena. His love for Azucena are always with him despite the guilt he harbours. He is now confident that his life with Penny is doomed. 'How could I consciously bring a child into the midst of this turmoil?' he questions.

His mind returns to Nicaragua, and to Azucena. Immediately, guilt attempts to govern his thoughts. 'Fuck it. Why should I feel guilty?' he rationalizes. 'I wasn't committed to Penny when Azucena and I made love.' The more he rationalizes the conflict, the guiltier he feels. The more guilt he experiences, the more he desires his true love.

'Should I just bite the bullet and tell Penny? Of course not. She'll blow a fucking gasket.'

* * *

To add more internal tension, Duncan is becoming increasingly discouraged about the college's attitude toward his unique teaching methods. Rather than follow the college's lesson plans, which he finds to be rigid and unrealistic, he adopts a more philosophical approach to teaching, with less emphasis on rules, theory, and technology, and more sessions that provide the students with opportunities for open discussions.

Sometimes he diverts completely, choosing to discuss seemingly unrelated topics that are otherwise useful to them in the long haul: the subject of PTSD affecting journalists, and the benefits of pursuing an alternative passion. He introduces the concepts of abstract art to the students who are obsessed only with images of gritty reality, in hopes that it will broaden their minds to wider horizons.

Duncan is encouraged by what he had witnessed during his visit to *Paraíso*.

'People want to learn; it's a natural desire. Rules, classrooms, and structures, that are created to control the act of learning, only place barriers against the desire to learn. That's why students drop out. When they start college they sincerely want to learn something, a subject that they are already excited about, but once they're dictated to, they close down. People learn far more when they're in a free environment. Teaching and learning amount to the same thing; they occur simultaneously. I learn as much from the students as what I expect them to learn from me … probably even more if the truth were revealed.'

Realizing that he's eligible to apply for a 12-month sabbatical for the following year, Duncan prepares a proposal that will take him to Nicaragua to organize a school of photojournalism for local students. The school will be twinned with the college he currently teaches in and will be a pilot project organized through the university in Managua. He plans to suggest Father Manuel as a reference and will rely upon him for connections with the university. He chooses not to tell Penny until the results of his proposal are known, for fear of creating any additional tension. Besides, he hasn't yet considered her role in his plans.

The project concept finally receives approval in principle from his Dean. Although it will not start until the following year, Duncan invites Penny out for dinner to tell her the news. When Duncan informs her, she becomes silent, gathering her thoughts, before she asks in an unusually calm voice, "What about having our baby? How will that work with you on sabbatical?"

Duncan is direct. "It won't work, Penny. There isn't going to be any baby."

"What?" Penny gasps, before retreating into silence. She stares vacantly into her wine glass.

Duncan knows the moment has arrived. He takes a deep breath to carefully prepare the words he will speak to relieve his guilt. In a sudden burst, he ignores his preparedness.

"I'm in love with Azucena," Duncan blurts "We made love the last time I was there."

Penny serenely swallows the last of her wine, sits quietly, carefully pondering her next move. She stands.

"Then it's over, you and me." She throws her napkin on the table before storming from the restaurant.

The following day, Penny's belongings are cleared from the townhouse.

PART SEVEN
1987 – 1988

CHAPTER 17

CONTRAS

Managua, Nicaragua, 1987:

Eight years have passed since the triumph of the revolution and Duncan's last visit to Nicaragua. Night has already fallen when Aero Nica touches down at Augusto C. Sandino Airport. From his window seat, Duncan notices how dark the city appears. 'There's either a hydro outage, or they've imposed a blackout. Probably both.'

He soon discovers that the official exchange rate at the *Casas de Cambios* (money exchange depot) is 900 *córdobas* per U.S. dollar, and the unofficial street value is in the thousands. Triple digit inflation, caused mainly by the U.S. embargo against Nicaragua, is playing havoc with their economy.

At the airport there are journalists arriving like flies to a rotting carcass and the customs officials are passing them through with little or no inspection. The majority of the international journalists are empathetic to the story of David defending itself against the bullying superpower Goliath to the north. There is renewed news interest in the revolution thanks to President Reagan's public ranting about Nicaragua allegedly exporting revolution, while he illegally funds a counterinsurgency known as Contras, who are waging war from across the northern border with Honduras. There are also anti-Sandinista skirmishes along the southern regions of *Rio Escondido*.

In recent years, the international news has focused on the war between the new Sandinista government and the Contras, sponsored and financed by the U.S. The conflict is commonly referred to as the Contra War.

Through the daily news coverage, Duncan is aware of the Contra war and of the violence and atrocities committed with intent to strike fear into supporters of the revolution. There is anxiety that the U.S. will eventually invade Nicaragua as they have done in the past. Evidence of the fear appears in the capital through the guards stationed at main intersections armed with AK-47s, and billboards shouting political messages: *'No Pasarán,'* (they shall not pass), *'Patria Libre o Morir,'* (free homeland or death), and *'Viva Nicaragua Libre'* (long live free Nicaragua).

Aside from the anxiety, Duncan notices an overall positive outlook from the people he meets and photographs in the streets. Hand-painted graffiti with similar messages appear on walls, homes, and fences everywhere.

The Pacific port of *Corinto*, and the Caribbean port of *El Bluff*, have been mined by the U.S. to discourage ships from entering Nicaragua thus limiting international trade. The U.S. has placed a trade embargo against the struggling nation and are waging a propaganda campaign on the English-speaking Atlantic coast.

One bizarre rumour of the propaganda being spread through the Atlantic Miskito Coast claims that the Sandinistas are administering vaccinations that contain the urine of Cuban President Fidel Castro, and that anyone accepting the vaccine will become a communist. This wild accusation is intended to counter the Sandinista's very effective immunization program underway against killer diseases like polio and measles.

It's late when Duncan finally arrives in the capital. Fortunately, he had booked a room in advance at the Intercontinental Hotel for two nights, unsure of what his itinerary would involve. His first night is spent catching up on the sleep lost in transit.

In the morning following breakfast, he eagerly walks to the Ministry of Culture, situated on an attractive, treed acreage once belonging to the former president. The offices are located in the main house adjacent to an empty dilapidated swimming pool. He enters and surprises Azucena in her office.

"*Hola*," he whispers, peeking around her doorframe from the hallway.

She looks up from her desk, hesitates, and covers her smile with her hand. Her eyes light up as she runs to embrace him. "Oh my God, Duncan." She jumps into his arms and smothers him with kisses, spreading her tears of joy across his face. "You've come back. I don't believe it."

"I couldn't stay away any longer," Duncan says, sharing with joyful tears of his own.

"I almost didn't recognize you. You've grown a beard."

"Yeah," Duncan replies, running his fingers through his fresh greying stubble. "It's a symbol of my independence," he jokes, alluding to his new freedom.

"How long can you stay? Forever I hope."

"I would love to stay with you forever but I'm afraid I must return by the first of September. I still have my teaching job, but we have the summer to be together."

Azucena pulls his arm to her. "Come with me Duncan. I'll take you for lunch."

They stroll, arm-in-arm, through the park-like setting of the Ministry of Culture until they arrive at nearby *Panadería Plaza España*.

Before entering, Duncan takes photos of a line of people waiting with empty baskets for baked goods. The people joke with him and he shares a smile with them. It feels good to be using his camera again.

Duncan asks Azucena. "Are these people suffering from the shortages caused by the embargo? If so, why are they so happy standing in line? They're not like the sad-faced people you see standing in bread lines from the great depression photos in the 1930s."

"The shortages are affecting everyone here of course," Azucena explains, "but these people are not waiting in a 'bread line' like you imagine. They are *vendedores ambulantes*, street vendors, waiting for their orders to be filled so they can hit the streets again. As soon as they have their fresh bread to sell, you will hear them shouting in the streets, *'Pan, Hay Pan.'* Some people call them *pregoneros*, shouters, like town criers."

After indulging in a light lunch, Azucena guides Duncan on a tour of post-revolution Managua. Realizing that they are only together for a limited time, she holds him close, often resting her head against his shoulder.

After passing the Inter-Continental Hotel, Duncan stops to photograph a block-long painted mural on a fence along *Avenida Simón Bolívar,* depicting the history of imperialism in Nicaragua and they arrive at a military base guarded by three young soldiers bearing automatic weapons.

Azucena shows her pass at the gate and guides Duncan into the military base where he registers as a *periodista* at the international media centre. Azucena assures him, "With this accreditation, you have access to most of the country as a *periodista*. We love journalists here."

Much of the devastation from the earthquake, 15 years before, remains evident as they approach the centre of the city. The shells of former commercial buildings are now occupied by families who are squatting in, what used to be, offices. Water is occasionally accessible from open pipes in the streets.

On streetcorners, plaques and monuments honouring the fallen heroes of the revolution are a constant reminder to the living.

Duncan trains his camera on a mother bathing her naked child in the street, while other children play baseball around them. He's ecstatic to be photographing again and senses a renewed vitality in his vision and approach. Sometimes a rest can be the best form of renewal.

From the downtown core, Azucena leads Duncan to an eternal flame, a monument to Sandinista founder, Carlos Fonseca. It is placed adjacent to the renamed *Plaza de la Revolución*. They stand for a moment to reflect. It is important for Azucena to also visit the Cathedral, still standing in ruin, for another moment of reflection.

She turns to Duncan and wraps her arm through his. "You have excellent timing Duncan. You have arrived just in time to accompany me to the mountains. In two days I begin teaching a workshop to women about sketching and painting from their dreams. The women are former sex workers, although there may be some more current than former, but we must do what we can to improve the outlook for our *compañeras*. Prostitution is mainly an economic decision for many of these women. They don't want to be forced into selling their bodies to strange men for a few *córdobas*; they would much rather be sharing their bodies with loved ones for free, do you agree?"

"Not that my opinion is valid but, it seems logical to me," Duncan responds, and tells her about the project he did while in college that focused on a Toronto sex worker. "For that woman, the incentive was economic as well; she was supporting a four-year-old child."

Azucena adds, "There are also many women who start into the sex trade as teens because they want to escape from bad family situations. They're looking for love when they haven't experienced love of any kind at home. Other girls, sad to say, are drawn into the trade because their mothers are already in it."

"I suppose they don't know any other kind of life," Duncan assumes.

"So, will you join me in the mountains? It will be a wonderful photo story for you. We'll be staying at a cooperative there. You should count on it being cold at night so bring warm clothing and a blanket with you. If you pay attention, you may also learn how to paint your own dreams," she winks. "Do you have dreams, Duncan?" Azucena nudges him with her elbow in jest. "Of course, you do. We all have dreams. Who knows, we may even be sharing some of the same dreams."

"I am sure we are sharing the same dreams," Duncan agrees, chuckling. "It sounds like a great story. I could use some variety in my coverage." He gives Azucena two thumbs up. "I'm in."

"I must warn you, though, Duncan." Azucena begins with a cartoonishly sad frown on her face. "I'll be sharing accommodations with the women who are taking the workshop. I hope you understand. You, unfortunately, must share sleeping accommodations with some of the male workers at the co-op."

Duncan imitates Azucena's sad face. She laughs and cuddles him.

"So we don't get too lonely in the meantime, we must celebrate tonight. What are your plans, Duncan?"

"I plan to make love to the woman I adore. I want to make up for the years I have missed with her since the last time we made love.

"And who is that lucky woman?" she asks with a teasing coquettish grin.

Duncan squeezes her arm. "It's a secret. I'll never tell."

* * *

Duncan arranges for room service to be left in the hallway outside his hotel room door. He hangs the *'No Molestar'* sign on the door handle. While waiting for the meal, he and Azucena waste no time in re-acquainting themselves to the fantasies they'd been imagining all afternoon, indeed the dreams that had kept the flames alive for the past eight years.

The knock on the door is well-timed. Duncan grabs a robe and opens the door, quickly hauling the food cart in. He rejoins Azucena in the king-sized bed where they dine in segments, separating the courses with passionate entremets.

They leave the hotel in the morning. Duncan relocates into Azucena's *casita*, a humble dwelling one street away from *Avenida Simon Bolívar*, in *Barrio Martha Quezada*.

Tomás, now 14, meets Duncan for the first time since he was seven years old. He is initially shy about the strange man obviously displaying an attraction to his mother, but soon warms up to Duncan's outgoing friendliness and his genuine interest in Tomás' preoccupation with baseball.

"Mamá says that you knew Roberto Clemente," Tomás poses to Duncan. "Is it true?"

"Yes, it is true, Tomás. We spent a bit of time together. When I return home I'll send you some photos I took of him. Would you like that?"

"Alright!" Tomás shouts, trading high-fives with Duncan.

It's arranged for Tomás to spend some time with Father Manuel while Azucena attends the workshop. Duncan promises to play baseball with him when they return.

It's a clear morning when Duncan and Azucena leave the capital for the mountains. They travel north along the Pan-American highway in the pickup bed of a *camioneta* driven by one of the workshop organizers. The air is fresh against their faces as the grey mountains loom on the horizon.

Duncan's eyebrows knit together as he leans forward over the cab of the *camioneta*. A cooler breeze brushes his face as they proceed northward into the foothills. Duncan points ahead to a moving cloud formation. "What's that?" he asks.

"*Zopilotes,*" Azucena responds, adding a translation. "Vultures."

As they pass what originally seemed like a cloud, a swarm of ravenous vultures battle over the skeletal remains of a once majestic, long-horned cattle beast. Duncan recalls the cowboy movies of his youth where a similar scene would signal an ominous warning of impending doom.

The cooperative is located a few kilometres off the highway past the city of Jinotega, an area known for its coffee production and a nearby hydro-electric plant that serves most of the country's power.

"We have arrived," Azucena announces as the *camioneta* enters the cooperative. They are greeted by an applauding assortment of workers and work-shoppers.

Azucena smiles as she meets and greets everyone personally. Duncan is impressed with how she can interact with people in all walks of life.

The women, all from poorer circumstances, represent a variety of age groups. The youngest, aged 15, was drawn into the sex trade two years earlier at the encouragement of her own mother, to earn extra money for the family of five. The children, all younger than her, have been sired from a variety of fathers, most unknown to their mother, who is also enrolled in the workshop. The oldest attendee appears to be in her mid-60s but in reality is only 45.

At the beginning of the workshop, the women gather in a circle. Azucena asks each woman to introduce herself by her first name only, and to offer a brief explanation of why they entered the sex trade.

As a male, Duncan is not invited to sit with the introduction circle so he wanders the grounds of the cooperative exploring photo opportunities. From afar, he can still hear the women's voices as they reveal their circumstances.

They offer their stories, most citing abuse at a young age and being forced into the trade for economic reasons. One woman explains that it was a deep desire to be loved, because she was abandoned by both parents as a seven-year-old child and forced to raise herself on the street in the only way she knew.

One woman introduces herself as Cecilia. She is shy and embarrassed about telling her story and sheds tears before she begins.

"My mother was a domestic at a rich man's estate when I was just a child. When I was 14, my older sister and I were enticed into a darkened room one night by the *patrón*."

Cecilia stops, turning away from the circle of women as she wipes her tears.

"He told us we would be playing games and that we would receive favours from him in the morning. During the night, we were both sexually assaulted. It wasn't until the morning that we recognized our attackers as the sons of the *patrón*, our childhood friends."

Azucena approaches Cecilia and wraps her arms around her. "Would you like to stop? It's OK if you want to."

Cecilia insists on continuing.

"You are among friends here," Azucena reminds her.

Cecilia continues, exhibiting a renewed strength. "They ruined our lives," she states in a stronger voice. Those bastards ruined our lives. My mother was relieved of her duties at the estate and resorted to selling her body to sailors in the port of Corinto. My sister …"

Her voice disappears and she chokes her tears back before starting again.

"My sister … who was only 15, became pregnant from those attacks and threw herself in front of a moving train."

"Let me help you, Cecilia," Azucena offers in a soft voice. Hold my hand while you finish your story. I'll stand here with you."

Cecilia takes a huge breath to build her strength.

"Naturally, I followed my mother into the trade, as my oldest of five children has followed me. This is my daughter beside me. She is Margarita, named after my dear departed sister. She is now 15, the same age as my sister was when we were attacked."

Margarita stands. She starts her story, shyly, "I am Margarita. I am …" Her voice chokes. She hides her face in her hands, weeping.

Azucena thanks Margarita and embraces her in consolation. "Your mother has told us everything we need to know."

After the introductions, they break for tea and coffee. When they regroup, Duncan is invited to join the circle as a guest. Azucena asks him to introduce himself.

"I am Duncan, a Canadian photojournalist. I have known Azucena since the earthquake, and I know that her commitment to the revolutionary process is sincere as is her compassion for what is right. As my Scottish name is difficult to pronounce for the Spanish tongue, you can just call me 'Canuck,' a nickname we often use for Canadians."

Variations on the word Canuck are heard around the circle that sound more like a flock of honking *gansos de Canadá* (Canada geese). A woman repeats in rhythm, "*Señor* Canuck, Canuck, Canuck," and the others join the singing in unison.

Duncan observes, with keen interest, how Azucena instructs the women to be sensitive to their dreams, to accept that their dreams may be related to their inner imaginations and not necessarily serving as a function of their realities. Her lessons involve physical contact and embracing each other to build trust between them and confidence within themselves. Duncan is asked to participate in the sensitivity building exercises, the sole male involved. There are sceptics among the women but most accept Azucena's wisdom and are moving forward.

One of the women jokes, "Is this how men react when I touch them sensitively? Do they start having dreams?"

Cecilia adds to the joke. "They just have wet dreams. Am I right *señor* Canuck?" She looks at Duncan with an open smile that displays several broken teeth. Margarita laughs as does Duncan.

Azucena responds with a message for the women. "This is not an exercise to please others. It is to enhance the appreciation of your own dreams, and to recognize pleasure from them. The benefits are for you to enjoy. That is where you will find the truth, within yourself. When you live with the truth, you live happy and satisfied lives, with an enhanced self-esteem."

"Satisfaction doesn't feed my children," one of them shouts.

Azucena responds. "But self-esteem will provide you with the confidence needed to get on with a better life, to enable you to find more suitable employment, and maybe even a partner who will love you with honesty."

The women are asked to draw or paint whatever they can recall from one of their dreams. Some attempts render realistic images, while others demonstrate a raw talent for expressing themselves in more abstract forms. Some of their dreams are futuristic and display idealistic images of their lives with husbands and children playing in heavenly bliss, as they wish they could be. Many however, are dark, ominous imaginations with lightning storms, erupting volcanos, military themes, and death.

Margarita offers a speeding train with her aunt's body silhouetted against the front. No doubt this is a nightmare she has experienced more than once.

Azucena encourages them to illustrate their dreams with only one simple stroke of the brush. Once again, a variety of images emerge; some are solid brave strokes in bold colours, others are weak slight lines fading in and out across the page with minimal force or commitment, as if afraid to face their realities.

After a few days, Azucena suggests that she and Duncan take some time off, starting with a picnic lunch in the mountains followed by a stroll through the streets of Matagalpa.

Duncan is confident that he already has the photos and information for an exceptionally powerful story on the workshop. "I'd welcome a break from all these women," Duncan jokes. "I get the feeling I'm being stared at all the time."

"You are," Azucena laughs, adding, "You're a funny man, Duncan, or should I call you *señor* Canuck, Canuck, Canuck? You are always making jokes."

"I think that, this time, I'm more the subject of jokes than the purveyor."

* * *

Azucena prepares a picnic lunch wrapped in large leaves and adds six bottles of *Toña* beer for refreshment. Duncan organizes his gadget bag and photo vest. They load everything into the *camioneta* and drive south.

Before arriving at Matagalpa, Duncan's eyes are drawn to a magnificent mountain vista. The sun filters through a soft mist hanging over a *laguna*.

"Stop the truck, Azucena. Just look at that view. It's beautiful. Can we stop so I can take some photos?"

"We have all day," Azucena says while steering the *camioneta* to the side of the road. "Take your time. Enjoy the beauty of our country."

Azucena kisses Duncan. "I'll be right here waiting for you when you get back."

Duncan wanders along the mountainside with his camera, searching for ideal vantage points. Below, in a valley, the tops of pine trees peek above the mist, a scene that reminds Duncan of La Cloche Mountains on the approach to Manitoulin Island, typical of northern Ontario. While composing the magical scene through his viewfinder a single file of mule riders emerge along a mountain trail. Duncan snaps a sequence of images before they disappear down into the mist-enveloped valley.

'It was so temporary,' Duncan ponders, checking the settings of his camera. 'Minutes later and they wouldn't have been a part of my life, a fleeting moment in my memory. Now, thanks to my photographs, I can relive the moment forever.'

Duncan continues exploring the mountain vistas as the mist slowly dissipates, revealing the verdant richness of the high country. When the bright sun approaches noon, he returns in the direction of the *camioneta*, and Azucena.

From a distance, Duncan sees that Azucena has laid out a blanket on a level section of the mountainside and is busily sketching. He takes candid photos as he approaches. By the time he arrives at her side, she has placed Duncan's image into the sketch.

Duncan steps behind Azucena to look at her sketch. He caresses her shoulders.

"Do you like my sketch?" she asks, turning her head toward him.

"There's only one thing missing," he observes. "Where is the lover I made love to in *Paraíso*?"

Azucena rises from her camp stool and kisses him. "That's because she is here, waiting for you in the mountains."

After lunch, Azucena returns to her sketches. Duncan lays his back down against the blanket and stares aimlessly, squinting into the sky. Billowing clouds pass over the mountain peaks causing cloud shadows to roll across the valley. When the sun re-emerges between the clouds, Duncan closes his eyes and quickly dozes into dreamland.

Miles Davis' muted trumpet improvises over a soft ballad and he sees his own photos from Paraíso pass in random order across his imagination. The images blend with details from Azucena's painting that hangs in his Toronto living room. Abstract forms of two lovers emerge from amidst the flaming inferno of Paraíso, materializing as Azucena and himself. The flames of the forest kindle in Duncan's mind and flutter about; he imagines a crackling sound.

His eyes scan downward to the white lily in the corner of the painting before it zooms outward to encompass his entire field of vision. He smells the lily close to him and senses a wisp of warm air pass across his face. Azucena's lips touch his.

The closeness of Azucena wakens him from his dream. His eyes snap open. Her face fills his visual field and her lips are smiling. She leans forward and kisses him again, a warm tender kiss, not the kiss from a friend, but from a lover. Duncan welcomes it and responds. She places her body close beside him and, with pelvic gestures, suggests her desires.

Duncan's curious hands caress her contours while Azucena welcomes his body with her own. Together they consummate the wonder of the moment.

In Matagalpa, they book into a hotel room. Rather than proceed directly to the dining room for dinner, they share intimacies that become more playful than earlier on the mountainside. Their endurance to resist each other is tested through teasing and sensuous allusions. Azucena reveals to Duncan what she wants but mischievously resists his advances when he approaches. There is no immediacy, only prolonged pleasure.

* * *

"Wake up Duncan. I'm famished." Azucena shouts childishly before striking him with her pillow. "Wake up. It's morning."

After a hearty breakfast in the hotel's dining room, Azucena is compelled to paint a vision she realized in her dreams during the night. She settles her easel on the patio garden adjoining the hotel while Duncan departs to photograph around the city.

When he returns to the hotel two hours later, Azucena is in a frenzy. A half-completed canvas lies on the floor, dominated by daubs of thick red, orange, and yellow textures.

"We must leave, quickly" she shouts. "Something is going wrong."

As they pass through Jinotega, the pungent smell of smoke penetrates their nostrils and intensifies as they approach the cooperative.

"Oh shit," Duncan points ahead as they approach the cooperative. What the fuck happened here?"

Buildings are burnt and smouldering in ruin. Smoke continues to rise from the ashes. Duncan jumps from the moving vehicle and runs toward a group of weeping women gathered around in a circle.

One of the women runs toward the approaching vehicle in a panic.

Azucena brakes and jumps from the *camioneta* to meet her.

"What happened here?" Azucena asks.

The woman's body trembles. She answers, stammering with fear in her voice. "Contras … they attacked the cooperative … early this morning … we were still asleep. Three women were killed, and …" The woman collapses against Azucena.

Azucena places her arms around the woman to console her.

"It's Margarita," the woman cries, flapping her arms haphazardly. "The Contras … they … they violated poor little Margarita."

Duncan calls quietly, but in an urgent panicked voice. "Azucena, I think you should come here."

Azucena discovers that Margarita's young body had been abused and mutilated; the Contras fastened her remains to a fencepost as a warning to the others. Further investigation reveals that other women and children were kidnapped. A few dazed and confused survivors remain, consoling each other and aimlessly picking up remnants: clothing, unfinished paintings, children's toys.

Duncan is traumatized by the atrocities inflicted on these innocent people. His stomach empties without delay while his mind churns.

'A natural disaster like the earthquake is tragic enough,' he ponders. 'But this … this abominable attack on human dignity is incomprehensible. Who? … no, not *who*,' he corrects his thought, '*what* despicable monsters could do such things? Even wild animals of the most vicious kind would never do this to their own kind, or any other kind for that matter.'

Despite his inner turmoil, he instinctively photographs the devastation as a historical record, fully aware that he will ultimately suffer the haunting memories forever. He interviews survivors who describe the details of how Margarita was tortured while they were forced to watch. He also learned that some men who worked at the cooperative were taken away at gunpoint.

Azucena tells Duncan, "The three women who were murdered … they were trying to stop the bastards from torturing Margarita."

"Oh shit." Duncan responds.

While Azucena busily helps the women prepare the bodies to be relocated to a *funareria* in the city, one of the women calls Duncan aside. She quietly whispers that the Contras asked specifically about *compañera* Azucena.

"They asked where she was and how they could find her. They referred to her as a '*puta comunista*,' (a communist whore). When we refused to tell them where she was, they started to torture poor Margarita. I tell you this secretly, because I want you to protect our precious *compañera*, but I don't want to put fear in her mind," the woman says, dirt-filled tears encrusted on her cheeks from having cried hours on end. "You must promise to protect her."

Duncan gives the woman his promise. He embraces her and vows to keep the woman's information secret.

* * *

When they return to the capital, Azucena pleads to Duncan. "Please

Duncan, don't return to Canada. Stay here. I need more of you." She embraces him and rests her head against his chest. "You also need me. You already know that. You proved that to me in the mountains and during the triumph. I even sensed that long ago in *Paraíso*. Please, Duncan. Stay here with me. I love you."

"I love you too, so very much, Azucena."

Duncan reminds her that he must return to his classes by September but reveals that he is planning a sabbatical so he can stay in Nicaragua for an entire year, but it won't start until the following summer.

"In the meantime, I want to know everything about this magnificent place you call home, and even more about the beautiful and mystical *compañera* Azucena," Duncan tells her, smiling while placing the palm of his hand softly against her cheek.

For the remainder of his stay, Duncan lives with Azucena and Tomás.

Tomás approaches Duncan during a game of catch in a nearby park. "*Señor* Duncan, can I ask you something?"

"Sure. Go for it," Duncan answers, bending down to pick up a wild pitch. "You can ask me anything, Tomás."

"Are you my father?"

Duncan is surprised by the directness of Tomás' question, but he understands why it was asked.

He places his hand on the boy's shoulder. "I'm not your father, Tomás. I couldn't be. I wasn't even in Nicaragua when you were conceived. I was, however, present at the very moment you were born."

Duncan pauses to allow Tomás to comprehend his answer before continuing.

"I want you to know that I love your mother very much, and ..."

Tomás grins. "You don't do a very good job of keeping that a secret, Duncan." He tosses a ball in the air and catches it in his glove.

"Yeah, I suppose you're right there. You're very perceptive for a 14-year-old."

"I'm almost 15, you know."

"Yeah, I know." Duncan pats his shoulder and leans down to where he can be face-to-face with the boy. "I want you to know that I can't be here all the time, Tomás, but when I am here, I would be happy to be *like* a father to you ... but only if you want me to be."

"I would like that, Duncan." He pauses, squeezing his face into a question before asking, "Should I call you Papá?"

Duncan backs up and signals Tomás to throw another pitch. When he catches the ball, Duncan rejoins Tomás. "Let me buy you some ice cream, son."

Before they arrive back at the *casita*, Duncan answers, "You can just call me Duncan, that's what everybody I love calls me."

"Right on," Tomás answers, offering a high-five to Duncan. "Mamá loves you. Does she always call you Duncan?"

"Hmm ... not always," Duncan chuckles. "Sometimes she calls me a pain in the ass."

Over the summer, Duncan and Tomás enjoy games of baseball together with his friends, and Tomás contributes to many of Azucena's and Duncan's discussions about politics, religion, and philosophy. When Tomás decides to learn to play the guitar he challenges Duncan with musical questions.

Azucena is busy preparing paintings for an upcoming August exhibition. Duncan documents her preparations by photographing her at work in the studio, a project that results in a comprehensive series of photographs of an artist in the act of creativity. His images include her down time, moments of tension and triumph, and some formal portraits and figure studies of her shrouded in the beautiful north light of the studio.

Duncan embarks on several photo projects of his own. He begins what could result in an extended project, documenting the arts and culture of the new Nicaragua. Remembering when Azucena and he visited the communities of *Masaya* and *Niquinohomo* years before, Duncan eases into a comprehensive documentary about the smaller communities of Nicaragua, with special interest in the unique artists and craftspeople of those regions.

CHAPTER 18

BLUEFIELDS

In July, before Azucena's show opens, Duncan plans a short research trip to the Atlantic coastal town of Bluefields, where Azucena's mother was from, and where she was conceived. When he proposes to Azucena that she can travel with him, she's ecstatic.

"I have always wanted to go to Bluefields to meet my grandparents. Mamá often talked about them and about Palo de Mayo when I was conceived. I wonder if my grandparents are still alive. I once made a painting of them based on my mother's dreams. From that dream I think I would recognize them. Can Tomás come with us? I want him to know where his roots are."

"Of course," Duncan answers, smiling at her tenderly. "I was going to suggest that. How could I possibly say no?"

Travel to Bluefields, the capital of the Southern Caribbean Autonomous Region, is limited due to occasional Contra activity and some resistance to the revolution by local citizens. Through Azucena's and Father Manuel's security connections, and Duncan's press credentials, they are able to acquire travel clearance through the Interior Ministry with little effort.

The route to the Atlantic coast is via a twisting secondary road to the village of Rama, and from there via the *Rio Escondido* ferry to the coast.

From the deck of the ferry, Tomás is exposed to the vast diversity of wildlife for the first time in his 14 years.

"Look Mamá," he says, excitedly pointing toward the shoreline. "There's crocodiles. We better not fall overboard."

"How fast can you swim, Tomás?" Azucena asks.

"Not fast enough," he laughs.

Duncan grabs some photos of the crocodiles and turns his camera to the landscapes that open new vistas with each bend in the river. A cluster of humble shanties, resting on stilts, provide housing for local Indigenous families totally dependent upon fishing and hunting. Children wave from their docks as the ferry passes. Azucena and Tomás wave back. Duncan makes a note to return to the area when time permits.

Azucena and Duncan were warned before embarking on the journey that there is a potential for military confrontations along the river, explaining why armed soldiers are located at both bow and stern, constantly monitoring for signs of danger.

As the ferry veers around a large bend hidden behind a cluster of mangroves, a sudden outburst of rapid-firing machine guns break the silence. The soldiers respond quickly, firing blindly into the forest.

More Contra machine gun fire is directed at the ferry from the southern shore. Duncan grabs Azucena and Tomás and forces them face down against the deck.

After more intensive and focused fire from the soldiers, a voice screams on shore. The soldiers continue their assault from the ferry, shooting toward the Contras as they escape into the dark protection of the forest.

Further along the river, in a narrow passage, the ferry travels through shadows cast by low overhanging tree cover. Two of the young crew members suddenly reach up into the branches and haul down a boa constrictor.

Duncan freaks out. "What the fuck?" he shouts.

The boys laugh and release the snake onto the deck, where it writhes in an attempt to escape from the crew members by heading toward Duncan.

Duncan steps backward in a panic, tripping over a cable and falling on his back. As he falls he catches a glimpse of Azucena and Tomás staring at the scuffle with their mouths wide open. Azucena pulls Tomás back, out of the danger zone. The boa moves closer to Duncan.

Duncan shouts, "Get that fucking thing out of my sight." He kicks his feet at the writhing *serpiente*.

The young crew members slide the snake overboard just as it reaches Duncan's foot.

Duncan stands up and swiftly approaches the boys, placing his face nose-to-nose with the main perpetrator.

"Don't pull another fucking stunt like that, you assholes." He threatens the boys, raising his fist at both of them, "or … or …" He searches for the right words. "… or you'll be lunch for those *cocodrilos*. Understand?"

"Si, *señor*." Embarrassed, the boys hang their heads and quietly return to their post.

The armed soldiers laugh at the entire episode, but especially at the embarrassed crew members who were routed out by the *gringo*.

Azucena, still gripping Tomás, slowly approaches Duncan, stroking his arm to calm him down.

Duncan is breathing heavily. "I have no problems handling Contras, but I don't do boas well."

* * *

When they finally disembark at the port of Bluefields, they're welcomed by a cacophony of shouting, laughing, and bartering, between local fishermen and shoppers wanting fresh fish from the daily catches. Further into town crowds gather at the market. A young boy passes, toting the freshly severed head of a butchered cattle beast over his own head; blood trickles through his hair and over his face. Another child carries two live chickens by their legs, their squawking heads bouncing against the gravel road with the rhythm of her gait.

To Duncan, the Caribbean atmosphere is both an exotic culture shock and a welcome diversion. He dances through the crowds at the market with a smile on his face, photographing the locals; it's a feeding frenzy for his creative energies. He loves concentrating his camera on the lively interactions of people going about their daily routines; customs that are vastly different from those he was brought up with in Canada.

Meanwhile, Azucena searches for her grandparents by asking people in the crowded market about her family name, Sosa. She carries the only photograph she has of her mother in hopes that her grandparents are still alive, and that they will want to see her if, and when, she locates them. Luck swings her way when a fish vendor directs her to a small house where an older couple, with the surname Sosa, live.

Azucena runs to tell Duncan the news and together, with Tomás, they search for a brightly painted bungalow.

"The fish vendor said we can't miss it. It's the only purple house on the street," Azucena tells them. Suddenly, "There it is. Look." Azucena points.

A demure woman in her seventies, her hands displaying signs of hard work and arthritis, answers the door. She peers at Azucena through thick glasses.

"Are you *señora Sosa*?" Azucena asks.

The woman nods her head in confirmation.

"Are you the mother of Lydia Sosa?"

The woman remains silent, studying Azucena's face. Azucena concludes that her silent response is affirmative and steps forward to embrace the woman.

"I am Azucena, your granddaughter, and this is your great grand-son, Tomás. He is now 14 years old."

The old woman returns Azucena's embraces. She pulls back to take a better look at her granddaughter, studying her up and down and finally speaks through her tears.

"Look at you. You are beautiful, just like my Lydia." The sudden shock sends memories of sadness and regret through her. She wipes the tears from her eyes with the corner of her handkerchief. "Thirty-four years have passed since Lydia moved away. I still keep count. Such a long, long time ago."

Señora Sosa cups Tomás' face with her hand and encourages the trio to enter her house.

The old woman explains. "It's a humble home we have, I know, but it's been our home since we were married. Lydia was born here, you know." Tears reappear at the memory. She wipes them away and sniffles. "I must apologize, the house needs a new paint job."

"It's a beautiful house," Azucena says, "Don't you think so, Duncan?"

Duncan agrees, nodding. "I love the colour, especially."

Once everyone is inside, the *señora* officially welcomes them with embraces to each. She points into the living room, "Come in, sit. If I knew you were coming I would have cleaned up."

It's a cozy living room with a flower-patterned sofa. There are well-worn dents and swells in the cushions that reveal someone often sleeps on it. Two soft recovered chairs, once matching the sofa, form a semi-circle around a wooden coffee table with a vase of fresh flowers in the centre.

The striped wallpaper reminds Duncan of his parents' home in Hamilton.

Señora Sosa waits until everyone is seated before sitting herself on a simple chair adjacent to a needle stitching frame. She sits upright and pats her hands on her lap before asking.

"So. What news do you have of Lydia?" she asks.

Azucena started worrying about this moment as soon as Duncan asked her to come to Bluefields with him. She knew it would come up in conversation so she prepared not to step around the answer.

"Mamá was lost in the earthquake," Azucena answers sadly, placing her hand on her grandmother's arm.

Señora Sosa acknowledges the sad news by patting her hand on Azucena's. "I just knew something had happened to my dear Lydia. She promised to be in touch when she became successful and I never heard more from her."

Azucena assures her grandmother, "Mamá was never wealthy but she was very successful. She operated her own business and was self-employed. She was a very proud and independent woman."

The *señora* is curious about the role Duncan plays in the scenario that confronts her. "Is this the father of Tomás, your husband?" she queries.

Duncan steps forward, introducing himself, while Azucena explains what happened to them during the earthquake and Duncan's role in saving her life.

"What about my grandfather?" Azucena asks, attempting to change the line of questioning, and afraid of having to explain too many details.

Señora Sosa explains that her husband is sleeping, but warns them that his memory is frail, and he may not remember their daughter, Lydia. "Sometimes he remembers many things well, but at other times he knows nothing. Maybe today will be a good day. I will wake him and make some tea for us."

Azucena joins her *abuela* in the kitchen to make tea.

When the old man arrives in the living room, he appears confused, staring intently at each of the strange visitors. When his eyes settle on Azucena, he slowly steps forward and embraces her. In a choked raspy voice, he says, "Lydia, my Lydia. I am so sorry."

Señora Sosa explains that her husband thinks Azucena is his long-lost daughter. "Of course, I thought the same thing when I saw you at the door. You look exactly like your mother. She was a beautiful young lady, just like you are so beautiful. You have the same colour of skin, a perfect blend of my husband's and mine."

Azucena thanks her and shows her grandparents a photo of her mother. The old man repeats, "Lydia, my Lydia." He kisses the photograph.

The conversation rolls around to Tomás, and what his ambitions are. "I'm planning to go to university in a few years," he tells them. "I want to be a lawyer."

Señor Sosa smiles and creates a gurgling laughing sound with his throat.

Tomás adds proudly, "Mamá was also at the university, and she's now a famous Nicaraguan artist."

Duncan seizes the opportunity to take some candid family photos in his unique documentary style, watching carefully for the subtle expressions and interactions, the tears and the smiles.

Leaving Azucena and Tomás to visit with their family and to review their histories of events, Duncan excuses himself and returns to the market and the fishermen's wharf to add more images to his documentary of small-town Nicaragua.

Like other areas in the country there is a noticeable military presence and graffiti on buildings and fences that offer both pro- and anti-revolutionary sentiments. The hand-painted graffiti and murals provide informative graphic backdrops for Duncan's street photography that focuses on human subjects. There are visual differences between the eastern *Miskito* coast and the western, more urbanized, areas of the country. Black Caribbean culture dominates the eastern regions offering contrast to the Spanish Latino dominance of the central and western regions.

Duncan thought the easygoing *'mañana'* pace of life in the capital was challenging to his urban North American expectations, but the Caribbean pace is from another world altogether. 'I could learn to love this life,' he thinks. 'Maybe when I retire.'

Duncan manages to expose 12 rolls of Tri-X black and white film before returning to the purple Sosa house, where a scrumptious traditional dinner awaits him.

CHAPTER 19

VACATION

Managua, Nicaragua, 1987:

The curator of the Bistro Gallery shows several of Duncan's photos as part of Azucena's show, including their first collaborative effort: one of Duncan's photographs from the aftermath of the Contra attack at Jinotega upon which Azucena has symbolically painted a group of women and a young man with fear on their faces. In the background of Azucena's painting, two men and a boy seemingly in his teens, are being forced into the forest at gunpoint by men in camouflage. Two mules, loaded with weaponry, wait for them amongst the trees. Dark gray smoke rises from the ruined buildings.

When Duncan asks Azucena why she chose to paint something that has already happened instead of her usual foretelling, she explains, "Maybe I'm becoming a painter of history, or maybe there are revelations yet to come that we're not aware of."

In addition to their collaboration, several portraits of each other are included. There is mixed response to their work from the viewers between those who like the work and those who love it. Azucena's reputation as an important Nicaraguan artist is spreading. The media, as Duncan predicts, focuses on an apparent erotic symbolism alluded to in a couple of intimate portraits.

A reviewer from one of the daily newspapers, headlines a glowing review of their work, '*Compañeros Intimos* (intimate comrades).'

Some of the attention, however, is more disturbing.

Azucena receives an anonymous letter referring to her as a communist whore and warning her to leave the country immediately or face execution. She maintains a strong appearance and dismisses it as an idle threat, but Duncan views it as serious. For him, it is an ominous signal that relates back to the Contra attack on the cooperative at Jinotega, where she was apparently the primary target. Of course, he has never told her about what he heard there. Rather than raise a fear alarm, Duncan suggests an alternative.

"I have a wonderful idea, Azucena. My contract requires me to return to teaching at the beginning of September, a few weeks from now. How would you like to go on a vacation with me to Canada? It's a wonderful time of the year there and I could show you some of the tourist sights, maybe even go hiking and camping in the bush for a few days. You will like my townhouse. It's located in the centre of the city with many activities you can amuse yourself with, like art galleries, shopping, and a wonderful international market. In the evenings and on weekends we can enjoy fine restaurants and entertainment of all kinds. I can arrange a return flight for you at the beginning of November, before the snow starts to fall. You wouldn't enjoy that part anyway. Unfortunately, I can't return with you then because of my contract."

"What about Tomás?" Azucena asks, hesitancy pegging her voice.

"Hmm." Duncan quietly ponders the ramifications of Tomás joining them. 'It'll give me a chance to become more of a father to Tomás. It'll also show Tomás another side of me, the practical side.

What if he doesn't like the other side of me?' He pauses his thoughts. 'Shit, what if Azucena doesn't like the practical Duncan?'

Duncan asks Azucena, "What about Tomás' schooling?"

"He's an 'A' student," Azucena answers proudly. "The change in culture will be more valuable to him than anything he will ever miss at school."

"Then we'll all go," Duncan decides without hesitation. "Get your passports and exit visas ready."

While preparing for the trip, Azucena is busy with questions about Canada, and about sleeping in the bush with only a tent between them and the wild animals. "Can we see Niagara Falls? How cold will it be? Can we visit the Indigenous people? I would like to meet them. Do the police really wear red uniforms and ride horses like in the movies?"

Tomás' excitement focuses on baseball and his new fascination with music. "Can we see the *azulejos* play, Duncan?"

"If I can scam a few tickets we could go to a Blue Jays game. Sure, that'd be great."

Before they leave the *casita*, Duncan calls to Azucena. "Bring the slides of our work with you. Who knows? It might be interesting to show them to people in Toronto."

* * *

Toronto, 1987:

After a gruelling series of connections and delays between their 5:00 am departure from Managua to San José, Costa Rica, and a direct flight from there to Toronto, they finally arrive after midnight. Customs delays and concerns about passengers with Nicaraguan passports keep them from leaving the airport until well after 2:00 am. After combing through their luggage, it's only when Azucena shows her and Tomás' return tickets, dated in November, that the customs officer finally passes them through.

"What was that all about?" Azucena asks Duncan during the limo ride. Is it always that difficult to enter Canada?"

"No. They just wanted some reassurance that I wasn't trying to sneak you into the country as an illegal alien, that's all."

Exhausted, they arrive at Duncan's townhouse, tip the limo driver, and haul their luggage to the front door. Duncan struggles to locate his keys. Tomás, who fell asleep in the limo, drags himself inside.

Duncan leads Tomás upstairs. "For tonight Tomás, you can sleep in the guest room where I also do my editing. I'll clean up this sorry mess for you in the morning. I'm sure you're eager to get right to sleep."

Duncan gathers some bedding from a linen closet and quickly makes the bed. He and Azucena give Tomás hugs before leaving him alone.

"I know it's terribly late but would you like a nightcap, Azucena?" Duncan asks. "Some wine before we head to bed?"

"That would be wonderful. I just need something to calm me down.

Duncan pours a pair of Merlots and sits beside her on the sofa.

"Mmm," Azucena sighs, throwing her head back. "Just what I need."

Duncan offers a toast. "*Bienvenida a Canadá.*" They click glasses.

* * *

Tomás' first day in Canada starts early. He's as eager as a spring stallion to check out his new environs. He rises with the sun and wanders around the townhouse. His curiosity is attracted to the photographs hanging on the walls; images from Duncan's past work, most notably from Nicaragua. For Tomás it is like being treated to a history lesson of his own life. The photo of his birth with the ruined cathedral in the background is particularly moving.

When he realizes that his mother and Duncan are still sleeping, he returns to his bedroom where he's surrounded by remnants of Duncan's photo projects, some still in progress. The light table reveals colour images from *Paraíso*, a mystical place his mother has often talked to him about and has promised to visit with him someday.

Scanning the small rectangles of brilliant colours on the light table, Tomás stops to examine several images of his mother, personal images not intended for the 14-year-old Tomás' eyes.

Sounds of movement from out in the hallway and downstairs in the kitchen cause Tomás to switch the light table off quickly.

"Tomás, are you awake?" Azucena's voice calls. "Get dressed. We're going out for breakfast."

They drive to a local pancake house where Duncan knows they use only authentic Canadian maple syrup. The walls are adorned with sports photos of the Toronto Maple Leafs and the Blue Jays, a subtle reminder to Duncan to buy the tickets he promised Tomás.

"We won't do this every day," Duncan warns. "It's just because we don't have any fresh food at the townhouse and I wanted you to taste one of Canada's treasures, genuine maple syrup. We'll shop for groceries after we eat."

Es muy dulce, " Azucena says to Tomás, licking the excess syrup from her lips.

Es magnífico, "he responds, pouring more of the sweet elixir over a mound of buttered pancakes.

A pass through St. Lawrence Market, a quick visit to the local supermarket, and a stroll through the liquor store prepares the trio for the next week.

"So much food," Tomás observes in the supermarket. He waves his arms in a circle. "All the shelves are full of food. I can't believe there's so much."

Duncan grins. "Not all of it is good for you."

"At least you have a choice," Tomás replies. At home, in Nicaragua, we may have to buy sardines because it's the only food on the shelves that week."

"Now you know that's not true, Tomás," Azucena scolds. "You're exaggerating things."

Azucena and Duncan prepare a dinner combining Canadian and Latin American fare while Tomás blitzes through the TV channels with the remote in the den, eventually settling on the highlights of a Yankees game from two weeks prior.

During dinner, Tomás accidentally mentions what he discovered from the images on Duncan's light table.

"You're even more beautiful than I imagined, Mamá."

Duncan adds, "Yeah. Your mother is very beautiful."

"Thank you both," Azucena says, "but that's an odd thing for you to say, Tomás. What brought that on?"

Tomás hesitates. "Um … I saw some photos of you upstairs, on Duncan's light table. They're from *Paraíso* I think."

"Oh shit." Duncan pounds his forehead with the palm of his hand. "I left the *Paraíso* slides out. They're not for you to see, Tomás." He turns to Azucena. "I'll put them away right after dinner, I promise."

Azucena runs upstairs to see what images Tomás saw. When she returns to the table, she discounts the fuss.

"There's nothing wrong with the photos. They're beautiful and I'm not ashamed. Tomás is right, I am beautiful in those photos. They were obviously taken through Duncan's eyes … with love." She passes her hand over Duncan's.

After dinner, Duncan stores the photos in boxes and reorganizes the room. Azucena and Tomás wash and dry the dishes.

Tomás returns to the den to watch TV. Duncan joins Azucena on the sofa.

Looking upward from the sofa, Azucena is impressed that Duncan hung her painting in such a prominent location, however, the image saddens her as it foreshadowed the tragic destruction of her beloved paradise, *el Paraíso de los Redespiertos*.

Azucena rests her head against Duncan's shoulder. "I must confess to you, Duncan," she reveals, a shade of pink tinting her cheeks. "It was there, in beautiful *Paraíso* where I first experienced the pangs of desire for you."

Duncan kisses her forehead.

She continues. "There was an uneasiness in the pit of my stomach that told me I wanted to be closer to you." She shakes her head, smiling. "Of course, my mind argued that the times were wrong. I was committed to the revolution, to the safety of my *compañeros*, and of course to Tomás who was so young at the time. There was danger lurking everywhere at that time, not a time for falling in love. My body wanted you, but my commitments told me no. But finally, we shared our love in such an intimate way, didn't we? Through connecting our inner spirit and our bodies."

Duncan agrees. "During our meditation when we held hands, I felt your soul vibrating in synch with mine, our hearts pounding a rhythm, like how the pulsing of drums build up a primal need to dance, to perform naturally, as if to complete a circle of life."

"That's very poetic, my dear Duncan. Are you certain that you're not really a Nicaraguan? All *nicaragüenses* are aspiring poets." Azucena clasps Duncan's hand, wanting to relive the experience from the island. "When I gave you the painting, I wanted you to have it as a reminder of that wonderful experience we shared," she says, pausing to peck an exploratory kiss on his neck.

"If you look closely," Azucena explains, as she points toward the painting, you will see that we are both there, in the painting. We are the two figures making love under the flames. It saddens me to see this painting again, because of what happened after we left, but I am so happy that we were able to consummate our love for each other. So much time passed by between when we were in the garden, to when we were finally alone under the stars in Costa Rica."

Duncan pulls Azucena close. "I wanted you close to me during the march to the capital but …"

"… but then you were shot." Azucena completes his sentence. "I was so afraid when I saw you laying on the ground with blood on your shirt. I thought I had lost you forever."

"But we're still here," Duncan returns to the present.

Azucena continues reminiscing. "I knew you would leave me after the triumph. I couldn't let you go without proving my love to you. That's why I wanted you the way I did, why I stayed the night with you at the hotel. I needed to know that you felt the same. It's why I told you that you would return, as if I could predict it. Sometimes, if you say something out loud, it becomes true."

"My grandfather used to tell me that, although he said it in French." Duncan recalls. "Of course, he also said things OUT LOUD that never happened."

Azucena laughs, poking Duncan before she continues. "Contrary to what some people believe, I don't possess the power to predict the future; I only paint what I see in my dreams. Some other force is predicting the future, maybe it's Mamá," she shrugs casually, unsure of what to believe. I prayed you would understand how much I wanted you with me."

"Oh, believe me, I understand, and I want to spend more time with you. You are always in my thoughts and my dreams, my precious Azucena." He strokes the back of his hand gently across the soft skin of Azucena's face.

Elated to hear that Duncan shares her feelings, Azucena nestles closer, settling against his chest. She raises her head and kisses him again on the neck, on the cheek, and finally a prolonged soft kiss on the lips, teasing Duncan with the tip of her tongue.

Duncan passes his fingers through Azucena's long dark hair, draws her head against him, and allows her wisps of hair to tickle the side of his cheek.

Azucena continues. "In the years following the triumph, we were all so busy and preoccupied with reorganizing the country." She pauses to contemplate her hand as it explores Duncan's chest.

"Suddenly, one night," she recalls, "I was sitting alone. Tomás had gone to bed. The pang in my stomach returned. It became unbearable. My thoughts wandered back to *Paraíso* and to your face and your lips. I could even taste the perspiration on your skin. I wanted you. I wanted you to be with me. I wanted to know you inside me again. The feeling was so intense."

"We're here, together now, and we're almost alone." Duncan whispers, following his words with kisses to her earlobe. "After all this time, we're together again."

"I had no idea what became of you. You didn't return as I prayed you would. That's when I wrote you the letter. I became bold about it. I didn't even care if you were married with children of your own. I was greedy. I wrote how I felt without it appearing like I was begging."

Azucena pulls back from Duncan and stares directly into his eyes. "But I *was* begging, wasn't I?" Can you understand how much I was missing you, my dearest Duncan? I was begging for you ... begging for love. I was begging for *your* love."

Duncan caresses her, shamelessly exploring her body, loosening clothing, feeling the warmth of her skin.

"You don't have to beg for me," Duncan tells her. "I do understand, my beautiful Azucena. I too, felt those same pangs. We now have what we both wanted ... to be together."

Azucena settles back. "Before I sent you the letter, I kept it for a week to make sure I was doing the right thing. I even edited the letter several times so it wouldn't offend you or your wife, if such a person existed. Finally, in a weak moment, when the pang was heavy and no longer bearable, I mailed the letter to you. When you arrived unannounced at my office, I had a renewed hope in destiny. I also realized that it might be my last opportunity to reveal my deepest emotions to you."

Duncan is filled with desire. His body is eager to make love to Azucena.

She asks, "How did you feel at *Paraíso*, Duncan? Aside from us making love, how did you feel about me, more importantly, about *us*?"

Duncan gazes back up at the painting, his desire placed on hold.

"It was at *Paraíso* where my feelings for you materialized. At the time, they bunched up inside of me and were confusing ..." Duncan pauses to stroke Azucena's arm. His eyes follow his hand as his fingers explore further.

Azucena's eyes scan Duncan until their eyes fix on each other's.

"It wasn't until later, looking at your painting every day and night that I realized how much I missed you." Duncan tells her, sending subtle messages to her through his probing fingers while he stares into her brown eyes. "I couldn't erase you from my thoughts," he adds. "That's when I knew that I'd fallen in love with you."

Azucena stares back. She responds to Duncan's amorous advances in kind. "Duncan, do you have any idea how many times I have painted you into my work?" she whispers. "There are so many."

"That's enough talking for tonight, my dear," Duncan whispers back. "It's time to create another painting together." Duncan starts to lift Azucena from the sofa to carry her upstairs to his bed.

"Wait, Duncan. What about Tomás?"

They find Tomás asleep in front of the TV. Highlights from a table tennis match are in progress.

"Tomás," Azucena whispers. "Go to bed. It's late."

Tomás straggles up the stairs to his room with help from Duncan. Azucena and Duncan kiss him goodnight.

After waiting to be sure that Tomás is settled, Azucena's fingers grope with the buttons on Duncan's shirt. They toy playfully with the hairs on his chest before roaming further.

Duncan's breathing intensifies. His lips explore the contours of Azucena's torso.

* * *

Azucena is in awe with her visit to Niagara Falls, although the circus of commercialism surrounding it upsets her. "Do couples actually come from around the world to have their honeymoons here?" she asks.

"Believe it or not," Duncan tells her with a grin, before leading her and Tomás into the Ripley Museum of the weird and bizarre.

"Can you imagine what we could accomplish in Nicaragua with the dollars spent here in only one single day?" Azucena reflects.

"Nicaragua would be debt-free," Duncan responds.

Tomás is excited about leaning over the edge of the Falls and the stories of the people who have tumbled over, whether by accident or for adventure.

Algonquin Park is more to their liking, particularly hearing nature's voices from their tents at night. Tomás has his own pup tent that Duncan picked up for him at Canadian Tire. His mother and Duncan share Duncan's two-person hiker's tent where they zip their sleeping bags together as one and share their warmth.

Azucena reflects, "This reminds me of my earliest days with the FSLN, when we were in the mountains, hiding from the military. Of course we didn't have tents; we just slept openly in the forest, disguised by leaves and branches. The natural sounds helped to disguise our movements, because we were only able to change locations in the darkness of night. Sometimes we passed within meters of the *guardia's* camp without them knowing."

Duncan jokes, "Well, right now, the denizens of the forest, the moose, foxes, bears, and raccoons, are sneaking around our tent in the dark, hoping we don't see or hear them."

During the daytime, Duncan leads them on a hike. He lends Tomás his second camera and offers some basic photo-taking hints to get him started.

While Duncan enjoys this quality time with Tomás, it also reminds him that there is a son somewhere, who isn't with him. 'I wonder what he's doing, the boy I've never met. Hopefully he's safe with a caring family.'

From Algonquin Park they drive northwest, through the mining city of Sudbury, stopping to visit the 'Big Nickel' before turning south through Espanola and La Cloche mountains. They stop to climb Dreamer's Rock, where they share their thoughts with the ancient spirits of young Indigenous men who sat, fasted, and waited for days to receive their names from the Great Spirit.

"Duncan?" Tomás asks, peering down from the cliff. "What would my name be if I was an Indigenous boy?"

Azucena reminds Tomás that a small part of him is Indigenous.

Duncan suggests he be named, *'Terramoto'* (earthquake).

They enter Manitoulin Island from the bridge at Little Current and continue to the village of Wikwemkoong. Duncan stops at the cemetery overlooking the village, where he places tobacco on the graves of the elders, to honour those who entrusted him with their knowledge and wisdom. The village population is swelled with thousands of visitors for the annual Powwow. Indigenous people of tribes from across the continent arrive to experience the magic of their own island of creation.

The dancers respond to the drumming, the heartbeat of Mother Earth, in spiritual recognition of her gifts. Most of the dances are either competitive or sacred, and specific to Indigenous dancers. Occasionally, the announcer invites visitors to join the circle. Azucena, Tomás, and Duncan take advantage of the opportunity to join the circle, stepping as lightly as possible in respect for Mother Earth.

For dinner, they explore the variety of traditional foods available from the booths of Indigenous vendors surrounding the park. They finally agree on bowls of corn soup and fried bread. After eating, they purchase double scoop ice cream cones and walk through the village as tourists.

Duncan introduces Azucena and Tomás to his friend, the Chief, who immediately recognizes Azucena's Indigenous features and shares experiences about natural medicines with her. They also compare stories they were told as children, like the stories about creation; the similarities are uncanny.

For Azucena there is a comfort seeing so many people like herself, and so similar to the Indigenous people from Masaya, celebrating their culture and heritage. For Duncan, it is a journey of reminiscence, to hear the pulse of the drums once again and to share the experience with Azucena and Tomás.

* * *

Back in Toronto, Duncan exposes them to the cultural and culinary diversity of Toronto, moving from one ethnic district to another.

With further explorations of St. Lawrence Market, Azucena is elated to discover foods that she's familiar with from Central America. Traditional fare like *gallo pinto* (rice, beans, and chicken) are common, but she and Duncan both agree on their love of paella, more of a Spanish dish than Latino. She organizes the menus and they share in the preparation.

"I wanted to cook iguana for you, Duncan, but I couldn't find any at the market," Azucena says. "In Nicaragua, as you know, live iguanas hang from market stalls waiting to be taken home, cooked, and eaten. They are a delicacy."

"Thank God, that custom hasn't travelled north," Duncan answers with praying hands.

Duncan's menus are more conventional, preferring slow-cooked chili or roast beef, with chick pea or leaf lettuce salads.

For either, fruits are always included, although it is frustrating for Azucena who is accustomed to having a large variety of tropical fruits to choose from.

During the first week they're in Toronto, Duncan takes Azucena and Tomás on a tour around the college where he works, and he shows them the displays of student projects on the walls.

"How did they do that?" Tomás enquires about a technique he sees in one of the photos.

"It's called a shallow depth-of-field," Duncan explains. "The main subject is sharp and the background remains out of focus. It's a device we use to place more importance on the main subject. The viewer's eye is always drawn to the sharpest point in the photograph. You can also see it used in many of my own images."

"Yeah, but how can I get that effect?" Tomás probes.

"The easiest way is to use the widest aperture in the lens," Duncan instructs. He demonstrates the technique to Tomás with his own camera. "There is more to it that I can show you later at home."

Tomás resets the aperture on the camera he borrowed from Duncan.

Azucena is impressed with the students' work and asks Duncan if there is a Fine Arts program.

"Absolutely. Come, I'll take you there."

Fortunately, the chair of the department is in her office. Duncan introduces Azucena and Tomás to Joyce Banerji.

Joyce and Azucena discuss trends and the passions of art, while Duncan visits the Dean's office to discuss his faculty loadings and timetables for the fall semester. He also submits his application for a year-long sabbatical commencing the following year. When he returns, Azucena is projecting slides of their work on the screen to show Joyce.

"This is magnificent work, both of you." Joyce pauses before continuing. "Azucena, how long are you staying in Toronto?"

"Until November, I think." Azucena looks at Duncan for confirmation.

He nods.

"Wonderful," Joyce says and looks toward Azucena. "Would you be interested in becoming an artist-in-residence here in Fine Arts for the next few months? I'm sure I could arrange it with the Dean if you're interested. Of course you will be well remunerated."

Azucena thinks about it, turning her eyes toward Duncan for any signs. His eyes confirm positively.

"It would be fantastic if it could be arranged," Azucena confirms. "Of course, I will have to contact my superiors in Nicaragua first, but I'm sure there will be no problem."

"Wonderful," Joyce says, extending her hand to Azucena. "I will confirm it with you right after the holiday weekend."

As they leave the campus, Duncan raises his hand to Tomás.

"Check these out, Tomás." Duncan shows him three tickets to a Blue Jays game on the 16th. "The Dean gave them to me; all I did was ask. They're playing the Tigers."

"Awesome," Tomás leaps in circles.

On the Labour Day weekend before Duncan starts classes, he takes Azucena and Tomás to the Canadian National Exhibition (CNE).

"There you are, Azucena," Duncan points. "The Mounties' musical ride."

Azucena's face comes alive with glee. "They do ride horses and wear red uniforms, just like in the movies."

After checking out the food building, an equestrian event, and the marching bands, they head to the midway where Duncan challenges his guests to a rifle shooting contest. Azucena wins herself a huge stuffed animal.

"Let's go on the roller coaster," Tomás challenges.

"Not a chance," Duncan resists, pulling Tomás in the opposite direction. "I'm a chicken-shit at heart."

Instead, they experience several moderately exciting rides, nothing that causes them to up-chuck their dinner. Most of the entertainment is earned by strolling through the crowds and watching the people.

Duncan, always with his camera around his neck, enjoys taking candid photos of people stuffing their mustard- and relish-coated faces with everything from hot dogs to candy floss.

Tomás tries his hand at taking photos, imitating Duncan.

"Use the same technique as I showed you at the college," Duncan says, showing Tomás the dial. Use the widest aperture you can. Same technique, different reason."

When classes resume, Joyce invites Azucena to sit in with one of her freshman studio classes and, after a few weeks, to deliver a lecture on the subject of 'painting from dreams' to the advanced students.

"Bring your slides to show the students. They'll eat them up," Joyce tells her.

"What do you mean?" Azucena asks with a quizzical expression. "Why would they eat my slides?"

"It's just a saying," Joyce clarifies, chuckling. "It means that they'll love them."

Duncan informally arranges for Tomás to audit his classes in the photojournalism program. When one of Duncan's students advertises to sell her camera so she can upgrade to an advanced system, Duncan secretly buys it for Tomás.

During a day off from classes, Duncan escorts Azucena and Tomás on an orientation walk along Queen and Yonge Streets, pointing out areas they might want to avoid in the process and recommending some excellent stores and cafés. He arranges visits for them at the Royal Ontario Museum (ROM) and the Art Gallery of Ontario (AGO), where an exhibition of Indigenous art is showing.

A block away, Azucena quickly orients herself to the sounds and diverse aromas of St. Lawrence Market. Duncan then explains how she can access Harbourfront if she chooses to while she's on her own.

On Saturday morning, Tomás awakens early, his heart beating with anxiety. Duncan is taking him and his mother to see *los azulejos* (the Toronto Blue Jays) play the Detroit Tigers at Exhibition Park. He arrives at the breakfast table wearing a Blue Jays cap his mother bought for him at the Eaton Centre. Azucena and Duncan wear matching caps.

Their seats along the first-base line offer excellent visibility. Duncan purchases a program and shows Tomás how to follow the game by filling in the box scores, play-by-play. They order three hot dogs, two Labatt's Blue, and a large Coke.

Tomás gives his all to the cheering and joins the wave as it passes through. By the seventh-inning stretch, his voice has disappeared. The Blue Jays take the home game 6 to 4.

After the game, Duncan announces. "Now for the big finale, Tomás. Through my media connections, I was able to get us access into the dressing room to meet the players. Your mother may want to stay outside, unless she wants to see a bunch of sweaty, smelly, naked jocks."

"Ugh!" Azucena grimaces. "I think I'll pass. I'll wait out here for you."

Tomás and Duncan follow the media crews into the dressing room. They meet George Bell and Tom Henke, who sign Tomás' program.

* * *

Duncan empties space in an upstairs room for Azucena to use as a temporary studio. Rolling around in the back of Duncan's mind is the possibility that Azucena may, in time, consider moving to Toronto. He tries to balance that consideration against the alternative of moving to Nicaragua himself.

One Thursday after classes, Duncan finds Azucena staring at slides on the light table. He watches her quietly for a moment, but she soon senses his presence. Looking up at him, she asks, "Which ones do you think I should show for my lecture, Duncan? I can't make up my mind."

After offering his suggestions, she vetoes most of them.

"Why did you ask me if you don't like my choices?"

"I just wanted to find out if we agreed on everything. Thank God we don't," she answers. "That would be so boring, don't you think?"

"That's a Catch-22 if I ever heard one. If I agree with your statement, I will be too boring. If I disagree with it, I run the risk of being antagonistic. I can't win that one."

"Nobody wins," Azucena says. "It's not a competition."

"Speaking of competitions, how do you feel about artistic competitiveness?" Duncan asks. "You know the kind of thing I'm referring to, competitions where prizes are awarded for the 'best' painting, or the 'best' photograph, that kind of thing."

"I hate them," Azucena responds without delay. "There are no bests, no firsts, no seconds, no thirds. There is no place in the arts for that kind of thinking. It's not a horse race."

"I agree with you wholeheartedly, my dear."

"Of course, on the other hand ..." Azucena teases.

"There is no other hand," Duncan answers firmly.

"I know. I was just trying to be funny."

Azucena cuddles up to him. "I love being with you, Duncan."

* * *

Azucena's lecture goes exceedingly well. The students listen attentively and have many follow-up questions about where her visions come from, and she's very tactful in explaining how she receives them from her mother's dreams.

When Azucena mentions that her mother died in 1972, and that she still receives dreams from her, there are the expected comments from sceptics, but one voice expresses her acknowledgement with, "Wow! My mother sends me messages in my dreams at night too."

There is, of course, snickering when Duncan's bare ass appears in one of her portraits. One brave student asks Azucena how it works to be collaborating with her lover, citing her own failed attempt to work alongside her boyfriend.

Azucena answers with a question. "Was it the work of art that failed, or just your relationship? Sometimes a breakup can be the catalyst for exciting new directions in your art."

"It wasn't for him but it was for me," the student answers with a chortle.

* * *

Finally, on a crisp November morning, Azucena's and Tomás' visit comes to an end. Duncan drives them to the airport, where they spend an hour in the lounge before they must pass through customs.

"I'll miss you, Duncan," Azucena says with a saddened voice. "You have made me so happy, happier than I have been since my childhood." Tears erupt from both of them. "I also want to thank you for what you have done with Tomás. He loves you; you know that don't you?" She places her hands against Duncan's dampened cheeks and stares into his eyes, crying. "You're the father he never had."

Duncan consoles her and makes promises that he doesn't know whether he can keep. "I've made it official. My application for a one-year sabbatical has been submitted. I should know within a few months whether it's been accepted. If so, I will spend an entire year with you and Tomás in Nicaragua."

She counters, "It would be better if we could spend a lifetime, at least whatever life we have left."

Tomás approaches Duncan with tears. He embraces the man who has accepted him as a son. "Thank you, Duncan, for everything. I love you, man."

Duncan pulls Tomás tighter. "I will see you soon, son. I promise." Duncan hesitates, pulling a package from his gadget bag. "This is for you, Tomás."

"You're kidding me, right?" Tomás reacts to the Nikkormat camera he holds in his hands. "My own?" he questions to make sure.

"It's only a second-hand camera, but it'll get you started. That's how I started."

Duncan hands Tomás another package. "You'll need some film as well. I know how difficult it is to buy film in Nicaragua these days. I look forward to seeing what you can do with it when I visit again next summer."

Tomás gives Duncan another hug. "*Muchas Gracias*, Duncan. *Hasta la próxima.*"

They share high-fives.

Azucena's face is coated in tears as she witnesses the closeness that has developed between Duncan and Tomás. "Thank you, Duncan. How can I ever thank you enough?"

"I will join you in June. In the meantime, talk to me often. Call me collect, I know how erratic the phones are in Nicaragua. Write me many letters. You write so beautifully, and your letters always make me miss you more, which is what I want, to miss you more each day." Duncan's voice breaks. "Send me photos of you and Tomás, and your new work, of course."

"My work won't have the same passion as when we work together. I will miss those times most of all."

As it is with their collaborations in art, their emotions in life often coincide. At this sad departure, they simultaneously succumb to uninhibited crying. Tears abound with no attempt to wipe them away.

"I love you, Duncan," Azucena declares aloud. "We must be together, soon."

Duncan folds his arms around Azucena and pulls Tomás into the embrace.

"I promise," he affirms. "I love you both, more than anything else in the world."

Suddenly, they stop searching for the right words and stare, blankly and speechless into each other's eyes. There are no words to replace face-to-face silence. Their embraces continue until they hear the dreaded announcement.

"Last call for boarding the flight to San José, Costa Rica." Lacking any direct flights, Azucena and Tomás must make a connection there for the final leg with Aero Nica to Managua.

Azucena turns away, and Duncan watches her leave.

She doesn't turn to look back; it would be too painful. Tomás takes one final glance toward Duncan and waves.

Duncan waves back and watches each step they take, further away from him, until they disappear through the gate altogether. Though they have already left his sight, Duncan continues to stare at the empty space before him.

He spends the entire night sitting and drinking, gazing at the abstracted lovers in Azucena's painting from their treasured *Paraíso*.

PART EIGHT
1988

CHAPTER 20

SABBATICAL

Managua, Nicaragua, 1988:

'Azucena was right,' Duncan recalls, 'I could get to like it here in Nicaragua.'

With his application for a one-year sabbatical approved, Duncan is committed by contract to plant the seeds for a photojournalism program at the university, document post-revolution Nicaragua, and prepare a report on arts education, with a possible book when he finishes.

Of course, Azucena is happy. They are together again, and she has survived the winter without further threats to her life, reinforcing her claims that they were merely the rantings of some harmless political rival.

Tomás, now 15, is ecstatic to have Duncan around. He knows that Duncan isn't his father but accepts him as the ideal surrogate. Before Duncan unpacks his luggage, Tomás is showing him some of the photos he had taken during the winter. Tomás, being a typical artistic Nicaraguan, has also started to express himself through poetry and song writing, which he performs for Duncan, accompanying himself on the guitar.

A small office and darkroom is secured for Duncan to use at the university, situated adjacent to Azucena's art studio. Duncan will be employing photography to document his research and will be writing stories to accompany his reports. In case any news breaks out while he's in Nicaragua, he renewed his connections with former magazine clients.

'Of course there'll be news; there's always news.' Finally, Duncan feels his creative desires emerging once again.

During the quiet of the evenings, Azucena, Duncan, and Tomás gather as a family to share ideas about art and life. Sometimes Tomás performs his latest poem or song but, when Duncan and Azucena become cuddly, or when they begin philosophizing, Tomás retreats to his room or gathers with friends in the barrio, leaving Azucena and Duncan alone.

The only available television channel is Sandinista TV. In the evenings it entertains its viewers with soap operas from Brazil or Mexico, unless there is an important message to be delivered by the president.

Azucena and Duncan prefer to curl up together on the sofa discussing life and art.

"When I started to paint as a young girl," Azucena reflects, "my first examples were naïve, unpolished, childish."

"Of course they were," Duncan injects. "You were just a child."

"Of course," Azucena agrees, laughing. "However, my goal was always to paint reality, with sharp lines and fine detail. I would take the dreams my mother passed on to me while she was still alive and attempt to accurately copy them. I became very good at it." She smiles with pride, placing an imaginary star on her chest.

"That's what people started to see in my paintings, and what they appreciated. It wasn't the art of it, nor my imagination. Instead, it was the accuracy of the painting and how closely it resembled real life. I always attempted to paint like a photograph."

"Why would you want that?" Duncan challenges. "A painting should be a painting, not a photograph."

"I appreciate that now," Azucena acknowledges, "but then it was all about achieving perfection and pleasing people. It wasn't until I visited *Paraíso* that my vision began to change. You witnessed that shift, Duncan, as I learned to bend reality into more of a child's out-look, a flat distorted perspective with awkward people interacting out of scale with each other, combined with a crude abstraction of the landscape, sweeping gashes of brazen colour with disregard for balance. I started to see things as a child once again. I passed from adulthood to childhood while I was there, as if my life was beginning all over again. What a revelation that was. At the age of 23, I was being born all over again, not in a fundamental religious way, but in a spiritually-free, emotional, and full-of-curiosity way."

"God, was that really 11 years ago?" Duncan asks, smacking his forehead with his hand. "I'm still learning how to approach my art like a child, and I'm already 40."

"You might be older than me, but you're very young at heart." Azucena smiles and strokes Duncan's arm.

"My dear Azucena. I love it when you tell me something import-ant, or when you discover an epiphany that you must share with me. Your eyes open wide and they stare intently with excitement."

"I am excited, Azucena agrees before continuing. "It's all about curiosity. Curiosity drives children, that's how we learn. The problem is that we also have a need to be taken seriously. So, we accommodate the power structures around us: our parents, priests, teachers, police, and we strive to please them all. When we do, we're rewarded, with grades, with food, with applause, with the promise of eternal salva-tion, all for obeying a set of rules. We're told to paint and live within the lines, but in doing so, we sacrifice our liberty, our freedom to believe in magic and to accept the unknown as real."

"You make it sound so Pavlovian," Duncan responds with a grin.

"It is. One day I was helping Tomás paint some animals, and I gave him a brush daubed in bright magenta paint. He loved it … until he showed it to his teacher. The teacher scolded him, saying, "Cows aren't pink or purple. This is wrong." Tomás tore the painting up and scolded me when he returned home."

Duncan laughs. "It's strange that you should tell me that. When I was a young child in school, the teacher told us to paint a scene from the Bible. I chose to paint the Red Sea. I took some red fingerpaint and covered the entire paper with red. The teacher wrote that I had a wild imagination. I always wondered. What's so wild about that? Why else would they call it the Red Sea? In retrospect, I was being much too literal."

"Too literal, yes," Azucena nods in agreement. She raises her forefinger, "But, you were being a normal child. You were striving for approval, like I was, and it was driving you toward literal interpretations and perfection."

"Exactly," Duncan responds, raising his finger. "Another time, during one of my earliest music lessons, I sat at the piano and smacked away at random keys. My teacher asked me what I was doing, and I told her that I was composing music, just like Mozart. She reacted by shouting, 'You cannot be a composer until you can play the piano. Only then will you know the rules.' She told me that my music had to sound like Mozart would want it to sound." Duncan pauses. "Now I ask you, who in hell, centuries later, knows exactly what Mozart wanted it to sound like, as if we all had access to his mind?"

"Or who really knows what was going on in Van Gogh's mind?"

"Did he even know?" Duncan jokes.

"He certainly knew how to paint, and in his own way. That's the true beauty of him."

Duncan recalls, "When I became a professional musician, and later a photographer, I had been taught so many rules that I was obsessed about detail and everything being in the right place." He shakes his head with disappointment. "Practice makes perfect, right? As I grew,

I followed the logical theories and technical etudes to make my playing sound like my teacher and others expected; in other words, what Mozart wanted. The teachers could only accept one prescribed way, because they went through the same rigorous rules and exercises their own teachers taught them."

Azucena reflects. "I was fortunate that way. Until I attended art school in my late teens, I had no teachers. Mamá was my only guide and she never told me how to paint. How could she? She didn't know how to paint. She was my mentor though, and she was also my inspiration. She still is." Azucena's face displays a sudden sadness that quickly reverts to a smile. "Until you came into my life, Duncan. You are my inspiration now."

"Wow," Duncan blushes. "None of my students have told me that."

"Not yet, they haven't." Azucena chuckles and adds, "One day you will become a legend, Duncan. Just wait and see."

"Speaking of legends, Miles Davis doesn't tell his musicians what to play," Duncan says. "His real talent is in choosing musicians who are willing to play how they feel, how they blend as a group, and to experiment in directions they haven't gone before. From that raw material, came the finest jazz that money can buy, and it reshaped all the jazz that was yet to come."

"That's what I appreciate about jazz, Duncan." Azucena says, nodding her head in agreement. "I'm not a musician but I love that the music is always fresh and alive."

Duncan embraces Azucena, appreciative of her true understanding of one of his passions. Kissing the top of her head, as she lays against his chest, he continues, "When I was travelling through the U.S., I came across a book of photographs by Robert Frank, called, 'The Americans.' At first glance I thought, 'What a piece of shit this is. Some of the photos are out of focus, the compositions appear random and disorganized like snapshots my grandmother would take.' I noticed that Jack Kerouac had written the introduction, so I decided to read 'On the Road.' It was then that the photos came alive to me. They were both telling the story about America, and it was the same rough and raw America that I was experiencing, not the America seen on calendars and advertisements. I decided that I wanted to photograph that way. I discovered that it isn't easy to shoot photos like that. My mind's eye, so accustomed to organizing the frame before pushing the shutter, and my deeply engrained fanaticism to fine tune the exposures to perfection, kept me and Mr. Frank far apart."

Azucena laughs, her eyes wide. "How far apart were you from Mr. Frank?"

"That far." Duncan spreads his arms to the extreme before continuing.

"Ha, ha," Azucena breaks up. She rubs her hand along Duncan's knee. "You're so funny sometimes, Duncan."

"It wasn't until later, when the colour films from *Paraíso* were processed, that I realized that I had freed myself from the rigidity of perfection. You, Azucena, were a large part of that epiphany. When you changed the way you approached your work, I followed your example, and I responded to your renewed spirit and energy."

Azucena raises her forefinger to correct Duncan. "It wasn't so much my spirit but the mysterious spirit of the place that changed us. *Paraíso* is magical. At the time, and the timing was ripe, we were allowed to share the 'epiphany,' as you call it. It also allowed us to share something even more special, our love." She plays with Duncan's fingers.

"While there," Duncan continues, "I adopted a laissez-faire attitude that enabled me to explore fresh ways of seeing. Notice that I said 'fresh ways' as plural because there is no one way to see. It opened up my eyes, but mainly my mind. I became free, not to copy another photographer, but to create my own vision. That is freedom. That is creative honesty, or 'integrity' as I prefer to call it, because it's not created for external purposes like commercialism or god forbid, those infernal competition prizes."

"Ugh!" Azucena reacts. "That's a whole other issue. Let's not go there right now."

"I know," Duncan says, caressing her back and pulling her closer. "I've talked enough for one night, maybe for a lifetime."

Before kissing Duncan, Azucena pulls back to inject another observation.

"Some paintings are like photographs and vice versa. It shouldn't matter what medium they are. If they are art it's not important," she hesitates, tapping her finger against Duncan's chest for emphasis. "In fact, regardless if they are paintings or photographs, they are also jazz and dance; selected slices of time that speak out as representative of weeks, months or years. Art is timeless."

"Yes, I agree, Azucena," Duncan's eyes light up. "But," and this is important. "All creative actions occur only in the present tense, whether it's a musical composition, a painting, a theatre performance, whatever."

"What about tapes and movies?" she asks. "Are they also limited to the present tense?"

"Tapes and movies only represent the presentation and consumption of the art. The creative force occurs when the work is made. A live theatre performance or dance, however, is active. The art of its creation is still in progress."

Azucena hesitates, cuddling closer to Duncan before continuing. "I believe that there are no differences between photos and paintings, between films and poetry or prose, or music, philosophy, or dance. These all amount to the same thing. They are expressions, thoughts and concepts passing between our senses and driven by our heart. The choice of a medium is of no consequence. It shouldn't matter which medium you use. Art lives within the soul and the soul encompasses everything. That's where it belongs."

Duncan agrees with her assessment, but adds jokingly, "So, if that is true, why do we hang pictures on the walls and rent studio space? Wouldn't it be more efficient, and definitely cheaper, to exchange these wonderful images, thoughts, and emotions between our souls and save money?"

Azucena punches Duncan on the shoulder, following it with a kiss. "Now you are being impractical, Duncan."

* * *

"One ... Two ... Uh, Uh, Uh, Uh." With fingers snapping on the off-beats, Duncan counts the musicians in for a grooving blues while Pablo takes the first chorus. The Bistro Gallery offers Duncan an opportunity to play jazz alongside his friend Pablo and a quartet two nights a week.

Opening night at The Bistro Gallery with Pablo turns out to be more successful than Duncan had originally imagined. The café fills beyond capacity even before the band starts to play. Duncan is gobsmacked. He tells Pablo, "I never experienced full houses like this back in Canada. This is amazing."

Pablo suggests, jokingly. "Maybe we're the only game in town tonight."

The band members agree to play only music they feel strongly about. Much of the music is based upon original compositions and exploratory free music with minimal structure. The audience loves the freshness, but Duncan believes it's because the music is 'honest.'

He explains his concept to Pablo. "We're not doing this for the money, right?"

"Speak for yourself, *gringo*," Pablo jokes.

"Point taken, Pablo, but we're really doing it for the satisfaction." Duncan places his hand over his heart. "For the love of it. Every note we play is an exploration for us, driven by our curiosity; we never know where it will take us next."

"Does the audience get what we're trying to do?" Pablo challenges, loosening his fingers by fluttering them against the valves on his horn.

"The audience understands our sincerity, Pablo, and they appreciate the fact that we're taking risks, we're enjoying ourselves, and we're not selling out to them. Nothing here is predictable. There's a surprise for them every time we play, and we're just as surprised as they are. Remember, they are going through the same angst as we went through. They question why and how they became pigeonholed into clones. We give them an opportunity to escape that, if only for a few hours. If they want predictable music that sounds like the radio, they should just turn on the radio."

"*Vaminos!*" Pablo calls to the musicians. "Let's get to work."

The band surges into an energetic blues that none of them have performed together before, but the energy and the collected simpatico of the musicians delivers a solid opener. A loud applause invites the band to continue. They follow up with a ballad featuring Pablo's expressive trumpet virtuosity.

Most of the crowd stays with them throughout the evening until the final tune, a medley of Miles Davis' classics that receive a rousing standing ovation.

CHAPTER 21

TOMÁS

Nicaragua, 1988:

"I am sick and tired of this revolution," Tomás yells at his mother. "It's going nowhere. The entire country is broke. The revolution, the war, the embargo, I just want it all to end. Where are the promises?"

Duncan hears Tomás and Azucena arguing in the kitchen. He goes to check what's going on.

Azucena is livid. Tomás, her only son, dares to question his mother's most precious values. She seethes in retaliation. "You have no idea how we fought for our independence. Do you even know how many people have died for what we have?"

Tomás counters without thought. "People died for this?" he asks, "For THIS?" Tomás waves his arms in an arc to emphasize. "Do you, Mamá, have any idea how many people are dying right now, as we speak, for THIS?"

Azucena turns her head away in disgust. Before she can compose herself, Tomás releases another barrage, waving his arms about like a madman. "We have nothing to buy in our stores, the shelves are empty. And we have no money to buy anything, even if there was something to buy."

Duncan enters from the living room. "Hey! Calm down you two." He attempts to step between them, but Azucena does an end run.

Her very soul is being threatened. She attacks with the rage of a wounded cheetah, this time going for the jugular.

"That's the trouble with your generation." She points an accusing finger directly at her son's face. "It's all about money and things to buy. What about our freedom, where everybody has the right to education and health care? Even in the United States, people die because they don't have free access to health care. We, proud Nicaraguans, have fought and lost lives for that and handed it to you on a platter."

"Fuck all that bullshit. I've heard it so many times. It's becoming tiresome." Tomás fakes a yawn.

"That's it," Azucena shouts. "I don't have to put up with your inso-lence. Get out!" She points to the door. "Get out of my house. Now! Come back when you can accept what we have given you."

Tomás, surprised but angry, grabs his backpack and slams the door behind him.

Duncan attempts to console Azucena. "Let me follow him. Maybe I can talk to him."

She reacts. "He'll be back. As soon as he discovers how brutal life is out there."

* * *

Days and weeks pass. Tomás doesn't return. Azucena sinks into a crater of depression.

Duncan wanders the streets, pleading with neighbours and strangers alike. "Have you seen this boy?" He posts photos of Tomás on buildings and billboards, adding one more 'missing' poster to the multitude of others already posted. His major concern is related to the threat he was warned about in Jinotega.

He rationalizes. 'Maybe someone is getting at Azucena through

Tomás, although she's just as accessible as Tomás is. Why take the kid? Why wouldn't they just kidnap her instead? God forbid. What am I thinking?'

Duncan maintains contact with some of the international journalists whenever they're in the capital. One day, while having a beer in the Inter-Continental bar, Duncan encounters a long-time friend, Kurt, a Dutch photojournalist who has been covering the Contra war from both sides of the Nicaraguan-Honduran border. He shows Kurt a photo of Tomás.

"Did you ever see this boy in your travels?" he asks.

Kurt studies the picture of Tomás. "There is something familiar about this kid." Kurt says, pointing his forefinger at Tomás' face. "There are families who gather on the weekends at *Los Manos*. It's a small community on the Honduran border. They go there with hope in their eyes that they'll find loved ones who have gone missing during the Contra war. Some of the missing crossed the border for ideological reasons and some kids went there to avoid being drafted by the Sandinistas, only to be kidnapped and used as mules by the Contras." Kurt pauses, his face revealing signs of sympathy. "There are too many sad stories here."

"Keep the poster with you," Duncan tells Kurt. "Maybe show it around up there. Here's how you can find me." Duncan gives Kurt his address. "If you see or hear anything, please let me know. His mother is going crazy without him. Tomás is not a Contra, he's just a boy who doesn't understand what's going on, like most people these days."

Kurt folds the paper and puts it into one of the many pockets on his photo vest. "I'm returning to the border in a couple of days. I'll look out for him. If I discover anything I'll send word to you."

When Duncan returns home he tells Azucena about talking to Kurt and mentions the weekend meetings at *Los Manos*.

"We must go there," she says. "Tomás may be looking for us. Maybe he can't return. Maybe he's in trouble. Maybe …"

"Maybe he's not there either?" Duncan warns. "I don't want you to get your hopes up and then be disappointed again."

"I can't give up, I just can't."

On the weekend, Duncan rents a car at the Intercontinental and they drive the Pan-Am highway north to the border town of *Los Manos*, a four-hour drive away. There is a small glimmer of hope fuelling their expedition, but hope is all they have to hang on to.

Their arrival is met by crowds of other people and families just like them, all hoping to catch a glimpse. They carry mementos — photos, teddy bears, and they play the missing person's favourite song on portable tape players — to attract the attention of their loved ones.

Azucena and Duncan pass out posters with Tomás' photo to total strangers who are also searching for their lost sons and daughters. Their rationale is that if a parent discovers their child, that child might have seen Tomás, or may know his whereabouts.

"There are so many people here," Azucena observes. "People of all walks of life with whom we share the same suffering, the same need to know the truth."

Duncan photographs the faces of the searchers, expressive combinations of desperation and hope, all massed together. Some hold their own posters out to Duncan when he photographs them, for others to see. Busy hands finger rosary beads and raise crosses above their heads, praying that their loved ones will magically appear from behind the barricades to return home with them, to a normal family life, as if the war never happened.

Names are shouted for the missing, primarily young men and women in their teens and early 20s: "Pablito, Juanita, Hermanito, Carlita, and Tomásito," applying the diminutive names of small children, as they are still cherished and remembered as children.

Duncan remarks to Azucena about this phenomenon. "They *are* children," he demands, "the child victims of war. It's always the fucking children who are sent to fight on the front lines. Regardless of their age when war begins, the ones that return are pathetic old men when it's over; dead and insane old men who just haven't been buried yet."

Overnight, Azucena and Duncan sleep in the rental car, grabbing meals from roadside vendors. The hawkers who sell food, souvenirs, and trinkets are everywhere in Nicaragua, wherever people gather.

The weekend comes to an end. There is no Tomás. Azucena and Duncan start the long journey home, disappointed.

* * *

Each morning, Duncan brings a chair outside and drinks coffee on the doorstep of their *casita*. He hears the early traffic grind past along the interlocking-bricked Avenida, a block away.

Azucena is sleeping in late, something she's been doing often, not unusual as she doesn't get to sleep until the early hours of morning.

A man approaches Duncan on foot, declaring he's a messenger for Kurt, the photojournalist. He gives Duncan an envelope marked private. Inside there is another envelope addressed specifically to Duncan. 'Read this letter in private before sharing it. Kurt.'

Duncan thanks the runner and places some *córdobas* into his hands.

"*Gracias, señor,*" the runner bows to Duncan.

He reads the letter.

My good friend Duncan:

The boy, Tomás, was kidnapped and used as a Contra mule. It is believed that he was killed trying to escape following an altercation with one of the Contras. Apparently, someone claimed that he was the illegitimate son of Col. Jorge, the Contra leader. Tomás was heard defending the honour of his mother, whom they called a communist whore. I'm sure you will understand why I addressed this to you privately Duncan. Please also understand that this information is only what I've been told. I'm not certain of any facts in the matter. As I'm sure you will agree, there are very few facts these days.

Kurt

Kurt's news stuns Duncan. He stares at the sidewalk in disbelief. Salty tears blur his vision. He stuffs the letter into his pocket, tops up his coffee and leaves for a walk. So many things occupy his mind.

'Should I give Azucena the news? Should I show her the letter or just tell her that Tomás has died? I know what Azucena told me, but it's hard to imagine that Col. Jorge could be Tomás' father? That brutal son-of-a-bitch who orders the killing and torture of innocent children and mothers.'

He walks aimlessly through the barrios, unaware of the comings and goings, so unlike when he's photographing and noticing every nuance. He's been consoling Azucena throughout Tomás' disappearance without considering his own attachment to the boy.

'Fuck,' Duncan realizes. He stops to sit on a streetside bench. 'Tomás is like a son to me as well. Why am I not more emotionally attuned to the loss? I miss him deeply. The kid's an intelligent young guy, always into our discussions and so advanced for his age. Why would he just take off? Where the fuck would he go? Where could he go? This country isn't that big after all.'

Delayed emotion finally catches up to Duncan. He collapses into a fetal ball on the bench, pulling his knees to his chest. His body vibrates in shock; tears flow hysterically and he struggles to breathe.

'What if what Kurt wrote is true, that Tomás was killed? Fuck, he's just a youngster, barely 15. If someone had kidnapped him, wouldn't they send a ransom note? Maybe he's just lost somewhere, or in some other country where he can't return from. Shit.' Duncan buries his face in his hands. 'The only fact is that we have no fucking idea where he is.'

Duncan resists telling Azucena the news for fear that it will destroy her. Azucena has already stopped painting because she's afraid that one of her horrifying nightmares will become real, that her son will appear painted as a corpse on the next canvas. She recognizes Tomás in every young boy that walks past her on the street. Her eyes are tired and dry from crying too much. She sees without focusing.

Recognizing that it's been eight months since Tomás left and a month since their disappointing trip to *Los Manos*, Duncan agonizes over whether to tell Azucena the latest news from Kurt or not. He decides to tell her. By not telling her will contribute to her failing health. Duncan chooses the moment carefully.

Duncan takes Azucena's arm and leads to her a chair in the kitchen. He makes her a cup of tea.

"I heard news from my old friend Kurt," Duncan says, "the Dutch photojournalist I told you about. He told me about a rumour, just a rumour, that Tomás had been sighted in the north, but of course, that could be any young boy, as you know. The boy in the rumour was involved in an accident … and died immediately."

"What kind of accident?" Azucena sits upright. She clutches Duncan's arm. "When did it happen? How? Where?" Her face pleads for more information. "I must know these things."

"They are only rumours, my dear." Duncan touches her face softly. "There are very few facts these days. I only tell you this so, if the worst is confirmed, you are not shocked. It is realistic to expect that something has gone wrong after all this time. Otherwise, he would have returned home, would he not?"

Azucena doesn't give in easily. "Maybe he's lost. Maybe he's …"

Duncan places his arms around Azucena's waist. "I'm worried about you. You're not eating, and you don't even leave the house anymore."

Azucena wipes tears from her face. "If this is only a rumour, and if there are very few facts these days, I can still have hope, can't I?" she asks, pulling away from Duncan's chest to look up into his eyes.

"Of course, my dear." Duncan consoles Azucena by rubbing his hand over her back. "I'm just concerned about you." He kisses the top of her head. "Regardless of the outcome, you must pull it together. You can't give up."

Days pass before Azucena emerges from the bedroom dressed in her finest. Her long black hair is freshly washed and combed soft.

"You are right about some things, Duncan. I have failed myself and my health, and by failing myself I am also failing you … I'm also failing Tomás. What kind of a mother will I be when Tomás returns if I'm sick and dying from worry?"

Duncan smiles at her fresh appearance. They embrace.

"I promise to start exercising and eating better. I want to start tonight. Take me out for dinner, somewhere nice. I so miss our dinner conversations."

Duncan takes her to *Costa Brava*, an upscale restaurant specializing in seafood. Upon entering, he realizes that they have the restaurant to themselves. Upscale restaurants are not well attended during the current embargo-imposed economy. He senses some guilt in his choice, but orders a bottle of imported French Chardonnay, a luxury in Nicaragua during these times. They both order *langosta*, the specialty of the house, and dive right into conversation.

Duncan admits to Azucena, "I haven't eaten lobster since I vacationed in Prince Edward Island with my parents as a child. *Es muy delicioso.*" He says, licking his lips.

Azucena admits, "I have never eaten lobster, but I will take your word for it."

No sooner has the food arrived, than they are surrounded by an ambulant band of four serenading musicians, playing and singing traditional love ballads. Spanish, the language of love and poetry, is just what the doctor ordered for this evening. For the first time since Tomás disappeared, Azucena smiles, and her eyes sparkle. She sings along with the musicians; songs she recalls from her childhood, songs shared with her mother. No doubt she also sang the same songs to Tomás as a child.

The band also smiles as they leave, their pockets filled with Duncan's monetary gratitude. No mention is made of Tomás' name throughout the entire evening, even at home, where they are intimate for the first time in months.

Soon afterward, Duncan asks Azucena if it might be possible that Tomás went searching for his father. Azucena is surprised by his question.

"Tomás doesn't even know who his father is. Nobody knows. I've never told anyone except you. It's our secret."

Duncan assures her. "Just for the record, I have never revealed your secret to anyone else if that's what you're implying. While it is your secret, it could also be the secret of his father, and we don't know if that bastard has told anyone."

Azucena explodes. "His father doesn't give two shits about Tomás. He's too busy arranging assassinations and taking money from the CIA. He's a disgusting, bloodthirsty bastard who wants to kill the revolution. If he ever steps foot in this country again, I will kill him myself, that's a promise."

Duncan's eyes widen at Azucena's outburst.

Realizing the scope of her anger, Azucena backtracks. "I'm sorry for ranting Duncan. I have said too much already. I'll shut up now." She adds an afterthought. "Of course, I wouldn't kill him. That would be too easy for him. I would want him to suffer."

CHAPTER 22

MOVING ON

Nicaragua, 1988:

One afternoon while out taking some street photos around the city, Duncan stops at *Los Antojitos* for a beer. Kurt is occupying a table by himself.

Kurt is a large burly man in all dimensions. He stands six inches above Duncan and sports a full salt and pepper beard. A black bandana prevents his long unruly greying hair from falling across his face. The multiple pockets of his Tilley photo vest bulge with the accessories of his trade: lenses, film cannisters (left pocket for exposed, right for fresh), a small flash unit, notebooks. Two Nikon F cameras sit on the table. An *Agence France-Presse* (AFP) ID badge hangs carelessly from a lanyard around his substantial neck. Without the camera gear, Kurt is a prime candidate for an outlaw biker gang. Aside from his gruff exterior and the terseness of his Dutch accent, however, Kurt's soft earthy voice displays his true disposition.

"Hey Duncan, my man." Kurt says, waving Duncan over. "Join me over here. I was going to call in on you anyway. I have a few more details on the kid, Tomás. Again, it's only based on rumours, but it doesn't sound too good." Kurt shakes his head with displeasure. "I confirmed that he was in fact, being worked as a mule. When one of the Contras said something derogatory about his mother, the kid blew out. There was a fist fight, and someone pulled a pistol. Shots were fired at the kid while he ran into the bush. I don't know if he escaped or whether he bought it. That's all I've heard, nothing firm I'm afraid. But at least someone recognized Tomás, so we know he was there. Sorry I don't have better news, man. If he got through it, maybe he'll make it home."

"Thanks Kurt. I don't know how I'll tell this to Azucena, but I'll think of something."

Duncan stands to leave but hesitates before returning to his chair.

"Hey Kurt," Duncan stares at the table before raising his eyes toward Kurt. "Do you mind if I unload on you?"

"No problem, man. What's up?"

"It's … you know … the thing … that delayed emotional thing we all have to deal with from time to time. You know what I'm talking about … the demons." Duncan's eyes gloss over. "We've always been able to do that, eh man? You know, talk … as friends."

"Yeah. I know the thing you're talking about, man. Who doesn't in our business, eh? I've always maintained that it's the sorry bastard who never feels this stuff where it hurts. Go for it. Let it out. I'm not going anywhere." Kurt waves his solid tattooed arm to the waiter. *"S-s-s-t, dos mas Toñas por favor."*

"The kid, Tomás," Duncan starts. "He's the kid I photographed being born during the earthquake, remember? His mother, Azucena, the artist I told you about … well she and I are a couple now. I'm kind of like Tomás' father. Not his real father, you understand, but I'm the only father the boy knows."

Duncan's tears begin to flow. He wipes at them with the side of his hand. "Sorry about the leaking taps, man."

"Damn you Canadians and your apologies, Duncan. You're always sorry about something. Just lay it out. I can handle it … and so can you if you just let it all hang out, man." Kurt pats Duncan's shoulder. "It's OK, man. I'm listening."

"Tomás is the only son I ever had," Duncan reveals, not wishing to tell Kurt about his son with Penny. "I can't lose him, Kurt. I'm trying to be the strong one around Azucena, but it's just a façade. I'm carrying it all inside me."

Kurt stands. "Come here, man."

Duncan rises and approaches Kurt with arms outstretched.

Kurt pats his large hands on Duncan's back. "It's OK, man. We're in this together. We're brothers, man."

Minutes pass before Duncan pulls back. "Thanks Kurt. I knew I could lean on you."

"So, Duncan," Kurt redirects the conversation. "When are we going to see you back in the trade, or should I call it the rat-race?"

Duncan wants to tell Kurt about his personal documentary project. Instead he answers, "Maybe never, man. We'll see."

"Yeah. I dig what you're saying, man," Kurt says. "It's starting to get me down too, it's the same old shit, eh? Of course, I don't have to tell you that, do I? You've been there."

Duncan stands and lays a handful of *córdobas* on the table to cover their bills and a tip. "Thanks again, Kurt. I owe you one, big time."

Kurt and Duncan share another man hug before departing.

* * *

With the end of Duncan's sabbatical approaching, Azucena and Duncan dread their impending separation.

"Do you really have to leave, Duncan?" Azucena pleads. "I need you here, at least until Tomás returns."

"I have no choice in the matter, Azucena. My sabbatical contract states that I must return to the college to resume teaching one year after it began. That's in one month. I'm sorry, my dear, but they'll sue the pants off me if I breach the contract."

Azucena plays the guilt card. "Do you not like living here, Duncan, with me?"

"You know I love it here. If it wasn't for the contract I'd move here to stay. But, I have to make a living. It may be cheaper here, but if I don't work, I'll have nothing."

"What about me, Duncan?" Azucena assumes a sad face. "Do I matter to you?"

"I didn't mean it that way. Of course, you are everything to me, Azucena." Duncan moves close to his lover, wrapping his arms around her waist. "You know that without having to ask. I love you, and being away from you will drive me crazy."

"Why don't you ..."

"Wait a minute," Duncan interrupts. "I just had an idea. Why don't you come with me to Toronto? Joyce said she would give you some teaching hours in Fine Arts."

"That would be wonderful, except for one thing. I can't leave Nicaragua until I know about Tomás. What if he comes home and I'm not here?" Azucena begins to cry. "Why is my life so complicated?"

Duncan wipes tears from Azucena's eyes. "We won't stop looking and hoping. I promise."

Azucena adds, as if an afterthought, "I also must keep working for the revolution. We worked so hard and it's always in constant danger of collapsing. I can't abandon my *compañeros* now."

Duncan sympathizes with Azucena's situation. He knows that he would feel the same way. The pressure to find a solution haunts Duncan through a sleepless night. In the hour before first light, while Azucena sleeps, Duncan picks up his camera and quietly leaves the house.

He avoids the main thoroughfares, seeking the small streets that meander through barrios, his mind tossing the pros and cons about like a busking juggler.

'I love Nicaragua. I love Azucena. I love Tomás. There's nothing I don't love here. I love the climate, the easy living, my friends, playing jazz with Pablo, the intelligent conversations with Azucena.'

Duncan recalls Azucena telling him early in their burgeoning relationship, that he should move to Nicaragua, that he would love it.

'Shit, she was right about that. So far, no cons ... well, except for this fucking war and the economy. And then there are the political assholes who threaten to kill Azucena.' He ponders for a moment. 'And, of course, there's the fucking bureaucracy that keeps me from getting the photojournalism school off and running. How will I explain that to the Dean in my sabbatical report?'

One of Duncan's attributes is that he's able to solve problems, quickly. It's the nature of a journalist, and especially a photojournalist when faced with glitches, like when equipment keeps breaking down, or when people don't show up for interviews. Duncan believes that problems only exist to be solved.

As morning breaks, he strolls toward the market, turns his camera toward shirtless men and kids struggling to pull heavy wagons of produce. He composes images of the posture-perfect women toting baskets of wares on their heads. A wooden-wheeled ox-cart plods slowly by, sharing a 'decisive-moment' image with the rusted mufflerless *camionetas*, overflowing with bags of grain and human cargo. Ancient, overworked city buses, tilting under the weight of passengers and long-collapsed springs, spew black diesel smoke into the traffic while grinding gears through the early morning rush. Commerce has begun again.

'God, I love this place,' Duncan reminds himself, chuckling and dancing his way between the crowds, snapping candid images, before returning to his problems.

'So, what are the problems?' he poses to himself, stopping for an early morning java. 'I have a contract for a job that I've stopped enjoying. The townhouse needs to be paid for ... or sold. My parents are aging and living in Canada; I hardly ever see them. I have no job here, and no way to make any money. Most of the population is unemployed.'

When Duncan returns home, Azucena has prepared a fresh fruit lunch: papaya, passion fruit, some mangos and pineapple. They eat at the small table set on the sidewalk outside their humble *casita*. She asks no questions of Duncan, knowing that he will speak soon.

In time, he does. He wipes pineapple juice from his lips. "If you are sure you want me to stay in Nicaragua, I must pull a few strings, and I will have to return to Canada for a short time. Of course, you could come with me. Consider it a vacation."

"Are you telling me that you will move here?"

"I'm telling you that I *want* to move here, my dear, and that I must manipulate the situation to allow me to stay here." He pauses. "What if I return to my occupation as a photojournalist, working for magazines? I could freelance like I used to do, specializing in Central American coverage; there's still a lot of news going on here, and I'm respected in the business. Managua is only a half-hour flight from everywhere else. I have magazine contacts in the U.S. and Canada, and maybe Kurt will help me with some international contacts as well."

"What about your teaching job … and your townhouse?

"Quit and sell, in that order."

Silence prevails while Azucena mulls Duncan's words over in her mind.

"Now it's time for me to be the practical one," Azucena offers. "I have also been thinking and searching for solutions. Here's what I think." She raises her forefinger toward Duncan.

"Don't quit your job. Plead a case that you must stay here because of Tomás. You have a union contract as well as your sabbatical contract. There must be some allowances for grief situations. Of course, you'll have to lie a bit, by claiming Tomás as your son, but maybe you can arrange a leave of absence. That would allow you to stay a bit longer, maybe a year. It wouldn't be permanent, but it will give you some time to establish yourself. You could also make a case to your superiors that the photojournalism school here is taking longer than you anticipated and you need an extension to your sabbatical. Maybe that could still happen, but only if you're still willing to push for it."

"What about my house?"

"Rent it out. How difficult could that be?"

"What about my grand piano, and …?"

Azucena places her hands on her hips to show Duncan she means what she says.

"Rent your house to a pianist, for God's sake, Duncan. You must know a few of them. Even better, find a pianist who is married to a photographer that would appreciate a well-equipped darkroom."

"Yeah, right," Duncan chuckles. As if I'm going to let some stranger use my darkroom … or my piano for that matter."

"Then, lock up the darkroom and put your piano into storage."

"But, how could I …?"

"Stop making excuses, Duncan!" Azucena stamps her foot on the sidewalk. "Listen to me. We can open our own gallery and café right here. The people from next door left for Miami a year ago. Their place is still empty and they're not likely to return soon, and then only if the Sandinistas lose the next election, and that's not likely to happen. We could arrange to set up a gallery of our work there. You could also play jazz with Pablo, here, in our own café."

"That would cost some *dineros* to set up," Duncan suggests, rubbing his fingers together. "You know, cash."

"Pfft!" Azucena lifts her arms in an expression of futility. "There you go again, Duncan, creating problems. In the gallery you can teach music and photo classes. I can teach painting. I know the money will be much less than you're earning in Canada, but at the very least, we won't starve. Maybe, once in a while, we can return to Toronto and conduct workshops, hang shows, and make some fast *dolares*. Your friend, Joyce, from the Fine Arts program, she would help us do that, wouldn't she?"

"Of course she would. In a minute. She already suggested it to you."

"So," Azucena concludes. "There you have it. Problem solved." She brushes her hands together in a gesture of finality. "Done!"

Duncan chuckles. "I should take photos of you when you're all fired up. I could make a living with those pictures."

Duncan has always envisioned Azucena as the free-spirited, ethereal artist, someone who floats above practical matters and watches the world pass without concern for details. Since moving in with her, he is learning about the down-to-earth Azucena who manages to cope with the trials of political oppression and poverty-line subsistence. She invites hard work and solves serious problems on a daily basis.

By the end of the week, Duncan has phoned the Dean at the college with a proposed one-year extension to his sabbatical and arranged immediate return flights to Toronto for he and Azucena.

There's a fresh vitality for both Azucena and Duncan, an exuberance they can enjoy together for the first time since Tomás left. They have plans for the future.

Azucena is in a quandary about what to pack for the trip. "Will it be cold? Do I need warm clothes? Can we go camping again in the forest?"

Duncan signals a pause with both hands up. "Hold the fort, Azucena. This isn't going to be a holiday like the last time," he warns. "This is a business trip. We fly in, take care of business details, and fly back to Nicaragua in two weeks; to our home together."

* * *

Toronto, 1988:

On the morning after arriving in Toronto, Azucena and Duncan proceed directly to the college. Azucena meets with Joyce for coffee while Duncan attends his scheduled meeting.

He presents his typed and spiral bound proposal to the Dean.

"Everything is in here, boss," Duncan promises. "It covers all the details of my leave of absence, complete with a suggestion for my replacement."

"Don't call me boss, understood? Now, tell me more about this Kurt fellow, Duncan," the Dean says, flipping through the report. "I assume you have already talked to him about this."

"Definitely. He has more experience than I have, and he's enthusiastic about the opportunity. He's thinking about the gig as a sabbatical from his normal routine, which is covering the world news. I've known him for many years."

While the Dean peruses the details, Duncan silently recalls his conversation with Kurt about the job.

'It's a piece of cake, Kurt. When you told me how tired you were about the 'fucking' globe-trotting game, I thought of you immediately. You're perfect for the gig. Besides, you can rent my place for half the going rate while you're in Toronto. It's the least I can do after all the help you've given me and Azucena. I owe you.'

"When can I meet this Kurt, Duncan?" the Dean asks, snapping his finger against the corner of Duncan's proposal before flipping it onto his desk.

Duncan grins at the Dean. "His name is Kurt, boss, not 'this Kurt.' One phone call, and he'll be here in a few minutes."

"That sounds a bit too convenient, doesn't it, Duncan," the Dean probes. "Are you telling me that the globe-trotting photojournalist is here, in Toronto, at this very moment?" he asks, his eyes stretched open in disbelief.

"Yup," Duncan answers with a grin. "In fact, he's here in the college right now." he chuckles, pointing toward the ceiling. "He's upstairs on the third floor in Fine Arts talking to Joyce."

"That really is *too* convenient, don't you think?"

Duncan explains, "Fate has it that he decided to come to Toronto to visit me while I'm here, and to check out the scene. He's staying at my townhouse."

"Call him, Duncan, before this … Kurt, is that his name? … takes a job with Joyce instead."

The Dean passes Duncan his phone, and punches Joyce's extension.

"Hi Joyce, it's Duncan. Could you send Kurt down to the Dean's office? I'll meet him in the hallway" … "Yeah, now." … "It's looking good." … "Tell Azucena I'll be up there in a few minutes."

Duncan waits in the hallway outside the Dean's office for Kurt to arrive.

"It looks like a sure thing," Duncan says, patting Kurt on the shoulder. "Just turn on the European charm and you'll have the job."

"Thanks so much, man. I appreciate everything you're doing," Kurt acknowledges with his fingers crossed. "I owe you."

"You owe me nothing," Duncan responds. "Especially after all the help you've given Azucena and me."

"I'm just sorry things didn't work out well for you guys, and for Tomás, Duncan."

"We still have hope, man. Like you told me once, There are very few facts out there these days, and that's a fact."

The two globe-trotting photojournalists embrace. "Good luck, Kurt," Duncan wishes him. "We'll get together later for dinner."

* * *

"Problems only exist to be solved," Duncan recaps to the other three celebrants at their table in the Casa Francisco restaurant in Little Italy. He raises his glass of Chianti. "Let's toast. To problems."

Kurt, Joyce, Azucena and Duncan raise their glasses in unison, "To problems."

"And to solutions," Azucena's single voice adds.

"And a special toast to my dearest, and most beautiful, Azucena, who solved, what appeared to be, an unsolvable problem," Duncan announces, leaning over to kiss Azucena.

"Another one of your circles has been completed," Azucena adds, proposing another toast.

"And another circle begins," Duncan adds, with embraces all around.

"There's more to this circle than meets the eye," Azucena announces, raising her wineglass again.

Duncan meets Azucena's eyes with an inquisitive twist of the head.

"What else?" Duncan asks with a quiet aside to Azucena. "Wait a minute. You're not … um … you know … um?"

"I am," Azucena toasts, waiting to see how Duncan reacts.

He starts his response with a slight, but positive, grin.

Azucena laughs and reveals her secret. "Joyce has offered me a residency for next year if I want it. Do you know what that means, Duncan?"

"Yeah. It means that it wasn't what I expected," he laughs.

"That was Joyce's idea," Azucena chuckles, sipping some wine "She told me to say it that way. She said it would get a rise out of you."

Kurt and Joyce tip their glasses together. "Good one," they offer in unison.

Later the same evening back at the townhouse, Duncan asks Azucena, "You're not playing Cupid are you?"

"What do you mean, Duncan?" Azucena answers with a coy expression.

"Are you trying to set Kurt up with Joyce by any chance?" Duncan winks his eye at Azucena.

"I had nothing to do with it. Nothing whatsoever." Azucena hesitates. "Do you really think that something's going on there?"

"Pure speculation, that's all," Duncan confesses.

Azucena suddenly becomes serious, the sheen of happiness in her eyes dim.

"What is it, Azucena?" Duncan worries. He strokes his hand on hers. "Are you alright?"

Tears emerge, streaming across Azucena's cheeks.

"Just talking about Kurt reminds me of Tomás." Azucena weeps openly, choking on each word. "My poor son ... my Tomás ... he should be here with us, to share the happiness we are enjoying."

She pauses to regain her breath. "Last night I dreamt that Tomás was with us, here in Toronto. You played baseball and music together, like father and son."

"You must paint that dream," Duncan tells Azucena. He pulls her closer. "Every once in a while, I have similar dreams, my precious." Duncan runs his fingers through Azucena's long hair, dampened by her tears. "My dreams include Tomás and I, playing baseball together with my other long-lost son, the son I never knew, the son with no name, and no face."

Azucena kisses Duncan's cheek; their tears blend together and flow salty between their lips.

PART NINE
1988 – 1989

CHAPTER 23

SEARCHING

Nicaragua, 1988:

"So! Here we are." Azucena begins, toasting Duncan with her morning coffee. "Together, in love, and about to be poor as *campesinos.*"

"Or maybe, as rich as old Don Ricardo," Duncan adds.

"Oh God, I hope not," Azucena grimaces and forms the sign of a cross. "Wealthy possibly, but in spirit only."

Duncan's sabbatical is extended for another year as a leave-of-absence without pay. He must decide over the coming year what his plans will be for the future and is obligated to confirm his decision with the college. He will have two options: either return to the class-room or resign. In the meantime, his pension remains in effect but won't grow further until he starts contributing again.

"Well, let's consider how things worked out." Duncan tallies up the pros and cons from their short trip to Toronto.

"I was given my leave of absence from the college," he notes, extending his right forefinger as the count of one. "That means I can stay in Nicaragua for at least another year."

Azucena raises her left forefinger. "Minus a monthly paycheque," she notes. "That equals zero *dineros*." She forms a zero with her fingers.

"Two," Duncan raises a second finger. "Kurt receives my paycheque and gives me $1500 *dineros* a month as rental for my townhouse. After expenses, that leaves me $500 income."

"That much?" Azucena's eyes widen. "We can live like the King and Queen in Nicaragua for $500 a month."

"Not quite," Duncan points out. "These are Canadian *dineros*, not American, my dear. That equals only $300."

Azucena stands up and approaches Duncan. She straddles his lap and kisses him with passion. "The main thing is that we are together, you and me … here, in Nicaragua. Together we can accomplish anything, *no?*"

"*Si*. Anything."

Without wasting any time, Azucena and Duncan begin collaborating on fresh works for a debut show to open in their new gallery/café, '*Galería de los Soñadores*' (Gallery of the Dreamers). The show, entitled '*Buscando a Tomás*' (Searching for Tomás), combines the painted interpretations of Azucena's dreams and Duncan's black and white photographs of locations where Azucena's visions imagine Tomás to have been since his disappearance.

The name for the gallery was originally Duncan's suggestion, an idea that Azucena initially rejected.

"It's too ethereal and removed from reality," Azucena complained, waving her arms loftily to illustrate 'ethereal.' "Nobody will take our work seriously."

A week later, when Duncan returns from a photo session, Azucena is busily painting a mural for the entrance to the gallery that includes two figures staring upward into a futuristic Milky Way. The words '*Galería de los Soñadores*' appear in hand painted script. Discreetly, in the lower right corner, her signature white lily motif and Duncan's initials, DM appear.

Duncan incorporates shooting the images for their collaborations with his documentary project on small Nicaraguan towns. Azucena often accompanies Duncan on trips around the country and sketches while he photographs. She also serves as Duncan's interpreter with the local citizens.

They invest a few dollars from Duncan's savings in a used Volkswagen camper van to transport them around to the rural towns and villages. It also proves helpful to haul paintings and supplies around. The vehicle is reserved for trips away from the capital, and when they plan to stay somewhere overnight. Around the capital they still rely on buses or taxis.

"What the hell happened to my van?" Duncan shouts to Azucena one morning while they prepare for a weekend in the northern mountains.

"Ha-ha," she doubles over, stepping out the front door with two pillows and sleeping bags for the trip. "Do you like them?" she asks.

"You could have at least asked my opinion about the colours you chose?"

"I missed all the excitement about Woodstock, hippies, and free love, so I thought a few painted flowers would bring some of that back."

Duncan runs back into their small backyard, picks some wild flowers, winds the stems in a circle, and places it on Azucena's head as a tiara.

He kneels before her. "I crown thee Your Majesty Queen Azucena Sosa."

"Ah, that's so sweet, Duncan." She feigns touching his shoulders with a sword and commands, "Rise, *Señor* Canuck, Lord Duncan of the Maple Leaf." She adds. "As official photographer of the *Soñadores* Clan, you are hereby commanded to take some photos of us with our royal flowered carriage."

Duncan adds, "Before it turns into a pumpkin, right?"

Once on the road, Duncan comments, "You look just like Janis Joplin with those flowers in your hair."

"Who is Janis Joplin?" Azucena asks, with a querying look on her face, as if she is missing something important.

"Well, listen to this," Duncan says, inserting a cassette into the tape deck.

Joplin's raspy voice starts into Me and Bobby McGee.

"Louder, Duncan." Azucena shouts, rocking in her seat to the pulse.

They drive the Pan-Am highway northward past Matagalpa and continue toward Jinotega and the cooperative where the dream-painting workshop was held.

"Look, Duncan," Azucena points excitedly as they pass the mountainside where they made love. "There's a memory for both us to share. We must stop and take photos."

"Why don't we stop here for lunch?" Duncan suggests. "We could even relive our memories." He jabs her arm with his elbow. "Eh? Eh?"

Azucena wraps her arms around Duncan. "We have the camper now. We can make love anytime, anywhere ... as long as the curtains are closed of course." She giggles amorously, following with an exploratory kiss.

After a light lunch, they continue toward Jinotega, and the cooperative. The land lays fallow, abandoned as wasteland. Some evidence of the horrendous Contra attack remains: charred boards, personal remnants from the people who toiled the earth there, a handmade scythe, and some other worn and rusted tools.

Duncan wanders through the overgrowth, kicking his boots and taking photographic details of the embedded relics, more for reminiscence that any other purpose.

They return south through Matagalpa and turn southeast on a secondary mountain road. Alongside the road, women with baskets balanced on their heads and men carrying machetes walk to and from market. Duncan is forced to stop the camper while a man on horseback steers a herd of cattle ahead of them.

They stop at the edge of a town called Muy Muy to stretch their legs. Azucena sketches details of an interesting row of humble *casitas*, while Duncan photographs a group of ambulatory vendors hawking their wares to travellers.

"Where are we going now?" Azucena asks.

"I'm not sure yet," Duncan admits, looking at a map. "At the crossroads, I'll turn east on a road that passes through a town called Matiguas, and then on through to Rio Blanco."

In Matiguas, Duncan notices a line of people waiting at the entrance to a medical clinic. He parks the camper and grabs his camera bag.

At the head of the line, a man stands with the aid of a crutch hand-crafted from a tree branch, his right leg is being held upward by a sling fastened to his belt. His foot is bound in a blood-stained bandage.

Azucena enquires of the man. "What happened to you?"

"Shot ... *con pistola*," he answers in a voice struggling with pain.

"Who did that to you?" she asks, grimacing while leaning forward to check the bandage closer.

"*Yo ... accidente*," he explains, pointing his finger toward himself. "Me, I shoot myself." He smiles, embarrassed, as if the pain has momentarily disappeared.

Azucena and Duncan enter the clinic. A nurse approaches. "You'll have to wait in line," she instructs. "We're very busy today."

Duncan explains that he's a Canadian photojournalist doing stories in and around small towns in Nicaragua.

"Canadian?" she responds, surprised. "So am I. Come in."

"Where are you from?" Duncan asks.

"Mitchell, Ontario. It's a small town near London. And you?"

"Toronto. Originally from Hamilton."

Duncan introduces Azucena and explains more about their projects. "Would it be alright if I take some photos for my project here, at the clinic?"

"Of course. I'll show you around."

Azucena touches Duncan's arm and excuses herself. "Duncan, I'm just going to walk around town while you're taking photos."

"OK," he says. They share a goodbye kiss. "I'll see you later."

"I'll come back to the clinic when I'm finished," Azucena promises.

The nurse introduces Duncan to some of the patients: a woman waiting for an abortion, two men with tuberculosis, a man and a child with malaria. In each case Duncan asks for permission from the patients before taking photos of them; there are no refusals. Far off in a dark corner of the clinic, lit only by a single 60-watt lightbulb, Duncan's attention is drawn to a mother and her child sitting patiently.

Initially drawn to the mother and child by the magic of the light and the way it falls across the child's emaciated face, Duncan asks the nurse, "What's their story?" He points toward the dark corner.

The nurse explains. "They just arrived and are waiting to be seen by the doctor, but he hasn't arrived yet today. She walked and hitched rides to get here from Muy Muy, carrying the child. That's 24 kilometres from here."

The nurse introduces Duncan to the mother as 'un periodista canadiense.'

The mother acknowledges by nodding toward him. "Hola señor."

"Mucho gusto, señora." Duncan responds and asks, "Puedo a tomar fotos?"

"Si," the mother replies, nodding. "No problema."

The nurse, whose Spanish is stronger than Duncan's, agrees to translate. Duncan starts his tape recorder so he can return to their conversation later.

"My child is malnourished," the mother starts. "We are extremely poor. I work part-time as a domestic. There are four other children at home … one of them is sick just like *Dooncan* here. *Dooncan* is five-years-old. I also have a small baby who needs my attention."

"Espara," Duncan asks the mother to wait, holding his hand up. "Repite por favor, el nombre de tu hijo."

"Se llama Dooncan, señor," the mother repeats. (He is called *Dooncan*).

Duncan is gobsmacked. 'How crazy is that?' he ponders. 'A Scottish name way out here in the Nicaraguan sticks.'

Duncan turns to the mother, placing his hand against his chest. "Me llamo Duncan, tambien," (That's my name too).

The mother places her hand on Duncan's arm. "Tocayos," she says, with a sudden smile. *"Tocayos,"* she repeats to her son, the Spanish word for namesake.

Duncan takes the boy's hand in his and bows. *"Tocayos …* Duncan and Duncan." He points his hand toward the boy and then to himself and repeats, *"Somos tocayos."* A fragment of a smile emerges from the child's dry lips.

Duncan can't restrain his emotions; tears obliterate his vision. This new revelation introduces a fresh dimension to Duncan's project, and it places an extra weight on why it must be successful. He exposes more than a hundred images of the mother and her child, his *tocayo.*

He carefully records the information about the mother and *Doon-can*, aware that he will want to communicate with them in the future.

Duncan can't wait to tell Azucena all about this new development. When she arrives at the clinic, she's breathing heavily and excited about something she's discovered.

"Duncan!" she announces with vigour. "He's been here … Tomás. He's been here in this town. A man on the street recognized Tomás' photo when I showed it to him. I had that same feeling while walking down the street. You know … that vibrating sensation I know so well. A man walked by and I showed him the photo I have of Tomás. He saw him, a few months ago, he wasn't sure exactly when."

The nurse asks who Azucena was talking about.

"My son, Tomás," Azucena answers. "He's been missing for more than a year now, but we still have hope that he's alive, and safe."

The nurse puts her hand forward. "Show me the photo. I see everyone who comes into the clinic. If something was wrong with him, maybe he came in here for help."

The nurse stares at the photo for several minutes before placing her hand across her mouth.

"Oh my God," she utters. "I have seen this boy. He was here in the clinic. I remember, there were wounds that I cared for and I bandaged him up. I don't want to alarm you, but one of the wounds was from a gunshot."

Azucena gasps, her hand covering her mouth. "No. please. Not my Tomás."

The nurse continues. "When he left the clinic he was healthy and would have been fine. It was just a surface wound on his leg, but from a gunshot nevertheless," she explains, touching Azucena with her hand to calm her. "Unfortunately, we don't keep accurate records. The war took care of that."

The nurse turns to Duncan. "It's not like back in Canada, where we have to report every gunshot wound to the police."

Duncan embraces Azucena. He whispers softly, "Think of it this way, my dear. There's still hope yet. We know now that he's alive."

"Oh thank God," Azucena crosses herself.

The nurse continues. "He seemed like a polite and well-educated boy. Not too many locals are well-educated. Some aren't very polite either," she quips an aside. "That's why I can remember him. When he was here, he was always looking nervously over his shoulder, as if he was being followed. I think he was running away from someone, but he never said anything about that."

Azucena probes for more information. "Did you see where he went after he left here?"

"No, I'm sorry. We're always busy here, I never even look outside. People come and people go."

Azucena places her hand to her lips and ponders deeply before speaking.

"So, Duncan ... is it just fate that brought us here today? I wonder. Is it merely coincidence, Duncan? We didn't even decide to travel north until two days ago."

"You already know how I feel about coincidences, my dear. What I do know, however, is that several circles have been completed. That's a very positive outcome.

Duncan introduces Azucena to the mother and his *tocayo, Dooncan.* Azucena acknowledges the child by taking his hand in hers and whispering his name.

Before leaving, Duncan thanks the nurse for everything and wishes her well.

Azucena embraces the nurse. "Thank you so much for the information about Tomás," she says. "You have been so helpful."

* * *

Azucena paints obsessively in the studio she has set up adjacent to *Galería de los Soñadores*. The gallery and the café are scheduled to open in two weeks, with *'Buscando a Tomás;'* their collaborations, a selection of Duncan's black and white prints from his current documentary project, and some personal paintings by Azucena.

"This is amazing work, Azucena," Duncan observes, perusing her new canvases that lean in rows against the walls. "You are continuing to evolve. It's so wonderful to see, especially since you haven't actively painted for more than a year."

"It has been a while, hasn't it, Duncan, but sometimes we need a break," Azucena responds without missing a brushstroke. "It's like a moratorium, or … how do you call it … a sabbatical? It provides us with the opportunity to re-energize, to see with freshness. Besides, I've had some very interesting dreams lately that I want to get onto canvas before they disappear from my mind's eye."

"Will it bother you if I take some photos of you working?" Duncan asks. "I promise to be quiet and I'll stay out of your way." When Azucena doesn't answer, Duncan accepts that she's totally absorbed in her creation. 'She won't even know I'm taking photos,' he concludes.

Duncan's trained eye observes Azucena's movements and expressions, both abrupt and subtle, and his shutter finger instinctively presses the button on his rangefinder Leica. He freezes sudden changes with precise timing while composing the frame in the viewfinder to emphasize her relationship to the studio environment.

During dinner, Azucena queries. "I thought you wanted to take some photos of me earlier, Duncan. What happened?"

Duncan laughs. "I guess I still have the magic."

"Oh-h-h," Azucena responds. "You did take some." She kisses him. "Can I see them when you develop the film?"

"The film is in drying right now. I'll make a contact sheet for you after dinner."

Azucena chooses six images from the contact proof sheet. "I love these ones. Let's use them in the show, as a sequence."

"Sure, no problem," Duncan agrees.

"Make them each this big if you can, OK?" She stretches her arms wide.

"Holy Shit! Why so big?"

Azucena grins. "There are some things that we aren't meant to understand."

Duncan embraces Azucena. "Sometimes you can be so evil."

* * *

For the *'Buscando'* series, Azucena paints likenesses of Tomás into Duncan's black and white prints, subtly positioning each image to challenge the viewer's curiosity. In the photograph of Duncan's *'Madonna and Tocayo,'* from the clinic, the image of Tomás appears as a low-key blue-gray figure overlooking the subjects in the background blackness, surrounded by a soft warm-toned halo shape that extends from Tomás' image over the child's head.

Another example shows Tomás as a *campesino* walking with his head bowed behind a pack mule on the mountain road to Jinotega, a symbolic *double-entendre* rendering of 'Christ entering Jerusalem on an ass,' and Tomás' apparent enslavement as a mule for the Contras.

In Duncan's sequence photos of Azucena painting in the studio, she has inserted subtle images of Tomás overseeing her painting other canvases in the *'Buscando'* series. In one, he appears pleading to the viewer from the canvas.

"This is it, my dearest." Duncan grasps Azucena's hand. "The show is hanging and the people are arriving."

Azucena stares up into Duncan's eyes; she squeezes his hand and grins. "I think Tomás would like the show, don't you?"

"No doubt about it," Duncan answers before chuckling. "I can tell how excited and how nervous you are, all at the same time. Your eyes are stretched wide open with enthusiasm but there's an apprehensive grin on your face."

"I always become nervous whenever I'm put on show," Azucena admits, gesturing her anxiety to Duncan with vibrating hands. "It isn't because of my work, I'm confident about that. It's just being in the public with all those people paying attention to me. I'd rather just let the work stand on its own merit and watch from the sidelines."

Duncan calms her with a hug. "Don't fret, you'll be fine." He offers her some advice.

"Enjoy the attention, answer the intelligent questions, laugh at the jokes, and shrug off the stupid comments, by diverting your attention to someone else in the room." He explains, "It's a subtle gesture that rejects the stupidity level of their comments and communicates to them that there is someone else in the room who is more important than they are."

Despite Azucena's anxiety, the show is immensely successful. Regardless of the economic setbacks in the country, there are still a few individuals who can afford to purchase luxury items like art. Fifty percent of the paintings are sold, with several pieces being purchased by the Ministry of Culture.

"Good news. We can afford to eat for another two months, Duncan," Azucena announces, waving a handful of money and cheques, many of the funds in U.S. dollars. "Some of your photographs sold as well."

Duncan suggests, "Why don't we go out and celebrate instead, and just count on eating for only one month."

Azucena slaps him playfully on the arm. "Shame on you, Duncan."

CHAPTER 24

PROJECTS

Nicaragua, 1988:

"Look at this god-damned letter." Duncan angrily waves a sheet of paper toward Azucena as he walks in the door. "I just received it in my university mail box. It's from the Ministry of Culture, the same people who spent hundreds of dollars buying our art. How can they do this?"

Azucena scans the letter and passes it back to Duncan. "Unfortunately they can," she says, tilting her head and shrugging her shoulder. "The Lord giveth and the Lord taketh away."

"In this case," Duncan muses, "the Lord taketh away more than the Lord giveth."

"It doesn't make sense to me," Azucena frowns in frustration. "They're also closing the Ministry of Culture offices near *Plaza España* to be handed over to some other level of government. They told us that it was to help pay for the war effort."

"There goes my sabbatical," Duncan continues, throwing the letter in the air. "I should have seen the writing on the wall. Everything was already so tied up in the bureaucracy. It was just a matter of time, I guess."

"Why don't you just do it by yourself?" Azucena suggests in an offhanded manner, as if it's an obvious practical solution. She picks his letter up from the floor. "Put up posters around the university and in cafés around the city offering private lessons in photojournalism. You could incorporate the lessons within your personal project."

Duncan responds, shaking his head. "Nobody joins me when I'm photographing. I do my personal projects alone!" Duncan demands. His face softens. "Except for my Queen Azucena. Of course, you are always welcome to accompany me."

"What about the private teaching idea, though, Duncan?" Azucena asks. "Would that work?"

Duncan cradles Azucena's face in his hands and kisses her. "You are brilliant, my dear. Fuck the bureaucrats … we'll become capitalists," he adds chuckling.

Azucena slaps Duncan with the letter. "Shame on you. That's just what Reagan wants to happen."

* * *

Azucena and Duncan both tend the café when it's open during afternoons and on weekend evenings when Pablo and the band are playing.

In the café, Azucena secretly bypasses the government regulations against domestic sale of Nicaraguan coffee beans. Through previous contacts with her *compañeros* at the coffee cooperatives, she arranges to access beans directly from the growers instead of importing Maxwell House and other North American brands.

"Nicaraguan coffee is difficult to get," Azucena complains. "The domestic beans are so much better but are reserved solely for the export market these days."

"Is that why our coffee tastes so rich?" Duncan notes, taking a sip of java from his cup and sampling a bite of cake.

Azucena slaps his hand.

"As you know, Duncan, some women in the barrio are making extra *dineros* by baking these traditional dessert items for us to sell in the café. The popular items like *Pio Quintos* (rum-soaked cakes), *buñuelos* (fried dough balls), and *Rosquillos* (traditional cookies made from masa and curd cheese that resemble donuts), sell very well."

"So we're sitting on a gold mine here," Duncan muses, stuffing more cake in his mouth.

Azucena snaps back, removing the plate of sweets from his grasp.

"Our profits would be higher if it wasn't for a certain sweet-toothed *canadiense* named Duncan."

Duncan quickly gobbles the remains of his cake and, with one sweep, salvages the final crumbs into the palm of his hand.

While Azucena looks after the culinary delights, Duncan takes care of general maintenance, framing and hanging artwork, and arranging weekend jazz performances with Pablo.

Between these chores, both Azucena and Duncan squeeze in a few students for lessons in painting, photography and music.

With the gallery show over, and especially since the Ministry of Culture scrubbed his photojournalism program, Duncan has more time to spend on his small town documentary project. He tries to group several towns in each *departamento* (states or provinces) to minimize the travel expenses.

Each *departamento* reflects its own cultural flavour and, through his own unique visual style, Duncan attempts to capture the distinctions and diversities in his photographs. Through his viewfinder he looks at the local industries, food markets, schools, housing, music, and arts and crafts specific to each region. He knows that only through comprehensive coverage can the true nature of a community emerge, and that a fuller and healthier understanding of the people will result.

"When will you be returning to the mountains, Duncan?" Azucena asks. "I would like to search for more clues to Tomás' whereabouts, especially now that we know he was there, and alive, well after we received Kurt's earlier messages from the front, the ones that say he had died."

"It's strange that you bring that up," Duncan responds, scratching the back of his ear. "I was thinking of heading up there soon."

Duncan walks to the darkroom and returns with a pile of 8 x 10 inch prints. "I made some prints of *Dooncan*, my little *Tocayo*. I'd like to give them to his mother. I know his family lives in the small village of Muy Muy. We passed through it when we went to the clinic in Matiguas. It can't be too difficult to find him and his mother there. All I have to do is show someone the photos."

Azucena proposes, "Why don't we drive up there at the beginning of the week? We can ask Father Manuel to look after the café while we're away."

"Excellent," Duncan agrees, adding a caveat. "Just be careful about Father Manuel though, Azucena."

"Why?" Azucena questions with a frown.

"He'll eat you out of business," Duncan laughs. "His sweet tooth is far more gluttonous than mine."

Azucena wraps her arms around Duncan. She presses her face into his chest. "Just think, Duncan. If Tomás was here, he could look after the café when we go away."

Duncan runs his hand on her back. "True," he whispers softly into her ear, "but we wouldn't be going away to look for him then, would we?"

Azucena pulls back and stares up into Duncan's eyes with a questioning frown. She slowly adopts a smile.

* * *

Their arrival in Muy Muy is met with a heavy downpour. The greenery of the valleys reflect a diversity of subtle verdant tones. The area is mainly agricultural, supplying much of Nicaragua with dairy products.

Despite the intense rainfall, *campesinos* continue walking along the roadside. Duncan is fascinated with how the men carry machetes as if it's a second nature, the palms of their hands gripping the blades without fear of being sliced.

"Wake up, Azucena." Duncan jostles her arm. "We're here, in Muy Muy."

"What, already?" Azucena asks in a foggy voice.

"You've been sleeping since we left the capital," Duncan tells her.

"What time is it?"

"It's almost noon. I took a short cut. There was no point in driving all the way to Matagalpa again."

Azucena offers to slide into the back of the camper to make something to eat but Duncan suggests, "I should top up with some gas, so why don't we stop and eat in that restaurant over there, next to the gas station?"

Azucena asks, "The one called *Comedor Sara*?"

"That's the one," Duncan confirms.

Duncan prefers eateries as a place to initiate conversation with locals. At home in Canada he opts for diners over the pretensions of fancy restaurants, except, of course, when he's trying to impress someone.

"This place looks ideal ... where the locals eat lunch." He points randomly around the property. "Look at all the *camionetas*, horses, and mules parked outside."

Duncan parks the camper next to a horse-drawn farm wagon. He takes his camera bag with him.

Inside, *Comedor Sara* is someone's humble home with many small tables and chairs of varying designs and origins spread through several rooms. A view into the steamy kitchen reveals an immense middle-aged woman standing over a stovetop, manipulating pots and cookware with the confidence of a mother who has raised a dozen children alone.

"I'll bet that's Sara," Azucena observes, pointing to the woman. She whispers, "That's how you will look if you keep eating those cakes."

"And that's one of Sara's many daughters." Duncan nods toward an attractive teen of similar body type carrying four ample plates of food to a table of cowboy-booted and hatted men.

Duncan is reminded of the images of the cowboy-hatted revolutionary hero, Augusto Sandino, that appear on walls and posters throughout the country.

Azucena and Duncan order a *Plata Tipica* meal to share between them, knowing that they won't need any more food until tomorrow.

It's when Sara's daughter delivers the plate that Azucena and Duncan realize the difference between the *Plata Tipica* of *Los Antojitos* in Managua (with its beans, rice, and chicken), and the mountain of steak, vegetables, eggs, and cheeses set before them.

"I'll bet the breakfasts are great here," Duncan offers with a grin, while spreading gravy over his portion from a coffee mug improvising as a gravy boat.

Azucena smiles and offers another observation. "They won't have any Merlot on the wine list, Duncan.

"Wine list?" he asks. "Do you see one?"

* * *

After the hearty lunch Sara leaves the kitchen to meet her customers. She's attracted to Duncan and Azucena's table, probably because they are strangers.

"Americano, señor?" she asks Duncan.

"No señora, canadiense," Duncan responds, showing her the maple leaf decal on his camera bag.

"Ah, canadiense," Sara acknowledges, with a huge smile, and announces Duncan's origin to the other customers in a loud enthusiastic voice. *"El gringo es de Canada."*

She turns back to Duncan and lunges into a Spanish-language barrage of friendly-sounding conversation and arm-waving about her brother who, Duncan surmises, has relocated to Canada.

Azucena recognizes Duncan's inability to keep up with Sara's verbal assault and offers her service as translator.

"Sara's brother left Nicaragua a decade ago during the Contra war to avoid serving in the military ..." Azucena explains, pausing to listen to Sara's next sentence. She continues, "He found a sponsor in Canada who helped him settle and find a job. Now he sends money to Sara and the family whenever possible."

Sara steps forward and envelopes Duncan between her ample arms. She rattles off more Spanish that brings tears to her eyes.

Duncan returns Sara's embraces while Azucena translates.

"On behalf of my dear brother," Azucena interprets, "I thank you with my heart for being a Canadian. Canada gave my brother a new life."

"*Gracias, señora,*" Duncan acknowledges, placing his hands together and bowing his respects toward Sara.

Duncan volunteers to take a family portrait of Sara, her daughter who served them, and three of her siblings. Sara gives Duncan the address of her brother in Winnipeg.

"*Por favor*, you will visit him, *mi hermano*, in Canada ... in *Wee-neepeg*," Sara makes Duncan promise. "He will embrace you as a friend and feed you well."

Before leaving the restaurant, Duncan shows Sara the photo of his *tocayo, Dooncan*, and the boy's mother.

Sara nods affirmatively to the photo. "*Si ... su nombre es Carmen y el niño es Dooncan. Ellos son muy pobres.*"

Azucena translates for Duncan that Sara knows the mother. Her name is Carmen and the boy is Duncan. Sara says they are very poor."

Sara watches Duncan's face quizzically as Azucena translates her words. Sara's facial expression reveals that she wants to ask a question but is afraid of the answer she might receive.

Azucena jumps to a conclusion. "I think Sara wants to know if you are *Dooncan's* missing father, because you have the same name."

"*No, no, señora,*" Duncan negates ahead of Sara's question, waving his head from side to side.

Azucena thinks ahead, asking Sara for directions to where Carmen and her family live.

Out in the parking lot, while Azucena enters the van, Duncan's attention is drawn to a parked blue *camioneta* with a group of teenage *muchachos* (young men) sitting in the back. They seem interested in Duncan's Volkswagen camper. Duncan had noticed them in the restaurant earlier, acting up and showing off their group *machismo* to Sara's daughter.

"*Ey gringo,*" one of the boys shouts to get Duncan's attention. "*Que pasa, canadiense?*"

"*Somos turistas,*" Duncan answers, before entering the van to join Azucena.

"*Tiene cuidado,*" the same boy warns them to be careful. Another boy flashes Duncan the bird and the others laugh as Duncan and Azucena proceed on their way toward Carmen's home on the outskirts of town.

Following Sara's directions, Duncan and Azucena arrive at a collection of humble one-room *casitas* haphazardly arranged in a muddy field. Duncan hesitates to call it a suburb of Muy Muy, but no other description enters his mind.

After showing the photograph to several locals, Duncan and Azucena are directed by gestures toward a dwelling constructed of miscellaneous building materials.

From outside, they hear a baby's cries and a mother shouting in desperation. Duncan calls, "*Señora Carmen.*"

The door creaks open cautiously. Carmen's eyes peer through the narrow opening to see Duncan and Azucena's silhouette pasted against the late afternoon sun which had only recently revealed itself.

"*Hola señora,*" Azucena speaks, "*nos recuerdas?*"

Carmen opens the door further as a positive sign that she remembers them. She steps outside to see them more clearly.

"*Si, los recuerdo. De la clinica.*"

Duncan offers Carmen the 8 x 10 inch glossy prints. Tears emerge in the mother's eyes.

Through Azucena's helpful translations, Duncan asks about *Dooncan's* health.

"Lo mismo," Carmen responds, "the same." She opens the door further as an invitation for Duncan and Azucena to enter.

The room is as dark inside as a tunnel. One small glassless opening allows a narrow stream of light to spread onto a floormat where Duncan's *tocayo* lays. The boy stares upward without any apparent focus. He rolls from side to side on the mat, issuing moans and grunts. A baby cries, and Carmen satisfies the tyke's demands. The odours of urine and vomit permeate the room.

Azucena asks Carmen whether the children have seen any doctors.

"No. No es posible," she exclaims, placing the baby on the floormat next to *Dooncan.* "When the Sandinistas came to power, they opened up the health clinics. They were free for everyone, even the poor *campesinos.*" Carmen touches her breast. "Like us."

Azucena's facial expression displays concern. She takes Carmen's hand to demonstrate her consolation.

Carmen continues. "Then Reagan's embargo prevented the clinics from getting any medicines. So, we had free health care, but no medicines."

While Azucena and Carmen are conversing, Duncan discreetly photographs *Dooncan* and his baby brother in the stream of light.

Carmen speculates. "It is being said that the Sandinistas will lose the next election. What then? The new government will close the medical clinics, but we will have medicines … for a cost beyond what anybody can pay … anybody but the rich. There is no justice. It will be as before, under Somoza."

Carmen offers her conclusion. "For the poor, there is no salvation. No matter what government is in power, there is no justice for us. Just look around." She sweeps her arm around the shanty in an arc as proof.

Before they retire for the evening, Duncan and Azucena return to *Comedor Sara.* They order a *Plata Tipica* to go. While they wait for their order, Azucena shows Sara the photo of Tomás.

"Did you ever see this boy anywhere?" Azucena asks, studying Sara's reaction to the photo. "He is my son."

"This boy," Sara begins. "This boy … your son … was here, in Muy Muy within the last few months. He was in the restaurant with some other boys about the same age as your son. They were travelling in a *camioneta*." She points her forefingers at her temples to challenge her memory. "Yes. I remember. They each had tortillas."

Azucena asks. "Do you know any of the other boys with him?"

"I don't know them, but one of them comes here often. Wait …" Sara extends her hand to her forehead again. "He was here today, when you were here. The boy I was talking about. Yes. I'm certain. He was here with three other boys."

Duncan interjects. "Were they loud and teasing the waiter?"

"Yes, those boys. They are still spoiled children."

Duncan turns to Azucena. "The guys in the blue *camioneta*, when we were leaving, they called me a *canadiense*. He told me to be careful and another boy gave me the bird. Remember?"

"Yes, Yes. I remember, now." Azucena concludes, "So, if we can find that *camioneta* and those boys, we will find Tomás, no?"

Sara agrees. "Yes. They drove a blue *camioneta*."

Duncan and Azucena are eager to find the pickup truck.

"Wait, *señores*. Don't forget your *Plata Tipica*."

They drive their camper back to Carmen's shanty. Azucena presents the package of food to Carmen. *"Para su familia, señora."*

Carmen is surprised and overwhelmed at the gesture. *"Muchas, muchas, gracias,"* she repeats and invites Azucena and Duncan to share the bounty with her family.

Simultaneously, Azucena and Duncan turn down her offer. "We must keep moving," Duncan explains.

After searching for a half hour in the impending darkness, Duncan locates a narrow lane leading to a fallow farm field, a quiet place to park the camper for the night. He chooses a level grassy clearing protected from the road by a row of trees and foliage for privacy. The day's driving, combined with their sumptuous feast at Sara's, prepares them for a sound sleep.

CHAPTER 25

CONFRONTATION

Nicaragua, Early 1989:

"What's that noise?" Azucena barks. "Is that you, Tomás?"

Azucena's sleep is interrupted by ominous sounds from outside in the intense darkness of the northern mountain sky, removed from any human illumination. She hears scratching at the doors and windows of the camper and imagines that Tomás is outside desperately trying to get in. She is tempted to open the door to let Tomás in but is also afraid of who or what may be lurking outside. She considers shining the flashlight but rejects the idea in fear that it may attract whoever might be outside the camper.

Finally, when she can't tolerate the anxiety any further, Azucena shakes Duncan awake. The digital clock on the dashboard reads 3:46 am, too early for first light. The outside remains ink black.

"Uh? What's wrong?" Duncan groans.

"I'm worried, Duncan. Hold me."

"What are you worried about? We're safe in here."

"Tomás is outside in the darkness. He wants to get into the camper."

"You've been dreaming," Duncan says, pulling her closer in their communal sleeping bag.

* * *

Morning pierces its fresh light through the striped curtains of the camper, casting patterns on the opposite wall. Duncan stretches his arms before sliding out of the sleeping bag. He tries not to waken Azucena yet, in appreciation of her disturbed sleep.

He steps outside to relieve himself in the fresh mountain air, following it with a short stroll to stretch his leg muscles. There are always surprises in the morning when you park the camper in an unknown location at night.

Intricate spider webs that didn't exist in the night, light up against the rising sun. Morning comes alive with birdsong and smells of dampness and fresh growth.

A car door breaks the silence from somewhere nearby. Duncan follows the sound to the narrow entrance access to the farm field. A blue *camioneta* blocks the lane at the main road. He watches from behind a growth of wild foliage.

A young man relieves himself against a tree before returning to the *camioneta*. It's the man who shouted, *"tiene cuidado"* to Duncan in Sara's parking lot the previous afternoon.

Duncan remains quiet, returning tiptoed to the camper. He carefully pries the door open without creating a sound and pulls it closed with the same care.

While Azucena sleeps, Duncan ponders how he should proceed.

'I want to find out who that guy is because he knows something about Tomás but is he dangerous? What if he's armed? Should I arm myself with a weapon of some kind? If so, what? All I have is the baseball bat I used to play with Tomás. I should, however, try to get a photo of the guy in case he runs for it. Maybe the licence plate number as well. Does that even matter here? Who knows if the government even keeps records of such trivial details?'

Azucena attempts to open her eyes against the bright sun. "Duncan?" she calls weakly.

"I'm right here, my precious. Stay where you are until you feel like getting up. There's no hurry."

"What time is it?" Azucena asks, yawning and rubbing her eyes.

"According to the camper's clock, it's 6:42."

Duncan hears footsteps outside.

"Shh," Duncan signals, zipping his lips toward Azucena. He whispers, "Be quiet. Stay where you are. Don't move around."

Duncan peers through the striped curtain but sees nobody. He listens attentively for any sound. Nothing. Finally, he reaches for his bat and eases the door open. Staying close to the camper and watching where the sun is casting his own shadow, Duncan sneaks around the vehicle to the opposite side. Nobody appears.

'Am I imagining ghosts?' he wonders. 'Am I becoming like Azucena, hearing things that don't exist except in my mind?'

"*Ey, canadiense,*" a voice calls from behind him.

Duncan turns. The young man from Sara's parking lot stares at him. Duncan raises the bat, fully aware that he could crush the man's skull with one blow.

The man raises his hands. "*No estoy armado,*" he declares his lack of a weapon, adding, "*Soy amigo, señor.*"

Before Duncan can react, the camper door opens and Azucena steps outside. She sees Duncan with his baseball bat raised toward the man's head. Azucena pushes the man to the ground from behind and threatens to pound him with a frying pan.

Duncan calls. "Stop, Azucena! No!" He steps between them. "I think this guy is friendly. He's OK."

"*Como se llama?*" Duncan demands of the man.

"*Me llamo Raul. Yo conozco Tomás, su hijo.*"

"He knows Tomás," Azucena shouts. "Don't hit him."

"Is there any fuel in the camp stove, Azucena? Duncan asks. "If so, let's make some coffee."

Duncan offers a handshake to Raul. It's reciprocated. Duncan introduces Azucena.

Together they sit outside the camper enjoying their contraband coffee from *Galería de los Soñadores*.

"*Es buen café,*" Raul complements, sipping from a camp mug.

"*Gracias. Es nicaragüense, de Jinotega,*" Azucena tells Raul.

The conversation goes immediately to Tomás.

Azucena wants to know everything, assuming that Raul has all the answers.

Raul explains. "Tomás and I were kidnapped together. We were *mulas* for the Contras. Do you know what *mulas* are?" Raul asks.

"*Si,*" Duncan answers.

"*Esclavos,* they are slaves," Raul confirms. "We carried all the heavy supplies for the bastards. *Mulas humanas.* That's why we were called *mulas.* We were forced to do bad things as well, whenever they ordered us to. After witnessing some terrible acts, they threatened to kill us. We, Tomás and me, escaped into the bush under gunfire. I am from these mountains and know every peak and valley. That is how we escaped."

"What happened to Tomás?" Azucena pushes for an answer.

"Tomás was shot in the leg. I took him to the clinic in Matiguas. I knew it was operated by the Sandinistas so it would be safe there. The nurse fixed his wound. I wanted him to stay here, in Muy Muy, but he wanted to search for his father. That's all he told me."

'What happened then?" Azucena probes after refilling the coffee mugs.

"I drove him to the *Costa Atlántica* in my *camioneta* where he connected with a fishing boat heading for Belize along the Miskito coast, with stops in Honduras. He had to stay away from the Honduran mainland to avoid the Contras. That's where we got captured in the first place. I know nothing after that."

Azucena's face falls into disappointment. "We still know nothing," she says to Duncan.

Raul speaks again. "I also remember that he talked about Canada.

He told me that, if he couldn't get into the United States, he would travel to Canada to find a friend."

Duncan lowers his head. "Fuck!" He stands up and walks in a circle, kicking the earth. "What if he looked for me in Toronto. I wasn't there. I was here. Shit!"

Azucena stands and wraps her arm around Duncan's waist. "It's not your fault, Duncan. How were you to know? Besides, if he went to the college, he would meet Joyce ... or Kurt. They would tell him immediately where you are. And, they would have communicated with us if Tomás showed up there."

"So, we know he must have gone to Miami," Duncan concludes. "That's all we have to go on, right?"

Azucena tightens her grip on Duncan. "That's 100 percent more than we had last night, Duncan." She smiles with fresh optimism. "If Tomás is in Miami, he will know how to return home."

Duncan adds, "But if Tomás was in Miami, he'd be able to telephone us, right?"

Duncan avoids discussing other possible options if Tomás had problems along the route. He decides to save that conversation with Azucena for another time. 'Besides,' he ponders, 'maybe Tomás will be home soon.'

Duncan embraces Raul. "*Gracias, amigo*. You have been very helpful. A circle is coming together for us. Let us treat you to one of Sara's breakfasts."

CHAPTER 26

ORDEAL

Nicaragua, Early 1989:

Duncan steers the flowered Volkswagen through the midnight darkness. An ink-black, starless sky forces him to squint into the highway, his vision only guided by the headlights of his own camper. After three hours he finally veers off the Pan-American highway at Tipitapa toward the capital where the increase of traffic noises wake Azucena.

"Where are we?" she asks, rubbing the sandman's dust from her eyes.

"Almost home, my dear. You've been sleeping since we left Muy Muy. Do you know that you snore?"

She tries to laugh. "I'm sorry, Duncan. I know you don't like me sleeping while you're driving but I couldn't keep my eyes open." Azucena yawns widely. "I was exhausted after such an event-packed week. So much happened that I still can't digest it all. It's like I've been dreaming everything. I don't know what to believe anymore. What is true and what is fantasy?"

Duncan proposes an answer. "That's why you have sand in your eyes. The Sandman drops it into your eyes so you can sleep soundly. When you sleep well you dream well."

"Yeah? I don't believe that. You know me, Duncan. I can dream while I'm wide awake. We're both dreamers. Just look at the sign above our gallery door."

"Well, we're almost home," Duncan promises, turning onto *Avenida Simon Bolívar*. He pulls the camper up to the front of their *casita*.

"I'll open up," Azucena offers. "You start emptying the stuff."

Duncan throws his camera gear over his shoulder and grabs their backpacks.

"Duncan." Azucena whispers. "Come quick. Somebody's broken into our house. Look. The glass is broken and the door is wide open."

"Stay where you are, Azucena," Duncan warns. "Don't enter the house."

Instinctively, Duncan grabs the baseball bat from the camper and slinks through the door into the darkness ahead of Azucena. "Stay here," he whispers. "I'll find out who it is. They'll regret doing this, I guarantee it."

"Be careful, Duncan," Azucena whispers, reluctant to step further inside. "They may be armed."

From the corner of her eye, Azucena detects a light burning in the studio. "Duncan," she whispers, pointing to the studio window. "Somebody's in the studio."

They slowly and quietly enter the studio together. Azucena follows Duncan, grasping onto his shirttail. Once in, Duncan shouts, "Show yourself, whoever you are. I'm coming in after you and I'm armed."

A muffled voice comes from a darkened corner, behind a row of framed paintings. "Duncan? Is that you? Don't shoot. It's only me."

"Tomás?" Azucena shouts, recognizing his voice immediately. "Is that you ... is it really you?"

"Mamá! Yes it's me, Tomás."

Tomás emerges from under a tarpaulin that Azucena had thrown over her recent paintings to protect them from dust.

Seeing the figure rise, Azucena rushes toward him, arms outstretched. "Oh Tomás ... Tomás ... my son!" she says weeping tears of joy. "You're alive."

Duncan drops the bat on the floor and runs to add his arms to the already entwined mother and son.

"I thought somebody was breaking in," Tomás explains. "That's why I hid under the tarp. When I arrived back, nobody answered the door, so I had to break my way in. I'm sorry. I'll repair the damage."

Azucena tightens her grip around Tomás. "You don't have to apologize for anything, my dear. We're just so relieved to have you home."

"I can explain everything ..."

Duncan interjects. "We're sure there is so much for you to tell, but now is not the time to explain anything, Tomás. We just want to celebrate your return. There'll be plenty of time to talk about the past."

As tired as Duncan and Azucena were an hour ago, sleep is far from their minds.

Azucena tells Tomás about their trips to the mountains searching for him, and about the reported sightings they heard about in Muy Muy and Matiguas.

Referring to information they had received at the clinic, Azucena prompts Tomás, "The nurse at the Matiguas clinic said you had a gunshot wound. Where were you shot? Who did that to you?"

Tomás pulls up his left pant leg revealing an indented scar below his knee. "It's really nothing. One of the Contras got angry with me when I told him to fuck off ... oops, sorry Mamá.

"I don't want to know the details right now. I just want to know that you're all right."

"What are all those paintings I saw in the studio ... the ones painted on photographs?" Tomás asks.

"Those are from our exhibition called, 'Searching for Tomás.' Duncan and I collaborated on a series in which I painted your image into photographs that he had taken in locations where my dreams envisioned you."

"Are you still having dreams, Mamá?"

"I have dreams every day and night," Azucena says. "I am always dreaming, most of the time about you."

"I have them too, Mamá. Sometimes I think that you send me your dreams like *mi abuela* sends you hers.

While Azucena and Tomás are talking and getting re-acquainted, Duncan candidly photographs their emotional reunion. "It will add some resolution to our next exhibit of the 'Searching for Tomás' collaborations," he justifies, as if Duncan needs any excuse for taking photographs. "More importantly, it's part of our family history."

Duncan removes the caps from three bottles of *Toña* and hands one to Tomás. "Sorry, but these are the only bottles left from our trip."

"Stop, Duncan." Azucena slaps his arm. "Tomás is only 16. He's too young to drink."

"Mamá," Tomás pleads. "I'm almost 17 now."

"That's right," Duncan agrees. "Tomás is a man now. After what he's gone through he deserves to drink like a man."

Azucena retracts her opposition. "In that case, after what I've been through, I deserve to drink like a man too." She tilts the bottle and draws a long swig. When some beer spills over her chin, she wipes it with the back of her hand ... like a man.

Their initial tear-filled emotions of the night evolve into episodes of unreserved laughter. Azucena plays some happy music on the stereo and drags Tomás and Duncan up for celebratory dancing.

* * *

It takes several days before Tomás feels comfortable enough to describe what his time away has been like for him. Both Duncan and Azucena urge him to wait until he can assess the events objectively, but Tomás insists.

"I want to clear it all out of my head so I can forget about it, Mamá. Then I can put it far into the past and get on with my life ... my new life."

"Would you be comfortable having Duncan join us when we talk?" Azucena asks.

"Definitely. He's my Papá, after all."

"Before I begin, Mamá, I am really sorry for blowing up at you the day I left home. I had no right to criticize you for all the hard work you did during the revolution. I've had the opportunity to look at it from the other side, and it's not pretty."

Azucena strokes Tomás arm. "Apology accepted," she says with compassion on her face.

Tomás begins. "When I left I was just eager to get out of the house and spend some time alone. I was only going to stay away for a few days, just to burn off my anger. I went to hang out with some of the guys from school, and I ranted to them about the shortages and the war, the same things I said to you. They thought the same way and told me that they were going north, to Honduras, and asked me if I would join them. I said yes. I thought it would be an adventure, and that it might show me the other side of the politics. I was curious, that's all."

"You'd make a good journalist," Duncan observes.

Tomás continues. "On our way to Honduras, we connected up with some other guys in the mountains, in a town called Muy Muy. Finally, in Honduras, we hooked up with a bunch of other guys who had already joined up with the Contras. One night, sitting around a bonfire, one of the guys said something that pissed me off. He said that my father was Col. Jorge, the Contra leader. I didn't believe him and we argued. Then he called you some bad things, Mamá. That made me madder than a rogue bull. I got into a fight. He was a tough guy but I stood up to him ... gave him a good thrashing before the other guys pulled me back and worked me over.

Azucena pulls Tomás close. "I've heard those things said about me before, Tomás. They're nothing to get upset about ... water off a duck's back. The people who say those things are ignorant. They just don't understand. You have to ignore them."

Tomás continues. "One of the guys, a guy a bit older than me named Raul from Muy Muy, sided with me. He got beat up a bit too. We soon became friends."

"Wait a minute." Azucena turns to Duncan. "Raul. Isn't that the same guy we met in Muy Muy just last week?"

Duncan nods.

Tomás adds. "Well … it turned out that the guy I fought with was one of the Contra militants. He reported me to his *comandante* and told him who I was related to. They recruited me, and Raul, as *mulas*. Do you know what *mulas* do?"

"All the hard slugging," Duncan says. "They're the slaves."

"That's right," Tomás confirms. "All the shit jobs. If you can't take it, or if you bitch to them, they shoot you, like a lame horse." He starts to cry.

Duncan places his arm over Tomás' shoulder. "You don't have to tell us everything today, Tomás. Give it a rest."

"No, I want to tell you everything, while it's still fresh in my mind."

"I'll tell you what," Duncan suggests, standing up and adjusting his belt. "I need some exercise. Why don't we all walk to *Antojitos*? Get some fresh air. We can continue our conversation over lunch."

"And a *Toña* I suppose," Azucena jibes with a grin.

"Exactamente," Duncan replies.

On their stroll to the restaurant, Azucena reminds Tomás, "You're home just in time for the 10th anniversary celebrations. It's only a couple of months away."

"It's pretty hard to ignore," Tomás answers, "with all the propaganda plastered around the city."

"Be careful, Tomás," Duncan warns, his hand shielding his voice from Azucena but speaking loud enough for her to hear. "Your mother had a lot of input into those signs and murals. She designed and painted many of them. The ones she didn't paint were done under her guidance by some of her students and volunteers."

Over lunch, Tomás revisits his story. "After I heard the rumour that Col. Jorge was my father, I couldn't erase the thought from my mind. I didn't want to believe it, but I wanted to know for sure. I searched for him in Honduras, then I found out he stayed in Miami, where he plotted all the Contra manoeuvres. It was then that I decided to search for him there. Do you know how hard it is to enter the U.S., especially for *los nicaragüenses*?

Azucena finally asks Tomás the difficult question that has been haunting her. "Did you ever get to meet Col. Jorge?"

"No. I never made it to Miami." Tomás reveals. "It's probably a good thing that I didn't get there. I might have killed the bastard myself after what I've seen."

"Be careful what you say, Tomás," Duncan warns. "So, what did you do then?" he asks, pouring some *Toña* into each of their glasses.

"Raul helped me connect with a fisherman sailing up to Belize, but we never made it that far. The boat landed in Honduras and we were forced to return to Puerto Cabezas in Nicaragua. I had to find my own way back through the jungle and the mountains."

Tomás turns toward Azucena. "I remembered all the stories you told me about being in the mountains with the *guerrilleros* during the revolution, about eating snakes and hiding from strangers. That's how I survived. I bartered with a man for his machete and carried it for my own protection."

Azucena strokes her son's arm.

Duncan asks, pointing to Tomás' leg, "When and why were you shot?"

"Once, before I tried to get to Miami, when I was a *mula*, I tried to escape. I was carrying a heavy load of supplies on my back and I thought I was going to die from the abuse. I was choking from thirst and my back felt like it would split in two. Raul and I gradually slowed down until the others had marched ahead of us. We dumped our loads and made a run for it into the deep bush. One of the Contras started shooting. We dodged from side to side, like in the movies. The Contra shooter must have been a newcomer because he couldn't hit the side of a cow if he was milking it at the same time. We were well into the bush when a bullet ricocheted off a tree and sizzled across my leg. Fortunately, the bullet didn't penetrate, so Raul bandaged it up with the sleeve of his shirt. I whittled a cane from a tree branch. It was hard walking for a while, but we made it through the mountains to Matiguas. That's where Raul dropped me off at the clinic."

Duncan confirms his story. "The nurse remembers you being there. She identified you from a photo."

"Raul and I split up after that. It was too dangerous for us to be seen together. I was still on the run at the time, afraid of being discovered. I remained in hiding for a while in the mountains until I felt it was safe to start travelling home. And here I am," he adds, stretching his arms.

"Let's drink to that," Duncan proposes, his *Toña* held high.

After the toast, Azucena turns to Tomás. "Now that you're back, you must get back into your studies. You'll be turning 17 this December, but you've missed more than a year of classes."

"I know, Mamá. I'm going to the school next week to sort things out. Maybe I can do some extra work to catch up. I'm sure that I'm not alone in this situation."

"Duncan and I will help you in any way necessary. I'm sure Father Manuel would pitch in as well."

PART TEN
1989 − 1993

CHAPTER 27

ANNIVERSARY

Nicaragua, 1989:

Interest in Nicaraguan affairs enjoys a renewed profile in world news. Duncan starts receiving photo assignments from InterNews to report on events surrounding the ongoing Esquipulas Peace Agreement (also known as the Central American Peace Accords and the Arias Peace Plan, named after Costa Rican President, Oscar Arias, who initiated the process).

Duncan's assignments are primarily to photograph the political leaders of each of the five Central American nations when they meet. His unique talent is in capturing the variety of their facial expressions and gestures when they share the podium (or refuse to). From a visual standpoint the assignments are not particularly exciting, but the political ramifications are substantial.

There are also assignments arriving for Duncan from InterNews, as well as other magazines, including referrals from Kurt's connections in Europe, to provide photo coverage in advance of the upcoming 10th anniversary of the Sandinista revolution. The event, anticipated to be a grand national festival is also bringing to the fore, public dissent from counter-revolutionary segments of the population.

Azucena is kept busy creating new art pieces for an exhibition in their own gallery and, for the Sandinista party, overseeing a staff of young artists in the creation of public murals promoting the anniversary celebrations.

"Kurt gives his regards to you, my dear," Duncan reads to Azucena from a letter he receives from Kurt. "Everything is going swimmingly at the college and he hasn't destroyed my townhouse yet."

Azucena offers some levity, giggling in advance. "By swimmingly, does Kurt mean that he's hanging out in Joyce's pool?"

"He didn't even mention Joyce," Duncan says. "Remember that Kurt is working in the Photojournalism faculty, not in Fine Arts with Joyce."

"I know, but I just thought Kurt and Joyce would hit it off."

* * *

July 19, 1989:

Buses, arriving in the capital from every corner of the country, deliver thousands of Nicaraguans to the festivities at *La Plaza de la Revolución*. A complicated decade has passed since the triumph of the revolution; years of joys and sorrows, or as Charles Dickens wrote, 'It was the best of times, it was the worst of times …'

Nicaraguans are joined in their celebration by thousands of visitors from around the globe. Hotels, pensions and *hospedajes* are fully occupied with sympathizers, political leaders and journalists.

For the past six months, Azucena has worked alongside her *compañeros* to help in the preparations for this day. Her contributions included painting huge murals promoting the event and the party: images of peasants working together for the cause, and soldiers bearing AK-47s in one hand and olive branches in the other. She has been instrumental in guiding younger artists who enthusiastically volunteered to join her in the mission. Throughout the process, she has also enjoyed the company of the older revolutionaries who arrived at the studios to offer advice and relay well-worn stories of valour.

Duncan seizes the opportunities to take photographic portraits of the veterans from the various campaigns of the revolution leading up to the Triumph.

While preparing to leave for the plaza, Azucena turns to Duncan. Her face reveals a sudden sadness. "I am often haunted by whether my own commitment and involvement in the revolution was the wrong decision," she reflects.

"Why do you think that?" Duncan asks, curious about her comment on the day intended to celebrate the triumph.

"Maybe Tomás was right," she confides with Duncan minutes before they leave home, hand-in-hand, to join in the celebration. "Maybe I was too rigid with him, Duncan."

Duncan grips her hand and squeezes. "Don't beat yourself up, my dear," he tells her, serving a dual role as consoler and listener.

"It was my fault Tomás left home," she says, banging her right hand against her head in an act of self-flagellation. "I should have listened to him, at least tried to have a calm discussion."

"It's all in the past now, my dear. Tomás is home. He apologized to you for what he said and did. He left as a boy and returned as a man. In the interim, he learned many lessons, albeit the hard way."

"I know, Duncan. It's just that these thoughts won't go away. They keep cropping up in my dreams."

"We can stay home instead of going to the plaza," Duncan offers.

Azucena gives Duncan a squeeze and steps back with a grin on her face.

"Look at me." She laughs hysterically at her image in the mirror. "I'm already dressed in my revolutionary regalia, *mi roja y negra*, my red and black. I look like an old wind-torn Sandinista flag that's waiting to be flown in the wind for one last time. Ha-ha." She laughs at her own joke.

Duncan joins her, embracing and kissing her. "We'll enjoy ourselves, *mi bonita compañera*, if only for the memories.

Azucena shouts, "Tomás! We're leaving for the plaza. Are you coming?"

Tomás appears at the door sporting a red and black bandana around his neck. "Let's go."

Azucena, Duncan, and Tomás join the throngs arriving at the plaza, first stopping to shed tears at Carlos Fonseca's eternal flame. A brass band performs *Himno del FSLN* (the Sandinista Hymn) in front of the podium where the President will soon deliver his address. The crowd sings along, *"Adelante marchemos compañeros …"* (Together we march, comrades). Tears are shed; of joy and of sad remembrance for those lost or disappeared during the revolution and in the conflicts that followed the triumph.

Azucena's tears blend joy and sadness.

From the rooftops of nearby buildings, military snipers stand ready against any disruption of the festivities by the Contras, while helicopter gunships sweep across the sky.

The President offers his anticipated promises of prosperity and peace. He ends his speech emphasizing with his fist, *"No Pasarán! No Pasarán!"* (they shall not pass) followed by the crowd's response, *"Viva Nicaragua Libre!"* (long live free Nicaragua).

A carnival atmosphere overtakes the capital throughout the day. Bars overflow and complete strangers dance together in the streets.

Before Tomás leaves to join his younger friends in the revelry, he gives a hug and kiss to his mother. "See you later, Mamá. He turns to Duncan. "I'm really glad you came to live with us in Nicaragua, Papá. They embrace.

Duncan had instructed Tomás to call him Duncan but he greatly appreciates being referred to as 'Papá.'

* * *

There is an ominous underlying reality to the revelry. One of the conditions of the Arias Central American Peace Plan proposal, currently being negotiated, is that Nicaragua must hold democratic elections. Many Nicaraguans are feeling betrayed about the prosperity promised them by the ruling Sandinistas, doubtful that peace will break out anytime soon.

Journalists, who have been talking directly to the people on the streets, already have a sense of how it will end. People are tired of the war and its enormous cost in human lives, of shortages caused by the embargo placed against them by the United States, and of the families broken apart.

Public debates and lively street demonstrations separate the factions representing the mothers of the revolution and the mothers of children who have left the county to avoid the draft, or who have been lost in the continuing conflict. Some hardliners demand that the ones who have left should not be allowed to return or should be imprisoned for abandoning the revolution.

Azucena refuses to be drawn into the argument. "It's a seesaw," she tells Duncan, " and I'm sitting on both ends."

Duncan compliments her on her metaphor. "Let me guess," he suggests an extra line, "that you are constantly being pushed up and down at the same time."

"We're so good together," Azucena tells him, affectionately punching her fist into his shoulder.

* * *

1990 – 1991:

An election date is scheduled for February 25, 1990. Prior to the election, the United States promises to lift the embargo if the UNO party is elected. UNO represents a coalition of 14 vastly diverse parties, from extreme left to ultra-right, that share only one common goal, the parties are all opposed to the current revolutionary government.

The UNO coalition party wins the election with a narrow 54 per cent of the vote, signaling the apparent demise of the Sandinista revolution.

"It's all over," Azucena laments, her eyes shedding tears over Duncan's shoulder. "What is ahead for us now? I hate to think."

"You keep fighting for the values you cherish, my dear," Duncan encourages. "That is who you are."

"I don't know if there is much fighting spirit left in my heart."

"Do you remember how you fought for your ideals before the triumph?"

"Of course, Duncan. How could I forget?"

Duncan grips her shoulders and looks directly into her eyes with a serious demeanour.

"Then you start all over again. I know you haven't stopped believing in your ideals. You practice them each and every day."

Duncan pauses. Azucena's dampened eyes stare back. She sniffles but remains silent.

He continues. "There will be another election. Be ready for it. *Entienda?*"

She nods. "I understand, Duncan. I truly do."

Duncan monitors current events as they unfold in Nicaragua through the three major daily newspapers: *Barricada*, *La Prensa*, and *El Nuevo Diario*. Each represents a different hue of the political spectrum, from Marxism to Conservatism. Duncan learned early that his quest for truth is only discovered by reading between the lines in all three sources. He did the same thing at home in Canada, and he encouraged his students to do the same.

"If you only read one paper, or watch one TV news station, you will always get one perspective, the same one every time. Unfortunately, that's what most people do, and it's the cause of narrow mindedness and social illiteracy; the breeding ground for bigotry and self-righteous intolerance."

He also keeps his eyes and ears open to the scuttlebutt from international journalists that come and go in the Intercontinental bar. Occasionally, Duncan receives his own assignments from InterNews to cover local events of global interest, but the world all but stops watching Nicaragua. It turns its cameras on earth-shattering events elsewhere.

One story that Duncan continues to cover, with personal interest, follows the migration of people returning to Nicaragua. With every photo he takes he quietly reflects on Tomás' story and how it affected he and Azucena. Every young person he sees through the viewfinder has Tomás' face.

In the year following the election, men and women who had formerly left Nicaragua to support the Contras gradually return home, mainly from Honduras and Miami. Many hope to reclaim property that had been occupied by the agrarian reform policies of the Sandinista government.

A rumour spreads that the brutal leader of the Contras, Col. Jorge, might be planning a return to the capital from his base in Miami. The news, whether fact or fiction, is met with public demonstrations and editorial opposition.

Finally, Col. Jorge attempts to enter the country incognito. The plot is discovered and results in an assassination attempt in the parking lot of the Intercontinental Hotel which he narrowly escapes, at the cost of two security guard's lives. Quickly, Col. Jorge is whisked back out of the country by his supporters.

CHAPTER 28

RENEWAL

1992:

"Tomás," Azucena shouts through the studio door. "We're leaving now."

"I'll be right there," Tomás answers from the studio.

"Will you be OK looking after everything while we're gone?" Azucena asks.

"Of course, Mamá. I'm not a child anymore. I'm 19-years-old, you know. Don't worry. If there are any unforeseen difficulties, I'll call Father Manuel."

"Of course I know how old you are. How time flies ... but you're still my baby."

Tomás leans forward for a quick kiss on the cheek. "When will you be coming back?"

Duncan answers while Azucena does a last-minute check through the studio. "We expect to be home in a few weeks, maybe a month. It depends on how the spirits treat us," Duncan jokes. "Give me a hug, son."

Tomás and Duncan share embraces.

"Have a great trip, Papá. Come back rejuvenated."

"That's almost a guarantee, Tomás. Anywhere I go with your mother, I come back rejuvenated. *Hasta pronto.*"

As soon as they're on the road, Azucena asks Duncan, "Can you believe that Tomás will soon be 20? So much has happened since then."

"That's the nature of life. It's always changing." He pauses to concentrate on the traffic. "Isn't that why we're returning to *Paraíso* ... to search for change?"

"What are you hoping to change, Duncan?" Azucena asks.

"I'm searching for peace and tranquility," Duncan poses. "That's what I need most these days. Only through peace and tranquility, will I discover what I'm looking for."

"So you don't know what you're looking for? Azucena probes.

"Do you?"

"Absolutely. I'm looking forward to a new, fresh vision in my work. I'm tired of what I've been doing. I need a new theme. I'm no longer searching for Tomás; I found him. Now I need fresh dreams and visions to move ahead to a new plateau."

"I always thought you received the visions from your mother. Won't your future work depend on what she sends to you in your dreams?"

"Of course, Duncan. It's up to me, however, to interpret those dreams. That's what I'm hoping to discover in *Paraíso*; new ways to interpret my dreams.

"Yes," Duncan agrees, "but for that to happen, you first have to find peace and tranquility. That's the foundation of it all."

"So, I guess we'll be spending a lot of time meditating in the forest," Azucena says, flirtatiously. She squeezes Duncan's hand for confirmation.

"I'm looking forward to that." Duncan squeezes back.

For the next hour, as they gradually enter the rain forest region, conversation in the camper surrenders to the sounds of taped music: a potpourri of Joni Mitchell, John Coltrane, Gary Burton, John Prine, and of course, Janis Joplin.

When they arrive at the end of the road, Duncan and Azucena transfer their belongings from the camper to the fishing boat. During the boat trip, Duncan reaches over to Azucena. He whispers in her ear.

"Remember what we promised each other. No politics this time, right?"

"No politics. I promise."

* * *

Azucena wraps her arms around Duncan's waist, as they step together from the boat. She looks up into his eyes. "Do you feel anything, Duncan?"

"Oh yes."

The first steps on *Paraíso's terra firma* send vibrations through Duncan's bones, a feeling he used to experience whenever he stepped onto the soil of Manitoulin Island. It's one of those unexplainable senses that welcomes his entrance into a special place, a magical aura where anything becomes possible.

In Manitoulin he was exposed to an enhanced level of wisdom and knowledge, and a deep appreciation of the spiritual domain of another culture. When he was exposed to *Paraíso*, 15 years ago, his heart was opened to love and to the power of imagination. He was also released from the shackles inhibiting his creative desires, enabling him to cross over the divide between restrictive structure and freedom.

'What awaits me this time?' he contemplates as the vibrations slither from limb to limb.

Azucena and Duncan share a celebratory embrace before gathering their gear and venturing toward their *cabaña privada*, a private cabin deep in the density of the forest secluded from other vacationers. Access to the cabin is via a narrow trail that extends from the small clearing where Duncan and Azucena had originally meditated and where they first enjoyed their passions for each other.

As they venture further, they are shrouded by the natural sounds of the forest: melodic breezes filtering between the leaves and the squawking calls of toucans. Their arrival at the private domain reveals less than a *cabaña*, more a hut or shack instead, where they will hopefully discover the next phase of their lives.

Duncan is comforted by the continuous row of marching ants passing from one tree to the next across the broad wet leaves surrounding the hut. 'It's nice to know that some things don't change,' he contemplates. 'Regardless of what happens to us while we're here, these ants will still be marching when we return for our next renewal. They were probably here before the dinosaurs.'

From their hut, Azucena and Duncan agree to explore the diversity of shapes, textures, patterns, and colours contained within the immediate environs. Azucena sets her easel in one place for days, staring into the verdant richness as weather and the time of day alter her subjects.

Duncan moves in close, using a macro lens on his Nikon SLR to isolate all but the smallest inhabitants and details. Of course, his precious ants become a primary focus for him.

When they're not creating, they renew their affections with all the liberties that privacy affords. They lavish in their isolation from radios, telephones, newspapers, music, traffic, political rhetoric, even clothing when weather permits. Occasionally they walk the narrow trail into the community to replenish basic supplies — food and water — and to commune with the locals, before returning to their much desired solitude.

The hut faces a small clearing where they join hands in meditation to welcome the freshness of each morning. Azucena believes the dawn of each new day provides them with the openness and clarity that can accept fresh thoughts and ideas. Their meditations clear the noise of unnecessary thought from interrupting the process.

At the conclusion of each day, they repeat the process, allowing their quiet spaces to contemplate the lessons learned from the experiences of the day just completed.

During one of the early morning meditations, Azucena conducts an experiment without Duncan's knowledge. 'Is it possible for me to share my dreams and visions with Duncan, like my mother shares hers with me?' she wonders. 'Could Duncan learn to share his dreams with me in the same way?'

While their hands maintain delicate contact with each other's and they are both comfortable in their personal quiet zones, Azucena imagines an image in her mind with intentions of sharing it with Duncan. Every muscle in her body is relaxed, willing to relinquish the tensions and energy to the power of her mind. The image dominates her inner space while she silently focuses her attention on Duncan's personal space and offers the image to him.

Azucena senses a slight twitching of Duncan's hand. 'Could it be a sign that he's receiving the image I'm sending?' she ponders, before realizing that the mere thought of her external concern has interrupted her focus and eliminated the image from her space. 'Did Duncan receive my thought? How will I ever know? Will he even suspect where the image came from?'

Following the morning meditation, Azucena maintains her lotus position and focuses her mind upon the diversity of greenery surrounding her. She uses her focusing mind to catalogue the images in all their verdant hues, with plans of reclaiming them later when in the studio with her paints.

Duncan photographs details of the moisture droplets that have formed on the waxy surfaces of fern leaves surrounding the hut. He is fascinated by how the droplets reflect inverted 'fisheye' images of the landscape behind him and the sky above, with images of himself and his camera in the foreground. By shifting his vantage point only slightly around the leaves, the droplets reflect a variety of fluctuating images.

The simplicity of life in *Paraíso* is addictive to Azucena and Duncan. It isn't that they are searching for a radical, 'back-to-the-land,' change in the way they live. They merely seek renewal.

Each night in the darkness, surrounded only by stillness and the ambient sounds of nature, Azucena and Duncan share a hammock and discuss the kinds of thoughts only possible in solitude away from the chaos of the city.

Duncan embraces Azucena, pulling her gently against him. She rests her head into Duncan's chest where she senses the steady pulsing of his heart.

Duncan inquires at the end of their first week. "Do you think continuous renewal is possible for us, Azucena … or any artist, for that matter? Isn't it possible that each of us has a limit to how much renewal we can tolerate."

"That's a funny question, Duncan." She raises her head to face him, a quizzical expression in her eyes. "Are you becoming bored, or are you asking me if God has placed specific timelines on us?" Azucena asks with a grin intended to provoke discussion.

"Assuming that there is a god," Duncan muses, "he must have really liked Monet, Matisse, and Picasso, who continuously re-invented themselves well into old age."

"Is that what we're searching for, Duncan? Are we trying to re-invent ourselves? Or is the Almighty just keeping us from blooming until we reach old age? At some point in our later years, will we suddenly produce our Magnum Opus and become famous?"

Before Duncan can reply, Azucena concludes, "Or not," before changing the topic. "Are you feeling any change in the way you approach your art?"

"It's a lot quieter," Duncan answers. "There's not a lot of action like I'm used to, although I'm having fun. I have no way of knowing whether it'll lead anywhere though."

Azucena admits that she's been having some interesting dreams.

"A few days ago, I dreamt that I was painting in a field of wildflowers. The flowers rose up from the earth very quickly but were suddenly overcome by thousands of those ants you're fascinated with. They were marching as if toward a battle. From the opposite direction came another army of ants. They looked just like the first army. Once they started fighting, I couldn't tell which were which. How did they even know?"

"The smell, that's how," Duncan answers. "I wondered the same thing after my first visit to *Paraíso*, so I asked an entomologist at the university. The progeny of each queen all share the same smell."

Azucena questions, "Why were they fighting each other? Do ants hate other ants?"

"Maybe they just don't like how they smell," Duncan grins, "or maybe they're just like people. Why do people go to war? Mainly for territory, money, power, or religion. Usually all four amount to the same thing."

"That's all too weird, Duncan."

"The whole thing is weird, my dear. In fact it's uncanny." Duncan admits, "I had a similar dream … almost identical in fact. How is that possible?"

Azucena digs further. "When did you have that dream, Duncan? What night?"

"Oh, shit. I don't remember. Let me think. It was two, or three nights ago. No, wait. It was when I was meditating … in the morning. Is it still a dream when it happens during meditation? Or, is it something else … a vision perhaps, or a prophecy?"

"That is uncanny," Azucena acknowledges, faking her surprise. "That's when I had my dream. How weird is that?"

Duncan describes how his dream came to him. "What's really weird is that I didn't dream the image in one piece, it came to me in small bits … teasers … like pieces of a jig saw puzzle waiting to be assembled. The pieces floated around in my space until they gradually found each other to form a final image."

"Hmm," Azucena reacts. "That *is* weird. In my dream it appeared all at once, as one solid image."

She ponders, 'I wonder how that happened. There must be some kind of filter between us, some interference that breaks the image into pieces.' She concludes that there must be something wrong with the delivery system.

Azucena takes a minute to contemplate before proposing, "I have an idea, Duncan. Tomorrow, during our morning meditation, when an image is strongest in your mind's eye, turn your focus to my mind. We'll see if we experience the same dream."

"If it happens again," Duncan offers, "there's something bizarre happening in this place. Are you sure *Paraíso* hasn't been invaded by aliens?"

"Better aliens from another planet than being invaded by *gringos* and the characters running our current government."

"Uh-uh," Duncan chastises by waving his forefinger. "No politics, remember?"

"Sorry, Duncan. It just slipped out."

During their late evening meditation, Duncan focuses on his own desires, imagining he and Azucena sharing their bodies and souls in the hammock. While at the pinnacle of his dream he simultaneously focuses on Azucena's mind and wonders if she's having similar thoughts. He senses Azucena's fingers twitching softly in the palm of his hand.

Their concentration is broken when Azucena leans toward Duncan with love glistening in her eyes and tenderness in her touch.

"I received your message in my dream," Azucena whispers into his ear. Their moist lips connect as Azucena leads Duncan by the hand into the hut.

Making love in a hammock shares similar dynamics as having sex on a water bed in a tall ship under full sail during a perfect storm. The hammock oscillates in motions diametrically opposed to the passionate intentions of the lovers, creating unexpected, but not unappreciated, calamities. Falling out of a tilted hammock interrupts the process but rapidly invigorates the desire to re-engage. Unlike in a traditional bed, there is no turning away afterward in the belly of a hammock; lovers are bound to each other for a night of total contact, engagement, and sleep.

It is during their satisfied sleep, that Azucena and Duncan's dreams co-exist. They sleep together, enveloped by each other's arms, Azucena's face imbedded into Duncan's chest, while dreams pass between them: visions of wildflowers and lovers, of beauty and ugliness, of peace and war.

The dream evolves until they are witnessing events occurring within a colony of ants. There are three separate groups, each serving their own Queen, but they live peacefully within the colony. When they march, they march together, to collect food and to fight their common enemy, the oppressive scarab, a beetle that destroys the plant leaves of the trees the ants call home. Each army exudes a different odour, sensed only by the ants themselves, but they tolerate each other for the common purpose: to rid the tree of the scarab beetle.

During the dream, there is a major battle. The scarabs are stripped of their shell-like armour and their flesh until the few injured survivors limp away, in search of a new home, abandoning the tree altogether. The ants gather in a celebratory feast. As time passes, however, there is developing intolerance for each of the three Queens. The smell of each group becomes offensive. Battles erupt within the colony.

* * *

"TOMÁS!" Azucena shouts into the darkness, interrupting the rhythm of Duncan's snoring.

"WAKE UP, DUNCAN!" Azucena shouts again, shaking her lover. "It's Tomás. He's in trouble. Wake up!"

They quickly gather their belongings, weave their way through the dark forest along the narrow pathway by flashlight, toward the community. First light is appearing in the eastern sky. They run to the pier where the fishermen are busy untying their boats for the morning's catch.

"Take us to the mainland, please," Azucena pleads with the same fisherman who brought them to *Paraíso* two weeks before. "It's urgent."

Before they reach the mainland, Duncan presses Azucena for an explanation.

"What is going on? Is Tomás in trouble? How do you know something is wrong? Is it just a whim?"

"I can't explain it, Duncan. It's like the time we were in Matagalpa during the workshop. I had a dream about the Contra attack at the cooperative. Remember?"

"How could I forget?"

"A similar dream appeared to me last night," Azucena describes. "This time it's all about Tomás. I can't see any details in my dream but I know something serious is wrong."

* * *

Their arrival at the studio is met with a police tape around the house and studio. Police investigators are inside searching everywhere.

"What's going on?" Azucena pushes her way toward the studio.

An officer prohibits her from entering.

"What are you looking for?" she demands. "Where's my son, Tomás?" She shouts his name, "TOMÁS! TOMÁS!"

The officer in charge introduces himself officially. "I am *Capitán* Noguero, *señora* Azucena, or should I say, *compañera*? I am looking after this investigation.

"I know who you are *capitán*. We fought side-by-side as *guerrilleros* on the southern front. Why are you here tearing up my studio?" she asks, "and where is my son, Tomás? I need to see him right now."

"Please, *compañera*. Come with me where it's quieter." The *capitán* looks toward Duncan. "You may join us, *señor*." He guides Azucena and Duncan toward the front door of their *casita* with his hand pointing the way. "Please sit. I will explain everything to you."

The trio gathers around the kitchen table. Azucena frowns in worry, fumbling with her fingers.

Capitán Noguero removes his cap and explains. "I am investigating the attempted murder of Col. Jorge in the parking lot of the Intercontinental Hotel last month. As you are aware, Col. Jorge escaped, but two other people were killed by the assassins. We believe there to be several suspects involved."

"What has that got to do with Tomás?" Azucena demands. "He couldn't kill a mosquito," she adds.

"Tomás was seen on news footage. He was in the crowd when the shots were fired. We don't know who fired the shots, but Tomás is a person of interest in our investigation."

"That's ridiculous," Duncan says, caressing Azucena's back with his hand. "He has no reason to be interested in Col. Jorge. He would have been an innocent bystander."

Capitàn Noguero turns to Azucena. "May I have your permission to speak frankly in front of *señor* Duncan?"

"Of course. He is like a father to Tomás. There are no secrets."

"Very well, *compañera*. We have reason to believe that your son, Tomás, has affiliations with some of our suspects. That would indicate to us that he may have been involved in a plot."

"No, not Tomás," Azucena discounts, shaking her head. "He couldn't ..."

The *capitán* interrupts. "With all due respect, *compañera*," the *capitán* places his hand on Azucena's. "There is some indication, based solely upon rumour, that Col. Jorge may be the father of Tomás. Can you verify that?"

"No. I cannot," Azucena denies outright.

Duncan sits passively beside Azucena. Finally, he asks the *capitán*, "What is the source of that information?"

"Of course I can't reveal the source, but it is widely known that Tomás was searching for Col. Jorge over the past couple of years. We have statements from several of Tomás associates during that time."

"Associates? What associates?" Azucena demands assertively, pounding her fist against the table. "Tomás doesn't have 'associates' for Christ's sake. He hardly has any friends, just Duncan and me, and of course, Father Manuel, who has always been helpful to Tomás, especially when he was a young boy." She pauses. "Of course, we haven't seen Father Manuel too much since Duncan moved here full time. Duncan is like a father to Tomás. The boy doesn't need to look for another one, especially one so twisted as Col. Jorge, that bastard."

Duncan softly taps Azucena's arm to calm her. "It's OK, my dear. I'm sure we can work this all out."

Capitán Noguero stands. "I think that's all we need at this moment. We will also be talking to Father Manuel in the coming days. I'm certain that everything will work out well for you … and for Tomás." He shakes Duncan's hand, nodding, and bows to Azucena, *"compañera,"* and replaces his cap while leaving the *casita*.

Before stepping outside, he turns. "I have always adored your paintings, *compañera*. I'm certain that no damage was done to them but please contact me personally if there is ever a problem."

"There is a problem now, *capitán*," Azucena takes the offensive with a stern face. "You have my son locked up. When can I see him?"

"Soon. I will let you know."

Duncan embraces Azucena. "I will get to the bottom of this, my dear, I promise. Right now, let's go to see Father Manuel. He will know a good lawyer, just in case we need one."

* * *

Two days of agony pass before Azucena and Duncan are allowed to visit Tomás in the jail. Father Manuel and a lawyer accompany them.

"Please let me do the talking," the lawyer advises Azucena and Duncan when they arrive. "You can have a few private moments with Tomás before we start, but please keep it brief. Our time is limited."

When they enter the large room, Tomás is sitting alone at a table. Two uniformed guards, each with a baton and sidearm, stand a metre behind him.

Azucena approaches Tomás with her arms outstretched. "Tomás, my baby," she cries.

There's a short embrace before one of the guards steps forward to separate them. *"Contacto esta prohibido, señora,"* he warns in a soft, but firm voice.

Azucena's glazed eyes, reddened from lack of sleep, stare directly into Tomás' eyes while he answers the lawyer's questions.

Duncan quietly analyzes the questions and answers, jotting his thoughts into his own notebook.

Tomás answers the most obvious of the lawyer's questions. "Why were you at the Intercontinental that day?"

"I went to the Intercontinental because I heard that Col. Jorge would be arriving to meet with his followers and would be delivering a speech announcing his interest in running for political office. I wanted to talk to him, but there were too many people gathered around him. Some of them were treating him like a hero. It was hopeless so I just watched from the crowd. I had hoped to confront him and ask him to confirm whether he was my father or not, but everything was too chaotic. Everywhere I turned there were press cameras and reporters."

The lawyer pressed further. "When did you realize that something was going wrong?"

Tomás answers without delay. "There were some loud noises from the parking lot as Col. Jorge stepped out of the building. I soon learned that they were gunshots. He had two security guards. They pushed the colonel to the ground and then fell themselves. I found out later that the guards had been killed. Everything became more chaotic: people running for cover, some falling down on the pavement. Some of us, dumbfounded, just stood there looking around to see what was going on."

"Did you see any of the shooters? Did you see what happened to Col. Jorge?"

"No. By the time I clued into what was going on, Col. Jorge had been removed from the scene and disappeared. I haven't seen him since."

"Were any of your friends in the crowd?" the lawyer asks.

"There were a few guys I'd seen around before, but none of them would be considered as my friend ..." Tomás pauses and exposes a simple grin. "I don't have too many friends," he adds. "I'm just a solitary guy most of the time."

A guard signals that their time is up.

Azucena defies the rules by pulling Tomás tightly against her. "We'll get you out of here soon," she whispers.

Father Manuel suggests dinner on the patio at Los Antojitos. The lawyer declines, citing other important business to take care of.

Duncan declines for both he and Azucena. "We haven't slept in three days, Father. We'll call it a night. *Ciao.*"

CHAPTER 29

PROPHESY

Nicaragua, 1992:

In the morning, Duncan walks briskly to the Intercontinental Hotel. He locates a couple of TV journalists having breakfast in the dining room.

"Duncan, come and join us," one of the ABC cameramen calls, beckoning with his hand. "We were just talking about you. How are you and Azucena holding up?"

"No secrets from the news media, eh?" Duncan answers, smiling. He orders a coffee from the waiter and joins the cameramen at their table. "We'll survive, thanks, but we won't get much sleep until Tomás is free. That's why I'm here. Can I ask you guys a favour?"

Without waiting for an answer, Duncan continues. "Do you guys still have footage from the night Col. Jorge almost got killed. Not so much the prime action, but the peripheral stuff, you know, the onlookers, the crowds, and all that."

"We could let you screen it, Duncan. After all, you're one of us."

"Thanks guys."

"What are you looking for, man?"

"Apparently, Tomás was seen there, somewhere in the crowd," Duncan says, stopping to sip his coffee. "That's why they're holding him. As far as I can tell, that's the only reason they're holding him. My suspicion is that the police were just looking at the action footage, and when they saw Tomás' face somewhere, they made assumptions by trying to mix facts with rumours. I'm just curious what Tomás was doing when all hell broke loose, when the shooting started. You know how a crowd takes a moment to respond. You guys were probably doing the same thing, taking some establishing coverage, fillers; we all do that. There should be a delay in your footage before your cameras refocus in on the colonel. If I can find Tomás in the crowd doing something unrelated at the same moment as I hear the first shots, it may prove that he was there as nothing more than a bystander … a curiosity seeker like the rest of the crowd."

The ABC cameraman offers, "I'll take you into the editing room right after breakfast and we'll look up that stuff."

The other guys at the table ditto the same offer.

For the remainder of the day, Duncan stares at the monitors watching images advance and reverse until his eyes refuse to focus any longer. He has noticed Tomás several times and has duped the immediate 'before and after' sections for more fine-tuned scrutiny.

"Sorry Duncan. Your boy doesn't seem to be doing anything," the ABC editor says. "Besides, he's so far back from where the action took place, it's a wonder that he could see anything at all."

"Perfect," Duncan says, removing his duped edits from the machine. "That's just what I was hoping to find. Thanks guys. Have a drink on me."

Duncan takes the edits immediately to the lawyer's office and explains his findings.

"Thanks Duncan. I'll look after it first thing tomorrow."

* * *

Capitán Noguero arrives at the studio entrance two days later.

"*Compañera* Azucena," he shouts through the open doorway. "Are you there?"

"I'm over here," Azucena responds from behind a series of paintings on easels. "It's the muse, I can't ignore it. I must paint while the muse is hot."

"May I enter?" the *capitán* asks, removing his cap before entering. "I brought you a gift, *compañera*. Something special."

Azucena peeks over the easel. "Come in, *capitán*. What have you brought me?"

Tomás steps inside following the *capitán*. "It's me, Mamá … Tomás. I'm free." He stretches his arms wide to accept his mother's anticipated embrace.

Azucena drops her palette knife and runs toward Tomás. "My baby," she shouts, throwing her arms around him. "Duncan, come here!" she yells. "Tomás is home."

Duncan and Tomás embrace. Duncan turns to *capitán* Noguero. "So. Is the boy free on bail, or is he free forever?"

"He didn't do anything, *señor*. He is innocent." The *capitán* turns to Azucena. "You can thank Duncan for that. He found news footage that proved his innocence."

Capitán Noguero places his hand onto Duncan's elbow. "Perhaps we could allow *compañera* Azucena a few minutes alone with her son, while we have a talk, *señor*, in private."

"Sure, what's up?" Duncan asks. "I'll get us a couple of *Toñas*. We can sit out front."

Once seated, the officer confides in Duncan. "There are forces at work in the country, who want to … how should I say this? … reduce the numbers of former *compañeros*, especially those who have connections."

"Like you, for instance, *capitán*?" Duncan asks, pointing his beer hand toward the uniformed officer.

"*Exactamente, señor*. Like me. And like *compañera* Azucena. There are some in the party who want us to return to being the hardcore *revolucionarios*, and to abandon the democratic process we now enjoy. Having to live with another party's government is one of the realities of democracy, no? Maybe we will win the next election, maybe not. We will see. But in the meantime, we carry on."

"Why are you telling me this, *capitán*? I'm just a *gringo*."

The officer draws a swig from his bottle. "I'm not sure, but I think *compañera* Azucena thinks the same way as I do, that we want the party to embrace the democratic style of government. I am relatively certain, that she doesn't want us to return to the kind of oppressive dictatorship that we fought so valiantly, and lost so many of our bravest *compañeros*, to overthrow. Unfortunately, that is what we will return to if some members of the party insist on reassuming power by force. Do I make sense, *señor*?"

Duncan empties his bottle and pauses to contemplate the officer's remarks.

"*Capitán*. I sincerely hope that you are not asking me to spy on my dear lover and partner.

"No no, *señor*. I would never do that. I was just wondering if the *compañera* might have spoken to you about her concerns."

"You should just ask her directly. Don't be afraid of her. If she agrees with you, she might just give you a big hug. If not, she will let you know her feelings with no uncertainty."

The *capitán* adds. "It is more important that nothing should happen to the *compañera*. There have been suggestions that she might be in danger by those who don't like what she says. They think that she is becoming unhappy about the directions the party is going."

"Like you are, *capitán*, unhappy. Don't worry about what Azucena will say. Most of what she has to say, she'll say through her paintings."

"That's what I am most worried about, *señor*. Sometimes her paintings cause heated discussion, even though many of them don't understand what she intends." The officer pats Duncan on the arm as he stands and replaces his cap to his head. "Please take care of the *compañera, señor*. She is very valuable to us all and could step into danger without realizing it."

"*Hasta luego, compañera*." *Capitán* Noguero tips his cap toward Azucena as he passes the studio entrance and returns to his unmarked cruiser.

Duncan contemplates the *capitán's* purpose. 'Was he issuing a threat or a sincere warning?'

* * *

Dreams continue to occupy Azucena's sleep time. Her observations of the ants from *Paraíso* haunt her until they begin appearing as rough suggestions on her new canvases. Initially there's an idyllic field of wild-flowers sprouting from the damp soil. Hidden among the wildflowers are thousands of small dots that gradually expose themselves as ants. The ants become personified, with human faces, hands, and legs. Their armies occupy a field and appear as *campesinos* wielding machetes and baseball bats as batons.

"What is this you're working on, Azucena?" Duncan asks, peering over her shoulder.

"I don't know where it's going yet, Duncan. I'm just following my muse."

Duncan surmises. "My first impression is that you are recreating the peasant revolution, but that would be historical. You don't usually look backwards. Your work is most often foretelling events. Is this one of the changes you experienced in *Paraíso*? To become an historian?"

Azucena answers while continuing to paint. "I don't think we were in *Paraíso* long enough to experience a radical change, Duncan. I did, however, experience persistent dreams about the ants; I still do. I have no idea where they will take me, but I am obsessed with their presence. Were you able to focus on anything there?"

"Ever since I first went to *Paraíso*, I've been fascinated by the rows of marching ants. I love their determination and the ritual. During our last visit I too had dreams about them, weird dreams. I took quite a few colour photos this time, hoping to make sense of it all. The films are out for processing. I'll show them to you as soon as they arrive."

Duncan senses that Azucena's project on the marching ants will eventually lead to something masterful. He starts taking documentary photos of her at work, for the purpose of accompanying future exhibitions and, with any luck, a published biographical collection of her work. She has been gaining recognition throughout Central America as a prophetic artist with exceptional vision. It is only a matter of time before her work will be seen in North America, maybe even in Europe.

Azucena's months of dedication in the studio begin to pay off with, what appears to be, another comprehensive project. More than 20 canvases based on the evolving theme of personified ants line the walls. They are intended to connect with each other as a continuing chronological history of the future. Duncan is reminded of the extended wall murals along *Avenida Bolívar* he saw and photographed when he visited in 1987.

When the finished canvases are revealed, Duncan realizes how provocative their message is; a vitriolic, politically-charged, critique of the very party Azucena has worked with since the 1970s. He begins to seriously consider the concerns from *capitán* Noguero concerning Azucena's safety, and the possible threats against her.

'The works are so powerful that they must be seen,' Duncan ponders, 'but it would be almost suicidal to mount a show here, in Nicaragua. The political suggestions would most certainly cause Azucena some grief, maybe even place her in danger.'

Without revealing it to Azucena, Duncan sends a query letter with several photos to Joyce at the college. Joyce has always suggested that Azucena should have a show in Toronto, possibly in conjunction with an 'artist-in-residence' appointment in the Fine Arts program; at the very least, a series of lectures.

Duncan rationalizes, 'It will give Azucena a chance to show her work abroad and provide a buffer from the local political dynamics that are beginning to reveal their colours here.'

Within a month, a letter addressed to Azucena arrives from Joyce.

My Dearest Azucena:

I hope this letter finds you in good health and happiness.

I am following up on my offer of several years ago. We are interested in having you teach in the Fine Arts faculty, either as an 'artist-in-residence', or as a special lecturer, beginning in September. If you choose the artist-in-residence option it could continue until the end of term in December.

Accompanying the appointment will be a one-person show of your most recent work at the exclusive Galería Profundo in the Village. I assume that you have some exciting new work. I am eager to see photos.

I enclose a copy of the contract, and a brochure from the gallery. Please note the impressive remuneration we are offering and that all shipping costs, to and from Nicaragua, will be covered by the gallery.

Note that the expenses for the show are covered through several arts and international exchange agreements. The work will not be for sale. You will, however, receive a handsome remuneration from the granting organizations.

Please carefully consider our offer and talk about it with Duncan. Also tell Duncan that we would like him to teach some classes and workshops as well, at the same remuneration of course. We would like to hear from you both within the next two months to secure the arrangements.

Sincerely,

Joyce Banerji

Chair, Fine Arts Faculty

"DUNCAN!" Azucena shouts. "You should see this. I just received an offer from Joyce, to teach and to show my work. It's amazing."

She roars into the house from the studio, waving the letter in her hand. "Can we go to Toronto?"

Duncan plays it cool. "Just let me read what she says before I can comment."

He muses quietly. 'Thank God Joyce didn't mention me sending her the letter and photos.'

"Hmm." Duncan nods. "It looks promising. What do you think, my dear?"

Azucena holds the letter to her heart and jumps gleefully up and down like a child on a trampoline. "Let's do it. Let's go. I could show my latest ant paintings. Do you think she'll like them?"

"She'll love them, I'm sure."

CHAPTER 30

ARTIST-IN-RESIDENCE

Toronto, 1993:

Duncan and Azucena's arrival in Joyce Banerji's office is met with fresh coffee and a large box of assorted Timbits including double chocolate, sour cream, and honey-coated.

Joyce greets them with double-cheeked kisses.

"Ah. The breakfast of champions," Duncan laughs, dipping his fingers into the box of Timbits to retrieve a double chocolate glazed.

Joyce glances around the room as if someone is missing. "I just noticed. Where's the boy, Tomás? Didn't he come with you?"

"He couldn't come this time," Azucena reveals. "He's no longer a boy, he's a man. I will miss him, but I'm very proud of him. He starts university next week. Can you believe it? My little Tomás is now 20 years old."

"He's not little anymore," Duncan adds, raising his hand to equal his own height. "He's as tall as me now."

"Let me guess," Joyce says. "He's enrolled in a fine arts program."

"No," Azucena shakes her head. "He wants to be a lawyer when he graduates. Of course there are many years before he has to decide. Maybe he'll change his mind."

"I doubt it," Duncan adds, rubbing his fingers together and grinning. "He wants the big bucks."

"Well. We have good news, folks." Joyce announces, slapping her hands together. "Your paintings arrived at Galería Profundo yesterday, just in time."

Joyce turns to Duncan. "Did you remember to photograph each of the paintings before they were wrapped and crated, Duncan?" Before he has a chance to answer, she answers for him. "Of course you did. You're a photographer after all."

Joyce's talent, aside from her excellent reputation as a creator of thought-provoking and emotionally-stimulating installations, is first and foremost, an organizer. She planned and created the Fine Arts program from the seed of an idea to one of the most successful programs in the country. She recognizes talent before the artist themself realizes it and will promote artists of any age when she believes in them. She has also curated several major exhibitions in the city. Azucena's work has fascinated Joyce since their first encounter.

"What would you like me to teach this time, Joyce?" Azucena asks, before inhaling a sour cream Timbit.

"You can do pretty much what you did the last time; it's a fresh bunch of students out there." Joyce points her arm toward the large studio where Azucena's classes will be held. "Make sure you address how you paint from dreams. The students really loved that workshop you did the last time. I assume that the new work is based upon dream sequences like your previous work, right?"

Duncan offers an opinion. "Azucena's new work is more provocative than her earlier material, Joyce."

"How so?" Joyce asks. "I thought her previous work was already quite provocative."

Azucena speaks up. "I think what Duncan's referring to is that my current paintings have a political edge, where my earlier work was sexually provocative. There are some politically disturbing outcomes in my new work that will cause some people to be … um … upset. I guess that's the best word to use."

"I can hardly wait to see them," Joyce says. "The gallery should have everything uncrated in a couple of days. Then we can inspect them and make sure they're ready for hanging. In the meantime, we can prepare your classes. On Tuesday morning, we'll meet and greet our new students and I'll introduce you to the returning students in the afternoon. You should be prepared to talk about yourself after I introduce you."

"Just out of curiosity, Joyce," Duncan asks. "What do you want *me* to do?"

Joyce laughs. "Oh, I forgot all about you, Duncan." She elbows him in the ribs. "You're just here as eye-candy. Just hang around the halls and look good. The students will love it."

After they all share the humour, Joyce adds. "Seriously, Duncan, I'd really like you to spend some time with the Fine Arts students talking about photography and the role it plays in the arts. We've never really delved into photography … yet. Of course, you and Azucena will spend some time doing workshops on your collaborations. Oh yeah. I think Kurt might like you to pitch in with him in Photojournalism, if you can fit it in; probably a workshop or seminar about your Nicaragua work."

"Hmm. I saw Kurt last night when we arrived at the townhouse but he didn't say anything."

Joyce chuckles. "Kurt was probably exhausted just trying to get the townhouse cleaned and organized before you arrived."

"It looked fine to me. I guess he succeeded."

"I think he has a cleaning lady come in," Joyce surmises with a wink. "A very attractive cleaning lady she is too."

"So that explains where he disappeared to," Duncan reacts. "He told me that he would leave the townhouse to us while we're in town."

Opening night at Galería Profundo is an overwhelming success, considering what Azucena expected.

"Why did so many people show up here, and why are they so interested in my paintings?" Azucena asks Duncan. "Nobody knows me in Canada; I'm a nobody outside of Nicaragua."

"Joyce has performed her magic, my dear. She placed ads in the major newspapers and in the Canadian arts magazines. She appeared on the CBC arts program and The Star did a brief interview with her last week about who you are and what they can expect to see on the walls. The Star wants to interview you here, at the gallery, tomorrow afternoon. In the meantime you may want to think about what you'll say to them."

"I'm not very good at talking about my art, Duncan."

"When you make 'provocative' art," Duncan explains graphically, "the work always requires some clarification. You can handle that, my dear. Just talk like we do at home."

"What if I say the wrong thing?"

"Resort to speaking English with a heavy Latina accent. They won't understand most of what you say but they'll be enthralled."

"What do you think about the show, Duncan? Do you like it?"

"It's fabulous. Some of your greatest work so far. It also is very edgy, a combination of your later abstract period with more realism than you've painted since before you went to *Paraíso* the first time."

"Is that a good thing, or am I slipping backwards?"

"To the contrary, I see it as a maturing. You've found a truer self this time. There is nothing contrived. There's no art-for-art's-sake."

"Do you think it's too political?"

"If you are foretelling the state of Nicaraguan politics, then there will be some in Nicaragua who will be very concerned. It's not a pretty future you have painted."

"I have just painted interpretations from my dreams, Duncan. It's my dreams that are upsetting. I don't anticipate what will happen. I can't help what dreams I have; they just come to me. I suspect that my mother has something to do with the dreams I receive. Besides," Azucena adds, "I doubt that anybody in Nicaragua will read the Toronto Star or see the CBC arts report."

"Never say never, my dear."

* * *

"So, Azucena," the Star arts reporter begins. "Your work seems to suggest a chronological evolution of contemporary Nicaraguan history, beginning in the mid-20th century with the formation of the FSLN that opposed the Somoza dictatorship and ultimately overpowered him during the revolution in 1979, is that correct?"

"*Si.* That is correct. It is a period that I am very familiar with."

"Of course you are. Can I assume that you were, in fact, a member of the FSLN at that time, and that you participated in the final assault in the south of the country?"

"*Si.* It is an action I am very proud of."

"Are you still a member of the FSLN Party, Azucena?"

"Um ... *Si.*" She hesitates. "Why are you asking me these questions, *señora?*"

The reporter alters her line of questioning. "You say that your paintings are derived from dreams you receive from your mother ... who died in 1972 during the Managua earthquake. Is that correct?"

"*Absolutamente, señora.* Mamá has shared her dreams with me since I was a young child. It was because of her that I started to paint."

"Was your mother a member of the FSLN before she died?"

"No. Mamá wasn't political. She was a poor, hard-working, single mother. Her situation, however, was instrumental in my choice to join the revolution while in university. I wanted to make changes that would improve life for women in my country, and to allow people of all ages to attend school and become literate."

"I'd like us to discuss the paintings in some detail, if we may? There appears to be a 'utopian' period during the centre of the chronology you present. Would that represent the current state of affairs in Nicaragua?"

"No," Azucena answers, shaking her head. "The current situation is not so utopian. Since the election of 1990, the new coalition government has unravelled many of the progressive changes we, the FSLN, made during the decade we formed the government, like free education, health care, and a better life for women in our society. For me, that would be the 'utopian' period, despite the economic embargo, the Contra War, and the disagreements with the United States. Of course there was so much more we wanted to accomplish. However, our current democracy still allows for the people to decide who should manage the country's affairs, similar to Canada, except there are many more parties to choose from."

"Thank you, Azucena." The reporter continues. "You have been credited as having 'special powers,' where you paint events that are yet to happen. The second half of your current show leads to a return to when it began. You seem to be 'predicting' an oppressive, dystopian future for your country. Will that be caused by your former nemesis, the United States, or some other influence?"

Azucena pauses to consider her response. "I can only paint what I dream, *señora*. I have no control over what is in the future, you must understand that. I am *not* a clairvoyant, as some people suggest. I only interpret dreams and follow my imagination."

"If I may be so bold to interpret the paintings I see on the walls, Azucena ... as a viewer you understand. I see a future that is being undermined by the very same people who created the 'utopia' of the 1980s. Could it be that the FSLN could become the new oppressor?"

After some hesitation, Azucena offers a response. "Art is meant to ask questions, *señora*. The answers can only be provided within the mind of the viewer. In this case, that is your mind. If you see what you claim to see, then it is your truth, only yours ... not mine, not someone else's truth." Azucena pauses again before continuing. "However, your truths and mine may coincide in some circumstances."

"Do you care to expand on that statement, Azucena?"

"There is no need to expand. It's just the way it is. In some things we will agree, in others, not necessarily."

The reporter digs deeper. "As a current member of the party, are you concerned about the future of the FSLN? What about the future of your country?"

"Hmm." Azucena pauses to contemplate her answer. "I would be very concerned if the party headed in that direction, to a time when they would become the oppressor and where the democratic process would be in danger of collapsing. I am certain that there would be serious dissent within the party against venturing in that direction. After all, *señora*, how would you feel if a similar thing happened here, in Canada? Wouldn't you be concerned? ... Would you allow it to happen without speaking out? ... Would you continue reporting objectively on the demise ... another day at the office, perhaps?"

The reporter probes further. "Will you be in difficult circumstances back in Nicaragua now that these paintings are being seen in public. I would guess that some powerful people may be offended by their suggestions."

"Like I have already stated *señora*, I only paint what has come to me in my dreams."

The reporter stands and offers Azucena her hand. "Thank you so very much for this enlightening chat. It's a fabulous show."

"*Muchas gracias, señora.*"

* * *

"Revolutionary Artist Predicts Doom and Gloom," reads the Star's headline placed above a photograph of Azucena beside one of her large canvases. "An outstanding exhibition of allegorical paintings by talented Nicaraguan artist, Azucena Sosa, opened Thursday at Galería Profundo. Developing the life cycle of personified ants, Azucena transports the viewer through a fantastical odyssey of the history (past, present, and future) of the Nicaraguan revolution. The chronological development of the ants, from humble beginnings to a military and political force capable of inflicting the same oppression against its people as the brutal regime they overthrew is, of course, pure fiction, but worthy of serious consideration and concern, nevertheless. Is it merely the state of another banana republic flexing its muscles against the world powers' demands for fruit, gold, and coffee, or is it more symbolic of a global shift to the right?"

"Where do they get this crap from?" Duncan shouts, slapping the back of his hand against the newspaper. "This is bullshit."

"Oh, it's just 'art speak,' Duncan," Joyce responds. "Don't get too upset over it. Readers won't care what she says. They will, however, flock to the gallery to see what it's all about."

"Out of curiosity, if nothing else," Azucena offers.

"Curiosity is good," Duncan adds. "If they weren't curious, they would never show up."

Joyce continues reading the paper. "O-o-o. Here's a separate article about Azucena on the international news page. It must be from the interview."

She reads. "Azucena Sosa, the revolutionary Nicaraguan artist, is a member of FSLN *(Frente Sandinista de Liberación Nacional)*. She was active as a *guerrillera* during the assault on the capital, Managua, during the final days of the revolution in 1979, and remains a member to this day. In her current show at Galería Profundo, she foresees a Nicaragua of the future that will be ruled by another oppressive regime, one that will rewrite the constitution and cede all power to a dictator. She further suggests that the oppressor may be within her own party."

"Ouch!" Azucena reacts. "That will hurt back home."

"I doubt that anyone will read this in Nicaragua?" Joyce contests, looking toward Duncan for a reaction.

"Everybody will!" Duncan states. His arms spread outward to encompass the entire world. "Once the wire service gets this, and they will, it will travel like a rocket. Just the tag, 'Nicaragua,' means that it will be available to *Barricada*, *La Prensa*, and *El Nuevo Diario*. They will already be reading this and will have a field day."

Azucena sighs. "Maybe it's a good thing we're in Toronto ... at least until this blows over. By the time we return they will have forgotten all about it. As you always say, Duncan, there will be other fish to fry."

"I'll arrange for Tomás to send us copies of *Barricada* and *La Prensa*," Duncan proposes, placing his hand on Azucena's shoulder. "The news will be a week late, but at least we'll have some feedback of how they're reacting."

* * *

Over the next few weeks, Azucena is pre-occupied with preparations for her lectures and Duncan is team-teaching with Kurt in the Photojournalism program. The first Nicaraguan newspapers finally arrive in the mail but remain folded on the coffee table between the latest Star, Globe, and assorted flyers for Canadian Tire sales, grocery deals, and weekly pizzeria specials.

Finally, on Sunday morning following a hearty breakfast, Duncan and Azucena take their coffees into the living room to relax on the sofa and catch up on the latest news events. Duncan consumes newspapers as if they're the staff of life.

"What's the big story for this week?" Azucena asks, following her question with a sip of java.

"The Oslo Accord," Duncan answers, folding the page to follow the story. "Israel and the PLO have signed an agreement that allows each other to exist."

"Does that mean there'll finally be peace in the Middle East?" Azucena inquires.

"It's about time, don't you think?" Duncan suggests, peering sceptically at Azucena over his reading glasses. "What are you reading?" he adds.

"*La Prensa*. It was stuck in between the other mail."

"What's news in Nicaragua these days?"

Azucena reads news about a dispute between the city workers over who should pick up the garbage, and how often.

Duncan rises. "Give me your cup. I'm going to the kitchen to replenish our coffees."

"Wait, Duncan," Azucena places her hand on his arm. "Read this." She hands him the paper folded open to the International News page. "This article here." She points to a headline, "Nicaraguan Artist in Hot Water."

Duncan's eyes widen as he reads. "Wow! Now we know what the right-wingers think about your show. It looks like they're stirring the pot, hoping to create some dirty laundry within the FSLN party. What did *Barricada* say?"

"You get the coffee, Duncan. I'll look it up." Azucena sorts through the pile of mail for a copy of *Barricada*, the Sandinista newspaper.

Duncan returns. "Hot coffee for the artist in hot water."

"There's nothing mentioned at all in *Barricada*," Azucena notes.

"The party is saying more by remaining silent," Duncan offers. "They don't want to hang their dirty laundry in public. They're going to let the *La Prensa* story fizzle out without any challenge," Duncan surmises. "Don't be surprised if they publish a rave review of your show next week. That's an easier route for them to take. It's a more positive, and useful, approach to glorify their favourite artist and her international achievements, than to wallow in the mud with their competitor. That would only give *La Prensa* more ink."

"I know. They're going to quietly boil me instead when we return, like those poor lobsters we ate, right?"

"When we return, it would be wise to keep your mouth shut and your eyes and ears wide open," Duncan advises. "I would keep the paintings crated for now ... or maybe even find another gallery in Canada or the U.S. that would show the work. For the meantime, keep the paintings out of Nicaragua until you know more. You can put them in my garage after the show's over ... if that's OK with Kurt."

Azucena looks worried. "Maybe I should stay out of Nicaragua as well, Duncan. Am I in danger?"

Duncan pulls her close, stroking his hand across her back as consolation.

"My dear. You have always been in some sort of danger. Up until now, it's been the reactionary far right you had to fear. I really don't think you have to fear your own *compañeros*. They all know who you are and what you've contributed to the cause. By the time we arrive back the whole issue will be forgotten. You'll be a hero again."

"I just don't want to be a dead hero."

PART ELEVEN
1994 – 1995

CHAPTER 31

ALLEGIANCES

Nicaragua, 1994:

Whether it's ignited through a previous conversation with Azucena, or some other influence, is uncertain, but one night, while Azucena is out attending a Sandinista party meeting, Duncan sits alone sipping some *Ron Oro*. A scorching Eric Dolphy flute recording surges from the stereo speakers while snippets of colours and shapes flutter freely about in the open cavity of Duncan's meditative mind, as if searching for a painting to belong to.

Brazen colours mimicking those of Azucena's 'Paraíso on Fire' paint-ing, but lacking form, suddenly explode into miniscule pixels that float about like a shaken snow globe, aligning themselves into a blazing inferno with smoke surrounding two figures kneeling on a bench. Gradually a composition forms, similar to the previous painting but with a cross rising above the smoke and flames.

Azucena's arrival at home coincides with the final cadence of Dol-phy's fiery solo and Duncan's awakening from his meditative state.

He smacks the side of his head at the coincidence and recalls the prophetic words of the Indigenous elder, 'There are no such things as coincidences, only things we are not meant to comprehend.'

Duncan tells Azucena about his meditative dream.

Azucena responds, raising her forefinger. "I had the same dream a few weeks ago. What a coincidence."

"How was your meeting?" Duncan asks while pouring *Ron Oro* into two glasses.

"Very productive. I was meeting with several of the *compañeros* to discuss breaking away from the FSLN party."

"Wow. That sounds heavy. Is that a wise move, Azucena?" Duncan asks. "Won't it break up the popular support for the party, especially with an election on the horizon?"

"We will still identify with the Sandinistas but some of us are dissatisfied about the hard line the FSLN leadership is taking. We want to work toward a more progressive and democratic Nicaragua. God forbid if we ever return to another embargo or civil war, and who in their right mind wants to go through another revolution? We'll be a party that listens to the concerns of all *nicaragüenses*, rich and poor, men and women." Azucena stretches her arms wide to emphasize the breadth of their diversity.

"There have been a lot of meetings lately," Duncan observes. "You must be getting close to solving everything."

"The big meeting is tomorrow … an all-day meeting. We hope to ratify our decision, vote on the official name of the new party, and draft a list of our priorities, including a list of constitutional reforms."

Duncan surmises. "It sounds like you've already decided to split away. What will you call yourselves?"

"*El Movimiento Renovador Sandinista, (MRS),*" Azucena explains, "The Sandinista Renovation Movement," she repeats for Duncan in English. "Of course, that depends on whether the name is approved. It's all very exciting," she adds, "except of course, for all the bureaucracy. I wish we could just get on with it and forget about all these meetings."

"I've poured you a glass of rum and lemon," Duncan passes her the glass. "Come. Let's just relax. Put your feet up."

"Not until I change into my sleeping wear, just in case I fall asleep."

When Azucena returns they retire to the sofa with their drinks. Duncan puts some easy listening music on the stereo and proposes a toast to the new political party. *"Viva los renovadores,* (long live the renovators)," Duncan toasts, touching his glass against Azucena's.

She cuddles against him. "I'm sorry I haven't been paying you much attention these days, my dear *Dooncan*," she says in a soft voice. Her original phonetics of Duncan's name are reserved for personal 'lovey-dovey' moments. "I've been so wrapped up in political stuff lately. Happily, it will soon be over."

Duncan is more realistic. "It won't be over until after the next election. That's still two years away."

Azucena opens her mouth to speak, but Duncan places his finger against her lips.

"Come with me, my dear." He prepares more drinks and they retire arm-in-arm to the bedroom.

* * *

Shortly after sunrise, Duncan prepares a breakfast and brings it to their bed where Azucena is slowly waking up. She stretches her arms and yawns.

"I thought you might like a big breakfast before your all-day meeting," Duncan says after leaning over to kiss Azucena.

"Thank you," she answers, kissing him back. 'Where would I be without you, Duncan?"

"Well," he speculates, "probably happily, or unhappily, married to one of your *compañeros*, with a dozen little children running around.

"Ha-ha. Like that could ever happen."

"What time does your meeting start?" Duncan asks, offering Azucena a second cup of coffee.

"At 10:00 am," she answers. "Jairo is picking me up at 9:00. You met Jairo, Duncan. He was at the anniversary celebrations. I introduced you to him. Do you remember? The meeting is out of town, at a retreat near Masaya. I should get dressed."

Duncan smiles. "Not at Don Ricardo's *'Finca del Oro,'* I hope.

Azucena places her hands on her hips. "Duncan. Do you really think that Don Ricardo would invite us *'comunistas'* to his estate?

"Just joking," Duncan responds, embracing Azucena before she steps outside.

Azucena kisses Duncan playfully at the door as her ride arrives. "Oh, don't forget to wake Tomás up," she reminds him. "He has exams this week."

Duncan waves at Jairo, still not recognizing him. He follows Azucena to the car, offering some last-minute advice.

"Whatever you do, Azucena, please *do not* volunteer for any official position in the new organization. You don't need that hassle."

"No?" she asks, smiling. "They want me to be their leader, to be the next *presidente*."

Duncan chuckles and promises Azucena. "I'll prepare a wonderful home-cooked dinner for you when you arrive home; a celebration for your new party. And who knows what will follow that?"

* * *

Darkness falls on the retreat before all items on the agenda are resolved. There is a short celebration before the members of the new MRS party depart.

After declining her nomination to run for the leadership, Azucena is subsequently nominated as vice-leader of the party but declines again. She finally agrees, with the party's backing, to run as a delegate in the next election, which won't occur until 1996. Her reputation as a nationally known artist is an attraction the new party leaders can't overlook. She will also organize and run the party's media campaign.

Azucena and Jairo leave the retreat close to 9:00 pm and head directly back to the capital. The driver becomes concerned about a vehicle that has been following behind them steadily since leaving the retreat.

"There's someone following us," he tells Azucena.

"It's probably someone from the retreat," she answers, turning her head to see for herself. All she sees is a pair of headlights surrounded by darkness.

"I'm going to make a series of turns," Jairo warns her. "Don't be worried. It's just to satisfy my curiosity."

Jairo takes a sharp left turn at a country intersection, driving a kilometre before stopping. No lights follow them, so he returns to the highway, veers left, and continues toward the capital.

Other traffic passes from the opposite direction. After a few kilometres, lights re-appear in Jairo's mirror.

"Don't look now, Azucena, but they're behind us again," Jairo says.

"It's probably just another vehicle, Jairo. You're becoming paranoid."

"I'm certain it's the same car," Jairo confirms. "It has the same weaker headlight on the right side as the previous car."

Azucena turns to see the headlights. She offers Jairo a simple solution.

"Once we reach the capital, take some detours through a few barrios. Then we'll know for sure. There'll be many places to hide there as well."

* * *

Duncan anticipates Azucena's late arrival for dinner. He knows that meetings never end on time, just as they never start on time. He plans a late dinner for 10:00. He is disappointed when she doesn't arrive by 10:00 and is upset when the clock reaches 11:00. At midnight, Duncan is conflicted between outright anger and worry. He avoids falling asleep by over-indulging in caffeine and is alerted to any vehicle lights passing by their *casita*.

"When will one of those fucking cars stop here?" he mutters aloud.

He checks the studio regularly in case Azucena has arrived late and doesn't want to wake him. "It would be just like her to do that," Duncan explains to a painting in progress on the easel.

He is reluctant to wake Tomás. He's already been studying hard for exams and was out pulling a late-night study and pizza session with some other students. When Tomás returned around midnight and asked about his mother, Duncan told him not to worry, that she's at an important meeting and could be late coming home.

By 3:00 am Duncan is in full panic mode, walking in circles through the house, the studio, and the gallery. He considers taking the camper out and following the route Jairo would have taken, except he doesn't know exactly where they were going for the retreat or what route they would use to return to the capital.

"Besides," he rationalizes aloud, "I have to be here when she returns."

"Something's happened. I know it," Duncan says to the umpteenth coffee in front of him at the kitchen table. He rubs his temples with both hands. "Azucena would never be this late."

The clock clicks to 4:00. Duncan calls Father Manuel's number. It rings itself out, leaving the priest's answering machine voice. "God hears you but is busy at the moment. Please leave a message so He can return your call."

"Cute, you motherfucker," Duncan shouts irreverently into 'God's' answering machine. "It's me, Duncan. Give me a call, ASAP. Something bad is happening."

Duncan's mind plays tricks, leading him into illogical problems to solve. 'Should I wake Tomás? He will only worry. I don't want him to fail the exam. What if something serious has happened? Then Tomás should know. Fuck, I don't even know anything. I'll wait another hour. If I still don't know anything by then, I'll tell him. I'll have to wake him up then anyway.'

More tricks challenge the sanity of Duncan's thought processes.

'Why do I always wait for the clock to arrive at a round number before making any decisions, like 3:00, 4:00, or 5:00? What's wrong with 2:37, 3:52, or 4:16?' He immediately realizes the futility of his internal question. "Who the fuck cares?" he shouts aloud, staring at the ceiling, his arms outstretched.

While talking to the ceiling, the phone rings. "Finally, it's Azucena," he assumes.

"*Hola, amigo. Que pasa?*"

"Oh it's you Father." Duncan rattles off his concerns about Azucena and mentions the meeting she attended yesterday.

"What meeting did she go to?" Father Manuel asks.

"You must have been there, Father. It was a meeting of ..."

'Oh shit!' Duncan suddenly realizes. Father Manuel may not have been invited. Maybe he's not included. Maybe he doesn't know anything about the 'Renovation Movement.'

Duncan quickly retreats. "Sorry Father. I must have been mistaken. There was no meeting last night. I'll get myself sorted out. I've had a bit too much to drink. You know how it is." Duncan backtracks, using humour as his exit. "Sorry for waking you, God."

Duncan hangs up the phone without waiting for a response from Father Manuel. "Oh Fuck!" He holds his head in his hands. "What have I done? Azucena's going to be so pissed at me."

He immediately calls the police to file a missing person report.

The officer on call informs Duncan, "If the *señora* is still not home by this afternoon, call us back and we will begin a search."

"Fuck," he curses in reply. "She's already missing."

The policewoman on the phone ignores Duncan's curse and informs him not to panic. "In most cases," she says, "the missing person is just involved in some other pursuit."

"Is that a polite way of telling me that she's having an affair behind my back?" he asks.

"Call us back this afternoon, *señor*, and we will do everything we can to begin a search, if it's still necessary."

Losing all track of time, Duncan finally passes out on the sofa at 5:00 am, succumbing to his fatigue. He'd been sleepless for more than 24 hours. A rooster crows the arrival of first light from the neighbour's yard, and the cacophony from the morning traffic speeding up and down the *Avenida* a block away fills the air, but Duncan sleeps through the chaos until he suddenly remembers Tomás.

'Shit.' He runs to Tomás' bedroom. The bed has been slept in but it's empty. Back in the kitchen Duncan sees a note on the table.

"Gone to my exam. Wish me luck. Didn't want to wake you, Duncan. Must be one hell of a meeting. See you later. Love Tomás"

CHAPTER 32

OPPOSITION

Nicaragua, 1994 – 1995:

"ABRE LA PUERTA!" a voice of authority orders through the barred glassless front window, accompanied by abrupt hammering against the front door. "POLICE! OPEN THE DOOR!" Duncan jolts from his dream, falling from the sofa onto the floor.

He shuffles to the door, squinting against the outdoor light. *"Momentito.* I'm coming."

The knocking persists. "Just a fucking minute," he shouts, getting himself organized.

"Señor Duncan?" an officer asks.

"Si?" Duncan responds. "Have you found Azucena?"

Two officers enter the *casita* and remove their caps. "Please sit down, *señor,"* one officer suggests to Duncan in a more pleasant, but compassionate, tone. He points toward the sofa. *"Por favor, señor."* The serious expression on the officer's face suggests that Duncan is in for some bad news.

"Am I in trouble?" Duncan asks.

"*No señor.*"

Duncan obeys the instruction and sits on the sofa. "Then what's happened to Azucena?" he asks, in a subdued, vulnerable, voice.

"There has been an accident, *señor.*"

"Is she alright?" Duncan pleads. "Please tell me she's OK."

"A car has been found on a road near the Santiago crater. Do you know this place, *señor?*"

"*Sí,*" Duncan acknowledges. "The volcano … on the road to Masaya. Yes, I know it."

The suggestion suddenly strikes Duncan. "Oh, fuck no. It can't be." He grabs his head in frustration. "Don't tell me that, please. Tell me she's OK."

"*Señor.* The car has been identified as belonging to *señor* Jairo, a *compañero* of *señora* Azucena. Can you confirm that they were travelling together yesterday?"

"Yes, they were at a meeting together," Duncan confirms. "It started yesterday morning and would probably have continued into the early evening. The meeting was somewhere near Masaya. I expected her home for a late dinner but she still hasn't returned home. I called the police early this morning and reported her missing. That's all I know."

"*Gracias, señor* Duncan. You have been very helpful. We are investigating and will keep you informed."

Duncan quit smoking more than 20 years ago but suddenly searches his empty pockets for a cigarette. His anxiety level surges. 'Accident. At the volcano. What can I do? Where is Azucena? FUCK!'

He's tempted to open a bottle of rum but realizes the futility of drinking when he may be called upon to react quickly or to make a critical decision. Instead, he paces the floor aimlessly.

"I can't leave," he mutters. "I have to stay here by the phone."

The phone rings. He picks it up after one ring.

"*Hola amigo.* It's God speaking."

"Hi Father. I'm sorry about earlier. I was confused."

"What's wrong, *amigo*? You sound strung out."

"It's Azucena. She hasn't arrived home. She left yesterday morning and she still hasn't come home."

"Where did she go yesterday?" Father Manuel asks.

"I'm not sure," Duncan answers, burying his white lie in the thread of truth that he really doesn't know *exactly* where she went.

Duncan adds, "The police were here a while ago. I called them last night when she didn't arrive home." Duncan takes a deep breath, hesitating before continuing. "They found a vehicle that was in an accident near the Santiago crater. There's a good possibility that she was in that car."

"Who was driving, Duncan?"

Duncan can't withhold information from Father Manuel any longer. "*Compañero* Jairo. He was driving."

While Father Manuel responds to Duncan's information, there's a heavy knocking on the front door.

"*Señor* Duncan. Police."

"I have to go, Father, I'll call you back later." Duncan hangs the phone up.

When he opens the door, *Capitán* Noguero addresses him. "May I come in *señor* Duncan?"

The *capitán* informs Duncan that the body of *compañero* Jairo has been found near the crater. "I am sorry to say that he was bludgeoned to death. It's obviously a case of homicide."

Duncan falls backward onto the sofa. "What about Azucena? Where is she?"

"We are still looking, *señor*." He places his hand on Duncan's shoulder. "We will find her, I promise."

Duncan folds over, weeping openly, his face buried in the palms of his hands.

After regaining some composure, he inquires, "What if you can't find her? What then? What can I expect in the next news you will bring? Will it be the worst possible scenario? Has she been kidnapped? Will she be lost forever in that cauldron?"

The *capitán* stops Duncan. "Don't even think what you are suspecting, *señor*. That only happened in the old days. God forbid that we ever return to those evil times."

Capitán Noguero pauses, tears flow from his eyes.

"*Señor* Duncan," the *capitán* places his hand firmly on Duncan's shoulder. "As you already know, I am a *compañero* of Azucena. We served together in *el triunfo*, along with *compañero* Jairo.' I give you my sincerest promise, *señor*, that I will find her. I will also keep you fully informed about every action we take." The *capitán* discreetly wipes some tears from his own eyes with his fingers and recomposes his official stance.

Duncan embraces the officer. "*Gracias, capitán. Gracias.*"

As they embrace, a junior officer runs into the house from the cruiser. The *capitán* regains his official composure, brushing imaginary lint from his uniform.

"*Capitán*, come quickly. There is news on the police radio."

Duncan waits on the doorstep. He notices a slight smile emerge on the officer's face.

Capitán Noguero returns to the door alone. He ushers Duncan into the house.

"*Señor*, we have located *compañera* Azucena. She was in the field away from the parking lot at the Santiago crater. I am happy to tell you that she has fared much better that *compañero* Jairo. She is alive. She has been rushed to the hospital."

Duncan crumbles against the officer. He shakes uncontrollably from his weeping.

Noguero explains. "*Compañera* Azucena has also been beaten, but she miraculously survived the ordeal. She is in the hospital in serious condition, but it is not life threatening. If you wish, *señor*, I will drive you there right now."

The *capitán's* cruiser is led through Managua's streets to the hospital by a siren-wailing gaggle of cruisers. Duncan is gobsmacked at the spectacle.

Capitán Noguero and Duncan rush inside and are ushered directly to the emergency room where Azucena is being cared for in a private enclosure. She is heavily sedated while a team of surgeons attend to her injuries. Duncan notices that her right leg seems to have received the worst of the attack. Her face and left arm are also badly battered.

"I want to stay here," Duncan says. "I know it will take some time for her to be revived but I want to be here when she comes to."

"She will be well-cared for here, *señor*," the officer takes Duncan by the arm. "Some of the doctors here are also *compañeros*. You should get some sleep while she's under anaesthetic. Why don't I take you home, now that you've seen that she'll be OK? You can return tomorrow to visit. Bring her some flowers for her room. She will like that to wake up to."

"You are probably right, *capitán*. I should be there when Tomás returns home from his exam, and I should also call Father Manuel to tell him the news. He will be wondering."

* * *

Duncan and Tomás alternate their time each day sitting with Azucena. It takes several days before she comes around, finally awakening to the sweetness of the many flowers.

"Welcome back to our world, my dear," Duncan greets Azucena with mild humour and a kiss.

Her swollen right eye struggles to focus while becoming accustomed to the brightness in the room. Injuries to her left eye remain bandaged.

"Duncan?"

"Yes. I'm here with you, my dearest. Tomás will be joining us shortly."

"Where am I?" she asks, in a state of confusion.

"You're in the hospital. You've been through quite an ordeal, but the worst is over now," Duncan tells her, sitting on the edge of her bed.

She aims her 'good' eye at the sling holding her right leg up. "What happened to my leg?"

"It's been broken. I'll let the doctor explain the details to you later."

On the following day, when Duncan arrives to relieve Tomás, Azucena seems brighter.

"Could you bring me some art supplies please Duncan? Just a few pens and some watercolours will be fine. Of course, my watercolour book as well."

"You must really be improving. Are you sure you're ready to start working again?" Duncan's face expresses his concerns. "Be careful you don't over-exercise your vision," he warns.

"You won't believe the dreams I've been having here. I just want to commit them to paper before they leave my imagination forever."

"That's probably the work of your pain medicine, right?"

"I don't think so. These dreams are more realistic than hallucinations."

"Like what?" Duncan probes with concern.

"You'll see. Just bring me my supplies."

* * *

During the following week, Azucena fills three sketchbooks with ink drawings and watercolour renderings, abstracted interpretations of her recent dreams. There are renderings from the meeting she attended, with abstracted caricatures of the new party members. Other sketches reveal the events that occurred after she and Jairo left the meeting.

A series of ink sketches toned in watercolour, reveal a sequential series of images, not unlike cells in a story board for an animated cartoon.

One sketch shows the rear window of Jairo's vehicle with two headlights from a car following them; one of the headlights is dimmer than the other. Another sketch reveals two hooded and masked figures, one at each side of Jairo's car. The figures are both wielding baseball bats. A third shows one of the masked figures dragging each passenger from the vehicle with raised bats. A fourth drawing of Jairo being beaten; he screams in pain. In the fifth and final, a dark masked figure looms over Azucena lowering a bat toward her. From her prone position, she raises her left arm in an attempt to protect herself.

"These are the only visions I can remember from my dreams right now, Duncan. I'm sorry."

Duncan pauses before asking another question.

"Who would do such a thing to you, Azucena? What reason would they have?"

"I don't know," she cries. "I'm trying to think, but the painkillers keep obstructing my thoughts."

"Did you hear any conversations from the attackers," Duncan asks. "Would you remember their voices if you heard them again? Did they sound familiar to you?"

Azucena breaks down. "I don't remember. Capitán Noguero asked me the same questions."

Duncan advises her not to show the sketches to anybody else, except *el capitán*. If Father Manuel comes to visit, keep the sketches in the drawer, just to be on the safe side. Don't show them to him and don't discuss any details for now. He will expect that you are still affected by the drugs. Just let him believe that. OK?"

Azucena manages to force a smile. "I will paint a silly picture, like a cartoon cactus in the middle of a baseball park with Wile E. Coyote chasing the Road Runner, just in case he sees my book. It will be placed on the top of my other sketches so he won't be interested. Besides, he will also think I've gone mad."

"You're not as out of it as I thought you were," Duncan jokes.

* * *

When Azucena returns home, she struggles to get around using crutches. A cast covers her right leg from the ankle to above her knee. The cast is autographed by the most famous politicians, artists, musicians, and poets, of Nicaragua; a virtual 'who's who.'

"When this cast is removed I'm going to auction it off to the highest bidder," Azucena jokes to Duncan, gritting her teeth against a sudden stab of pain. "With all these famous signatures, I could raise money for the new party."

"Sit here," Duncan offers. "I'll get you the painkillers."

"No painkillers," she shouts, stiffening her body against another shot of pain. "I don't want to become an addict."

Azucena slowly sits on the sofa. Duncan takes her crutches and helps her raise her leg.

"I'll put your painkillers and some water right here on the side table … in case you need them," Duncan says. "Do you want the TV on?"

"For what?" Azucena asks, frowning. "There's nothing worth watching. Bring me my sketchbook instead, the one with my latest drawings."

While Azucena studies the watercolour sketches she made in the hospital, Duncan peruses the autographs and comments on her cast.

"You had a shitload of visitors," Duncan comments. "There's hardly any room left on here for more signatures."

Azucena jokes, "I guess there's no need to keep the identities of the new party members secret, their names are written all over my cast."

"There are some I don't recognize," Duncan says. "Wait, what's this?" he asks, squinting his eyes to read a small block-printed comment. After studying the printing, he carefully reads it to Azucena.

"*TIENE CUIDADO!* BE CAREFUL," Duncan reads "That's all it says. There's no name beside this one, Azucena. Who would have written that?"

"I have no idea," Duncan. "There were people coming and going all the time," she answers. "Half of the time I was asleep or dozing into La-La Land."

Duncan carefully reads the printing, paying close attention to the exclamation mark.

"This isn't from a well-wisher, my dear. This is a warning. Somebody is warning you to be careful."

"People are always warning me about one thing or another," Azucena responds, attempting to twist her body to a more comfortable position. "I can't worry about every little thing somebody says."

Duncan snickers. "Says the brave woman with the broken leg who was beaten to within an inch of her life."

"Can you give me a hand here please, Duncan? Just help me turn to my side."

The adjustment allows Duncan to read the underside of Azucena's cast. "Some of your admirers must have had an exceptional view while they wrote on the bottom of your cast," Duncan jokes. He tickles her toes.

"Don't Duncan. That drives me crazy, and I can't move to stop it."

"Here's another message in block-printing. Let me see if I can read it." Duncan rolls onto his back and slides underneath Azucena's cast.

Duncan tries to taunt Azucena with another tickle but is stopped abruptly.

"Oh shit!" he curses. "Here's another warning."

Duncan whispers the message to himself, *'ERES UNA MUJER MUERTA!'* He mumbles it quietly in English, 'You are a dead woman!'

"What did you say, Duncan?" Azucena prods. "I didn't hear what you said."

He kisses Azucena on the lips. "I'm getting my camera to take photos of some of these signatures and sayings … for posterity."

Duncan records images of some of the signatures and sayings on Azucena's cast. He also takes photos of the block-printed warnings.

PART TWELVE
1996

CHAPTER 33

TRAGEDY

Nicaragua, 1996:

Throughout the summer, Azucena recuperates magnificently. The cast is removed and she moves about freely, first on crutches and finally, with just the help of a single cane for support. She stores the two halves of the cast in a cupboard in the studio. Suggestions for the future of the cast include creating an art piece combining the cast and the unintelligible watercolours from the assault that she painted in the hospital while under the influence of painkillers.

Under the direction of *Capitán* Noguero, the police continue to investigate the brutal attack on Azucena and the murder of *compañero* Jairo, but no leads are forthcoming. Suspicions lie in two distinct camps: members of the former Contras upset with Azucena for her leftist political affiliations, and former *compañeros* from the FSLN who are upset about the formation of a breakaway party. No information has been forthcoming about the warnings printed on Azucena's cast.

Even Col. Jorge's name is mentioned as a person of interest but, of course, it is believed that he remains in Miami.

Since the initial furor in the press about Azucena's provocative show in Toronto, there's been no further mention about her 'militant ant' paintings nor any suggestion of future oppression by the FSLN. Most of the news recently is about the upcoming October election. Both the MRS and FSLN parties are running. Azucena struggles, campaigning on her crutch.

The ongoing investigation considers the possibility that *compañero* Jairo was the prime target, not Azucena, but Jairo was much less a public figure than Azucena. There has been no evidence of previous threats against him. Most of the people interviewed didn't even know Jairo's name. Some well-connected members of the FSLN knew the *compañero* only as 'the quiet *guerrillero*,' more suited to espionage than to battle.

"That explains why I don't remember him being there during the march from Costa Rica," Duncan tells the *capitán* when interviewed over a drink at *Los Antojitos*. "I haven't come across him in my photos of the time. Come to think about it, I didn't see him at the bungalow in San José either. The first time I met Jairo was at the 10th anniversary celebration. Azucena introduced us."

"What if …" *Capitán* Noguero proposes a possibility to Duncan. "What if the perpetrators were out to kill *compañero* Jairo and to merely warn *compañera* Azucena? If so, what would their incentive be?"

Duncan suggests to the *capitán*, "If, as you say, Jairo was better suited for a career in espionage, he might have known things that should be kept quiet. You know, secret information that he was privy to."

"Hmm," the *capitán* ponders, stroking his chin.

Duncan suggests. "Maybe Azucena was only collateral damage because she was riding with Jairo."

The *capitán* raises his forefinger. "You bring up a very interesting point, *amigo*."

"Sst," the *capitán* signals the waiter. "More drinks, *por favor*."

Duncan asks, "So, what happens next, *capitán?*"

"We look for whoever wants to keep secrets quiet, *señor.*"

"Isn't that everybody in Nicaragua?" Duncan suggests with a Cheshire cat grin. He raises his glass to the officer. "To secrets."

* * *

In the final weeks before the October 20 election, Azucena toils night and day for the MRS party. There are polls to study and analyze, signs to paint and erect, interviews, speeches, and endless strategy meetings.

Duncan is relegated to the home front: cooking meals, cleaning house, and answering the telephone. He finishes washing dishes and sits on the sofa to read his three newspapers. The telephone rings. He answers. It's the voice of Father Manuel.

"Sit down, *amigo,*" the priest orders.

"What's happened," Duncan asks.

There's hesitation, a sign that the priest is unsure of how to tell Duncan the news. Finally, in a monotone unusual for Father Manuel, he speaks.

"Col. Jorge, my brother, has been assassinated."

"What happened, Father? Who killed him? How? When?" Duncan hesitates to consider whether he should speak what's on his mind. "I am sorry for your loss, Father, but to be blunt, your brother was not my favourite human being. He had many enemies who would gladly pull the trigger."

"There was no trigger pulled, *amigo.* It was an explosion and fire. He was at *La Finca del Oro* … in the chapel. There was another person with him. They are both so badly burned that identification is proving difficult. It will take some time to confirm any suspicions."

"Thank you for telling me, Father. If there are any further developments, please keep me informed. I wonder how Azucena will take the news?"

"I'm not sure but the police have identified her as a person of interest."

"Oh come on, Father. What reason would she have to do a thing like that?"

"Apparently she was identified on the security camera footage at the estate just prior to the explosion."

"What in the name of God was Azucena doing at your father's estate? With, of all people, your brother, Col. Jorge, that son-of-a-bitch. In fact, what in the name of Christ was Col. Jorge doing there? He's supposed to be in Miami."

"Nobody can answer your first question, I'm afraid. I was hoping that you might be able to offer some explanation."

"I have no idea, Father. As far as I know, she was out campaigning."

"As for your second question," Manuel answers. "My brother apparently arrived incognito through his network of sick *bandoleros*. He was taken to *La Finca del Oro* secretly a week ago."

Suddenly, the conversation hits Duncan.

"Jesus Christ, Father. You can't honestly suspect Azucena. She couldn't have been there to kill him … no, that's not possible. She hated his guts, but she would never kill anybody, or anything for that matter."

Duncan recalls her verbal threat when Tomás went missing. It occurs to him that she might have gone to talk to Col. Jorge about Tomás. When Azucena confided in Duncan about Col. Jorge being the father of Tomás, he promised not to reveal that information, so he defers mentioning anything to Father Manuel.

Instead, Duncan offers, "Maybe she went there to confront Col. Jorge about what really happened to Tomás while he was away. After all, there were rumours that the boy had gone to the Honduran border in search of the Colonel."

Father Manuel explains. "According to the news I've heard, Col. Jorge was occupying a private suite on the second floor of the estate, the same suite where he slept as a child. In the morning he was visited by a servant delivering his breakfast. The servant reported to Don Ricardo that Jorge was feeling ill. Our father rushed to his room to find the

Colonel vomiting into his toilet. His condition failed to improve as the day passed and, by suppertime, his condition had become critical. Col. Jorge apparently requested to be taken to the family chapel and once there, to be left alone with God."

"But you said he wasn't alone. He was with someone else."

"That is only one of the rumours, *amigo*. Why he wanted to talk to God at all is beyond me."

Duncan offers, "Maybe he wanted to atone for his sins … his many, many sins."

"He never talked to God before. Could it be that somebody poisoned him? Maybe that's why he became ill in the first place."

"The whole thing sounds very confusing," Duncan says. "Were there any witnesses?"

"Some of the domestics, I suppose, and of course, there were the security cameras. Apparently there was a very loud blast before the chapel burst into flames. The heat was too intense for anyone to approach the building. When the investigators were called in, Don Ricardo told them that he didn't know anybody who would want to harm his son, apparently telling them that Jorge was a serious, warm-hearted man, who loved God and his country."

Duncan comments. "It's funny how the rich can live in their own little bubble, immune to the real world."

Father Manuel continues. "I heard from *Capitán* Noguero that, when Don Ricardo spoke about Jorge's warm-heartedness, the officers glanced at each other, wondering if he was talking about the same Col. Jorge. One officer asked whether there was more than one Col. Jorge. Another was quoted, 'There must be more than 100,000 people who hate his guts. I don't even know where we'll start looking for suspects.' Most of the police officers would have popped him off themselves if they'd had the chance."

Duncan spurts, "Put me on that list, Father" He pauses. "Oops, I guess that makes me a person of interest as well."

Father Manuel continues. "When the intense heat dissipated

enough for a crime scene investigation to be started, two bodies were discovered among the ashes of the chapel, one assumed to be Col. Jorge, the other believed to be a woman who still remains unidentified."

* * *

Azucena fails to return home. "I can't take much more of this," Duncan wails aloud in the early hours of the morning, cradling his head in his hands. "AZUCENA! … Where are you? Come home, please."

Duncan leaves messages at *Capitán* Noguero's office. Understandably, the officer's attention is embroiled in the Col. Jorge case, but for Duncan, his concerns for Azucena are paramount.

Tomás arrives home late. He's been drinking, apparently at a university class party. When Duncan tells him about Col. Jorge's death, his reaction is bland, unresponsive, except to shrug his shoulders and say, "He had it coming."

In the morning, Duncan attempts to explain to Tomás that Azucena hasn't arrived home.

"It is rumoured that your mother might be a person-of-interest by the police. I find that to be ridiculous; she would never hurt anyone, even Col. Jorge. Tell me Tomás. Is there anything you know that would support that suspicion?" Duncan pauses, but Tomás doesn't offer an answer.

"We have to search for her, Tomás. If you can think of any place she would go to hide, especially if she knows the police are looking for her."

"Why wouldn't she call us, at least to let us know she's OK?" Tomás asks.

"When people are afraid, they often act irrationally," Duncan offers, pulling Tomás to him. "I'll do everything I can to find her."

"What about that place, you know, that garden where you and she went to create and meditate. She would go there, wouldn't she?"

"*Paraíso*, of course. She would go there. Unfortunately, there's no way to communicate with her there. Besides, it's too far to travel there, especially when we should be staying close to home."

Despite Duncan's and Tomás' searching, a week passes with no word from Azucena. Duncan spends late nights pacing around the studio, looking for clues in her art. He starts drinking heavier than usual and even buys a package of *Alas*, a cheap unfiltered Mexican cigarette.

Late one night while Tomás is out with friends, Duncan hears a cruiser pulling up at the door. He watches through the window as *Capitán* Noguero places his cap on and walks alone to the front door. Duncan opens the door before the officer can knock.

"Please sit down, *señor* Duncan, the officer orders.

Duncan obeys without words.

Capitán Noguero removes his cap, placing it under his arm.

"I don't know how to tell you this, *señor* Duncan, so I'll just say it. Our beloved *compañera* Azucena died in the explosion at Don Ricardo's."

"What?" Duncan is in shock. He mouths words that can't be heard … "That can't be true," he finally blurts. "It's not true. I can't accept that."

"I'm so sorry, *señor*." The *capitán* stands before Duncan and places his hands on Duncan's shoulders.

Duncan shakes uncontrollably in the officer's arms. His voice blathers unknown words as if speaking in tongues. "Not my beautiful Azucena, surely not. There must be some mistake." His voice quivers, his throat chokes up, he cries, shouting like a hungry baby. "No, No, No!"

Capitán Noguero outlines the details of the police investigation.

"My officers confirm that *compañera* Azucena was seen on security camera footage outside the chapel minutes before the blast. We don't know why she was there. It's possible she just intended to confront Col. Jorge, and things escalated from there. I have even considered the possibility that she took her own life, but that wasn't something she would contemplate; she had so much to live for. We have discovered enough evidence to confirm that she was the second victim. I am so sorry, my good friend. We will both miss her dearly."

Duncan gathers his composure and proposes. "What if Col. Jorge wanted to commit suicide, and Azucena was just there at the wrong time? Is that a possibility? After all, he had much to be guilty about. Maybe he was feeling remorse. Maybe he tried poisoning and had second thoughts. Maybe he needed to atone for his sins in the chapel before his life disappeared."

"Those are all thoughts to consider, *señor*."

While Duncan talks to the officer, the phone rings. Duncan answers in a voice of desperation. "Hello?"

"*Hola amigo*, it's Father Manuel."

"Hold on, Father." Duncan covers the phone with his hand.

Capitán Noguero rises. "I'll leave you for now. You have enough to deal with. I'll be in touch as soon as we have more news."

"What possible news could follow this? She's dead. That's the last news that matters."

The officer embraces Duncan and turns to leave. He replaces his cap once outside the door.

Duncan pauses and returns to the phone.

"I guess you have heard the news, *amigo*," Father Manuel utters with a priestly consoling voice.

"The *capitán* was just here. He told me."

"I'm here for you if you need anything," the Father offers,

"There's only one fucking thing I need, Father."

"Anything you want. Just say the word, *amigo*, and I'll look after it."

"One word, that's all. AZUCENA! That's what I want. She's the only thing I want." Duncan breaks down, weeping openly.

Father Manuel waits in silence.

When he regains his voice, Duncan shouts into the phone. "AZU-CENA! That's her name. Get her back!"

Father Manuel attempts to address Duncan's desperation. "I only wish I could …"

"You're the fucking priest," Duncan interrupts, waving his fist in the air. "You're supposed to be God's messenger. Well send him a fucking message for me. Send her back! SEND MY AZUCENA BACK!"

Duncan's voice fades into a garbled echo. He slams the phone back on its cradle and lights up an *Alas*.

Duncan's rage against Father Manuel is tempered the following morning when the priest arrives at the door with a bouquet of flowers and a bottle of rum.

While they're in the kitchen, Tomás crashes through the front door. "DUNCAN! DUNCAN!" Tomás shouts. "Turn the news on." He steps into the kitchen and sees Father Manuel and Duncan with a bottle of rum and tears in their eyes.

"You heard … about Mamá."

Duncan rises to console Tomás.

"I just heard the news on the way home, Duncan." Tomás weeps as he places his arms around Duncan's neck. "Mamá's gone … Mamá's gone … Mamá's gone …" he repeats, gasping, his throat choking the words.

Duncan embraces Tomás. "I'm afraid it's true, Tomás."

Turning to the priest, Duncan insists, "There won't be a funeral, Father. There will be a celebration of her life. That's what she wanted. She told me her wishes during the revolution and reiterated them more recently when she was being threatened."

"I know," Father Manuel agrees. "She told me the same thing."

Tomás agrees. Mamá told me the same thing as well."

"Who would do such a thing, Father?" Duncan challenges. "Could former Contras still be angry with her ideology? But why would they also kill Col. Jorge? He was one of them."

Father Manuel offers, "As we once discussed, *amigo*, there are some things we're just not supposed to understand."

"This is one thing I can't understand, but I demand answers," Duncan insists.

"I will pray for you, *amigos*," Father Manuel promises.

"Great. You do that." Duncan answers with sarcasm. "That's just what we need."

Duncan is not religious, but on Azucena's behalf, he secretly thanks God for bringing them together and for giving them the short time they shared. His most recent memories transport him to their precious visits in *Paraíso*.

He retrieves a bottle of vintage Merlot that he brought with him from Canada during their last trip. He's been saving it for a special anniversary celebration with Azucena, the 25th since they first met at the cathedral. It's a year early but the time has arrived.

"Tomás," he shouts. "Come with me." He takes the bottle to her studio, uncorks it and, surrounded by her paintings, her art, her life, Duncan and Tomás toast the life of Azucena.

Duncan speaks aloud to her. "Wherever you travel, my dearest Azucena, take us with you. We belong together." Tomás returns to his room to remember quietly. Duncan stares at her paintings the entire night and weeps rivers of tears.

An early edition of *Barricada* reports that a country-wide investigation has opened with expectations that the killer might never be found. The police have started a list with names of people who have a direct association with the Colonel including relatives, close friends, and associates.

The following week, it reports that, as the investigation continues, there are some revelations emerging. There is speculation that the artist, Azucena Sosa, might have gone there with intent to kill Col. Jorge as a suicide bomber. It is rumoured, but not confirmed, that the Colonel fathered the artist's son, Tomás, when he raped her at the estate of Don Ricardo when she was only 17 years old.

"God, I hate fucking journalists," Duncan complains aloud. "How did I ever get mixed up with this bunch of assholes?"

Several weeks pass with the news occupying less space with each issue. Most of the references that do appear are purely speculative, leaning toward the sensational. Duncan finally stops reading the papers altogether.

Finally, the date for the celebration of Azucena's life is scheduled. While discussing arrangements for the celebration with a funeral director, Duncan and Tomás are informed that, because of the nature of her death, there is little of her remains to be saved. They decide that, regardless of the quantity, whatever remains should be evenly distributed into two ceramic urns; one for each of them.

CHAPTER 34

CELEBRATION

Nicaragua, 1996:

Tomás and Duncan arrive at *Teatro Nacional de Rubén Darío* together. Duncan places his arm around him as if he was his own true son.

Duncan expects a quiet, reserved gathering, and has prepared a humble eulogy, words that he's certain will suffer from an emotional delivery.

The theatre, where Azucena has delivered lectures and presented her work, is now where her *compañeros* are gathered to remember her. Her paintings and Duncan's photo portraits of her adorn the walls. Tomás and Duncan are seated in the front row, along with Father Manuel, who will deliver the service.

Señora Sosa, Azucena's grandmother arrived for the celebration from Bluefields, and sits next to Tomás, her great-grandson. Her husband, *señor* Sosa was unable to make the trip due to illness.

Music is performed before any eulogies are delivered; a classical guitarist plays Bach, some children from her *'Clases de Arte para los*

Niños' sing a song they wrote for the occasion. Mourners stand and blend their voices with a chorus of *compañeros* singing a reverent version of *Himno del FSLN*. An aged Indigenous man from Masaya, softly but confidently recites one of his own original poems that he wrote while Azucena was teaching him to read and write during the Literacy Crusade.

Father Manuel's words are brief, a few Biblical references about creation and the Garden of Eden, and about rebirth and life ever after. He then calls upon Duncan and Tomás to deliver the eulogy.

Duncan and Tomás have arranged to deliver the eulogy together, as father and son. Duncan is to begin. He turns and whispers to Tomás.

"Tomás, on this paper is my eulogy. I am almost certain to fuck it up. If I lose control, I will nudge you; please take over from wherever I leave off."

Duncan clears his throat, hesitates, and begins. "I first met Azucena the moment Tomás was born, in the ruins of the cathedral. I had no idea at the time, how she would change my life. But it was not only my life that would change. It would be Nicaragua's life that would change."

He pauses to calm a lump in his throat. "I don't have to remind anybody in this theatre how absolutely beautiful Azucena was …" He pauses. "I mean, how beautiful she is, because she is still with us."

Duncan pauses again. His moist eyes gaze toward the ceiling of the theatre before continuing.

"I have no doubt that she is probably watching us now as we gather in her name. Her beauty is not only in what we see, but in what she radiates to each and every one of us through her spirit. Her spirit is the beauty we now feel as we honour her this afternoon. There is no one here …" Duncan pauses. "Let me correct that. There is no one in all of Nicaragua who has escaped the beauty of *compañera* Azucena. Everything she represents, everything she has ever done, everything she has ever painted … all of it reflects the beautiful spirit of Azucena, and it has always been for the people of Nicaragua … all of the people of Nicaragua."

Two hands somewhere in the theatre come together. Soon, the applause spreads throughout.

"I have been in love with her ever since I first encountered Azucena, although I didn't realize it until several years later. I don't have to tell you how much I loved her; the evidence is hanging everywhere on the walls of this wonderful theatre. Every piece of art was produced from our hearts. We shared a love of creation, of the environment, of the human spirit and of the magnificent dreams and visions that we selflessly shared between us. I shall miss those dreams as I will miss her. But I will have memories that I can share.

Duncan recalls to the audience, Azucena's suggestion to him during their first day together, that he should read, 'A Roosevelt,' by Rubén Darío. "I believe that it would be most appropriate to recite it in this special theatre named after him, as it reflects the pride, love, and commitment that Azucena had for her country and for all of Latin America."

Duncan pauses for a sip of water. "Of course, it should be recited in the original Spanish language, the language of love. As my Spanish is insufficient to do justice to this important gathering, Azucena's son Tomás has offered to recite it this afternoon.

"A Roosevelt … " Tomás begins, completing the entire poem from memory, while others stand to join him, speaking the words aloud. He makes it to the end before emotions overcome him, when the tears flow unabated. The theatre waits in silence.

Tomás restarts. "I am Tomás, the son of Azucena. I am a *nicaragüense* … a very proud *nicaragüense*. I was born at the very moment the earthquake shook our nation, and I lived through two more decades of violent shaking. My mother was born to a poor single mother, under a tarpaulin in Mercado Central, where she survived by selling cigarettes one-by-one. Her mother, my grandmother, died at the very moment I was born, under the rubble of the cathedral."

He pauses to wipe tears away. "My mother, Azucena, spent her life dedicated to changing the lives of those who are born into poverty … into illiteracy. She taught people to love each other, and to love art. She believed that art is life, and life is art. When I look out among you, I see some who are wealthy, and some who are not. Those of you who were born into poverty would not be comfortable within these walls, and probably would not have even been welcomed here, until my mother encouraged you to love and embrace the world of art. Yet, here you are, the wonderful people of Nicaragua. Here you are, in the company of such greatness … my mother, Azucena."

There is an swelling of applause and emotion from the audience as Tomás turns away from the lectern. Before he reaches the edge of the stage, he stops, and returns to the lectern.

"I never knew my father. I only knew Duncan. He was there when I was born. He wasn't here all the time, but when he was here, he and my mother provided me all the love a son could want. Together we were a family. I know Duncan will miss my mother dearly and I recognize that he will soon be returning to his own home in Canada where he has a mother and a father eager to see him, I'm sure. I want him to know that I will continue our relationship and maybe someday, join him in Canada. My mother would want that to happen. I also know that she would really appreciate it if Duncan would perform her favourite ballad on the piano this afternoon."

There is applause. Duncan agrees and begins playing 'Body and Soul.' It was her favourite because that's what they shared together. From the side of the theatre, the rich tones of Pablo's muted trumpet join him. When they're finished, Duncan acknowledges, *"Muchas gracias, Pablo, mi buen amigo."*

Following the eulogies, there are voluntary, heartfelt words from so many others whom Azucena had touched in her short life: a homeless man to whom she had given a sleeping bag on a cold mountain night in Matagalpa; a battered woman who, unable to find a shelter was welcomed into Azucena's home; several men and women from the streets, for whom, with her own money, Azucena purchased raincoats and tarpaulins on the eve of a major storm, risking her own life to deliver them; the frail woman from *Niquinohomo*, aged beyond her years, places an Indigenous corn doll next to Azucena's photograph; the famous Nicaraguan poet and *compañero*, Father Ernesto Cardenal rises to reflect on their times at *Paraíso* and working together in the Ministry of Culture. He reads one of his poems in Azucena's honour.

An attractive well-dressed, obviously pregnant woman, who looks vaguely familiar to Duncan, humbly asks for permission to speak. She begins, "I am Cecilia. Only a few years ago, I was destitute and selling myself to any man with a few *córdobas*. I attended a workshop with *compañera* Azucena near Jinotega. *Señor* Canuck may remember me; he was there too. The *compañera* gave me the courage to change my life. Some of the women were not as fortunate as I was; some were killed by the Contras when the cooperative was attacked, including my beautiful daughter, Margarita. I have brought this painting with me that I made that week. I look at it every day, and because of that, I have since met a wonderful man who loves me. As you can see, we are having a child," she says, resting her hand on her stomach, "a child bred from love, not from destitution and despair. If the child is a girl, she will be Azucena, if it is a boy, he will be *Dooncan*."

Reduced to tears, Duncan assists the woman from the stage. "I do remember you, Cecilia, and I'm proud to have met you. Congratulations and *buenas suertes. A Dios.*" She embraces him before she rejoins the new 'wonderful man' in her life.

* * *

The following week, Father Manuel, Tomás, and Duncan arrive for a scheduled appointment with the attorney. He reads Azucena's last will and testament. Her monetary worth is limited; most of what she earned, she gave to others or spent on her artistic passions. The balance, combined with the value of her modest home, is left to Tomás.

Her art was priceless. Selected pieces are designated for Father

Manuel, particularly ones painted early in her career that have recently gained some interest for their historical value. Others are earmarked for Tomás. The remaining portion of her work is left to Duncan, in recognition of his role as her 'muse and the keeper of her inner spirit.' Duncan is uncertain and can only speculate about what she intended as 'the keeper of her inner spirit.'

Arrangements are made through Father Manuel, for the transport of the paintings to Canada and the insurance for their safe arrival. They make promises to continue communicating by both letters and phone calls.

Tomás and Duncan share a lobster dinner at Costa Brava restaurant the evening before Duncan's departure. Tomás informs Duncan that, as soon as he graduates with his bachelor's degree, he will start studying for his law degree.

Duncan promises him that he will never forget his mother. "She will occupy my heart and soul for all time. As for you, Tomás, I will always consider you as my son. If you ever want to be adopted, I'll volunteer."

CHAPTER 35

CONDOLENCES

Toronto, 1996:

"Why in hell did she go to Don Ricardo's?" Duncan shouts aloud staring at the empty walls of his Toronto townhouse. "There were only bad memories there. It's as if her time was just up, that fate reached down and scooped her away, but she was far too young."

Duncan is reduced to weeping episodes and sleepless nights. He agonizes trying to accept Azucena's death. There are so many memories that haunt him, not only in his sleep but in every waking hour.

During the most emotionally charged period in Duncan's entire life, the first months back in Canada prove difficult. Aside from dealing with the fallout from Azucena's passing, he is officially unemployed.

When Duncan opted against returning at the end of his sabbatical extension, Kurt accepted an offer for the fulltime position, replacing Duncan in the photojournalism faculty. More recently, when Duncan called Kurt from Nicaragua to tell him about Azucena's death, the writing was on the wall for Kurt; Duncan would be returning to Canada and would obviously want his townhouse back. Fortunately, Kurt was able to find suitable accommodations elsewhere in the neighbourhood.

Duncan carefully places Azucena's urn on the mantelpiece close to her painting from *Paraíso*. Tomás and Duncan agreed that each should have a symbolic urn, her name and dates inscribed, with only a modicum of ashes, but containing small items of personal memorabilia.

Duncan's urn contains some small stone remnants from the cathedral, a palette knife with her fingerprints embedded into the dried paint, his press credentials from the military base, and a red and black neck scarf from Azucena's days as a *guerrillera*, the same scarf she wore to the anniversary celebrations. It's not, of course, that Duncan and Tomás will ever forget her, but they need a tangible memorial, something they can look at and hold in times of difficulty. Duncan often finds himself talking aloud to the urn.

"Hello in there," he usually begins, before carrying on a one-sided conversation.

Word about Duncan's loss had already been spread by friends throughout the college and the music communities. Upon arriving in Toronto, there were many wishes for Duncan placed by Kurt into a box of unopened mail. He received well-intentioned messages and cards of condolence from faculty and students at the college, fellow musicians, and artists of all disciplines. Many contained invitations to get in touch when he feels ready.

'How does one know when one is ready?' Duncan ponders. 'Will it be weeks, months, years?'

A neighbour from across the street, whom Duncan has never met, arrives at his door with a casserole dish of cabbage rolls to express her sadness. Apparently, she had met and talked to Azucena while she was visiting.

Duncan also receives an invitation for dinner from Joyce Banerji, the Chair of Fine Arts at the college. He knows that dinner with Joyce will also involve many conversational references to Azucena and to his collaborations with her.

Penny calls offering her condolences "I'm so sorry, Duncan. I know how close you were."

Sarcastically, Duncan corrects her. "It's how close we *are*, not *were*. We are still close. She is just no longer here. But we're still close."

"Don't be weird about this, Duncan," Penny says in her own inimitable way. "I'm not trying to be an asshole. I honestly feel for you, and I certainly don't want to upset you. When you feel up to it, or should I say, *if* you ever feel up to it, we can have coffee somewhere. No agenda, just coffee and conversation."

"Maybe in a few weeks. I'll let you know. Thanks for calling, Penny. I really do appreciate it." She recites her new phone number to Duncan.

A phone message from FedEx informs him that a shipment of paintings is ready to be delivered. They want to know when he'll be at home to receive them. Duncan really hasn't given much thought to where he might store Azucena's paintings. He has some space in the basement and could hang some up around the house.

His editing room is already stuffed with work in progress, projects that he was working on when he heard the news while still in Managua. There are contacts and work prints from various self-assignments littered across his light table, as well as boxes and files from his life's work. He still isn't ready to return to his projects.

'Who knows?' he contemplates. 'I may never get back to them.'

When the FedEx truck arrives, Duncan is gobsmacked; there are so many paintings. Some are massive and will only fit along one wall in his garage. The paintings from Azucena's last show in Toronto are still stored in the garage as well. Once they're all inside, he has a renewed sense that Azucena has come home; they are finally together again.

He eats his neighbour's cabbage rolls over several nights and returns her empty casserole dish with thanks. He never cared for cabbage rolls, but he thanks her just the same.

A few weeks later he accepts Joyce's invitation for dinner. It proves to be an enjoyable evening. She's obviously an art lover but the bonus is that she loves jazz as well; Coltrane's wonderful 'Ballads' album plays in the background through dinner.

Afterward, they have drinks on her patio overlooking an inground pool. Joyce laments over Azucena's passing. "I was really looking forward to having her return to teach with us again. I love her work, but I admire her passion even more."

Duncan adds, "She enjoyed working with you, Joyce, and the students as well. She was looking forward to another semester with you."

Joyce touches Duncan's hand. "Duncan, would you be comfortable talking to my students about Azucena and her work, and also about how you worked together?"

He draws his hand back. "I'd love to. It would allow me to relive some of our most wonderful moments. I should remind you though, our work together also involved some intimacies, if that's permitted. Just a warning though. I may start weeping during the presentation."

"The students will relish the intimacy references and will probably cry with you."

After some silence while eating, Joyce says, "Besides the interesting conversation we're having, and the music, there's another reason I invited you here tonight, Duncan. I was wondering if you would consider …"

Duncan interrupts Joyce, raising the palms of his hands toward her in hopes of avoiding an embarrassing conversation. "Before you go any further, Joyce, I'm not looking for another companion, or a relationship."

"Heavens no, Duncan. You're far too vulnerable for that right now. I was wondering if you would consider joining the faculty in Fine Arts. I know that's a surprise for you, but there's an opening for another faculty member and you would be perfect for the position. We've never embraced photography in the program, and maybe it's about time we do something about that. I already know you are popular with students; I've done my research. And, here's the best part.

You can continue your seniority in the system where you left off, and your pension is still intact."

"Wow," Duncan takes a big breath. "That's a surprise. I didn't see that one coming. There've been a lot of surprises lately. I'll have to give it some thought, Joyce. I've been thinking a lot about what I'm going to do. As you can probably guess, I'm not as active in photojournalism as I used to be and it bothers me. The industry quite frankly, sucks; its head is stuck in the toilet."

"Is that because of the emerging digital technology?" Joyce asks before sipping her wine.

"Hell no. It's how the big publishers are reorganizing their newsrooms and gobbling each other up. They're trimming their budgets and cutting back on talent, all to improve the bottom line. What they're doing now is just the visible damage. It's going to get uglier; the icebergs will start to melt. Wait until technology catches up with them. Or should I say when they catch up to technology. Realistically, they haven't got a clue what they're going to be faced with when it hits them, and the technology will always be ahead of them. Besides it will be far more expensive than they can handle, and none of them have figured out how to monetize the technology. After all, no money, no news, that's reality."

"What will happen to the talent, especially the graduates, the young photographers and journalists who are breaking into the industry?"

"The very talented ones who are willing to roll with the changes will be fine."

"Can I get you another drink, Duncan? Incidentally, I'm not trying get you drunk, and I don't have any hidden personal agenda to this evening. I just thought you'd like some company."

"I thank you for that, Joyce, but no, I should be moving on. I'm not terribly sociable these days. Don't get me wrong. I've enjoyed the meal and the conversation immensely. It's the first conversation I've had since ... well, you know. It's also great to know we can talk about jazz. I can't do that with most people."

Joyce gives Duncan a solid squeeze at the door as he leaves. "You will give that offer some thought, right?"

"I'll let you know soon, Joyce. Thanks again."

In the following weeks, Duncan reorganizes the townhouse to accommodate the new paintings. He clears out a small guest room that was previously used for storage; he never has any guests. He repaints the walls and ceiling of the room a matte-surfaced, velvet deep rust tone, almost a warm black. Once the paint is dry, he moves a love seat into the room and, on the opposite wall, rehangs *Paraíso*, the first painting Azucena gave him, and places a soft light above it. His stereo system is located on a low table under the painting. Several times he tests the angles and distances from the love seat, where he can operate the lighting and the stereo with a remote.

Later in the day he takes a stroll around the neighbourhood. Walking is a great stimulus to inspire creative thinking. He finds that he can meditate while walking, especially when walking at a steady pace. Once his mind clears, there's space for random thoughts that often lead to new story ideas or trigger fresh motifs that inspire musical compositions. When he returns home there's a voice mail from Penny, a blunt message as usual.

"It's time, Duncan. Coffee tomorrow morning at Starbucks, around the corner from your place. See you at ten."

In the morning, he stares at some transparencies on the light table but resists becoming too involved in the process before his coffee date with Penny. He considers cancelling it in favour of his muse but decides to show up anyway. With any luck, he'll still remember what he was planning to do next when he returns home.

He takes a relaxed stroll to the café and arrives late. Penny is already sipping her first latte. Duncan orders an Americano Grande. She rises to hug him.

'God there's a lot of huggy people around these days,' Duncan thinks. 'In Central America everybody hugs, but it never used to be a habit here up north. It's just not formal enough for our uptight Victorian sensibilities I guess.'

Penny is unusually polite. She offers her condolences once again before asking Duncan how he's doing and what his plans are. His guard is up against any possibility of becoming re-acquainted with Penny. That's a rocky road he doesn't care to travel on.

They don't talk much, certainly not about anything important. She's still at the university. She asks if he's getting out socially.

"Do you mean am I dating?" he asks. "It's a bit early for that, don't you think?"

"I was just wondering how you're dealing with your grief, that's all."

"Well … I had dinner with someone, but there was nothing date-like about it."

"Where did you go?" Penny asks.

"What do you mean?"

'Like, what restaurant did you go to?"

"None. She made dinner for us. It was at her house." To deflect the attention away from himself, he smirks, with a pinch of sarcasm, "Are you getting any history lessons lately?" Duncan realizes his error in judgement and anticipates a blow-up but, surprisingly, she remains quite calm.

"We don't see each other very often, but we still get together for the occasional drink. So, what are you going to do for work? You've been away for a while."

"Yeah. It's been a while. Nine years actually. I was freelancing down in Nicaragua but there won't be many assignments for me up here. Prospects for the job front is a long story, Penny. Far too long for a coffee break."

"Then perhaps we should think about a dinner date some night."

Duncan sucks back the rest of his Americano and rises up from his chair. "I have some editing to catch up on. I'm so far behind. I should get moving."

"Is that a no?"

He pauses ... "It's not a no, it's an, 'I don't want to go through that scene again,' especially not now while I'm struggling to get my life back on track. Take care Penny."

Instead of returning home, Duncan takes a streetcar to the college to see Kurt and to reaquaint himself to the environment. He checks into his old office. A secretary, different from the one he remembers, tells him that Kurt is out today.

"Kurt doesn't have any classes today," she tells Duncan with an officious demeanour. "I believe he's at home marking assignments. Whom may I say is looking for him?" she asks.

"Just tell him Duncan was here. He knows where to find me."

"Yes sir. I will pass that message on. Have a nice day."

'Fuck,' Duncan reacts as he walks down the hall that he has trodden so many times before. 'Have I been away that long?'

Duncan takes the stairs to the third floor. He taps on the door. "Anybody home?"

"Oh. Hi Duncan. What's up?"

"Just putting in time, that's all, Joyce. What are you up to?"

"Just finishing up my marking. Feel like grabbing lunch?" Joyce proposes. "Someplace off campus, where we can have a drink, relax, and discuss the faculty position. I'll drive if that's OK with you."

"It's perfect because I rode the 'red rocket' in."

It's a warm autumn afternoon so they opt for lunch on the patio. When the wine arrives, Joyce cuts to the chase and presses Duncan for a decision.

"There's only a week remaining before I must advertise the position. Internal hires can be made without opening it up to public competition."

"This is hardly an internal position, is it?" Duncan challenges. "I haven't been teaching here for nine years."

"We'll just keep that to ourselves, Duncan," Joyce winks. "Your employment file is still on the books; I checked."

Duncan has already decided that it would be the best move for him but has delayed contacting her. "I read somewhere that psychiatrists advise against making major changes during bereavement," he tells Joyce.

"Getting a job when you're unemployed is hardly a major change, Duncan; it's a necessity."

"Good point." He hesitates … "OK, I'm game." Duncan jumps in with both feet. "Let's draw up the paperwork."

"Fantastic." She offers a handshake over the table. "The Dean has approved an upgrade to the pay scale, so you'll receive a higher salary."

"Higher than what?" Duncan poses with a snicker.

"I didn't mention that increase to you before because I didn't want you to accept the job just for monetary reasons."

"I *am* accepting it for monetary reasons, Joyce. It's a job, something I don't have at the moment."

"You haven't lost your sense of humour, Duncan. You're still quick with the comebacks."

"Maybe you should tell me what I'm expected to teach, like what courses?"

"Good point. I want you to supervise some of the studio courses and to conduct a special new course that will embody the metaphysical aspects of dream interpretation, using meditation as a catalyst. In other words, working directly from the imagination. Could you organize lesson plans around those parameters, Duncan? I know you and Azucena practiced meditation; she mentioned that to me when she was here."

"A piece of cake," Duncan responds. "But will I be required to use that complicated, long-winded, *fine art speak*?" he jokes, before promising, "I'll have the lesson plans on your desk tomorrow?"

They click their glasses in acknowledgement of the agreement.

Joyce adds, "I'll have the paperwork ready to sign tomorrow and you can start at the beginning of the next semester. In the interim we'll arrange some get-togethers to work out the kinks of scheduling and so forth. Would you agree to use examples of your personal work, and of Azucena's as well, in lectures and for demonstrations?"

"For sure. I'm certain that Azucena won't mind. They represent the fundamentals of my experience. I also have some of her unfinished work, and some things that she and I were collaborating on before she died."

Duncan suddenly realizes that he spoke about her death without crumbling into tears and without hesitating, or searching for softer words like passing away, moving on, or being called to the great beyond. He wonders if that's a step forward, or is he becoming callous?

"I'd love to see some more of her work sometime, and of course, yours as well," Joyce suggests.

"I just received a shipment of her work from Nicaragua last week. At the moment it's scattered throughout the house and the garage. I feel like a hoarder."

"Maybe you're not a hoarder, but a sensitive person who's fortunate enough to be surrounded by the love you shared with her. Think of it that way. Anytime you want, you can relive memories through her art, and the art you made together. What can be more satisfying than that?"

"Having her here with me. That would be much better."

Joyce expresses her understanding by stroking Duncan's arm.

After their extended lunch they walk casually around the neighbourhood browsing through several small galleries before Joyce drives him home.

"Would you like to see some of her work?" Duncan asks.

"If you're up to it."

They start in the hallway leading to the living room. Duncan has managed to hang several smaller pieces, but many still lean against furniture and alongside the grand piano in the living room. More are hung in the stairwell leading to the second floor and in the master bedroom, leaving only a small space around Duncan's bed.

"You *are* a hoarder, Duncan," Joyce chuckles. "You should find a gallery that'll show this work. At least it wouldn't be cluttering up the hallways."

"Wait until you see what's in the garage."

Before exposing her to the garage, Duncan opens a door to reveal his newly painted dimly-lit room. He clicks a remote that turns on the soft light above the *Paraíso* painting. With a second remote, Miles Davis' muted trumpet begins to play 'Blue in Green.' Joyce says nothing, appreciative of the sanctity of Duncan's special place. He feels her hand rubbing softly across his back in consolation.

"This is my cocoon," Duncan explains. "In this special place, there is no clutter, it's the only neat space in the entire house. I suppose it's really a shrine to Azucena. I meditate here and whenever possible, quietly commune with my memories."

Tears appear on Joyce's cheeks. She daubs them with the corner of a tissue. "I feel like I've been given an honour, that I'm in a place where very few are invited."

"You're the first."

"Why me?"

"Well … I watched as you viewed the paintings," Duncan says, "and I saw your reactions. You understand."

Duncan offers Joyce a seat. "I'll pour us some wine and join you. In the meantime, just quietly absorb what the painting is saying to you."

When he returns with their wine, Joyce has settled into a reflective state, her eyes remain open, fixed on the painting. Duncan sits beside her and settles into his 'contemplative zone of nothingness.'

He soon feels Azucena's presence; she is with him in the room, approaching him from the painting, as she does when he's in the room alone. He's taken back to *Paraíso* and senses that he's on the cusp of a new awareness. Azucena embraces him and returns to the painting. 'Is she giving me a message?' Duncan wonders. The music ends.

Joyce and Duncan sit quietly beside each other. Finally, she speaks, "Holy shit. I can't believe I can feel like this without chemicals. What just happened here, Duncan? Can you even explain it to me?"

"I don't know what happened to *you*. I do know, and you can accept this or not, that Azucena is in the room. Not physically, of course, but in spirit. It's the same as when she and I visited *Paraíso*."

Joyce explains her own experience. "I was drawn directly into the painting, as if I were there when the painting was being created. A woman, I must assume it was Azucena, waved her arms in shapes in front of a fresh canvas allowing her spirit to create the image before any paint was applied. Then with a heavy brush in her hand she applied random strokes of green, brushing in all directions, before placing the two figures. When the figures were as she wanted, the reds and yellows were added with a knife. The blacks and greys were smeared with her bare hands."

"What about the figures?" Duncan asks her. "What do you see there?"

"They may appear as just blobs of drab colour to some people, but they are a man and a woman to me, and their gestures are totally consumed in the ecstasy of love. I see two lovers in a forest and the forest is being consumed by fire. This is a painting by someone consumed by passion. There may be an environmental comment to the painting as well, but it's very personal. I must conclude that it is Azucena and yourself, a self-portrait, therefore. I interpret it as the ecstasy of creative reawakening, like a second coming of Genesis."

"Wow." Duncan contemplates Joyce's reaction. "You are the only person who has seen the painting in this room, and the first who has really understood it. A previous friend of mine saw only jealousy and rage. She called it 'that fucking painting' on several occasions and attempted to take a knife to it."

"Some friend." Joyce offers an opinion. "She must have been a jealous person."

Duncan fills in some details. "Azucena presented it to me as a gesture of love as we departed *Paraíso* for refuge in Costa Rica before the soldiers attacked and ransacked everything there. People were killed and the entire community was destroyed by fire. Azucena had … no, I'm beginning to sense that she still has … the ability to foresee events. This was painted several months before the soldiers arrived."

Joyce touches Duncan's arm. "I have great respect for what you and Azucena have experienced together and obviously still do. I want you to know that I would never violate that connection. You do, however, fascinate me, Duncan. I'm not going to lead you anywhere you don't want to go, but I would very much like to spend more time with you, if only on a purely platonic level. Our minds connect. Do you know what I mean?"

"I have a sense that we share some instincts, to put it safely for the moment. I'm very reluctant to get involved in a romantic relationship, as I've already told you. But I am tuned in to your sensitivity toward the creative process that Azucena and I share. I would like to work with you as I develop the course material because I believe that you have a depth of understanding and empathy."

"I think we're going to be eating out a lot," Joyce quips, sipping the last drops of her wine.

While leaving, Joyce leans over to place a 'kissy peck' on Duncan's cheek and rubs her hand along the small of his back. He accepts her gestures of intent with grace.

PART THIRTEEN
1996 – 1999

CHAPTER 36

A NEW LIFE

Toronto, 1996 – 1998:

Duncan has fleeting second thoughts about accepting Joyce's offer to join the Fine Arts faculty. He broods over how it will affect his own photography and his belief in the truth of his images. He has always been concerned about the human condition and his commitment to portray the truth about the subjects he photographs. After all, that's the reason he adopted photography in the first place.

'Am I becoming a traitor to my principles? Am I selling out?' he agonizes. 'Will I become one of those art-for-art's-sake guys who care only for their own product and image without regard for the truth of the message and how it will impact the people who see it? Will I start writing those self-indulgent manifestos about the universe that take longer to read than the artwork itself? Christ, I hope not. Is it possible for me to incorporate the documentary tradition of factual information into my art? Did I already cross the line when I started collaborating with Azucena? Maybe, but we were both trying to communicate our messages with integrity, weren't we?'

So many concerns complicate Duncan's ability to think clearly. He misses Azucena so much and worries that his sadness is clouding his real purpose in life.

'Who's life? What life? At the moment I don't really have a life. Can I find a way to get on with my life without worrying that I may be violating Azucena's memory, or her principles and influence in some distorted abstract manner? Why should she care? She's gone. It's my life to live, to continuing to live; it's mine and mine alone.'

He searches for answers during meditations in his private cocoon and ponders the questions while taking solitary walks in the park. Since Azucena died, Duncan hasn't used his camera nor played any piano. The life he's currently living parallels the zone of nothingness he escapes to when faced with chaos.

'If art is life and life is art, then both of us are in a damned sorry state.' His mind continues to wander, finally resting on his own mandate, 'teaching is learning and learning is teaching.'

"Of course," he states aloud. "I'll let the students teach me about art and I'll teach them about honesty and responsibility." Suddenly, without further pain, his lesson plans find shape. He works through the night forming them for presentation.

"Good morning, Joyce. I have the lesson plans ready for you. I have just one question. Can we alter the name of the course, or has that already been fixed?"

"It's already established and printed in the calendar, so the title can't be changed. Why?"

Duncan explains his reasoning. "What if I veer off course during the semester, or even during a class? I like it when a class finds its own energy and direction. Sometimes, for instance, a student will recall some issue they've been challenged by, not limited to technical issues, but life issues as well. Can I, within the broad spectrum of art, open the lesson plan up to accommodate the philosophical ramifications of the issue, hopefully accomplishing a universal solution that all of us, students and profs alike, will benefit from?"

Joyce provides Duncan with a practical response. "There's no problem, Duncan. Once the lesson plan is submitted, we still have flexibility within the course outline to customize material week-by-week, as we wish. You're a jazz musician after all. Improvise. Isn't that what you do? It should be a piece of cake for you. Just don't make a big splash about the changes you make. The main criterion is that, at the end of the term, the objectives have been met and the students aren't occupying the Dean's office and hanging effigies of you from the chestnut tree out there in the quadrangle."

"Oh. That reminds me, Joyce. I almost forgot. Can we organize field trips?" Duncan asks.

Joyce's eyebrows rise. "Like what? A trip to the local art gallery? Sure, no problem. Wait ..." she hesitates, detecting a red flag waving. "Where are you going with this, Duncan?"

"This is just a wild thought, and it would be voluntary for a limited number of students, maybe five or six, and they would pay their own way. I would like to organize a field trip to *Paraíso* in Nicaragua. It would place the students in the midst of where Azucena found her muse, and where mine came to fruition as well."

"Can I come?"

"Sure, why not?"

"Then we'll do it. Maybe I'll be able to find my muse there too. I can almost guaranteed it'll pass the Dean's approval, especially if everyone pays their own way. Here's the caveat, Duncan. If only some of the students attend the field trip, it can't be applied to the overall course grading. Understand?"

"Got it. We don't have to grade it at all. The satisfaction will be enough for everyone.

"Great idea, Duncan. Create a field trip proposal and I'll submit it to the Dean."

"It's right here," Duncan says, passing the paperwork to Joyce.

***

Duncan calls Nicaragua the day before Christmas Eve and wishes Tomás the best on his birthday. Twenty-five years have passed since he encountered Azucena at the Cathedral, the day Tomás was born. They talk about how much they miss his mother and how his studies at university are going. Duncan tells Tomás about teaching in the Fine Arts department, adding, "You're mother would be proud of me."

Tomás tells Duncan about a classmate he's been dating. They promise each other that they'll continue to keep in touch and consider the possibility that Tomás might come to Toronto for a visit someday.

Duncan wants to tell Tomás about the potential field trip planned for the students but opts to keep it a secret for the time being, at least until it's finalized. "Give my regards to Father Manuel. *Te amo, Tomás, ciao.*"

Tomás delays hanging up the phone. "I don't see much of Father Manuel these days, Duncan," Tomás says. "It's like he's been hiding from me. I think Mamá's passing has dealt him quite a blow. If I see him I'll pass on your wishes. *Te amo tambien. Hasta la próxima.*"

Duncan spends the balance of the evening in his cocoon with a bottle of Merlot, his memories, and Miles Davis. He recalls playing the Baldwin piano with Pablo, but his memories morph together with the celebration of Azucena's life.

That night, Duncan receives a visit during a fleeting dream. Azucena's face appears in images from the cathedral that fade into *Paraíso* and pass through the mist in the mountains outside Matagalpa; memories, but more than memories. Fresh images intersperse with the familiar; to places and events that are both new and foreign to Duncan. Her lips move without sound as she accompanies him like a tour guide on a journey of images that travel in and out of reality.

Joyce calls Duncan on Christmas Day to wish him a Merry Christmas and to ask how he's coping.

"I managed to survive the anniversary with alcohol," he tells her.

"If you're feeling up to it, I'm having a small New Year's Eve party

396   Doug Wicken

at my house. Just a few friends and some neighbours, that's all. Nothing extravagant, just a few laughs." she promises.

She catches Duncan on a good day. "Why the hell not," he answers. "If I stay at home alone, I'll only get drunk again, and hate myself in the morning. What can I contribute?"

"Nothing, just bring yourself, but here's the proviso; it's a dress-up party."

"Oh no, not one of those," Duncan complains.

"No Duncan. This will be fun, you'll see. You must choose a character you admire from the arts or literature — either a character, an artist, or a writer — as the basis for your costume," she tells him, "and you can't reveal who it is to anyone."

"What? A dress up with rules to boot? Wow! I can hardly wait," Duncan laughs sarcastically.

"Be serious Duncan. It's just for fun. Besides we'll be half drunk anyway, so it won't matter. Make up your own rules. You always do. Just so you know, we're having a contest so pick a subject that'll challenge us all. Who knows, you may win a prize."

"Oh wonderful, a contest, with prizes," Duncan responds with a chuckle. "I just love contests."

Duncan spends the next day agonizing over who he's going to dress up as. He's not a great costume person and usually avoids costume and Halloween parties. He reminisces, 'The only memorable Halloween was in high school, the first time I danced with Penny, and look how that ended up.'

He decides to choose someone obscure, someone that nobody will recognize. After studying his own image in the mirror to imagine someone he could morph into for the party, he reaches a decision.

He arrives at Joyce's by taxi sporting a black beret and wire-rimmed glasses, a long, embroidered cotton *guayabera* shirt hanging over a well-worn pair of baggy trousers. His feet are sandal-clad. 'If anybody can identify me, they deserve a prize.'

Joyce, provocatively dressed in a shapely 19th century corset and an exposed crinoline, open at the front to reveal fishnet stockings and high black boots. Her face is over-adorned with makeup; a curly, bleach-blond wig hides her black hair. She welcomes Duncan into her living room where two other couples are already diving into the alcohol and finger food. She attempts to introduce him to her guests while Coltrane's 'Live at the Village Vanguard' tests the speakers.

"Is that music for me?" he shouts.

Joyce shouts something back but it passes without being heard.

She brings Duncan a scotch and sits beside him on the sofa. The only conversation possible is between closely positioned people who shout directly into their listener's ears.

"I'm so glad you could make it, Duncan," she shouts. "How are you doing?" She pats her hand on his knee. "Everything OK? That's an interesting outfit. I can't wait to find out who you are."

Duncan counters with, "Not as curious as I am to discover your character. Whoever she is, she's very alluring. Is it safe to sit this close?"

She laughs and rubs her fishnet-stockinged leg against his. "You'll just have to wait and see."

A third couple arrives, one bearing a full-face mask, the other with a white-painted face. 'It'll be interesting to see where this evening leads to,' Duncan contemplates.

After an hour passes, Joyce turns the music down to make an announcement. "I think it will be wise to run our contest before the midnight hour. It'll make it easier to eat and drink without all the face paint and masks and it'll allow us to relax more. Does everyone agree?"

"Let's do it," someone shouts from the dining room where the food is laid out.

The guests attempt to identify each person; some are easier than others. The white-painted face is quickly identified as the famous French mime, Marcel Marceau. His partner is revealed as Colette, the author of Gigi. A man with shoes on his knees, standing a mere four feet high, is not surprisingly, Toulouse-Lautrec.

Joyce announces, "We are narrowing the field down to only five. I'm curious why everyone so far has been French."

Several attempts to identify Duncan fail. One guest suggests that he is Mahatma Gandhi; another thinks he's a pirate of some description.

"If I wanted to be a pirate," he answers, "I would have worn my wooden pegleg and brought my parrot. I decided to leave him at home because his language is too disgusting for mixed company."

Somebody calls Joyce a harlot. She challenges, "But which one?" Finally, the contest narrows to between Joyce and Duncan. It's left for her to guess his identity and for him to guess hers. Her eyes scan the length of him before writing something on a piece of paper.

Duncan already assumes that Joyce is a harlot, but from what work of art? He can't peg her down to one specific character. 'A painting, a play, a novel?' He finally takes a wild guess.

"The way everything has been going so far, I'm going to narrow it down to someone from France."

Joyce assumes a surprised grin.

Duncan reads it as a weakness. "I know, I know, I've got it," he blurts excitedly, pointing toward her. "You're one of the whores painted by Toulouse-Lautrec at the Moulin Rouge."

"Whew! Close, but no cigar Duncan. You're getting warm though; you're in the right country." She assumes a provocative 'harlot-ish' pose in front of him. "Go ahead. Take another guess."

"I'm at a loss, Joyce. I need more time. See if you can guess who I am," Duncan challenges.

Joyce outlines her train of thought. "Since you walked in here, I've done some mental calculations to figure you out. I've considered where you've been, what you've experienced, and what you've probably read, and I've arrived at a final answer that I honestly believe is correct." She hands Duncan the folded piece of paper.

"I can't believe it," Duncan responds. "How did you figure that out?"

"It was quite simple really," Joyce admits. "Considering that you were in Nicaragua during the revolution, I mentally recalled some of the photographs you had taken at that time. There is a photograph on your wall that was taken at the island community you attended, the one you call, *Paraíso*. This is the priest who started that community. He is a renowned Nicaraguan poet, a priest, and one of the revolutionaries, Father Ernesto Cardenal."

"Amazing. I didn't think anybody would know that."

"I win!" Joyce shouts, parading about the living room with her arms waving.

"What's the prize?" someone asks.

"I haven't decided yet. I'll figure that out later. Let's eat. I'm starved."

"Wait a minute," Duncan demands. "You won because no one could guess who your harlot is. Now you have to reveal who you are."

"I am Nana, the courtesan in Edouard Manet's painting, and also the subject in Emile Zola's novel of the same name."

With the competition over, the guests top up their glasses for the countdown to midnight.

"Ten ... Nine ... Eight ..." By now, most have shed portions of their costumes and are stuffed beyond belief with food. "Seven ... Six ... Five ... Four ..." Joyce places her arms around Duncan's neck, his hands rest on her hips, while they sway slowly with each other, eye to eye, toward the final count. Their thoughts are synchronized. They both know where this is going. "Three ... Two ... One ..."

Black and white images of Guy Lombardo's Royal Canadians flicker on the television screen. Everyone at the party is coupled up. Joyce and Duncan bring their lips together. At that moment, Duncan abandons any guilt for having her in his arms. They dance closely with their lips together, the harlot and the revolutionary priest, her pelvis pressed against his. She probes her tongue against the roof of Duncan's mouth. At this moment he'd rather be here than anywhere else.

Auld Lang Syne is just a melody for the moment. The meaning of the words, 'Let auld acquaintance be forgot,' strike a chord in his heart. He must never forget. But right here and now, Joyce's tongue is creating fresh memories.

When the guests leave, Joyce stops Duncan from calling a cab. "You're not going anywhere tonight, Duncan. This is a fresh new year, a time to make new friends and to restart your life. There will be many opportunities for you to remember the past. Tonight is about the present."

"I don't know about this, Joyce; it just doesn't feel right." Duncan pulls back. "It's like I'm cheating on Azucena."

Joyce looks directly into Duncan's eyes. "I will never ask you to stop thinking about Azucena, Duncan, nor to stop loving her. I want you to continue making virtual love with her and producing the wonderful, exciting work that you produce in collaboration with her. I hope that never stops for you."

Despite his guilt, Duncan allows Joyce to draw him closer. Their lips connect. He's overcome with the sweetness of her perfume.

"But tonight, Duncan, you're all mine. I won you in a contest, fair and square. You're my prize." She pulls Duncan to her room where they share passages from Pablo Neruda's love poems as foreplay.

Duncan worries about facing an awkward situation on their first day back at the college, but everything seems normal. They see each other at the 'welcome back' meeting with the Dean and other faculty members over coffees and boxes of Timbits.

Joyce asks Duncan how he's doing without references to New Year's Eve or smiling and jabbing him in the ribs. He responds honestly. "There were moments I questioned everything, but I'm back on track." Privately, he thanks her for the party and for including him. "I needed that, Joyce."

She leans over and whispers, "I'm sure you did. You're welcome."

* * *

The first summer Duncan spends at home in many years allows him some opportunities for local exploration. Because of his extended sojourn in Nicaragua, he has lost touch with what's happening in his own domestic environment. He manages to plug into some of the jazz festivals, even performing a few concerts with friends, old and new, and explores the diversity and exotica of ethnic neighbourhoods around the city with his camera. With new images, he revisits Jack Bryant, the editor of 'Human Interest' magazine who gave him his first big break. They meet for lunch and compare experiences over the past quarter century.

Jack is impressed. "I love these images, Duncan, so I have an assignment for you, if you're interested. Keep shooting your impressions of this entire city, not only the ethnic areas, but everywhere … in black and white of course. You still have that traditional documentary enthusiasm that I can't find in most younger photographers, and nobody captures those subtle candid moments like you do. You know the ones I mean, Duncan, the interactive shots with gestures and facial expressions that ask questions."

"That's what I do best, Jack. I'm always asking questions."

Jack complains. "Too many damned photographers are just lining people up against insignificant backgrounds these days. They lack context, you know what I mean, Duncan? I want to see the images that challenge the readers, where they get to interpret their own conclusions; the who, what, where, when, and most importantly, the why. It's time to get people thinking about their own environment again, before it's lost forever."

Jack points his finger at Duncan. "When you're shooting, watch how people are reacting and adjusting to the changes in the air and water, and their anxieties of facing the next millennium. It'll be a challenge for you but just think about those historic photos of Bresson and Kertész during the '30s leading up to the second great war. Whether you realize it or not, we're facing the lead-up to the third great war, the war for human survival. Just keep that in mind while you're shooting, but keep looking at the human condition, both positive and negative. I chose you because I know you can do it. Our children and grandchildren will want to know what it was like before all hell broke loose."

Duncan is ecstatic. He's out every day, wandering through busy streets and alleyways, practising his art with a smile on his face, capturing lovers and fighters, sellers and buyers, rich and poor, hookers and clients, musicians, painters, and dancers; the life and breadth of the city.

Duncan and Joyce meet occasionally over lunch to organize details of his new responsibilities. She's extremely professional during business meetings. Outside of the meetings however, they are far less formal, not to suggest that they fornicate like rabbits. In fact, their intimate episodes are sporadic, but enjoyable and exciting when they happen. Usually, they are unscheduled, a knock on the front door with an 'I was just in the neighbourhood' ruse. On occasion, one will phone the other and bluntly express a need to get together, often prefaced with a simple question, "Do you feel like a drink?" or more honestly, "Let's have sex."

Duncan asks what Joyce is keeping busy at during the summer vacation.

"Mostly I walk, casually. I prefer to walk alone with my thoughts. Often, I'll think of a project I could work on, maybe some conceptual installation I haven't considered before. The rest of the time I spend in the studio creating stuff. What are you up to, Duncan?"

Duncan talks excitedly about the assignment he's working on. "It's just what I need right now, a project I can sink my teeth into, a challenge."

"So you like what you're doing, that's the main thing, isn't it?"

"Shit, I'm in love with what I'm doing."

"Is that a habit of yours, Duncan, falling in love?"

"Ah, c'mon, Joyce. Have I ever told you that I'm in love with you?"

"Never, because you're still in love with Azucena, and your work, of course. I know that. But I also know that you desire me, you crave my body. That's more important to me than hearing you whisper that you love me over and over. I represent lust to you ... you want me, and I need to be wanted. Azucena represents love ... she is idolized, like a Goddess. We are very different. I even think she understood that, and that's why she'll continue to be in your thoughts forever. You'll see. I'll even go so far as to suggest that we will share you. Think of it as a virtual *ménage a trois*. Right now, however, you only have me to satisfy. I don't ask much from you, do I?"

"Only what you need … which ironically, is what I need."

Recalling what Joyce alluded to, Duncan ponders the differences between she and Azucena as lovers. 'There's no question that I lust for Joyce and that Azucena's meditative romanticism still entices and arouses me. There is no distinct line between them, however. It's a blend, like watercolours wet-on-wet.'

Duncan's new position as Professor of Fine Arts introduces him to a more *laissez-faire* approach. In photojournalism, everything is about deadlines and scooping the competitors. In fine arts, it's more about waiting for the muse and pondering, offering more time for coffees and meditative walking.

After learning that Joyce walks to find herself in much the same way as Duncan does, they start walking together, usually in silence, allowing their mental and emotional juices to flow freely. Of course, Duncan carries his camera at all times, prepared for any surprises. Occasionally, one of them offers a comment or some observation about what has just entered their consciousness, but most of the time, they keep their discoveries to themselves.

Joyce started in the performing arts as a child attending ballet lessons. As a teen, she followed her fascination into jazz and inter-pretive contemporary dance. A knee injury during university forced her to re-consider her ambitions. She changed her field of study to fine arts where she discovered the art of installations, often combined with live theatre performance, which explains to Duncan her keen talent for conceptualizing. When they discuss Azucena's and Duncan's collaborative projects, Joyce recognizes how active they were, how the participation of two people can contribute creatively, similar to an improvisational theatrical performance.

Organizing his course work with Joyce is an exhilarating process. She concedes total control over the methodology to Duncan but offers fresh insight and depth to discussions of philosophical and presentational concerns.

Joyce helps him settle in during the first few weeks of the fall semester. She's generous with her time, introducing him to the students and assuring that he has the materials necessary for the studio sessions.

"Let me know if there's anything you need, Duncan," winking to suggest a double entendre.

One sleepless night during his first week at the college, Duncan experiences a series of dreams, related to each other by a single thread, Azucena. Initially, he receives some visions in the form of unfinished images, similar to a few smears of watercolours to preserve a sketchy idea on paper. After several of these, a more closely finished product enters his mental hard drive, to be retrieved later toward something more tangible. It alludes to a photograph that Duncan took only days before. The final dream is her voice talking directly to him; he can see moving details of her face, her lips, and eyes, as she speaks.

My dearest Duncan.

I'm glad you have returned to taking photos. I really liked the series you did on the dance school; very poetic.

I miss you, just as you miss me. This will sound strange to you, Duncan, but I want to encourage you to embrace Joyce as a friend and as a lover. You need someone in your life, someone you can love and who will love you. I can no longer be that person. Joyce is a beautiful person, and she already has strong honest feelings for you, I sensed that while I was there visiting. You will be good for each other. She too, needs a lover. You both share so much intellectually, and I know that you have already experienced each other physically. I will communicate with you again soon, through our innermost thoughts. Hopefully that is not a problem for you. Please accept this news in good faith and understanding. Give my best to Joyce. Be good to her and she'll take good care of you. You'll be needing her someday soon. Hasta la próxima. I'll keep in touch.

Love forever, Azucena.

Duncan attempts to answer but there's no sound to his voice. He wakes and stumbles around in the darkness. When he arrives at his office in the morning with a large dark roast to keep him awake, Joyce is waiting at his door. They peck their lips together.

"What's up?" Duncan asks.

"I had some weird dreams last night, Duncan, I haven't been to sleep since. You will think this is bizarre, but Azucena talked to me in my sleep. She said some strange things. It sounded so real that, for a moment, I thought she was alive and standing next to my bed."

"What did she tell you?" Duncan asks.

"You won't believe this, Duncan, but she told me to embrace you as a lover, that you had strong feelings for me, and that I needed someone just like you."

Duncan confides with Joyce. "You're not going to believe this either, Joyce. I too, had a visit from Azucena last night. She said pretty much the same thing to me."

"Go on," Joyce jabs Duncan playfully in the ribs with her knuckle. "You're just saying that."

Duncan observes, chuckling. "It sounds to me like we have a match made in heaven."

CHAPTER 37

THE ABYSS

1998:

Life without Azucena gradually takes a toll on Duncan's spirit. He recedes into periods of depression and loses his desire to create. Each day, at the college, he goes through the motions of appearing interested in what the students are working on, but there's a mundane similarity to it all, the same feelings that he experiences about his own work. There's nothing new, no freshness, no growth — no passion. Eventually, he avoids heading out to take photographs altogether.

'Do I miss Azucena?' Duncan questions. 'Of course I do. It isn't that I want her to replace Joyce. There is no competition there. I consider Azucena as my lifelong spiritual partner, the one person who knows everything about me and who shares her most intimate thoughts with me. But lately, with her gone, there are no thoughts. In her last communication she promised to remain in touch. She also told me to be good to Joyce, that I'll be needing her someday soon, whatever she meant by that. Joyce is already taking excellent care of me, especially since I've plunged into the doldrums.'

Duncan and Joyce still live alone in their own houses, according to the agreement they decided upon when their relationship became serious.

'Maybe that's the problem,' Duncan ponders, scratching his uncombed hair. 'Maybe I need her living with me. Maybe I'm no longer suited to solitude.'

Joyce tries her damnedest to brighten up Duncan's days by offering her well-intentioned solutions and advice.

"Talk to someone about this crater of lethargy you've fallen into, Duncan. Maybe there's some simple solution that can pull you back up. God knows I've tried everything. Do you want me to ask around? What about the counselling office at the college? They might be able to help."

"I don't need professional help, Joyce," Duncan denies, cradling his head in his hands. I'll get it figured out, just give me some time."

Time passes as it always does. Three months become six, and the depth of Duncan's depression increases.

Joyce, having exhausted all of her solutions, finally delivers an ultimatum.

"I can't take any more of this, Duncan. You need professional help. If you're unwilling to seek it, then I can't do any more for you. I think we should go our separate ways for a while."

Joyce takes Duncan's hand in hers. "I know that sounds awful, but the truth is that you're pulling me down with you, and that's not good for either of us. Maybe we just need some space and time apart to think things through. If you're ready to get professional help, I'll be here for you, but I can't continue the way things are now."

"What if you move in here, in the townhouse, with me?" Duncan asks, squeezing Joyce's hand.

Finally, Joyce pulls her hand away. "Not while you're in this condition, Duncan. That would be suicide for both of us."

"What about at the college, Joyce? We'll still have to deal with each other there."

"I'll stay out of your way as much as possible. You might want to think about taking a leave from work for a while, but that's a choice you must make on your own; unless of course, this depression you're in starts to affect your work. Then it'll become a matter for human resources to deal with. That's out of my hands."

Duncan wants to explode with anger, but he could never treat Joyce that way. She's not a confrontational bully like Penny; Joyce is compassionate, and he recognizes that she's done everything she could to help.

'I'm beyond help,' he concludes to himself, while assisting her to load her few personal belongings from the townhouse into her car.

Joyce blows Duncan a kiss. "You know where I am, Duncan," she says through the open car window before driving away.

What Duncan doesn't need to do, but does anyway, is sit in his cocoon with a bottle of Merlot staring at Azucena's painting of *Paraíso*. The soft, distant strains of Miles' muted trumpet encourage him further into his self-inflicted misery, while he yearns to hear Azucena's voice.

"Send me a sign, for Christ's sake," he shouts, flinging his glass at the wall, still cognizant enough to aim away from the painting. "I need a fucking sign."

No signs have arrived by the time he awakes in the morning, folded into the loveseat. 'No surprise there. Azucena would be totally pissed at my behaviour.' He closes his eyes and quietly apologizes to her as if she's listening.

Working at the college proves to be a trial by fire. Joyce is friendly, but at a distance, not displaying any of her usual tenderness. Instead of spending time with the students beyond classes, Duncan retreats to his office with the door closed, listening to angry music through the solitude of his headphones. He wastes time staring at sudokus on his Mac, or he leaves the campus altogether to walk alone along the waterfront, a mickey of Jack Daniels his only sidekick.

Walking used to be his solace, the activity where his creative thoughts came together, where decisions were made that affected his life, and where new visions were decoded. Now, he's surrounded by a dense fog that rejects all positive thoughts and ideas. Avoiding routes that will expose him to friends, his walks now draw him along paths where he encounters others just like him, wandering dazed as if shackled in comas. Misery loves company.

He misses both Azucena and Joyce. One afternoon, while secluded in his office, he calls Penny and arranges to meet her for a drink. After numerous whiskies and sharing their despondencies through gradually deteriorating conversation, they fumble through meaningless sex in drunken disarray.

In the morning, Duncan's memory is still locked in the fog. His early morning studio class passes without him, despite the voice messages begging him to answer. It's afternoon before he checks the messages; several from Joyce beginning with, "Are you OK, Duncan? Call me if you need any help," and concluding with "Get your sorry ass in here, Duncan, or I'm taking this to the Dean."

There's a message from Penny stating, "I had a great time last night, Duncan; we should do that again soon."

'Like that's going to happen again,' Duncan mumbles, aware in his fog-filled mind, that it likely will.

The last message, from the Dean, creates some anxiety. "Duncan? Be in my office at 10 tomorrow morning. We have to talk."

The Dean is more conciliatory than Duncan expected as he's welcomed into to the office. "Hi Duncan, I'm glad you could make it. Come in, have a seat."

Duncan's first instinct is to apologize for missing his class yesterday, but he wisely remains quiet, waiting for the Dean to state his case.

"I understand that you're having a few difficulties, Duncan. Missing a class isn't the end of the world, we've all done it at one time or another. Usually illness is the reason, and the respectful action to take is to phone in and let us know. If I understand your situation correctly, what you're experiencing is a form of illness. The problem is that it's a bit more complicated than the sniffles or lower back pain. The good thing is, that the treatments for depression are covered under the college's health plan. Are you aware of that, Duncan?"

Duncan nods but says nothing.

"My suggestion is that you follow this meeting up by arranging for some treatment. Your doctor can prescribe the treatment, or our counselling office can arrange it for you. Either way, you should follow my advice. You're one of our finest professors, the students love you, and it's no secret that one of our faculty members loves you even more. It would be such a pity for you to throw all of that away, Duncan. We all want you to pull through this, every one of us, and we'll do everything we can to help, but you have to start the process."

After sitting quietly for a moment in the wake of the Dean's comments, Duncan folds forward, burying his face in his hands. Efforts to subdue his impending tears lead him to choke before the dam breaks. The Dean passes him a box of tissues.

"Thanks," Duncan offers, sniffling. "I'll let you know what I decide." Before he leaves, Duncan adds, "Life has been the shits lately, Dean. I'm not sure whether I can keep going. I can't even lift my camera. It feels like the floor has dropped out of my life."

"Wait just a minute, Duncan." The Dean picks up his phone and dials.

"Can I book an appointment with you? ... No, it's not for me this time, it's for one of my teachers. He seems to be going through the same crap as I did last year ... When? The sooner the better ... Tomorrow is good ... No name right now, just go ahead and book a time. He'll be there."

The Dean hands Duncan a sticky note with a room number and 10:30 written on it.

"Thanks," Duncan says, shaking the Dean's hand, his head lowered in embarrassment. "I'll be there. I promise."

* * *

The therapist listens intently while Duncan dumps his fears and anxieties out onto the table. He also describes some details of the dreams he used to receive from Azucena. The therapist nods knowingly and advises him to continue walking and to use the walks for contemplation as he used to do.

"I see walking as your salvation, Duncan. Keep walking the paths you used to when you were being productive. Let your thoughts lead you to fresh ideas instead of wallowing in the quagmire of your problems. Make new dreams for yourself and never say never. For the meantime, we're going to try and solve this without medication. A positive attitude, combined with the fresh air, will help carve a new path for you. Stay on the paths you used to walk, say hello to the friends you meet on the way. Don't avoid them; there is nothing about your situation to be ashamed of. If you have a close friend you can rely on, one that you enjoy sharing conversation with, that will be a big plus. If they'll walk with you, even better."

"So," Duncan concludes, "it's all about talking and walking. That seems too simple."

"Precisely, but it's not just that simple," the therapist warns. "It must become a new normal for you. You must restructure your life, Duncan ... a *new* life. You can't view this as returning to what used to be ... some past life that remains only as a memory. Embrace the new; make the best of today. When you start mumbling and complaining to yourself or thinking negative thoughts and blaming others for your doldrums, get out of the house. Walk. Breathe fresh air. Learn to respect yourself; be kind. Most importantly, laugh."

"Got it." Duncan rises from his chair.

"And one more thing I should mention. If you feel like talking to your spiritual friend, Azucena, while you walk, that's OK, even if she doesn't respond. So what? Maybe she just doesn't have anything important to say to you right now."

"Maybe she's just pissed at my bitching all the time," Duncan chuckles.

"That's a distinct possibility. Give it a try. I'll see you next week and you can tell me how it's all working out."

Duncan heads for the door.

"Oh, and one more thing," the therapist issues a final afterthought. "Booze is never a solution. It can sometimes be the problem, though."

* * *

Duncan returns to his office following the session. His mind circulates the therapist's suggestions. He picks up the phone.

Joyce answers. "Hi Duncan. How are things with you?"

"Better today. I've had some rough times, but I met with a therapist this morning and she was positive."

"That's great. Do you feel like talking?"

"Yeah, I do. How would you like to talk and walk? If so, I'll meet you at our usual trailhead."

"Sounds wonderful, Duncan. It's a gorgeous autumn day."

The air is fresh and many of the leaves have already turned. Joyce holds Duncan's arm as they stroll, her way of telling him that she's there with him.

"I'm sorry, Joyce, for the way I've treated you. It wasn't fair, and it wasn't like me to act that way."

"Let's not dwell on what's already passed. Let's concentrate on right now. That's something you told me when we first met. Live for now, you said. Well, here we are, now has arrived."

"Are we going to be OK, you and I?"

"As long as you can stay the way you are right now, we'll be just fine." Joyce squeezes Duncan's arm.

About mid-walk, Duncan tosses a fresh thought into the conversation. "Maybe I've been placing too much emphasis on the dreams I receive from Azucena, or should I say, the dreams I *hope* to receive from her; she hasn't been communicating with me much lately. It's time for me to be myself, to create my own *marque*, in other words. What do you think?"

"I would have told you that a long time ago, Duncan, but I didn't want to get wedged in-between you and your muse, just like I didn't want to declare my love for you while Azucena was still your lover, albeit your spiritual lover. As you know, I have communicated with Azucena in the past as well, and I too, love her very much. She's been very supportive of both of us, but I think, if you're open to my opinion, it's time to accept the fact that she died. Yes, she's a spirit to be appreciated, even to be loved, but she can't hold you and caress you like I can."

"I've never wanted to give up on her, you know. There are so many memories. She influenced me in so many wonderful ways."

"But, Duncan, this is now, not then, it's now. I'm right here, I'm not a spirit. Touch me just to make sure. Fuck that, just kiss me for Christ's sake."

They embrace. Her kisses feel soft and sensuous. So much time has passed them by.

Over pizza, they discuss art, as they used to when they first met.

"I think you should start right now. Stop digging through your basket of vision particles. Start fresh. Clear out your mind. Start the same way you tell the students to start. Your life is a blank canvas; make a mark that comes from your own desires, from your own heart. Don't think about anything else. Just do it. BANG, like that." Joyce slams her hands together.

"But, what about …?"

Joyce interrupts. "No buts, Duncan. Just do it. And besides, I think you should also start playing the piano again, not as an obsession, but just because you love doing it. We should also start making love again, don't you think it's about time. This walk is to celebrate your new beginning. The flames have destroyed the past. We have an opportunity to plant some new seeds. Open some space up for a new forest to grow. I'll support you in whatever you choose to do."

They spend the night together. In the morning, Joyce leaves for the college. Duncan has no classes scheduled.

Acknowledging that a casual stroll would feel good, Duncan

reaches for his camera. It feels good in his hands. He attaches a 35mm lens and places the camera around his neck.

Initially, he points the camera at abstract inanimate objects: peeling paint on a wooden shed, random arrangements of bird feces on a granite stone. He tests his comfort zone of moving the camera until he finds an agreeable abstraction, then works into the shots from there. While the quiet inanimate still life images are cathartic, he still misses the more active people shots from his photojournalism days. With every moment, people are different. Their faces and gestures, their emotions, and their relationships with others, all provide an unfettered variety of opportunities.

As he approaches the entrance to the university campus, a group of students are forming the nucleus of a demonstration; they tote 'Pro-Choice' and 'It's My Body' signs. Duncan takes a few images of them interacting and more when they start marching down Bloor Street. There are some great photo moments when pedestrians react to their shouting. A few blocks further, a church group lines the street holding signs reading 'Murderers,' 'Abortion Kills, and 'Death to Baby-Killers.'

Remembering his 'good old days,' Duncan prepares for possible confrontations and public reactions by choosing vantage points before the clashes begin. Police arrive at the scene in preparation as well. They direct traffic around the demonstrators by erecting barricades while other officers attempt to keep the two factions apart. Fortunately, Duncan has his favourite lens, the 35mm, that allows him to work in close to capture the nuances of expressions. He was never fond of telephoto lenses because they're too removed from most action, and zooms are just bulky, slow, and contribute to lazy photography.

Duncan dances through the confrontation, capturing a few decent images, nothing up to his previous standards, but enough to boost his enthusiasm. He celebrates with a large dark roast and chocolate croissant at Dizzy's, his favourite neighbourhood café.

At home, he confronts the piano. There are no clouds of old information between him and the keyboard, just a blank canvas. His first chords familiarly lead toward the introduction to 'Body and Soul,' but Duncan quickly, and wisely, diverts his hands to a random series of turnarounds that open new corridors. Not sure where they're taking him, he allows his fingers to explore directions that lead to fresh, spacious soundscapes. He attempts to analyze his actions but soon accepts the space without questions or answers.

'I have no idea where I'm going,' he internalizes. 'I'm just starting something for the sake of starting something. I've always appreciated the minimalists and envy them for their courage, and the tastefulness that allows them to stop before everything gets messy.'

After a few minutes he feels the space and stops. 'Whatever I just created, it's all mine. I don't even care whether it's good or bad. That'll be revealed through time, if at all.'

Duncan's challenge is to find his own voice, the one that speaks to him, for him, and from him. That, it seems, is the most difficult hurdle, but day by day he manages to create work that he can call his own.

While he continues attending sessions with his therapist, Joyce and Duncan gradually return to their previous norm. They talk openly, socialize, walk regularly, and enjoy cavorting during private moments. In-between, they plan a vacation.

Duncan asks. "Joyce, where would you go if the world opened its doors to us? Pick anywhere."

"Two places," Joyce answers, raising two fingers. "Europe to visit the great art galleries of history, and *Paraíso*, to visit the place where you and Azucena changed your lives." Joyce hesitates before continuing. "That, of course, is assuming you wouldn't mind taking me there. I know it has personal memories for you, and I don't want to stomp on those, but the stories about your paradise have always fascinated me. I guess I just want to experience the magic. Of course, I would never go there alone, it wouldn't be the same as being there with you."

"Hmm ..." Duncan strokes his chin. "I'm just a bit concerned that, because I'm struggling to wean myself away from Azucena's influence on my work, it may be a step backwards for me."

"That's OK, Duncan, maybe another time. I just thought I'd be ready for an artistic rebirth, like how you were affected when you went there."

"That's interesting. I hadn't thought of that angle. My current struggle is really about being reborn into my own independent voice, isn't it? Maybe what I need is another visit there. Give me a day or two to think about it. I'll let you know."

Before Duncan reaches a decision, Joyce arrives at his office door.

"The field trip, Duncan," she says with enthusiasm written on her face. "The field trip. Remember? We'll arrange a field trip to *Paraíso*."

"God, you're brilliant, Joyce."

"It was your idea, Duncan."

'Was it?" Duncan responds. "I don't remember."

CHAPTER 38

OBITUARY

1999:

Penny's obituary appears in the morning paper. Duncan needs someone to share the news with. He calls Joyce, who didn't know Penny personally, except through Duncan's comments.

"It states that she died quietly in her sleep surrounded by a loving family. What family?" Duncan rants. "She doesn't have a family. And how does one pass quietly? She didn't pass through life quietly. There must be noise, trumpets and drums, a shouting fucking resistance at least, that says, hey, you motherfuckers, I'm getting out. I've had enough of this bullshit. Life is too fucking important to pass quietly. Where is Dylan Thomas now that we need him?"

"Calm down, Duncan. Why are you so upset?" Joyce queries. "I know you were once close, but you haven't kept in contact, and you had such negative experiences together."

Duncan hesitates to consider the question.

"Because she's a part of my past, my history. It's sad when you lose someone who played a part in your life, regardless if you had disagreements or not. Besides, she's the mother of my son, whoever and wherever he is. Hell, I even wept when Elvis died. Not because I was a fan, but because he was there when I was a young teenager. He was part of my life, my growing up, like Penny, I guess."

Duncan commits to going to the service for Penny and asks Joyce if she will join him. They arrive at the funeral home, just as the minister begins his service. They sit quietly in the back row.

A small gathering is clustered at the front where family members and close friends are usually seated. A frail, older man, assumedly the well-mentioned history professor, sits alone several rows behind. A decorative urn is placed on a pedestal. There's a framed photograph of Penny that Duncan had taken of her years before.

Tears dampen Duncan's eyes and his spirit. 'The final nail,' he muses, referring to the end of another who shared his early life. 'I'm the only one left. The sole survivor. The last of my generation. Who will be here when it's time for me to go? Nobody will even know who I am.' His selfish thoughts grind to a halt as he remembers that Joyce is sitting beside him. He squeezes her hand and takes a moment to recompose himself. 'What the fuck?' he ponders, recollecting his priorities. 'This isn't about me. Today, it's about Penny.'

Outside, Duncan and Joyce pass through the gauntlet of apparent relatives: a tall handsome balding man, accompanied by an attractive middle-aged woman, and two younger women, one holding the hand of a toddler. Duncan shakes their hands while passing, uttering a tired, overused phrase from his life as a journalist, "I'm terribly sorry for your loss," and walks toward the parking lot. He stops while opening the car door for Joyce, considers his next move, and excuses himself to return alone to the mourners still assembled on the church steps.

Duncan introduces himself to the balding man. "Hello, I should have introduced myself earlier. I'm Duncan MacGregor. I was a close friend of Penny's many years ago."

"I'm pleased to meet you, Duncan. I'm Gerald, Penny's son." the man answers with an educated British accent.

The accent provides Duncan with the courage to continue. "Is your father here?"

"I'm afraid not. He died in Central America while covering the conflicts there; in a fire, I believe. He was a journalist. Mother thought of him as some kind of hero, someone she could never quite live up to. I didn't know my mother until just a few years ago. I was adopted in the UK as a baby. When I became curious about my birth parents, I started searching through the records in London. It took me a number of years before I discovered that Penny was my mother."

Duncan asks with compassion on his face, "Were you ever able to meet Penny ... your mother?"

"We finally made contact in recent years. I came to Canada and met her. She was living alone in Toronto. When we went out for dinner, I asked her whether she could provide me with information about my father. That's when I learned of his death." He hesitates. "Were you a friend of my father's as well, Duncan?"

Duncan hesitates before responding. "I believe that I could help you fill in some of the blanks, but it may require more time than you can spare this afternoon. Could we get together at another time?"

"Unfortunately, we're returning to the UK tomorrow; work and all, you know. But you are invited to join us at the restaurant this evening for an informal reception, we could talk more there."

Returning to the car, Duncan asks Joyce if she would accompany him to the restaurant, warning her that it could be an emotional experience.

Joyce answers with a grin. "My life with you is a never-ending emotional experience, Duncan. Of course I'll come."

On their drive to the designated restaurant, Duncan decides to avoid any small talk. He will tell Gerald the truth up front.

At the first opportunity after their arrival, Duncan approaches Gerald.

"Gerald, I happen to know that your father is still very much alive," Duncan states, swallowing the saliva built up at the back of his throat.

"Oh really?" Gerald questions, his face lighting up. "Where is he? Do you have an address or an email where I can reach him?"

"He is talking to you right now, at this very moment."

Gerald appears gobsmacked; he steps backward. A quizzical look causes his right eyebrow to rise. "Is this … some kind of a joke?"

Duncan continues. "If I tell you that you were born in May 1968, would you believe me?"

Gerald delays his response. "My God, can this be true? Are you really my father?" He pauses for a moment. "Then why would she tell me you were dead?" he asks.

"Probably because I was dead to her. We departed on difficult terms, I'm afraid, the details of which are no longer important. I did, however, spend time in Nicaragua after we split up, that much is true, but I survived. I am unbelievably happy to meet you, Gerald."

They clasp their hands together, firmly.

"I'd like you to meet my wife." Gerald turns to the woman seated next to him. "Karen, this is my father, Duncan … um …" He turns to Duncan to confirm his last name. "MacGregor?"

Duncan nods affirmatively.

"Can you believe that Karen? He's my father."

Karen examines Duncan's face before turning back to Gerald. "There is a similarity I suppose." She offers Duncan her hand, "Finally we get to meet you. We thought you were dead."

Duncan takes the opportunity to introduce Joyce as his dear friend. She is warmly received by the family.

Continuing around the table, Gerald introduces their daughter, Ariel, and her partner, Greta. "And this little ruffian is Jason, my grandson," he says, placing a hand on top of Jason's little head to scruff up the toddler's hair. "Jason, this is your great-grandfather. Give him a big hug."

It all suddenly closes in on Duncan, another circle completed. The sudden leap into fatherhood, grand-fatherhood and great-grand-fatherhood is proving too much for him. He can't express himself between the tears. In consolation, Joyce places her arms around him and is soon joined by Ariel.

Before parting, Duncan exchanges addresses, emails, and telephone numbers with his new-found family.

Ariel invites Duncan to keep in touch. "I want to know everything about Nicaragua," she says. "Greta and I would love to visit there someday."

"I promise," Duncan says with a final embrace.

*   *   *

The discovery of his new family nourishes Duncan with a reason to go on, like new greenery emerging from still-smoking ashes in the wake of a blazing forest. A new vitality appears in his step; there's a smile on his lips, and brightness in his eyes. He returns to photographing with renewed enthusiasm. A gallery expresses interest in mounting a show featuring the combined talents of Azucena and Duncan. Joyce commits to being his assistant and curator.

The night before the opening, Joyce and Duncan carefully peruse the walls, checking for consistency, general eye-appeal, and for any drooping pieces or mismatched information. With Joyce as curator, no problems are anticipated. They dine at a nearby restaurant to celebrate their achievements before retiring for the night.

As Duncan final succumbs to sleep, he starts to dream.

Collages of random images pass through Duncan's sleeping mind; fragments of his own photographs from the show, daubed with paint, seemingly intentional, but entirely abstract. He watches from a distance as the pieces reorganize themselves on the gallery walls. In other visions, photographs and cropped images he had taken over the years appear, affixing themselves to some of Azucena's paintings, as if they were meant to be there all along. Azucena fails to appear, but Duncan has no doubts about the source of his visions.

The following day, Joyce and Duncan arrive at the gallery an hour before opening for a final inspection of the show. Members of the press are already gathering outside, gabbing and smoking amongst themselves. The gallery manager and host for the evening, unlocks the door to allow Joyce and Duncan in. The manager seems irritated and eager to meet with them.

He expresses a concern. "Something just doesn't seem right. It's not as I remember the show. There are pieces that have been moved and others that have changed. I can only assume that you folks returned here later through the night, but how did you get a key?"

They assure the manager that they have been at home sleeping, or at least, attempting to sleep.

Both Duncan and Joyce are beside themselves. Duncan's dreams have materialized on the gallery walls. Photographs and paintings share the same spaces. Duncan examines several at close range, taking careful notice of the signatures. A white lily and the letters, DM, appear on every piece. The entire body of work is now a collaboration. Joyce's first response is that the show must be cancelled. Duncan pulls Joyce aside and describes his visions from last night.

Joyce answers. "Are you suggesting that this may be the work of Azucena, that she, through your dreams, curated this reconstruction of the entire show while we slept? Of course, if it was your dream, you're as responsible as she is."

"Before you jump to any conclusions, Joyce, hear me out. The work that now hangs on the walls, is the show we would have put together if Azucena and I were collaborating; if she hadn't died. This is exactly how it would have been. Don't you see?"

"I know what you're trying to say, but …"

Duncan interrupts. "What's your opinion of the show as it hangs now, Joyce? Be honest with me."

"It's outstanding, Duncan." Her eyes flutter as she speaks. "I can't explain it though. How can this all happen?" she asks, waving a hand in the air to showcase the room.

"How it happened is not up for discussion or explanation right now, Joyce."

Duncan raises his hands to his temples as if in pain. "Christ, I'm just as confused as you are, but let's be realistic, if that's not an oxymoron at this moment." He removes his hands from his head and points to the entrance door.

"The critics out there, who are chomping at the bit to get in, have never seen any of this work before. Hell, *I've* never seen this work before, either," Duncan admits, rolling his eyes upward and stretching his arms in confusion. "The public doesn't know what to expect. Regardless of how it happened, it is the collaborative work of Azucena and me. Look at the signatures. This is our show, and it's fantastic."

The doors open to an enthusiastic crowd. The pieces Duncan and Azucena created while in *Paraíso* attract the most attention from critics. There are many questions from visitors about the visions and how much information is communicated from one artist to the other, particularly in regard to the painting that stretches from the floor to the peak of the gallery's vaulted ceiling showing two tall buildings with people jumping from windows.

The show's publicity referenced Azucena's tendency to foretell events. Critics attempt to apply logic to the claims with each painting, even applying mathematical and scientific theories.

Duncan's response is predictable. "I have no idea what event, if any, Azucena was predicting. She had a wonderful imagination. The buildings are from some skyline photos I took while in New York, and the little people are from my photographs as well, but she adapted them to her own vision."

He pauses to gather his thoughts before continuing. "Allow me to quote the words of Azucena herself, words that I wholeheartedly agree with."

"I am not the answer, I am the question. My paintings are not the solutions, they are problems yet to be solved. The answers, and the solutions, are buried within your own soul."

Duncan is asked to comment on another large canvas that's receiving attention.

One reporter asks, "What's going on in the painting of the yellow-haired clown sporting a red baseball cap and playing golf in the rain? It looks like he's teeing off on the White House lawn."

In the painting, a lightning bolt breaks above the clown at the peak of his follow-through. Thousands of miniscule people, like ants from Duncan's photos at *Paraíso*, clamor around their sandy-holed homes, some wearing masks over their mouths and noses while others vomit and cough amid wooden crosses. Along the fairway, children scream from wire cages.

The reporter comments, "It's a bit overwhelming and disturbing, don't you think? Certainly surreal. Was Azucena influenced by the work of Hieronymus Bosch?"

"I agree," Duncan answers. "It is disturbing, and it is surreal. I certainly hope that it's not a sign of the future." He adds, as an afterthought, "I have never bothered to look at the work of Hieronymus Bosch. He never interested me, and Azucena never mentioned his name."

The Arts reporter from The Star, who interviewed Azucena during her previous Toronto show, asks, "Why are none of her revolutionary works on display?"

Duncan responds sarcastically. "All of Azucena's works are revolutionary. Besides, you've already seen them. Why would she show them to you again? Unless, of course, you've had time to change your mind."

* * *

Duncan is invited to play jazz piano with a group of young innovative musicians and is excited to be challenging the boundaries. They record an album of free expression jazz titled, 'Beyond,' featuring the title track, one of Duncan's own original compositions based on an abstract painting Azucena completed in *Paraíso* while there together. Duncan and the other musicians distribute the CD during live engagements at clubs and festivals.

Life is good, again.

He remains in contact, through emails, with his granddaughter, Ariel, and with his son, Gerald. Ariel is creating a family tree and asks Duncan if he is willing to have his DNA tested. Duncan is reluctant but finally agrees. The results confuse him with information quite different from what he expected.

Duncan is definitely the father of Gerald, and, by extension, the grandfather of Ariel. He is curious however, that he has Gaelic and German lineage. His parents after all, were both born in Canada. The Gaelic can be explained through his father's Scottish roots, but his mother is French-Canadian. The German lineage confuses him.

Duncan shares his new knowledge with Ariel. Her email response, "You are becoming more interesting all the time, Grandad. I am eager to learn more about your fascinating life. You should write and publish your memoirs."

Duncan remains curious about the German connection. He decides to confront his parents. His father, Mac, now lives with advancing stages of dementia at Happy Acres Home, a long-term care facility on the shores of Lake Ontario. Duncan must rely on his mother's account.

He calls her. "Hi Mom. It's Duncan."

"Of course it is. I only have one son, and you called me Mom, so you must be Duncan."

"I wish it were that simple," Duncan says. "Why don't I take you out for lunch. I have some questions I'd like to ask."

* * *

Duncan picks up his mother and takes her to a quaint café that serves light lunches and a host of teas and freshly roasted coffee beans from around the world.

"Where would you like to sit, mother?" Duncan asks. He points to a table in the corner. "There's a nice spot over there next to the window. It has a view of the patio outside."

Once settled at the table, Duncan orders a Sumatran dark roast.

After some careful consideration and a level of confusion, his mother admits, "I always get confused about those foreign foods," she explains. "I think I'll have … an Earl Gray."

Once the tea and coffee arrives, Duncan gets immediately to the point.

"Where am I from, Mom?"

"Whatever do you mean?" she asks. You're from Hamilton."

"OK," Duncan twists the conversation. "Let's try it this way. Where are you and Dad from?"

"Well … let's see. Your Dad was born in Hamilton and I was born in Québec. Why?"

"Well, apparently there's a German connection shown in my DNA."

"Well, there's no Germans in our family, at least not that I know of. I was born in Quebec to French-Canadians, and your father is as Scottish as they come. He still has a Scottish brogue, even though he was born here." She attempts to imitate her husband's Scottish accent with her own Québécoise but breaks into laughter. "Ha-ha. We used to joke that we were from the Hudson Bay trappers."

"Would you and Dad be willing to have your DNA tested?"

"Well … I don't know. I supposed it would be all right. It might raise more questions than answers though. Does it hurt?"

"No, of course not, Mom," Duncan answers. His mother's hesitation, however, raises suspicion for him. Finally, Duncan delivers the big question. "Mom, am I adopted?"

His mother peers down at her teacup, twiddling it with her aging fingers.

"Oh my. This is a conversation I didn't think I would ever have." After an extended pause, she looks up. "We chose not to tell you; we didn't want you to be confused. We both loved you so much and we were ecstatic that you came along when you did. We thought that if you knew, you'd leave us to search for your birth parents, and we worried that we'd lose you. Your father and I, we couldn't have our own children you see, and we thought we would remain childless forever. Suddenly, we heard about a baby whose mother had died in childbirth."

"Where, Mom? Where was that baby born?"

There's another long pause before his mother answers. "Well ... it wasn't in Germany, if that's what you're thinking." She pauses, and twiddles with the handle of her teacup, hoping that Duncan will interrupt and steer the conversation in another direction.

Duncan remains silent. He sips some coffee, waiting.

His mother begins talking, still staring at her teacup.

"I always thought it was ironic when you started to travel to Nicaragua." She pauses again. "Your father was a mining engineer at the time. He travelled to different countries where Canadian mining companies were located. When you were born, he was overseeing operations at a gold mine in Nicaragua. I didn't always travel with him but for some reason, he invited me to join him there for a brief holiday, only a few weeks. I found the place a bit too remote for my liking, but it was his job; that's how he made his living. The mine was located in a small mining town in the mountains. What was the name of that town anyway?"

"It doesn't matter Mom. The town isn't that important."

"Wait ... I think it was called Two Rivers, or something like that. I remember because it was similar to *Trois Rivieres* in Quebec. Oh dear. I'm glad your father isn't here with us. He would be so confused." She continues explaining. "One day, we had a visit from one of the nuns at the convent. There was an abandoned baby who needed a good home. His mother died at birth. I don't know who the father was. The nun never said. We wanted a child so much. Your father and I looked at each other and we knew our prayers had been answered. There you were, as if God sent you to us special delivery. That's what your father first called you before we decided on a name, Special Delivery."

She smiles at the name, raises her eyes to look at Duncan and begins to cry. She blows into her handkerchief. "I'm so sorry, Duncan. We should have told you. I know that now. Please forgive us."

Their lunch arrives while his mother is drying her eyes with a tissue. She adds, "I've often wondered what would have happened to you if we hadn't been there."

Duncan answers for her. "I would probably have ended up in an orphanage somewhere, I suppose."

"You were the cutest little guy. You had this little reddish spot on your behind. Whenever your Dad changed your diapers he always said, 'That's a hell of a place for God to sign his work of art.'"

Duncan and his mother laugh together.

She continues. "Your father used to have a great sense of humour, especially when he started into that Scottish brogue of his." She hesitates. "I could hardly understand him … but of course, then he lost the humour when he started forgetting things." Another pause. "Where were we, Duncan? … Oh yes, the red mark on your backside. That mark gradually faded away as you aged. I don't imagine it's still there, is it, Duncan?"

"Do you want me to take my pants down here so you can check?"

They share howls of laughter. "Don't make me laugh any more, Duncan. I might pee myself."

Equipped with the information he was seeking, for better or worse, Duncan takes his mother home.

On the doorstep, Duncan's mother leans over and plants a kiss on his cheek. "Thank you for the wonderful afternoon, Duncan. We haven't laughed that much since you were a toddler."

Duncan hugs his mother. "I know. Back then you were probably laughing at the red spot on my ass."

* * *

During the night, Duncan has difficulty sleeping. His confused mind wanders between two families, and two separate cultures. He envisions himself as a child, pleading for another bowl of soup at an orphanage where other kids laugh at the red spot on his ass, or begging on a street-corner in some sleepy mining town where nobody spoke his language.

Worse still, he pictures himself as a child labourer struggling to haul iron ore up a steep mountainside from the pit of an open mine. It's three in the morning and the phone rings.

"Duncan, is that you? What are you doing up at this hour? I thought I'd just get your answering machine."

"Of course it's me, Mom. Who else would answer my phone? What's wrong?"

"Nothing's wrong. I just found the name of that little town in Nicaragua, where you were born. It was called Dos Rios. I was right. It means Two Rivers in Spanish. After I returned home, I looked through some old papers from when you were adopted and guess what? I also found the nun's name. Your father must have written it down because it's in his handwriting. Her name was Sister Hortencia. That's H-O-R-T ..."

"I've got it. Thanks Mom. That really helps. I have to get some sleep right now. I'll call you soon. Love you."

CHAPTER 39

FIELD TRIP

Nicaragua, 1999:

A heavy downpour greets the Canadians as they arrive in *Paraíso de los Redespiertos*. Five students from Fine Arts join Duncan and Joyce for a two-week field trip in hopes of connecting to their inner selves. Personally, Duncan wishes to relive fond memories. Joyce pins her hopes on experiencing a rebirth of her creative directions.

Duncan conducts an introductory meeting so students will understand what they've signed up for, and what they should, or should not, expect.

"*Paraíso de los Redespiertos* interprets as 'Paradise of the Reawakened,' Duncan begins. "We just call it *Paraíso*. Don't be misled by the title. This is not some trendy, feel-good spa, nor is it a born-again cult," Duncan states, making sure it's understood. "What it becomes to you depends on what you're willing to accept. There will be quiet meditations, but they're not mandatory, and they're not affiliated with any religious doctrine or sect. There are no guarantees that you'll be reawakened to some new age art form, and nobody will be lecturing you on technical theories or fail-safe methodologies."

"Oh shit," a student named Jason complains, with a silly grin on his face.

"What's your problem, Jason," Duncan asks.

"I want my money back," Jason responds. "I need religion and guarantees, otherwise I'm wasting my money." His grin widens.

A student chuckles with Jason. Another shouts out, "Give us a fucking break Jason. Just shut up."

"It will be to your advantage to think of yourself as an empty container," Duncan begins, adding a personal put-down to Jason, the class clown. "Jason has already proven that he's prepared; he arrived here as an empty container."

The students contribute a bevy of laughs and groans. Joyce applauds and high-fives. "Good one, Duncan."

Duncan continues his introduction. "That empty container … each one of you … should be ready and willing to be filled with the unknown. If you are someone searching for spirituality or mysticism, you can either be enlightened or disappointed. The trick is to be open to whatever happens. Don't preconceive anything. When conversing with the locals, especially with the Indigenous people, listen to what they have to say. Their words are based upon their local knowledge and experiences gained over millennia, and what they say is always more interesting than anything you could offer."

Jason, the clown, inserts another gem. "Will we fall in love here, like you did, Duncan?" This time the entire group laughs, more at Jason's gall. Joyce initially covers her face with her hand but joins the laughing students.

Duncan replies with a grin of friendly revenge. "Only you can answer that question, Jason, but if I were you, I wouldn't count on it. Besides, it'll be cheaper if you fall in love at home."

"It's been a long day," Joyce suggests, yawning. "I suggest we all get some much-needed sleep so we're ready to get started bright and early."

The students settle into their *cabañas* for some catch-up sleep. Joyce and Duncan, also sleep-deprived, opt instead for hammocking under a thatched roof gazebo with rums and limes.

A penetrating early morning sun casts long deep shadows across their hammock. Half-filled glasses empty their contents on the ground, attracting a row of genetically-obedient marching ants. It isn't the light that awakens Duncan but the sweet fragrance of early morning vegetation following the rain. Verdant heavily-laden leaves bend groundward with massive raindrops clustered on their waxen surface. Like security mirrors, they reflect inverted curvatures of the surrounding landscape.

When Duncan rises, Joyce rolls inward toward the centre of their communal hammock, barely wakening but groaning at the disruption.

"What time is it?" she prods, her right hand shielding her half-opened eye from the sharp rays.

"It's sunrise, around five o'clock, I guess," Duncan offers without referring to his watch."

"That's too early," she complains.

"Get used to it. In 12 hours it'll be dark again." Duncan adds some trivia, "We're only a thousand klicks from the equator right now."

Across the courtyard Duncan detects the stirrings of student movement toward the biffy. "Beautiful morning," he calls and waves, without response.

During breakfast, Joyce complains about stomach problems. One of the Indigenous women prescribes a concoction of lime juice and politely suggests that Joyce remain close to the portable bathroom.

Duncan asks Joyce, "Are you going to be alright? Should I stay with you?"

"No. You go ... do whatever you planned for today. I'm sure this kind woman will look after me. It's just a combination of travel fatigue and maybe a touch of tainted food. It could also be the water I suppose."

Duncan leans over to kiss Joyce. Joyce pushes him away.

"No kissing, Duncan. We're not sure what I've got. Whatever it is, you don't want it."

Duncan decides to revisit the special meditation spot where he and Azucena privately shared their souls and so much more.

While reflecting deeply in a lotus position, he enters a trance-like space he has only experienced previously with Azucena. Time disappears. A natural ambience provides the base for whatever his inner soul can accommodate. A soft warm voice whispers garbled messages until Duncan's meditative zone allows for clarification.

"Follow me," the voice says.

The invitation maintains a soft monotonal quality while Duncan obeys, following it through the thickening undergrowth. It's hard to imagine that only 22 years ago, the entire island had been burned and is now green, vibrant, and healthy.

Duncan follows the voice without attempting to answer or question its message or even its existence. There is no visual presence, only a voice. Momentary lapses challenge whether he's still in a meditative state or if reality is driving him blindly into the deep unknown. As the trees and foliage thicken, colours become muted with the diminishing sunlight; a mist obscures detail.

The voice repeats. *"Follow me."*

Finally, he's instructed to stop at a clearing. The mist lifts, revealing a small dwelling, a hut constructed of natural materials, the same hut he shared with Azucena during their previous visit. A robed and hooded figure emerges from the hut. It turns toward Duncan, but the shadow of the hood prevents any facial features from being seen.

"Please, have a seat," the hooded figure motions with a hand toward a decorative cushion placed upon a meditation mat.

Duncan moves toward the mat and looks back toward the hooded figure. "Who are you. Why have you brought me here?"

"Hola, Duncan, my dear. It is me ... Azucena. Well, it's not really me, but a reincarnation. I will guide you toward a new path, a path of renewed enlightenment, to a place where you can accept the revela-

tions that are about to unfold. You need only to accept your imaginative visions as reality You'll be able to communicate with your inner soul, and with me."

"Azucena. I have missed you so much, my dear. Please, show yourself. Let me see you."

"In due time, Duncan. For now, just accept my voice and the thoughts that I will share with you."

Duncan sits on the cushion, forming a lotus position. Silence prevails, while he centres his breathing toward the zone, broken only by the vibrations of the forest; animal sounds and soft breezes provide impromptu musical performances as they filter through the leaves. Nearby, an endless singular file of ants continues on its silent journey, passing alongside Duncan. He ponders the possibility that it's the same column of ants he witnessed during his previous visit.

"Through our shared visions I have encouraged you to make this voyage with Joyce, but it is only you I can discuss the details of my journey with, at least for the time being. We can include Joyce in due time. From my lofty position as a reincarnated one, I have learned much."

Duncan struggles to ask questions, but his voice remains mute.

"Shall I continue?" the voice asks.

Duncan nods his acknowledgement.

"I have discovered who my father is. My mother disclosed his image to me in one of her visions. Even in my heavenly state, I continue to communicate with Lydia, my mother. I can also continue sharing my dreams and visions directly with you and ..."

Duncan's meditative mind attempts to process the revelations he's experiencing but, in the process, he slips from his zone. He refocuses inward, concentrating on the pulse of his breathing. Azucena's voice returns.

"It is critical that you are aware that the twins, Father Manuel and Colonel Jorge, are my half-brothers, for it was Don Ricardo who assaulted my mother at Palo de Mayo. It would be advisable for you to contact

Sister Hortencia at the convent in Dos Rios. *You will find her knowledge very interesting."*

Duncan is in disbelief that Sister Hortencia's name is the same as the nun his mother had mentioned. He attempts to raise questions with the voice but is muted.

The voice continues. *"I have so much more to share with you, my dear Duncan. I will gradually reveal more, but you are not yet prepared to comprehend the magnitude of the details. There will be a time soon when you can share my visions and conversations with Joyce and others, but for now, you will be unable to disclose anything you are experiencing this afternoon. That is all for now. Hasta la próxima. Abrazos y Besos."*

The hooded figure blows a kiss toward him as the mist reappears, enveloping the figure and the hut.

Duncan remains seated in a silent space for an unknown passage of time. When he finally emerges from his meditative trance, he's seated in the original location, where he and Azucena first meditated. A gust of scepticism forces him to question the narrative.

'Who was she? Was she really Azucena? Is Azucena still alive? Was I listening to Azucena's spirit? Am I going fucking crazy?'

Hours later, when Duncan returns to the community, Joyce is feeling much better.

"That lime concoction really works," she tells him. "I'll have to remember that when we return home," Joyce says with a chuckle. She positions her hand on Duncan's knee, sliding it back and forth. "So, what kept you busy today, Duncan? Were you able to get any photography done?"

"I …" His lips move without words. Instead there's a gurgling noise that sounds like a bad throat infection. He's physically unable to respond to Joyce's question.

Joyce's eyebrow rises. "I think you're getting a bad cold, Duncan. Try some of this lime juice," she says, offering a cup to Duncan. "It should help."

Stunned, Duncan hesitantly takes the cup from Joyce.

In the evening after a dinner of local fare, Duncan and Joyce gather with the students to discuss their first full day. As usual, some started sketching immediately. Others chose to ease into the ambience of *Paraíso*, with faith that their muses will discover them before the two-week field trip is over.

Joyce explains. "The advantage of jumping in right away is that you get an immediate sense of what you're dealing with, at least what it looks like on the surface, and that's OK, if the surface is all that matters to you."

Duncan adds his perspective. "The nature of photojournalism, which is where I come from, is to jump in and get the shots before your competition, but this isn't a race. I learned over time that great photojournalism results when you also put in the time, do the research, and fill the spaces between the big pictures with smaller details, the ones that you miss on the first, or second, visit. I further believe that this applies to all the arts."

"So what's the best way, then?" a student asks.

"There is no 'best' way," Joyce responds. "We each find our own way, our comfort zone."

The student probes further. "So Joyce, what approach did you use on your first day?"

"Hmm … well … I spent my first day sucking limes and barfing into the biffy." Her joke makes everyone laugh. "How about you Duncan?' she asks, turning her attention to him. "How was your first day? Did you take any great photos?"

"I … I … spent the day wandering through the forest and reflecting on past memories. I think that's the best way to put it. I didn't take any photos. I'm like a couple of you, praying that my muse will appear."

"And did it?" the student asks.

"Indeed, Duncan," Joyce asks. "Did your muse appear?"

"Hmm," Duncan ponders. "The jury's still out on that."

Joyce pats Duncan's knee as a gesture of understanding and turns to address the students.

"The danger in procrastinating is obvious," she says, raising her forefinger as a warning. "If you wait too long the muses may forget you're here. Just consider that it could rain for the entire second week. This is, after all, called a rain forest for a reason. Tomorrow, after dinner, we'll have a throwdown. Everybody, me included, will have something to show, something that reflects our first impressions of *Paraíso*. Duncan is shooting film that can't be processed here, so he's excluded."

"Not so," Duncan interjects, raising his finger. "I promise to have something to show tomorrow. You'll see."

In the early morning, Duncan strolls to his familiar meditation spot with a tin of watercolours, brushes, some water, and a pad of paper that he's borrowed from Joyce. He's never tried to paint before but has watched Azucena and Joyce often. With any luck, the muse of Azucena's presence will guide his mind, as well as his eyes, hands, and brush.

He sits quietly, eyes open, inviting the ambient sounds and colours to enter; they are music and perfume to his senses, but chaos blocks his desire to meditate.

'Are my memories of the previous day reality or fantasy?' he ponders. 'Was that really Azucena reincarnated? A mirage, a figment of my imagination? Where is that hut?'

Duncan's ethereal questions lead to attempts at analysis. 'What are fantasies anyway? Is what we imagine less authentic than what we know? Can fantasies also be realities?' The questions only add to the clutter echoing against the shell of his brain.

Duncan's eyes close in an attempt to isolate his mind from the chaos until he finally lands in a quiet space.

Wispy clouds of complementary colours float about him, blending into malleable shapes of pastels. Soft flute music surrounds him like an audio halo, carrying primary colours into the mixture. Together they create compositions as fresh and vibrant as spring. Small creatures of the forest find refuge in the solitude of his imagination.

Suddenly, a bolt of lightning cracks the shapes into stone-like frag-

ments, the earth beneath him vibrates, and plumes of smoke and fire vault in a thunderous explosion toward the firmament. Memories clash with the present. Concrete competes against nature. Death challenges life, darkness is bent on destroying light, evil absorbs good.

Upon regaining a path to reality, the colours in Duncan's palette pan have fused together into one drab grey mass. His clothing and skin are water-soaked and spattered with saturated blotches of colour. He gathers his supplies and returns to the camp, throwing the paint-splattered clothes into a laundry bag and retires to the hammock with a rum and lime.

* * *

Joyce's voice jostles him. "Wake up, Duncan. Let's eat."

At throwdown, the students display some impressive work. There are charcoal sketches of huts and people, watercolour landscapes, and abstracts that seek to interpret *Paraíso's* ethereal magic. Considering the limitations of film processing, a student majoring in photography shows some striking Polaroid portraits of an Indigenous family.

"Bravo." Duncan applauds him for his problem-solving. "Why didn't I think of that?"

Moved by the freedom to express her true self, Joyce chooses to dance her impressions of the local wildlife, from toucans to reptiles.

Again, Duncan shouts, "Bravo." The students join him. Joyce curtsies.

Duncan is reluctant to announce his failure to produce a work of art but decides to turn the disaster into a learning experience for them. He retrieves the laundry bag containing his paint-soiled clothing.

"Inside this bag is my magnum opus," Duncan announces, "the result of intense reflection and, I might add, misadventure."

"Are you going to pull a rabbit out of that bag, Duncan?" Jason laughs.

"Au contraire," Duncan states, emptying the bag slowly with a flair of showmanship.

"Ta-da." He produces the paint-spattered clothing he was wearing earlier, as proof that he had attempted something but failed. The clothes, however, appear surprisingly clean and unblemished.

The students and Joyce laugh. One of them shouts, "Mr. Clean, I presume."

"This is a setup. You're putting us on." another student offers. "Show us what you really produced."

Joyce reaches for Duncan's watercolour pad and opens its pages. "Is this your work?"

"No it can't be mine. I didn't …" Duncan's face stares wide-eyed, aghast.

"This is amazing, Duncan," Joyce says with a surprised look. "I didn't know you painted." Joyce places the pad on the table for all to see. There is page after page of vibrant abstracts displaying images that had passed through Duncan's imagination while meditating.

"I have no idea how …"

Joyce interrupts. "Never apologize for your work, Duncan. That's the first rule of portfolio presentation."

Duncan grabs his camera to take photos of the pages as proof that they actually exist. While concentrating on the images through his viewfinder, he notices a small white lily appearing in the bottom right corner of each page, next to the letters, DM.

* * *

The following morning, Duncan introduces Joyce to the place where he and Azucena meditated. There were still blotches of paint on the grass and the surrounding leaves, reminders of his sketching attempts the day before. He takes a few portraits of Joyce, shows her the row of marching ants, still dedicated to their quest, and suggests they sit for a while.

Joyce remarks about how peaceful it is and offers a thought.

"I'm wondering whether this is as magical a place as you believe it to be," she suggests, taking in her surroundings. "While I was meditating the other day, it occurred to me that a place is only magical to those who are magical people, people who are willing to allow magical thoughts to enter." Joyce looks at Duncan. She touches his hand. "You and Azucena have that talent, that ability, especially when you can share it together. This place is magical to you because you both brought the magic to it."

Duncan remains silent, privately absorbing the thoughts Joyce is sharing with him.

Joyce's eyes fall to her hands as she fiddles with her fingernails. "I was wondering, however, if it is still magical to you, without Azucena being here, I mean. Why are some places more important and mythical, or spiritual, than others? You have also talked about Manitoulin Island in the same way, that there's something magical about that place for you. Maybe it's because you brought your magic with you. Maybe it's because you met other magical people there who offered to share their experiences."

Duncan remains still.

Joyce looks back at Duncan. "I guess what I'm wondering is, can everyone experience the magic, or is it an exclusive club, a limited membership to only a few special people?"

Duncan hesitates before attempting a response. 'How can I answer this without revealing my latest experiences?' he ponders.

"Wow," Duncan finally begins. "Maybe you're experiencing the magic already. You said this occurred to you during a meditation yesterday. Was it before or after you conjured up that dance routine? That had to come from somewhere, right? Maybe it was the magic. Was it also magic when you received a vision from Azucena a few years ago?"

"Oh that?" Joyce says, thinking back. "That was just a dream, maybe a weird dream about something I wanted to happen, like you and I getting together, and Azucena was on my mind. Maybe I was worried that she would be offended if I made a play for you. By believing that she gave me her OK, my guilt was relieved. How does that sound?"

"That's just bullshit," Duncan says, raising his voice. "I'm suggesting that you've had many visions, or call them dreams, where Azucena has talked to you, or sent you images. Maybe she's encouraged you to pursue something. Besides, you call it magic, as if someone is pulling a rabbit out of a hat. It really is something more than magic. You won't believe this when I tell you, but the other day I ..." His words die on his tongue as he tries to speak them.

"What's the matter, Duncan?" Joyce asks, tilting her head. "Are you OK?"

"Yeah. I'm good," he responds, shaking his head to clear his thoughts. "I'm just having a bit of trouble getting my breath. It must be this heat."

"I thought you were having a heart attack."

"No. I'm OK. I think, before we leave here, you will experience the ... um ... magic that this place has to offer. I also believe that everyone has the ability to accept that magic. Yes, it appears to happen in specific places and to affect certain people, but those people have opened themselves to allow it to happen. Some of our students will feel it too before they leave. Of course, not all will."

"I don't doubt that Duncan. Jason, for example, is spending a lot of time with one of the local girls. Is he feeling the magic, or is he ignoring it? I'd place bets on where he's planning to spend his summer vacation."

The suggestion hits home for Duncan. "I can relate to that."

"No kidding," Joyce chuckles, poking Duncan in the side.

After some silence, Duncan introduces a new topic. "I have a special favour to ask, Joyce."

"Ask me anything. How can I resist." She inserts her arm through Duncan's and leans her head on his shoulders.

"Would you mind supervising the students during our second week in Nicaragua? There is some personal business in the capital that I want to take care of. I'd also like to visit with Tomás before I leave. Don't worry, I will meet you all at the airport for our departure."

"Is there something wrong, Duncan?" Joyce asks, stroking her hand across his back.

"No. Nothing wrong. Quite the contrary."

"Because if there is something wrong, I'll do anything I can to help," Joyce offers. "Are there any problems? Tell me truthfully, Duncan." Joyce places both hands on Duncan's cheeks and looks directly in to his eyes.

"No problems, Joyce, but there's some important research I must look into while I'm here. I don't know when I'll be able to return to Nicaragua and by then it may be too late. I'll explain it all to you when we meet at the airport."

"Of course I can take care of the students," Joyce answers, "they're adults, aren't they?"

CHAPTER 40

LINEAGE

Duncan catches the first fishing boat from *Paraíso* and hitches a ride to the capital.

He hires a taxi to Father Manuel's church in the barrio. No one there can provide information about the priest's whereabouts, only to suggest that he might have retreated to a monastery somewhere in Europe, possibly in Spain. One of the nuns reveals that he was seen researching a pamphlet on the pilgrimage at *Santiago de Compostela*.

Another taxi takes Duncan to visit Tomás at the *casita*. When he arrives, Tomás is in the former studio jamming with some friends.

"Hola Tomás," Duncan shouts, placing his overnight backpack on the floor.

Tomás looks up. "Papá," he shouts in return, before running to embrace him. "What a surprise. What are you doing here?"

"Joyce and I have a group of students on a field trip at *Paraíso*, but I didn't want to leave before seeing you, so here I am. I can only stay for one night. I have some research to look into before I leave the country at the end of the week when I have to meet the others at the airport."

"We can have supper together, Duncan. We'll just walk over to *Los Antojitos* … like the old times, eh?" Tomás nudges Duncan's arm.

"Sounds good," he agrees. "Who are your friends?"

Tomás turns to his friends. "Hey guys, this is Duncan, my Papá. He lives in Canada."

He tells Duncan that he and his friends have formed a band. "We play only original songs."

"Wow. That's great," Duncan acknowledges. "Who writes the songs?"

Tomás calls toward his friends in the corner. "Leandra, *venga aqui*." Tomás waves his arm to signal that Leandra should join them. A tall attractive woman approaches and wraps her arms around Tomás.

"This is Leandra, Duncan. We write the songs, together. It's like a collaboration." Tomás introduces Leandra to Duncan. "Leandra, *mi Papá*."

"*Mucho gusto, señor,*" she offers her hand. "I like your photographs very much."

"*Gracias,*" Duncan answers, shaking her hand.

Tomás explains. "Leandra is more than just a songwriter, Duncan."

"I gathered that," Duncan responds, accepting that Tomás and Leandra are collaborating on more than writing songs.

"Leandra is also a talented photographer," Tomás reveals. "You would like her work. Oh, and in case you were wondering, she is also my girlfriend."

"I wasn't wondering at all, Tomás," Duncan says, sporting the grin of a Cheshire cat.

"We met at the university. She's a graduate student in Fine Arts."

'And the circle continues,' Duncan ponders.

During supper at *Los Antojitos*, Duncan and Tomás catch up on recent events and personal accomplishments while occasionally touching on a few memories.

"What's up with Father Manuel, Tomás? I went by his church but nobody knew where he was. It's like he just disappeared. One of the nuns thought that he may be on a pilgrimage in Spain."

"That's what I heard too," Tomás says. "If that was the case, he would have at least called me, wouldn't you think.?"

"Yeah," Duncan agrees. "Something doesn't add up."

Tomás offers his opinion. "I think that he's a troubled soul. He's probably joined a monastery in some remote location to atone for something in his personal life." Chuckling, Tomás jokes, "Maybe he's sitting alone in an unheated cell in the mountains, self-flagellating with poisoned branches or whips. Seriously though, he was noticeably upset when Mamá died. The only time I've seen him since the celebration of her life was when we went to the lawyer's."

When they return to the *casita*, Duncan asks to see some of Leandra's photographs. She retrieves a portfolio case from the bedroom she obviously shares with Tomás.

Duncan is flattered that she pursues a documentary style similar to his own. Leandra honours Duncan by saying he's been an influence on her work.

Before they retire, Tomás and Leandra perform duets of several of their songs. Tomás sings harmony and accompanies her on guitar. Their songs blend romantic lyrics into the backgrounds of political messages.

Duncan sleeps at the *casita* in the bed he shared with Azucena. He imagines her familiar essence in the pillow under his head.

In the morning, after a light breakfast, he bids farewell to Tomás and Leandra, with embraces and promises to visit again. Duncan extends invitations for them to visit him in Toronto, reminding Tomás that he once considered studying law in Canada.

"For the time being, I'm pretty locked into staying here, in Nicaragua. I can't go into details right now, Duncan, but law school has me thinking about pursuing something in politics."

"*Tiene cuidado*, my son, be careful what you wish for." Duncan pats Tomás on the back.

Duncan walks the short distance to the Intercontinental where he rents a car. He drives north toward Matagalpa but veers eastward through the mountains toward the small village of Dos Rios. The cool mountain air offers a welcome contrast to the tropical heat and humidity of Managua.

Duncan considers the similarities between Nicaragua and his home in Canada. Both nations stretch between the Atlantic and Pacific Oceans and boast the diversity of mountains, forests, and plains. It's as if Nicaragua was Canada but squeezed into a smaller package. Of course, the seasons differ, and snow is unheard of in Nicaragua.

There is no road sign announcing the town of Dos Rios; it just exists, as if it had always been there. Anyone who comes to Dos Rios already knows where it is. The mine is still in operation, but Duncan is more interested in locating the convent. He inquires at a small café for directions. When Duncan asks about the convent, a woman provides vague directions, pointing further east and raising her arm indicating that Duncan should drive up the mountainside. *"La cima … de la montaña,"* she finally utters, adding in broken English, "top … mountain … *a la derecha."*

"Está bien, señora. Gracias," Duncan thanks the woman.

"Quién estás buscando?"

"Who am I looking for?" Duncan repeats. *La Monja* … the nun, Sister Hortencia. *La conoces?"*

"Aah, si," she nods to confirm that she knows the nun. *"A Dios, señor."*

Duncan interprets the woman's response as a positive sign that the nun is still alive.

The convent appears without signage on the right, across the road from a large hacienda. Duncan parks the car and starts walking toward the doorway. Suddenly he's attacked by a gaggle of geese, Canada geese, ironically. A nun steps out to scatter the geese with a broom and agrees to introduce him to Sister Hortencia. The aged nun has a brightness in her stare, a positive sign that she might still have control over her faculties. She welcomes Duncan in English as if she were expecting him.

She explains. "I was trained in *estados unidos* by the Maryknoll

Sisters, so I'm glad that my English is still useful. Besides, you are obviously not a local *nicaragüense*, you're not wearing cowboy boots. How can I help you, *señor*?"

Duncan is relieved that she has a sense of humour. "I am interested in a birth that occurred here in Dos Rios in 1948. You served as a midwife at the birth."

"Test me. I know everybody and everything that happened here since I arrived at the end of the war. That's World War II, not the Contra War," she clarifies.

"I am told that I was born here, and that you delivered me. If the records are correct, it would have been on August 14, 1948, or within that week. I was placed up for adoption and was accepted by a Canadian couple. My adopted father was an engineer at the gold mine. Do you remember?"

Sister Hortencia appears to be counting the memories in her mind. "Why do you want to know about the details. Obviously you are a healthy man and are living a good life. Is history that important to you?"

Duncan replies bluntly. "Yes, the details are extremely important. I'm a journalist, and the facts are always important to me. Besides, by law I have a right to know who my birth mother and father were." Duncan fakes the last statement in hopes the nun isn't up to date on the law. "I understand that my mother died during childbirth. Does that help your memory?"

Sister Hortencia is equally blunt. "There are two laws, *señor*, the law of the land and the law of God. In my profession, I live by the latter. How about you?"

"I live by three laws, Sister." Duncan exposes three fingers and starts counting. "The law of the land, if it is just; the law of God, if it is sincere; and the law of dignity." He holds the three fingers up to Sister Hortencia for clarification. "When all three laws are lived by, we have a wonderful world. Will that help you decide?"

The nun nods in agreement.

Duncan continues. "I have obviously come a long way to solve my dilemma. You are my last hope. Please, Sister. My mother is very old, and my father is approaching his final resting place. They would like to know that a circle has been completed."

Sister Hortencia appreciates Duncan's sincerity. "You seem like an honest man, not the devil you were accused of being. Your mother was Doña Isabel, and she died at the moment you were born. It was tragic. She was the daughter of a German industrialist before she married a *nicaragüense*."

Finally, the DNA results start to make sense to Duncan. "Do you remember if I had a birthmark?"

"Ha-ha," the nun laughs. "You know more than you reveal. Yes, there was a mark on your behind, a small one, but one that upset the *patrón*."

"The *patrón*? So my father was an important man. Why did he abandon me?"

"He not only *was* an important man, but he still *is* important. He believed you to be the son of Satan, because of the birthmark, and that you caused the death of his beloved Isabel. He called you a murderer. He would only accept the others, but not you."

"Others? What others, Sister?"

"Aha. That's when your story becomes interesting, *señor*. You were the third of triplets, but you were different than the other two. Of course you had the birthmark, but you were also fair-skinned and blond-haired, very unlike your siblings who are both darker with black hair."

Duncan absorbs every detail of the nun's description with intense seriousness. He attempts to analyze the information as it's delivered.

"But if my mother was German, would that not account for my blond hair and fair complexion?"

"Possibly," Sister Hortencia agrees. "But it also indicated that you were not an identical triplet, you were a fraternal triplet, which is not unusual by itself; it is more common within twins. The main reason you were rejected was because your mother died before you left the womb and you had the mark of Satan on your bottom. People here were much more superstitious in those days. Some still are."

Duncan's curiosity continues. "What happened to my other two siblings?"

"The other two remained in Nicaragua and became famous," the nun says. "One of them became infamous and should have been abandoned instead of you, I'm afraid to admit." She crosses herself and peers upward, appealing to her God for forgiveness. "But, alas," she crunches her face with determination. "He met his demise and is now suffering in the bowels of Hell with Satan himself." After a brief pause to calm herself, she adds, "So there, *señor*. Now you know."

"Tell me one more thing please, Sister. Who is my father? I must know before I leave."

Sister Hortencia crosses herself and utters some words toward heaven. "Your father is Don Ricardo," she offers. "He used to live in that large estate across the road. That's where you were born. He now lives on a private estate near the capital, a place called *La Finca del Oro*." She hesitates. "He would not have been a good father to have. That's my opinion, not God's. Your brothers are …"

Duncan interrupts, raising his right hand to Sister Hortencia. "With the knowledge of who my father is, I am now familiar with who my brothers are, Sister, and I totally agree with your assessment of my father. Thank you so much for your help."

He clasps her hands in his. "What you have told me is both a blessing and a curse, but my soul will rest with the knowledge. I will, however, edit some of the information I pass on to my mother; she would never understand."

Before turning to leave, Duncan adds, "Oh, by the way, my birthmark disappeared on its own when I was still a toddler. Maybe it was some kind of exorcism," he jokes.

Sister Hortencia laughs and embraces Duncan firmly. *"Buen viaje, señor. A Dios."*

For Duncan, another circle appears to have been completed.

PART FOURTEEN
1999 – 2000

CHAPTER 41

DREAMING

Toronto, 1999:

'Shit! Azucena is my half-sister!' The truth hits Duncan like a barn roof in a tornedo. He sits alone in his cocoon, his hands clamped to his temples. 'How in hell can that be?'

While his mind grinds the fragments of information that led him to this conclusion, there are still lingering questions. What he struggles with most is the visit he had from the reincarnated Azucena.

'That was bizarre. Was it even real?' he muses. 'Or did somebody feed me acid? She sat right in front of me and talked to me as if she were Azucena herself, which I know is impossible. As hard as it is for me to accept it, Azucena is dead.'

Duncan knows that he should just pass the strange visit off as a dream, but the thoughts refuse to disappear.

'It didn't feel or look like a dream. There wasn't that silky, film-like veil over it like my other dreams. The image was vivid, with sharp detailed texture, and her voice sounded vaguely like Azucena's voice … Shit, that was no dream, that was real.' His rational mind kicks in. 'Of course, there was all that mist. That was a bit surreal. And, how did I get back to the original place after being at the hut?'

"Fuck," he shouts aloud, pounding his hands against his temple. "I'm losing my mind."

Being a brother to Manuel and Jorge is upsetting enough to Duncan, but being a son to Don Ricardo is tragic. Sister Hortencia's surprising information partially explains his puzzling DNA analysis, that there are German ancestral links, but they must be from Doña Isabel. What is missing is a Latin American link that would provide evidence that Don Ricardo is his father.

When he puts the pieces together, things become stranger. 'This is all just too coincidental. How can it be?'

A flashback returns him to the elder's cabin in Manitoulin. "There is no word for coincidence in our language. There are some things that just aren't meant to be understood." The contradiction strikes him. 'But I'm a journalist … a curiosity seeker.'

Duncan's life is a compendium of dreams and truths, each battling with the other for acceptance. At nights his sleep is interrupted by dream references to Azucena. Sometimes they're merely thoughts or brief images that pass through without leaving any traces. In other episodes, Azucena talks to him, in her own voice, not the monotone of the reincarnated Azucena.

Later, a month before the new millennium arrives, Azucena speaks to him in a dream; she appears alive, wandering through the forest at *Paraíso* as she talks. Duncan sees the hut in the background.

Her voice asks. *"Are you alone, Duncan? Do you have time to talk?"*

"I always have time to talk to you my dear Azucena."

"Good, because what I'm going to tell you is extremely important. Promise you won't discuss this with anyone, not Joyce, not even Tomás when you talk to him at Christmas. Promise?"

"OK," he agrees reluctantly. "You have my word."

"I knew I could trust you, Duncan. I didn't die at Don Ricardo's

estate ... not really. I am still very much alive through my spirit, like my mother is still alive."

"I'm having some difficulty following all of this Azucena. Forgive me if I sound sceptical."

"It is true what I told you when we met at Paraíso. I am the daughter of Don Ricardo and Tomás is the son of Col. Jorge. That's why I appeared at the estate the night of the fire. I wanted to confront Col. Jorge about Tomás and tell him that he was my half-brother."

Duncan blinks in disbelief. He has trouble making sense of what's occurring in his dream. 'I don't even know whether I'm asleep or awake.'

He speaks aloud to Azucena's voice. "What am I supposed to believe? What about all the rumours?"

"The rumours claimed that I was responsible for the explosion and fire, that I wanted to kill Col. Jorge. I could never do that. You must know that. I couldn't kill anyone, especially the father of my son. Besides, I could never tell who was who between Col. Jorge and Father Manuel; they are so alike. Even now, I don't know for certain who actually died in the chapel. Maybe it was Father Manuel. From what I can tell, nobody has seen him since the celebration of my life, and that could easily have been Col. Jorge imitating Father Manuel."

"You know about the celebration?" asks Duncan. He shakes his head. "Were you there?

"Yes, but I was there above the rafters, peering down through the skylights. It was a beautiful send off. Thank you for the wonderful loving words and for playing our song."

Duncan suddenly bolts straight up in bed. "Jesus Christ. This is insane. I can't handle this right now." He rubs his eyes, attends to Mother Nature and pours a straight double Scotch. In the solitude of his cocoon, he listens to Coltrane's, 'A Love Supreme,' and cranks up the volume. He chooses a second Scotch rather than return to bed in an effort to distance himself from his bizarre dreams. 'If they were dreams,' he second guesses.

During his third Scotch, a voice is heard, apparently emanating from the urn on the mantle. Duncan dozily obeys.

"Can you please turn the music down, Duncan. I haven't finished. There's more to tell you. I miss you, Duncan."

Duncan can't believe he's talking to a wall. "I miss you too, so much. When will I see you again?"

"Soon. All I can reveal at this time is that I am considering running for President in the next election in 2001. Of course, I will be running in the MRS party. The original party of the revolution has veered from its commitments to democratic freedoms and is starting to look like the old regime that we fought so hard against. They need to be sent a strong message. Another woman President wouldn't hurt the country at all. Of course I can't become public but I can provide spiritual guidance."

"What do you hear from Father Manuel? Have you contacted him?"

"No, and I mustn't either. He is not to be trusted. Please don't utter any of this conversation to him. I can't say any more about it at this time, but I assure you, he isn't who he seems to be."

Duncan attempts to digest what Azucena is telling him about Father Manuel. Recalling the information he was given by the nuns at his barrio church, he says, "One story I heard was that he had sought hermitage at some monastery in Spain. Another said he was walking the *Santiago de Compostela* pilgrimage."

"He needs to do a pilgrimage, Duncan. He has a lot to atone for. Enough said. Gotta go. Hasta le próxima."

Duncan sits dumbfounded in the dark. His hand vibrates as he swallows the rest of his Scotch. His mind attempts to churn out the real from the unbelievable. Every communication Duncan receives from Azucena transports him to a deeper zone of confusion.

He remembers, as a student of photography, the professor used the phrase, 'Circles of Confusion.' It could have described Duncan's lack of mathematical prowess; the topic alone was thoroughly confusing to him. In later years, when he stood in front of his own classes, he explained the concept in layman's terms.

"The circle of confusion is a measure of the largest blurred spot that can be determined to be a point. In other words, if you can see a sharp point, the circle of confusion begins immediately adjacent to it. In photography we use it to determine what is blurred and what is sharp, as in the depth-of-field observations; for example, when an object or person in the foreground is sharp and well-focused while the background appears blurred, or out-of-focus."

Duncan's personal confusion challenges how one could possibly measure that miniscule point. Aside from mathematical concerns, however, Duncan sees the phrase relating to the confusion he experiences in determining what aspects of his life are real and what are fantasies. When Azucena appears in his dreams he is drawn into continuous circles of confusion, swirling zones of cognizant acuity witnessed through filters smeared with petroleum jelly.

Faced with the recent messages from Azucena, Duncan is torn between believing what seems to be real or what may be pure fantasy.

'Can a dream even pass as reality? But was it a dream? After all, I was awake, albeit three double Scotches into oblivion. If it wasn't a dream, what in hell was it? I carried on a seemingly intelligent conversation with a dead person. Not even with a dead person, but with a few remnants of her ashes. She talked about running for politics, for Christ's sake. Who dreams that? I can't even discuss this with a therapist; I'd be locked up.'

The dream conversations blend with his recent discoveries concerning his parents, and deeper memories from the past cause further confusion. The confusion leads to more questions that haunt him in his darkest hours.

The memories that linger, however, are those wondrous intimate experiences between he and Azucena that are indelibly imprinted within him. Her smiles, her soft kisses, and exploratory touches, her exceptionally curious mind and, not to be forgotten, the beautiful soul enclosed within her golden caramel skin that has kept Duncan younger than his years.

'She still dwells within me. I feel her presence in the pangs of emptiness that ache in the pit of my stomach. If she wasn't here, I would feel nothing. I long for her visits that arrive in my dreams while I sleep, and for the thoughts of encouragement she offers me.'

Duncan, becoming unsteady on his feet, pours another Scotch.

'It's during the quiet spells, the private moments of contemplation, when I yearn for something more from Azucena; another word, or just a piece of a vision. I'm anxiously waiting for the news she promised in my latest dreams. I'm not a great one to hold secrets from the ones closest to me. I know that Joyce must worry about my erratic behaviour these days.'

CHAPTER 42

MILLENNIUM

Toronto, 1999 – 2000:

With Christmas season approaching, Joyce visits Duncan for a Saturday marathon of baking. Duncan is domestically challenged, but for one exception, his Scottish shortbread cookies baked annually each Christmas. Duncan follows, to the letter, the recipe discovered years before in his Scottish grandmother's attic following her death.

Tin boxes of the cholesterol-pumping goodies stack up on the kitchen table with gift tags to his mother, his father, and for distribution to his students at the college during their final lecture of the semester. There's a special box for Jack Bryant, Willa, and the staff at Human Interest magazine. Of course, Joyce claims a hefty sampling to take home with her. Duncan, as usual, saves the 'not-so-perfect' samples and slightly charred end pieces for his personal consumption.

On December 23, Duncan calls Nicaragua to wish Tomás a happy 27th birthday, and Tomás updates him on his relationship with Leandra and his new appointment as an associate professor at the university. He also offers comments on the current political situation in Nicaragua.

Although it is tempting, Duncan resists discussing any of the fantastical dreams he's experiencing, especially of those involving Tomás' mother. In fact, Duncan resists discussing them with anyone for fear of being labelled insane.

'That's all my students need to hear,' Duncan contemplates.

While it is difficult conversing with Tomás as if everything is 'tickety-boo,' there is still a small dose of doubt that lingers within Duncan that the messages he receives from Azucena in his dreams may be anything more than wishful imagination.

On Christmas morning, Duncan and Joyce drive to pick up Duncan's mother at her apartment, before continuing on to Happy Acres Home overlooking Lake Ontario. Duncan's father waits anxiously in his room for the visitors, and especially, for the delicious Scottish shortbreads.

Duncan is careful not to reveal his discoveries from Nicaragua to either of his parents, but his mission this visit is not solely to deliver shortbread cookies.

"Dad, I'm going to take a sample of your DNA. It'll be interesting to find out about your Scottish heritage. Besides, I'm putting together a family tree for all of us. You can do this too, Mom. I'll just take a swab from each of you and send them away to a lab where they research your ancestry."

"Why would we want to know that stuff, Duncan?" his mother probes, expressing some reluctance.

"It's just for fun," Duncan lies. "Haven't you ever been curious about your history ... about your ancestors? Did you know, for instance, that my name is taken from King Duncan the Stout, and he fought at the Battle of Bannockburn. Don't you find that interesting?"

"Duncan was your grandmother's maiden name," Mac reveals, in a surprising surge of clarity. "What about the MacGregor clan?" he asks.

"The MacGregors were one of the first clans to adopt the bagpipes.

I bet you never knew that, eh?" Duncan had prepared for the question after discovering that little-known tidbit in a Scottish genealogy book.

His father wants more. "Can you get all that information from my spit?"

"Eat your cookies, Mac." His mother insists, trying to veer the conversation elsewhere. "They're even better this year. Must be because Joyce helped him."

* * *

New Year's Eves are becoming celebratory milestones for Joyce and Duncan, recalling their first intimate experience only three years ago. They allow Duncan the luxury of transitioning from what is lost to what's been found. While still assuming their hidden identities from the arts, like the dress-up exercise that first drew them together, they no longer dress up as other celebrities. Instead, over a late evening dinner, they each assume a secret identity which, accompanied by a series of skill-testing questions, decide who the winner will be. Of course, each wrong answer must be punished with a drink. The first to reach five drinks becomes the overall loser and must perform every duty the winner demands. In the end, there are no losers.

New Year's Day starts late with a hefty *huevos rancheros* brunch of steak and eggs, before Joyce settles in to watch the Rose Bowl parade on TV. Duncan retires to his cocoon for an hour or two with Miles and Azucena.

Instead, on this first day of the new millennium, Duncan attempts to mine details from the latest vestiges of Azucena's fragmented images, ones that still reside beneath the surface of his brain, residual pieces that appear like floaters in the eye after cataract surgery. They used to trickle in at night, unfinished sketches to be imagined toward completion, like the paint-by-numbers from his youth. All that's required of him today is to follow his heart, where the fragments have settled, waiting to be interpreted and manifested into virtual works of art. Some of the images recall pleasant reminders of their lives together, soft, and malleable, evocative, and sensuous. Others serve as enigmatic warnings, webs of labyrinthine messages to be decoded as they are being processed.

Duncan is now at an age where time matters little. The inevitable looms closer with each sunset, and with each arrival of dawn, a promise of old dreams and hopefully, new visions.

His memories are littered with the images of those no longer here: family, friends, associates, lovers, even adversaries; escaping this earth like lemmings, leaving Joyce and Duncan alone to pilot their own ship of life to safety, but is there ever a safe harbour on the horizon?

* * *

The DNA results arrive in the mail and add to Duncan's confusion. He shudders at the news they may reveal. Before opening the envelope, Duncan pours a Jack Daniels, tapping the envelope against his chest with anxiety. He pours a second JD before gaining the courage.

'Oh God," Duncan pleads to a deity he doesn't even believe in. 'Don't let this contain the information I'm expecting. Surprise me God." He pauses with the realization that, no matter what the tests reveal, neither option is ideal.

Sophie MacGregor is not his birth mother. She had already admitted to adopting Duncan, and the DNA results prove it.

Mac, his apparently adopted father, however, proves to be his true father. The results eliminate Don Ricardo from the mix, and subsequently, removes Azucena from being his half-sister. This is good news for Duncan, at least it's the better of the two options but it raises other questions. He pours another JD.

Instead of being elated, Duncan's confusion deepens. 'How in hell can I be a triplet to Manuel and Jorge, but not be Don Ricardo's son? How can Mac MacGregor be my father when I'm a brother to Manuel and Jorge?' The answer strikes him after another Jack Daniels.

'Fuck! What if my father had an affair with Doña Isabel? He was in Nicaragua at that time. My mother was only there for a few weeks, visiting. So,' Duncan rationalizes, 'my father was there by himself while my mother was here, in Canada. He could easily have carried on an affair with the Doña. Is it possible that my father is also Manuel and Jorge's father? Wow! Wouldn't that shake up old Don Ricardo?'

The new revelations about Duncan's father weigh heavily on him. After several weeks of agony, he decides to conduct some research, beginning at the Toronto library. Eventually, he's referred to a researcher in genetics at the university.

The researcher offers Duncan a possibility. "The most likely scenario is that Mac, your Scottish father, had an affair with the woman identified as your birth mother, Doña Isabel. Your fair skin and blond hair indicate that you are only a fraternal triplet to the other two, who are probably identical, both having darker skin and black hair. My suspicion is that the affair occurred within a few days of the conception by Don Ricardo. Therefore, Doña Isabel was pregnant by two contributors at the same time."

Duncan tries to follow the confusing puzzle outlined by the researcher. "Is that even possible?"

The researcher tilts his head from one side to the other in thought. "If you hadn't had the paternity test that identified Mac as your birth father, my assumption might have been that your fair complexion and blond hair were simply a result of Doña Isabel's German lineage. That may still have been the case, considering the Scottish lineage could very well produce darker results, closer to those of your siblings. There was, after all, sufficient contact between the Scots and Mediterranean travellers. However, with the paternity test proving Mac's DNA, you are most likely the result of 'heteropaternal superfecundation,' where two fathers have contributed to multiple conceptions and births."

"Wow! I wouldn't want to describe that at a cocktail party after a few drinks," Duncan says, jokingly.

"It's a rare occurrence," the researcher states, as he smiles in acknowledgement to Duncan's joke, "but it has shown up in a variety of paternity lawsuits. You're very special, Duncan, a one-of-a-kind."

Duncan stares at his feet. "My worry now, is whether I should tell my mother the news."

"I'm not a psychiatrist, Duncan, just a humble scientist, but I will offer you a non-professional opinion. Keep your mouth shut."

Duncan agrees with the researcher. "I don't think I could handle the stress when my 80-year-old mother throws in the towel on a 55-year marriage to my 83-year-old father with dementia."

* * *

At the beginning of February, a bulky envelope arrives at Duncan's townhouse. It was sent from *Santiago de Compostela, España*, on December 23, 1999, the 27th anniversary of the Managua earthquake.

My Dear Brother Duncan:

By the time you read this letter I will have descended into whatever incendiary inferno Satan has reserved for me. I am not worthy of the heavenly garden where I suspect our dear Azucena has retreated to, and where you will join her when the time comes.

My reasons for writing to you are numerous, so please read with patience and understanding, although the latter will prove difficult.

I want to thank you with all my strength for giving Azucena your love and your undying support through her difficult times. I too, admit that I have lived my life consumed by her beauty, both in love and in lustful cravings. Since being ordained I should have fought against the cravings as best as I could.

I am not the man you know, but another. I am not sure whether I am even the man I know, for I have lived a mixed and confusing life. It all began when I was only 14 years of age, a teenager with burgeoning hormones. My father, Don Ricardo, forced my brother and me to undertake a series of tests, designed to challenge our mettle as young men about to enter the world as his demented reality imagined it to be. The tests were to determine which of us would be destined for a military career and which was better suited for the priesthood.

In the first test, we were instructed to shoot our beloved Afghan dogs,

Marta and Max, behind the woodshed. We obeyed, but my brother was a coward; he always was the sissy. I, on the other hand, was willing to do anything necessary to get ahead, even if it required me to destroy our family pets. There were two shots, one from each rifle, but only one of us pulled the triggers. My brother was emptying the contents of his guts on the grass.

The second test required us to sleep with two women of our father's choosing. We were expecting two prostitutes to show us our way into adulthood. When they arrived in the darkened bedroom I was excited at the possibilities, eagerly leading them to the bed, where I had my way with them both ... several times I might add. My lust became more uncontrollable and violent with each encounter. My brother sat on the edge of the bed sobbing. He couldn't raise the flagpole if I may describe it that way.

The third test was very simple. We were to stand before the President and declare our allegiance to him. My brother prepared a speech that was exactly what my father wanted. I, on the other hand, prepared one that disagreed with all his policies and sided with the revolutionaries. Before our delivery to the President, we switched our identities to deliver the speech of the other, just for laughs.

My father just assumed that we had both succeeded in the first two tests, so it was necessary that the third test be one that determined who was going where. It was the only test witnessed by my father, so my brother and I decided in advance that one of us had to declare our allegiance and the other would deny it. The bottom line was that my father was never able to tell us apart. Throughout our lives we switched our identities to whatever served our needs. Even while we were studying in the U.S., we regularly traded places between West Point and the seminary.

The most shameful of my actions that I am revealing to you now will destroy our friendship, if such a friendship still exists. It is these actions that have caused me to end my life and live in the dungeon of fire for eternity. I can only ask for your forgiveness, but I cannot expect you to provide it.

When my brother was away with his troops in the mountains, I lusted so much for Azucena, but my priestly occupation prohibited any advances toward her. So, I dressed in one of my brother's uniforms and purchased a sexy dress for her, which I asked her to try on. She undressed shyly before my very eyes. She was stunningly beautiful. I used my charm to convince her that she wanted to lay with me, to give her innocence to me. She provided it willingly, but it wasn't for me, it was for a man in uniform. She was merely 16, and so vulnerable, so very pure. I am the father of Tomás, a declaration I could never reveal before now. Tomás, of course, must never know this fact.

When we met at the Cathedral following the earthquake, I was a fraud. I deceived you and Azucena alike. You were the best person for her. She needed compassion and love that was true, and you provided it. My jealousy of you remained with me throughout the years, and it haunts me even now, as I ignite the flame.

My brother believed that the truth of his weaknesses the nights of the tests would emerge, and he would become a priest. It would have been perfect for him. He was sensitive and he was chaste to the very end. He proved to be a horrible leader for the Contras. He was totally incapable of ordering the crimes he is accused of. Those were my doings. I interceded by giving the violent orders to his subordinates in his name. That was a simple maneuver as he was located in Miami and had no concept of what the real situation was here on the ground. I knew every move the revolutionaries were making before and after the triumph. For me it was a chess game.

Before he returned to the estate, he contacted me to discuss details of our lives as twins. He was planning to publish his memoirs, segments of which included how we switched roles throughout our lives and posed as each other during the Contra war. He even included details of the atrocities performed under my orders. I couldn't allow him to proceed any further.

I arranged the unsuccessful assassination attempt at the Intercontinental. It would have been so simple; anybody could have done it. There *were so many people who hated him after all ... but they hated him for what I did, not for what he did.*

I admit to you now, that I finally killed my brother at La Finca del Oro. He was such an easy target, and someone who was hated by almost everyone, except of course, our father, who admired him, but he didn't even know who we were. I had poisoned my brother earlier in the day. When he became ill, vomiting in his suite, he wanted to atone for his sins at the chapel. He had no sins; the sins were all mine. I arranged the explosion and fire to disguise the poisoning.

I assure you that I had no knowledge that Azucena was in the chapel with my brother. In my most evil moments, I could never have caused her death. But alas, my actions did destroy her. For that I stand guilty.

My life ended that evening. The remainder of my existence was merely the agonizing process of entering the inferno, day by day, hour by hour, year by year. At the celebration of Azucena's life, I could only utter a few well-worn phrases from the Old Testament, where it's eye-for-an-eye and tooth-for-a-tooth. My guilt would not allow Christ's forgiving heart to enter my demonic soul.

My sins have recently been confessed to the Bishop and I have been forgiven in the eyes of God. In what other bizarre system than this church, can a man be forgiven for murderous heinous crimes against humanity, but condemned to eternal damnation for his own suicide?

A Dios, amigo,

Manuel ... or am I Jorge? I no longer know who I am. But, as things turned out, it doesn't matter. We have switched our identities so many times.

"Shit!" Duncan shouts to the walls. "That bastard is even more confused than I am. I thought I knew who I was drinking with all those years. Apparently not."

The letter slips from Duncan's hands and falls to the floor as he sits stunned, facing Azucena's painting. His eyes are insanely dry; he can't remember the last time he blinked. The overwhelming emotions swirling inside his chest are too much for him to handle alone.

'He called me brother. Has he known all along that I'm one of the triplets? Or was it simply a naïve affectation? I will never know of course. But then, why would I even care?'

* * *

Duncan's townhouse is filled with Azucena's paintings, and with their collaborative works, but when he needs her for comfort, it is *Paraíso* that offers him the deepest consolation. He can't ignore the flames that consumed the garden, but with the flames came the freshness of new life, in whatever form that manifested. His relationship with the painting always brings Azucena closer.

"I need you more than ever my dearest Azucena!" he shouts to her. "Send me a message!"

In that precise moment, the phone rings. Duncan jumps to his feet and rushes to the phone. 'It can't be …'

He answers the phone in desperation, "H-hello?"

"Hi Duncan, it's Joyce."

Duncan's chest deflates. 'It's not her,' he sighs to himself. 'I was expecting Azucena's voice.'

"How are you?" Joyce continues, completely unaware of what her simple phone call has done to Duncan's heart. "I've been worried about you lately. Is everything OK? I'd like to drop over if you're OK with that."

Duncan is ready for some diversion. "Yes, Joyce. Please come over."

When Joyce arrives, they exchange hugs and casual conversation before retreating to Duncan's cocoon.

"What's your choice of music, Joyce?"

"The Bill Evans Trio. 'Sunday at the Vanguard' … with a glass of Merlot."

"Perfect."

The Bill Evans Trio is apparently also to Azucena's liking because she makes her presence known in the middle of Scott LaFaro's bass solo in 'Jade Visions.'

"Hello Duncan, and to you too, Joyce. It's been such a long time. I hope everything is well with you. I'm glad you are both together because I have some news."

"What's going on?" Joyce whispers to Duncan. "Is there something wrong with your stereo, or am I going mad? Did you hear that too?"

"It's OK, Joyce," Duncan consoles, patting on Joyce's knee. "Carry on, Azucena."

"It's now official. I am a candidate for the presidency. Well, not me, as Azucena, of course, but as my reincarnation."

Joyce's mouth is agape.

Duncan asks, "How is the news being accepted? Do the people know that it is really Azucena, the artist? Normally, people just don't wake up from death. It's a hard narrative to sell. What are people saying about this?"

"Well," Azucena answers. "Some are suggesting that it's a divine act. Some are calling me a witch who should be burned at the stake. Good luck with that, eh? Been there, done it. Nicaragüenses are religious people. Most can accept that a spirit can become president."

Duncan asks, "Why did you wait so long before coming forward?"

"I had no choice. If I hadn't died there, I would have been charged with the murder. It was a Catch-22, as you call it. Oh, by the way Duncan. Did you hear about Father Manuel? He died."

"I did know that. He wrote me about his own death in a suicide letter, but I didn't receive it until a month after he died."

"So it was intentional, then. I thought so. I was in Spain at the time, and I worried that I'd be accused of his death as well. He was in a monastery there when he died. I had painted a vision that I received several months before. It showed a priest battling against the challenges of the church amid a blazing inferno. I sent you some fragments of it I think. For obvious reasons I couldn't publicly show any of my latest paintings, the ones I completed after my death."

"Now that you're officially back among the living," Duncan states, raising his shoulders and arms toward Joyce as a signal of disbelief.

"You should mount a show of the paintings from your death days. Your fans will love them, and the critics will have a field day."

Joyce's jaw drops. She rattles her head to regain her senses. "I'm getting another drink, Duncan. Do you want one?"

Duncan nods.

"I've officially rejoined the Sandinista Renovation Movement, the MRS. The compañeros, at least the good ones, are happy to have me back. There's an election next year. I'll just work behind the scenes helping with the campaign for now. Unfortunately, I already know that we will lose the election; Mamá sent me a vision. I will forward it to you."

Duncan chuckles while offering Azucena a suggestion. "You do know that there's a thing called e-mail now, don't you? You can send me your thoughts that way and they'll show up on my computer. Maybe then I'll be able to sleep at nights."

"Ha-ha."

Joyce chokes on her Merlot. She whispers to Duncan. "You do realize that you're sharing jokes with a wall, don't you?"

"And how are you Joyce? Are you two happy together?"

"Um … I'm fine … we're fine," Joyce answers with a shaky voice. "It's wonderful that you're back with us."

"Oh yes it is. I feel so free. I can go anywhere I want now. I saw you briefly at Paraíso, but I couldn't reveal myself. I am truly sorry. Did you enjoy it there?"

"Um … I had a wonderful time, thank you." Joyce answers, still unsure of why she's talking to a ghost. "It's truly a magical place," Joyce adds. "By the way, Azucena, when you gather your newest paintings together, the so-called 'death paintings,' you might consider a show here in Toronto. I'm sure there would be fantastic response. I'd be happy to work with you on it. And I could offer you another residency at the college when it's convenient. I'm sure the students would love to hear your story. Think about it."

"I will, Thank you, Joyce."

PART FIFTEEN
2001 – 2006

CHAPTER 43

A NOVEL IDEA

Toronto, 2001 – 2006:

"You should write your memoirs, Grandad," Ariel suggests to Duncan during a phone conversation. "You're not getting any younger, and you have to start sometime. Now seems to be as good a time as any. I'm sure there are stories behind every photograph that you've taken. Aside from the photos, all of your firsthand experiences will be unrecorded history, and nobody will ever know about them, unless you write them down. That would be a bloody shame, Grandad."

The seed is planted. Duncan starts by jotting a few memories on scraps of paper and organizing them into chronological order. He creates a new folder on his new Macintosh laptop containing categorized and dated files of events and personal reflections. Gradually, the memoir begins to take form.

As the project evolves further into something feasible, Duncan agonizes over formatting issues: first- or third-person narrative, factual truths versus emotional memories, chronological or topical chapters, authentic or fictitious names, etc.

Despite his journalistic ethics regarding truth and objectivity, he also recognizes that there are fictional accounts containing more accuracies than many non-fiction essays.

'What is truth anyway?' Duncan challenges his brain. 'How much truth is there in a memoir? After all, it's basically one person's account of what happened. Even an idiot knows that, for each event, there are as many true accounts as there are witnesses. As a photojournalist, my photos are records of the truth because I was there and I recorded what was directly in front of me, but photos are interpreted in so many different ways. I take hundreds … hell, even thousands … of images at an important event and only one or a few are chosen to publish.'

Duncan seizes an opportunity to rant to himself.

'Editors, not photojournalists, choose the photos that are seen by the public. They aren't even on the scene; they're sitting in offices and newsrooms thousands of kilometres away from the event. They can choose an action-packed image with lots of smoke and fire, an emotional weeper, or some silly scene-setter like a street sign or dormant building. I feel like I'm just a broker, a middleman, as if I'm flogging used cars or insurance policies. Do the images they choose reflect the truth? Any truth? What about the so-called facts of history? Are they universal truths or are they just a few random photos chosen in a hurry to satisfy some artificial deadline? STOP THE PRESS! Worse still, are they chosen to satisfy the publisher's biases and obligations to advertisers and politicians? Of course. All of the above.'

His internal concerns about truth soon occupy more time than writing anything down. 'Maybe I should write a novel instead. How much truth could I put in a novel?'

* * *

Five years later, after daily grinding away at freewriting, editing, re-writing, and re-editing, Duncan's novel, '*Azucena*,' finally arrives in bookstores. He opens the first copy and breathes in the freshness of a newborn; the odours of paper, ink, and sweat permeate his nostrils.

The response is expectedly slow. However, Duncan is satisfied with the work and is confident that he made the right choice to fictionalize his experiences. After all, he reasons, 'Who would want to read my boring memoirs anyway? This way, they're still drawn from my memories, but they're spiced up a bit.'

Duncan is just happy that the book has become a reality. For him, the creative act is in the writing and editing. As far as he's concerned, his contribution is finished. 'All art is created in the present tense,' he reminds himself.

Fortunately for Duncan, Joyce assumes the duties of agent, office manager, and marketing kingpin for Duncan's novel. She coordinates the diversity of his life into one major project. In Joyce's world, Duncan MacGregor becomes a brand.

She contacts galleries and libraries with proposals to exhibit the art work of Azucena Sosa and Duncan MacGregor, in coordination with book release parties and readings for Duncan's novel, 'Azucena.' She even arranges for Duncan's jazz group to perform at the book release parties.

Joyce uses her gallery connections to organize an Ontario-wide tour of selected art pieces from Duncan's and Azucena's collections and coordinates the shows with book signings. Student volunteers from the Fine Arts program create posters and mailings for each of the events, for which they receive remunerative incentives.

The dates for the tour are chosen to coincide with summer activities in cottage country galleries and libraries throughout Muskoka, Haliburton, and Prince Edward County, and to continue through the fall and winter in universities: Queen's, Waterloo, and Western. In early March, immediately following spring break, the tour wraps up at the University of Toronto with a major retrospective of Duncan's life in photographs at the university gallery, including some of his collaborations with Azucena. Simultaneously, Azucena's controversial 'militant ants' show returns to Galería Profundo.

Duncan is invited to present a weekend of events at the university, including a Friday evening jazz concert, a Saturday gallery opening, and a Sunday afternoon lecture that addresses his numerous passions: photography, writing, cultural fascinations, music and, of course, his new novel. He accepts the offer at Joyce's insistence and promises to discuss the collaborative process shared by him and Azucena.

After a whirlwind final weekend, Duncan fumbles with his notes backstage, anxiously waiting to be introduced at the Sunday lecture. The university's Chief Librarian introduces Duncan from the stage of the lecture theatre.

"Welcome everyone, to our afternoon with the acclaimed photojournalist, writer, musician, and probably a few other talented occupations that may be disclosed during tonight's lecture. This is not a reading but, following the lecture, Duncan has agreed to sign copies of his book, 'Azucena.' He has requested that I keep my introduction brief with few adjectives, and to limit it to the basics, which I have just done. With hearty applause, please welcome Mr. Duncan MacGregor."

Duncan steps to the lectern amid enthusiastic applause from a 'standing-room-only' audience. He can't see their faces in the darkness of the theatre, but nods toward their applause. He is confident knowing that Joyce is seated in the front row directly in line with the lectern.

"That was the briefest introduction in history. Thank you for that Ms. Chief Librarian. And thank you all for coming out on such a wet and blustery afternoon. I sincerely hope you are not disappointed. Um ..." Duncan struggles to begin, unsure of what to say first. He shuffles sheets of paper in front of him on the lectern before releasing his first words.

"OK ... Here we go," he says. "During my lecture, I will touch on a variety of topics. Of course, they will include references to photography, music, writing, some poetry, and maybe even some baseball. I will also discuss dreams and visions, politics, Central America, racism, gender issues, ignorance, world dominance, famine, Indigenous cultures, love, hatred, and who knows what else. Oh yeah, also some adoptions, sexual assault, and a suicide. If you came this afternoon to hear me talk about only one of these topics, you could become bored. If you are offended by any of these topics, please note that you have been duly warned."

There is collective applause. Nobody leaves the theatre.

"My philosophy is that these topics are not only related to each other but are, in fact, the same thing. They represent to me, a single obsession ... it's called life. I believe in the concept that art is life and life is art. As I have only one life, I consider that all of the arts I dabble in come to me from the same places ... my heart and my soul. As I contemplate life, they all enter my consciousness together. I am not a guru sitting on a remote mountaintop in the Himalayas contemplating the breeze. I am a just a normal everyday schmuck who has been fortunate to encounter some extraordinary people. In the process, I have learned everything I know from them. I am not an expert on any subject. I don't provide answers, I ask questions. I have spent much of my life in journalism, I am driven by questions, and by curiosity."

Duncan stops before proceeding further. To cover for his apparent loss of concentration he resorts to improvising. "At this point, are there any questions?"

"What would be the point in asking you a question?" a smart-assed voice offers from the darkness. "You don't have any answers."

Some of the audience members react with snickers.

"You are correct, sir. I will give you an A-plus for your perception." Duncan's response receives heartier laughter. He continues his lecture with fresh confidence.

"Some of the people I learned from early in my career were Indigenous elders in Manitoulin Island, among the wisest humans I have ever encountered. They spoke slowly and softly, contemplating each and every thought before speaking, and every word they spoke was important and mind-blowing. From those elders I learned to listen, and to respect the wisdom and the experiences of those who have spent more time than I have on this earth, and who have different, more interesting, cultural experiences than mine."

Duncan pauses to sip water from a glass.

"Um …" He shuffles the papers. "Oh yeah, here we are. Another person important in my development is someone I never met but have admired since I was a child. Um …"

Duncan searches internally for the name of his childhood hero but it's hidden somewhere in the void. Joyce's voice whispers from her seat in the front row, "Jackie."

Duncan picks up the cue. "Jackie Robinson was my hero, a man who confronted the indignities of intolerance and ignorance and won. His courage shaped the world, and the mindset I chose to embrace. The photographer, Robert Frank, opened my eyes to a world I was already seeing, but, due to my obsessive demands for perfection, I was too uptight to follow his example for a very long time. The photographer W. Eugene Smith opened my heart and gave me the courage to weep at the world's tragedies and triumphs alike. Jazz musician Miles Davis opened my ears to fresh sounds, and to the concept that I should follow my own muses instead of the status quo."

Duncan's voice breaks. "I apologize to you, the audience, for the occasional gaps in my delivery. I have just completed an exhausting book tour culminating in this weekend's busy schedule."

The audience responds with applause. He uses the moment to sip a drink of water and calm his emotions.

"The Nobel prize-winning author, Gabriel Garcia-Marquez, opened another world of possibilities to me and proved that magic is truth, and that fiction is real. He also made it possible for me to open my mind and soul to accept the love and mysticism of my beloved Azucena, the artist whose visions foretell the future, and whose images are still shared with me from another plane of reality."

During the applause, Duncan is momentarily distracted by Azucena's voice.

"Thank you for the credit Duncan but what about thanking Joyce as well? She's doing most of the work."

"Before I continue, there is one very important person I want to acknowledge. Joyce Banerji, my very dear friend, curator, copy editor, and life partner. She gives me the courage and a fresh desire to continue with life when I'm faced with darkness. Without her I would not be standing here today. Joyce, please stand up and accept your applause."

Joyce rises from her front row seat while Duncan raises his water glass toward her.

"At this time, I want to share with you, some of the tenets that have shaped my life and work. Like you, I was raised within guidelines, rules of etiquette and of laws passed down by generations of parents, community leaders, politicians, and religious clerics, not to overlook a few Kings and Queens. As a child I obeyed my parents; I still remember some of the rules they enforced. Always wash behind the ears; you don't want potatoes to grow there. Never cross the street without looking both ways. Always wear clean underwear, you might be in an accident. What will the neighbours think?"

There is laughter of acknowledgement.

Duncan's confidence seems to be intact as he dives back into his delivery.

"I still follow most of my parents' rules to this day, but the last one always returns to haunt me. As a photojournalist, I have witnessed many disturbing scenes involving death and serious injury. Regardless of how clean your jockey shorts were before the incident they will fill with caca when you die. The neighbours might puke, but they won't care about your underwear."

More laughter. The same smart-assed voice shouts out.

"Have you ever thought of being a comedian?"

This time, there is no laughter from the audience, only hissing. Someone from the darkness quietly suggests to the heckler, "Why don't you just shut up, or get the hell out."

Polite applause follows the suggestion.

Duncan addresses the heckler with his own response. "I'm sorry, sir.

That's a question, and I don't have any answers for you." Duncan adds an aside. "Why is there always one of these guys in every gathering?"

"That was a good one, Duncan," Azucena's voice encourages. *"You're a lot better without a script. You're a jazz musician after all."*

Duncan departs from the lectern, walking freely around the stage as he addresses the audience. He envisions Azucena walking by his side.

"Don't worry. I'm right here beside you."

"When my granddaughter suggested that I write my memoirs, I struggled with how I would handle the names of the people I have met over the years. Some of them night be upset with what I may say about them, I thought. Some will challenge the details of events involving them. Some will be embarrassed at how they are revealed or spoken about by myself and others whom I may quote. Some may have wives and loved ones to whom they have lied to, only to discover their indiscretions described in detail. People value the truth, but do they really want it?"

Duncan pauses, returning to the lectern for a sip of water before he raises the question.

"What is the truth? Is there only one truth? Is the truth of what you see more factual than the truth that you hear or smell? Do all your senses lead you to the truth or are some less reliable? Truth is much more than a series of dates and events. There is also the spirit of the truth that must be considered, a gut faith that one's inner conscience will guide the integrity of the message. One's truth becomes another's lie. How many people here remember a few minutes ago when I talked about my good friend Miles Davis?"

Many hands are raised.

"My point exactly. I have never met Miles Davis, although I possess every one of his recordings and I did see and hear him perform live in concert in 1969, an event in my life that transported me to another musical dimension. In short, I was blown away. He was not a friend of mine, rather an important influence on my life. From that perspective, I know him well. There are some members of the audience who assume that I was a good friend and will later explain to their friends that Duncan MacGregor was a good friend of Miles Davis. That would not be true, but it may be an honest response based upon supposition."

Duncan steps away from the lectern again to stroll about the stage.

Azucena walks beside him. *"Are you going to tell them about our time in Paraíso?"* she asks.

Duncan turns to where Azucena is walking. "It's in the book," he says aloud to her, before turning back to address the audience.

"How much of our lives and beliefs are fictional? How often do we spread rumours that are unfounded but which we firmly believe in as the truth? Do you always believe what you've been told? Are the stories told to you by friends absolutely truthful, and do you repeat them to others regardless? If so, how much do you embellish them?"

He takes another pause for a sip of water, gazing out into the darkness. He struggles with his notes, searching for his next cue.

"Um … OK, here we are," he mumbles.

"In preparation for this project I began assembling my memories on slips of paper, gradually transferring them to my laptop. Yes, I have embraced digital technology," he adds with a chuckle. "I had arrived at a point in my life when I started to worry that my memories might not always be there when I need them. Life is all about memories. If they disappear, what's left? So now, like most people these days, I have a hard drive."

He pauses to ponder his last statement before continuing.

"When I concluded that I had enough to start the writing process, I tested myself. 'How much of this is true, or only true in my personal recollection?' Unfortunately, most of my friends and acquaintances have passed from this world so I couldn't call them up for fact-checking."

Sporadic laughter follows.

"Think about it this way." Duncan raises his forefinger as he often does when lecturing to his students. "Memories are only truths to the person with the memory. Other people witnessing the same event have different memories. Their truths differ from yours. Your memories are based upon your entire life's experiences and the influences that have shaped how you will accept the truth of an event. Often, they become truths because you want them to be true. If you tell your friend about an event that happened to you 20 years before, you will tell it differently than you would have a decade ago or when it originally occurred. The story will be embellished with emotional elements and will contain portions of how you wished the story would have turned out. You will also format the story in a more interesting chronology, considering that you've had 20 years to make it more exciting ... more worthy of being told."

Duncan pauses yet again, fumbling in his jacket pockets. He returns to the lectern.

"Are you still here, Azucena?" Duncan asks aloud. "Give me a sign."

Joyce, sensing Duncan's difficulty, immediately comes to his aid. There is mumbling between them. The audience sits patiently quiet. Joyce reorganizes some papers on the lectern and rubs her hand across Duncan's back before returning to her seat.

He turns to the audience, shaking his head with a smile on his face. "Sometimes I think I reside in a zone of mist between truth and memory."

He stares at the papers and starts. "What is it about memories? The older we get, the more memories we are plagued with, until they start to disappear, of course ... and they do. Oh, they're still up there." Duncan points to the side of his head. "It's just the retrieval system that starts to break down."

Duncan doesn't wait until the audience stops chuckling.

"The memories haunt us in our dreams at night and rear their ugly truths to us during the day. A popular adage suggests that before we die, our lives recur through memories and dreams like old movies being replayed on late night TV. We remember the characters and the basic plots but can never remember how they end. In Hollywood movies the heroes usually ride off into the sunset without a care in the world, their duties to society fulfilled. Have you ever noticed that they're usually singing a song at the end? In life it doesn't work that way. We never get to see how it all ends, and we won't remember the words to the song anyway."

Duncan is, once again, confident that the audience is with him. 'I'm on a roll,' he congratulates himself.

"If we're fortunate enough to survive an extended span of time, our final years are spent alone with our memories. There is no one to share them with; most of our lifelong friends and relatives have passed on ahead of us, like emissaries clearing a passage for us when our time arrives. We can, and we must, however, share our memories with those younger than ourselves. Otherwise, what's the point in having them at all?"

Duncan struggles with his papers. He briefly loses his continuity.

"Here we are," he continues. "Our memories are biased by a massive sampling of influences: our ideologies, the history of our experiences, how we felt under the prevailing weather conditions, if we had a disagreement with our spouse before the event, how much alcohol we consumed, if we're trying to give up smoking, or if we felt the call of nature at the time."

Ironically, someone leaves the theatre at the suggestion. Duncan takes advantage of the distraction to regroup. He abandons his notes on the lectern again and steps to the edge of the stage.

He stares out into the void and continues, this time improvising with strength and commitment.

"My story is one based upon truths. The seeds were sown in the soil of a memoir, but as they were nourished and fertilized, they assumed a new life of their own; a fictional novel blossomed. The characters are people I have known, and others I have imagined knowing. Some are composites of several people sharing one fictitious name. That this work is fictional by no means suggests that it is less truthful than some works of non-fiction. As you peruse the pages, believe what you want to believe. Discover yourself in the characters. Allow them to enter your dreams and visions. Become."

Duncan takes a breather before finalizing his lecture. He attempts to sip some water but the glass is empty.

"Can I offer you one last, but important thought? What I have learned from this wonderful experience is that dreams and memories keep you alive. Dreams allow you to look forward and memories exercise your brain. Memories lead to dreams, and dreams fuel memories. Together they lead to circles being completed."

He spreads his arms out toward the audience. "That concludes my talk. Now I will answer questions?"

From the darkness of the theatre, a voice asks, "Is Azucena a real person, or is she a figment of your imagination? An illusion perhaps?"

Duncan squints into the audience before responding. The voice is not from the smart-ass heckler but is a voice vaguely familiar to him.

"I can't see you in the darkness sir. You are only a voice in the void. Can I assume that you are, therefore, not real? An illusion perhaps? Maybe you would like to step forward so I can confirm that you are real."

There is laughter from the audience while their heads turn, searching for the mystery person.

Duncan continues answering. "Azucena is very real. She is as vivid and alive to me now as she was when we were together in *Paraíso*, or is it possible that *Paraíso* was an illusion? I see Azucena, and still communicate regularly. Every time I take a photograph, she guides me. Every time I play the piano, she dances and sings along with me. She walks beside me and lives within me. We eat and sleep together. She is here with me, in the theatre, at this very moment. To answer your question more fully sir, Azucena is not a figment of my imagination, she *is* my imagination. We are one and the same."

At that moment, a figure appears at the foot of the stage. As a backlit silhouette, the details remain hidden from Duncan. The figure waves toward him and calls out, "*Hola,* Papá." Duncan stops to consider the voice before his body starts to tremble.

"*Hola ...*" There's a momentary lapse ... until, "Tomás?" ... "Could that be you, or is my mind carrying me away to some remote mystical paradise?"

"*Sí*, it is truly me, Papá. I am Tomás."

Duncan loses sight of whether he's living in a present reality or in some past fantasy. The figure approaches.

Duncan outstretches his arms. "Come here, closer, so I can see you."

His entire being vibrates as if shaken by an earthquake. The man rises to the stage. Tomás and Duncan stare before embracing, both reduced to tears of sheer happiness. For minutes, Duncan forgets completely about the audience, which has remained silent and cemented to their seats, wondering what in hell is happening. Some have the foresight to snap photos of the reunion. Others remain sceptical, interpreting the entire episode as a setup, a cheap gimmick to sell more books.

The silence continues until Duncan turns to the audience, his voice cracking.

"My dear friends, I can honestly tell you that I had no idea that this was about to happen." He stops to wipe the tears before taking Tomás' arm.

"This handsome young man is Tomás ... I repeat, this is Tomás, the son of Azucena ... and he is my son."

The audience stands, applauding with screams and whistles. Tomás embraces Duncan again.

As the audience responds, several other silhouettes appear at the edge of the stage. Joyce emerges from the dark and leads the silhouettes up the steps, helping one of them leaning on a walker. With the continuing parade of strangers emerging, the audience remains in the theatre, spellbound by the strange events unfolding before them.

Joyce approaches Duncan, taking his arm. "Sophie and Mac are here as well, Duncan. They've come to hear you speak."

"Mom," Duncan reacts. He embraces and kisses his mother. "Did you enjoy my lecture?"

Sophie answers. "It was difficult to hear you out there, Duncan. My hearing isn't what it used to be. I'm sure it was excellent."

Duncan's father struggles on his walker to approach his son. He stares and grins when Duncan embraces him and mumbles some coded words. His glassy eyes tell Duncan all there is to know.

Duncan breaks under the emotion. "Thank you Dad."

Joyce continues the introductions. "You remember Gerald and Ariel, Duncan. They've travelled all the way from England to see you."

Duncan stares into the group with tear-filled eyes. "Oh, my God. Gerald, of course, and my beautiful granddaughter, Ariel. Have you met Tomás? Where's Tomás?"

Joyce explains that Tomás just left the stage. "He'll be right back, Duncan."

Tomás returns to the stage with a woman by his side.

Duncan stares at the silhouetted woman. "Azucena? Is that you, my dear, Azucena?"

Tomás addresses Duncan. "Do you remember Leandra, Papá?"

"Yes … of course. Leandra. You look radiant." He embraces Tomás' partner.

Tomás addresses Duncan quietly, so the audience can't hear. "You will notice that Leandra is expecting, Papá. I too, will be a Papá. We are having a daughter. She will be Azucena."

Duncan's tears flow unabated. With a smile on his face, he says, "I knew she was here. I told everybody that Azucena was here, in this room, didn't I?"

"Yes Duncan, you did." Joyce whispers into Duncan's ear, adding, "Don't forget, you have an audience."

"Oh shit." Duncan turns and apologizes to everyone.

"Please folks, take your seats," he pleads in a breaking voice. "This has been a complete shock to me; I'm totally gobsmacked. No doubt it is an extra bonus for you folks as well. Can we please have some extra chairs up here for our surprise guests? I would like them to share the stage with me."

Library assistants scurry onstage with chairs for everyone.

"Could we have some quiet in the room, please, folks?" Duncan asks, his hands raised. "Let me officially introduce my very special surprise guests. In the interest of brevity, please hold your applause until I've introduced everyone."

He turns to stage right, facing the lineup of seated guests.

"This handsome man is Tomás, the son of Azucena, and beside him, his beautiful partner, Leandra, soon to be the mother of a new Azucena."

Duncan's voice breaks. "If you have read the novel, you will know the names of our other guests as well. My son, Gerald, and my granddaughter, Ariel, from the UK. This elegant woman is Sophie, my mother, who has endured my strange life since I was born with the mark of Satan on my ass. Mac, my father sits next to her in his walker. The woman standing immediately to my right is the always magnificent Joyce, without whom I would not be standing here today."

Duncan turns to an empty portion of stage left and extends his arm. "And this beautiful woman, my friends, is the spirit of my beloved Azucena who is always by my side."

When the applause wanes, Duncan continues. "There was a question on the floor that I was answering when Tomás appeared. Yes, Azucena *is* real. Need I say more? Thank you all so much for such a gracious evening. I will sign books for the next half hour, but I must depart to spend some quality time with my family. I'm sure you will agree that a huge circle has definitely been completed here tonight."

The elusive Azucena whispers, *"I have to go now, Duncan. I'll be in touch soon. Nice job on the book. Thanks."*

A familiar figure stands at the beginning of the book signing line.

Duncan looks up. "Kurt, I didn't know you were here."

"I wouldn't miss a party like this for anything. You have to thank Joyce for making all the arrangements. She contacted everybody and told them about the show, the book, and the lecture. She even made reservations for travel and hotels. Man, you gotta hold on to her."

"Join us after, Kurt. We're heading to … oh damn … some restaurant. Joyce knows which one."

Kurt laughs. "You didn't even recognize my voice, did you? I did the best I could to hide the Dutch accent."

"What do you mean, Kurt?"

"I'm the heckler."

"Oh, you bastard. I was going ask them to throw you out."

CHAPTER 44

MAGNUM OPUS

Toronto, 2006:

With the book release and the university lecture behind him, Duncan enjoys the freshness of the first day of summer with a brisk walk alone through the neighbourhood, stopping at his local café for a dark roast and a chocolate croissant. He stares blankly into his coffee; it stares back. The past few months have overloaded his senses: the book, the tour, the lecture, and of course, all the visitors.

Duncan's extended family, the surprise guests that Joyce invited to his lecture, spent the following week visiting and dining out. Tomás and Leandra joined Duncan and Joyce at the townhouse. Gerald and Ariel remained at the hotel for a few days before returning to the UK. Of course, Mac was taken back to his room at Happy Acres and Sophie returned to her apartment.

Soon afterward, on the Easter weekend, Mac suffered a massive stroke and passed away. He never learned about the results of the DNA. Duncan didn't reveal them to Sophie either.

At the café, Duncan reflects on the events of the past year. 'So many things happening, and then suddenly, there's nothing … a blank canvas.' He recalls an old Peggy Lee song and starts singing aloud in the café. "Is that all there is? Is that all there is? Is that all there is, my friend? Then let's keep dancing …"

Dizzy, the owner of the café, applauds and dances across the floor to Duncan's table. "That's the way it is, Duncan. There's no more to it than that."

"Shit," Duncan confides with Dizzy. "How can I still remember the words to that old song but can't remember Joyce's name half the time?"

"Sometimes I can't remember my own name," Dizzy reveals so Duncan won't feel so sad.

Duncan drains the dark roast and orders a second. "It was great seeing … um … Tomás, that's it, Tomás," he tells Dizzy. "So many memories, both great and sad."

Dizzy remains silent while topping up the dark roast.

Duncan stares into the coffee mug, hoping in vain that more information will magically appear.

"You know what's weird, Dizzy? Someone's dead, and then I see them in a dream, and they're alive again. I have parents, and then they're gone, or they're not my parents after all. I had a son but never became a parent. Then I became a parent to somebody else's son. How quickly one's life can be altered in such a short span of time. Or, are those just the memories fucking around with my mind?"

"That's probably it," Dizzy agrees. "Memories always fuck me up too."

"See you tomorrow, Dizzy." Duncan waves and leaves the café for home.

'I'm glad she … um … oh yeah, Joyce. I'm glad Joyce moved in with me finally. She helps me keep track of things from time to time … makes sure I don't starve to death or set the place on fire. She still works at the college, poor soul. I had to quit. Just couldn't handle the paperwork and those fucking meetings anymore.'

Suddenly, Duncan stops in his tracks. He pats his hands over his chest and checks his pockets. 'Oh shit … I'm missing something. My wallet? Whew, there it is. Something's missing. Something doesn't feel right.'

His eyes scan the neighbourhood from where he stopped. He peers in all four directions. Two teens walk hand-in-hand down the street as lovers. Recognizing the photo potential, he grabs for his camera. "Shit," he shouts aloud. "Where's my camera?"

In a panic, Duncan backtracks to the café, a familiar landmark as he's been going there for years.

"Hey Dizzy," he calls. Duncan nicknamed him Dizzy for his fat cheeks, similar to the great jazz trumpeter, Dizzy Gillespie when he blows his horn. "Have you seen my camera gear? I think I left it here."

"Somebody must've ripped it off," Dizzy jokes with Duncan, quickly reverting to the truth to avoid confusion. "Sorry Duncan." Dizzy pats him on the shoulder. "You didn't have it with you when you got here, buddy. You need a ride home?"

"No, I can find my way. Thanks Dizzy. You're a pal."

A year before, Joyce sold her own house and moved in with Duncan when things started to become too challenging for him.

During the day, while Joyce is at the college, Duncan indulges in the comfort of his solitary existence. He searches the cupboards and the linen closet for the sugar bowl until locating it on the kitchen table where it always sits. A hand-printed sign on the table reminds Duncan that Kurt is coming for dinner.

'Kurt? Who's Kurt?' The question weighs heavily on Duncan's mind. It dissolves when he begins exploring the keyboard of the grand piano for some fresh voicings to 'Body and Soul,' until none emerge. He concludes that he has outlived the possibilities.

Duncan retires to his cocoon to reflect on recent events only to realize there weren't any. Amidst the initial cacophony of long ago memories he manages to centre in on the silence. He ponders the meaning of what has happened throughout his active life. To paraphrase an old joke, some memories remain like remnants of feces stuck on a wall; others leave blanks.

'What has it all meant? Have I made the best choices? Would my life be that much different if I'd continued at … um … you know …" He snaps his fingers together … "that jazz place in Boston … oh yeah, Berklee? Why did I go there in the first place? Oh right, to be a jazz musician. Of course life would be different. I'd be a lot poorer as a jazz musician, or … um … or maybe not.'

Once back on track, Duncan continues the thread. 'Would I have made it on the jazz scene, or would I be stuck in my hometown playing weddings and bar mitzvahs like so many of the graduates I've encountered who have lost the dream, the desire? Maybe I'd have been happier that way, living in a vacuum, just putting up with whatever happens. Who knows? What if I'd married what's-her-name and had a house full of kids? Penny … that's her name. What ever happened to Penny? I should give her a call. Would I have gone to Nicaragua? Why did I go there anyway? Baseball, of course. Wow! It's hard to imagine how my life would be without baseball. I'd probably spend my days staring at the TV with bedroom slippers on. Hell, what am I doing now? Is it any different? I'm sitting in a dark room staring at a painting on the wall and talking to myself. Shit. Who's painting is that? I wonder.'

Duncan wanders back to the living room where he keeps his booze. He opens the cabinet and pours a Scotch.

'Why do I remember some things and forget others? How are some events selected? How do I process and edit my thoughts, choosing which ones to send to the trash and which should be archived for history? And why, without warning, does some memory suddenly raise its ugly head from the trash bin to clutter my mind, or to steer it toward other forgotten, unimportant details? Why do I sometimes forget the important details? What's the story on those marching ants anyway? What drives them? Why can I even remember those fucking ants? Do they even know what they're doing, or where they're going? Do we humans even know what we're doing or where we're going ... or why? Maybe we *are* the ants. Maybe the ants are just reincarnated people. Do we even care where we're going? That's the big question. Shit, we're no different than those ants.'

Duncan wonders why he's struggling with so many questions and so few answers. 'I am not the answers, I am the question.' He asks himself, 'Who said that?' He concludes that it must have been that guy ... what's-his-name ...? 'Oh yeah, Kurt ... the guy who's coming for dinner, whoever he is.'

In his cocoon, Duncan sets the stereo on shuffle. Chick Corea and Gary Burton begin by playing 'Crystal Silence,' taking Duncan on a reflective journey through the ages. Visions from photos he took on his first visit to *Paraíso* appear, with gentle fades between them, blending colours and movement. Azucena appears, adding brushstrokes or taking swipes at the canvas with her palette knife. The gracefulness of the sequence is occasionally abrupted by lightning-like slashes, disturbing images of police bludgeoning an innocent demonstrator, before returning to the solace of the quieter images.

Coltrane's 'Giant Steps' encourages an increase in the tempo of the image sequence, gradually reaching the motion of a flipbook animation where faces and gestures change in the jagged style of a Charlie Chaplin or Buster Keaton silent film. Images from *Paraíso* merge with ones Duncan took of elders and powwow dancers in Manitoulin; scenes from Mississippi, New Orleans, and Rochester, blend with fishing boats from Nova Scotia and Bluefields, or mountain scenes from Matagalpa and British Columbia. They all cram together inside one collaborative recollection.

The sequence stops abruptly. He's on a plane waiting for takeoff at Toronto International airport. His camera gear accompanies him as carry-on luggage. The pilot announces they are passing over the Florida Keys and then the island of Cuba. Duncan sees flotillas of sailing yachts as small as ants. Several of Duncan's images from through his window reveal endless white beaches. Roberto Clemente sits in the seat next to him. They are the only passengers; the rest of the plane is filled with boxes and crates. The plane begins to vibrate, and the wings start flapping, slowly, like the wings of an eagle. Clemente and Duncan talk baseball when the aircraft starts to tilt. Duncan is suddenly laying on his back against the deck of a sailing yacht staring at a plane while it plunges from the sky into the crystal blue ocean.

"Would you like some breakfast, sir? Coffee or tea?"

"Yes, coffee please."

The photo sequence returns Duncan to Managua. On his stereo, The Bill Evans Trio performs 'Jade Visions.' Roberto Clemente poses for a portrait. Kids play baseball in the barrio. They laugh at the *gringo*, and he laughs back. He wanders through the barrios and takes photos at the market. Vendors shout their wares from stalls and by walking through the crowded corridors. *"Cigarros, cigarros."*

He eats lunch on the patio at *Los Antojitos* where a small, emaciated girl named Maria begs for food, and he walks to the plaza where he takes images of a cathedral. Two women are sitting alongside the stone wall of the cathedral. They're waiting for something or someone. Maybe they're waiting for a message from God. A closeup shows the steeple clock winding rapidly counter-clockwise toward midnight. He reaches out to stop the clock, but his arms won't cooperate. There's a blank in the sequence, total darkness.

Suddenly people are dancing to salsa music. It's dark but for the array of coloured lights surrounding an outside dance floor. Everyone is happy and friendly. Duncan is moved by the beat of the music and dances with Juanita, the owner's wife; he feels the floor vibrate and he snaps his fingers in synch with the pulse. The vibration increases, and the photo sequence begins to shake violently. The lights flicker, dim, and disappear.

"Gutierrez! Gutierrez! Where the fuck are you?"

People are sucked from their homes into the street. A constant grinding sound accompanies screams and weeping as pavement buckles and electrical wires break and snap like fireworks. The sequence of Duncan's photos travel across the road and jaggedly along *Avenida Bolívar* while smaller dwellings crumble into ruin. Comatose people stagger and stare mindlessly at the ruins. Somebody plays the trumpet. A voice says, 'Miles Davis.'

Duncan grabs quick photos as he runs toward the cathedral; stones tumble from above upon the two women sitting below. The clock stops at 12:35.

Workers hear faint cries. They struggle to remove the layers of stones. A small newborn baby remains connected to its mother. A nun severs and ties the umbilical cord.

A priest shouts, "No matter what happens, do what you can to save the baby."

"What about the other woman?"

"*Esta muerta*, she's gone," a worker says, shaking his head.

"Life and death amid the ruins." A circle completed.

* * *

Pellets of colour and random shapes rain down on Duncan MacGregor as he gazes toward the last remnants of his memories hanging on the wall. Labyrinthine details — questions more than answers — litter his vision like the kaleidoscopic compositions of his childhood.

Extemporaneous sounds blend the cacophonous irritations from traffic and verbal disagreements, with sighs of still vivid ecstasies, and harmonious laughter. Duncan's senses explode in a relentless audio-visual confusion, a thunderous big bang of destruction and new creation.

Love, compassion, revenge, mystery, all components of his obsessive passion for being, rotate like comets, planets, asteroids, and cosmic dust, in some pre-ordained circle of confusion around a life force; a fire that flickers before the final embers succumb to the freezing night and the black hole that sucks the debris into nowhere; or to somewhere else.

Memories: a collaboration between the facts and the fictions of our life.

The completion of another circle.

Such is life.

The cocoon is empty but for a final image that occupies the frame where Azucena's *Paraíso on Fire* painting once hung. Colours of the entire spectrum swirl in a mass into the centre as if being sucked into a vortex toward a black hole. In the lower right corner, the image of a white lily. Beneath the painting, on the frame, a brass plaque.

'Circles of Confusion.'
for Duncan MacGregor
by Azucena Sosa

ABOUT THE AUTHOR

Photo by Scott Wicken

Doug Wicken is a passionate photographer, jazz musician, writer, occa-sional painter of abstracts, and a retired professor of photojournalism at Loyalist College in Belleville, Ontario, Canada. He currently lives in Kitchener, Ontario. His published works include two books of docu-mentary photojournalism: 'MANITOU MINISS, Island of the Man-itou' (1982), and 'NICARAGUA PORTFOLIO' (1991). A youthful octogenarian, he remains active with all of his creative passions.

Email: dougwickenauthor@gmail.com

www.dougwicken.net

Milton Keynes UK
Ingram Content Group UK Ltd.
UKHW040644120924
1608UKWH00030B/209

9 780969 122845